ACTION!

BRIAN B. HAWTHORNE

ISBN- 978-1-68506-022-0 (sc)
ISBN- 978-1-68506-071-8 (eBook)

InfusedMedia Co. LLC
www.infusedmedia.co
1-888-251-6088

Books by Brian B. Hawthorne

Outlandish! Fairhome, a world isolated in space and time, where women rule, and men -- there are none! Just a poor but useful substitute...

The Day of Magic Rain Change has come to Fairhome. But is the Race of Women ready to rejoin the Human Race?

Action! A tale that mind-bendingly mixes everyday reality with science fictional unreality, as the Future comes to the Present!

Reaction! ... Would you like to go back and live your life over? Be young again? Live for a very long time? -- Are you _sure?_

CONTENTS

TAKE ONE:

One thing more remained

The naked boy skipped merrily across the courtyard, and entered the side door of the hotel. Running up the stairs two at a time, he easily dodged the occasional pedestrians with a happy grin. He stopped in front of a particular door and rapped lightly on it. A hotel cleaning woman rolled her cart past him, lightly whisking his exposed rump with her feather duster as she went by. He flashed+ a bright smile at her and tapped again. Listening closely, he heard the sounds of someone stirring on the other side. Patiently, he waited. Two doors down, someone came out into the corridor for the morning paper. The boy smiled and raised both arms in greeting, wriggling his hips as well, like a puppy wagging its tail. The lad seemed to be infectiously enthusiastic, waving with his entire body. With a casual gesture, the guest retrieved his paper and disappeared again. In front of the boy, the door opened.

"Oh, good morning, Paulo. You are looking very happy this fine, and very early morning." The white-haired old man was smiling at him.

"Good morning, Uncle-Papa. I am very happy this morning, for I have good news. I have been selected for the lead role in your movie!"

"That is wonderful! You are going to become very famous now, and perhaps very rich, too."

"I hope so. And my Mama is very much hopes so, too." The boy rushed to him as 'Uncle-Papa' leaned down. The old man wrapped his arms around the boy and embraced him, holding him close and casually patting his naked posterior with a large hand. Paulo pushed the door shut as the man led him back into the room. Then the man went to the desk and picked up the phone.

"Would you like some breakfast, my friend?"

"No, thank you, sir, but I would like some juice perhaps." Paulo flopped in the center of the bed and spread his body out, looking up at the ceiling.

Papa Brian as some called him, requested coffee and his breakfast, ordering a small pitcher of juice as well. He looked fondly at the boy, the very picture of contentment as he lay spread-eagled on the bed, like a cat luxuriating in the heat from a fireplace. "Now, Paulo, while we're waiting for that, why don't you tell me why you woke me up so early?" He moved to the verandah doors and spread them open wide, for the pleasant breezes of the morning.

"I wanted to invite you to come with me for my first make-up session. They are going to shave off the rest of my hair, and put on the tattoos today. I thought you would like to watch."

"I would enjoy that, Paulo! Thank you for thinking of me." He sat down in one of the padded wicker chairs near the open doors. "How did you come to be the lucky one to be the star?" Brian was delighted that they had selected Paulo. Of all the boys who had been contending for the role, this one reminded him most of the character in the book.

Paulo sat up with his arms stuck stiffly behind him. "All of us have done everything they asked us to do. The townspeople call us the 'Wingless Angels' because they say we look like the paintings of cherubs in the hotel. We all got our hair cut very short, and we have been spending a lot of time outdoors getting our tans even, while we do our exercises and study English and other things. The casting director said he selected me because my coloring was more even all over, and my head had a nice shape to it which will be important when I become bald for the camera. I have also been hanging around here all the time, trying to be helpful, and learning what I can." Paulo moved from the bed to stand in front of Brian in the clear light, turning to show his flawless and even-toned skin. "Mama says I fell into a camera a month ago." He smiled, showing beautiful white teeth.

Brian pulled the young boy closer, rubbing his skin and checking his muscle tone. The flawless skin had no visible lines to indicate he had ever worn clothes in his life. Down the length of his back and across his buttocks and upper thighs was all the same even tone. Paulo stood calmly, and seemed not at all self-conscious. That selfless demeanor might have been one of the things the casting director noticed as well.

Brian looked up into bright, intelligent eyes within a placid and serene face. The face of an uncomplicated child, or a saint. "How old are you now, Paulo?"

"I may not look it, but I am a couple of years older than my companions. Most of them are about twelve or thirteen. Mama said that when I was very young, I became ill for some time. I am small for my age. They asked about that as well. I think they were worried that I might grow too fast, or too tall, for the movie. But I think I am almost as tall as I will become." Brian nodded; like a lot of the youngsters here, the boy seemed somewhat physically immature for his age. It may have had something to do with the recent decline in their living standards a few years ago.

Paulo was exactly what they needed for the role, someone who looked youthful, and malleable, who would not change much during the filming. The character was to be a docile and timid slave, an affectionate and unthreatening servant to women. Paulo seemed to exhibit that behavior already.

The breakfast arrived, and they ate and chatted briefly. Brian walked with Paulo down to the hotel courtyard where the first make-up ceremony was going to be held. The film company had leased this hotel, and practically the whole community, for filming this movie. It didn't require a large cast. But an ideal climate and a population willing to let the 'Hollywood Morality' control their lives, for a price, were essential ingredients to the success of the enterprise. The lavish spending made it easy to accept the rather unusual demands of this project.

Paulo's nudity, for example, and that of the other 'Wingless Angels' was to a degree a test to see if the people would accept the other requirements. The boys had been running all over town as if the whole island had suddenly become a nudist colony. They had been cautioned to not get into trouble, and to be very helpful and polite to everyone like a troop of naked boy scouts, and the townspeople had come to accept them without complaint.

Other children and young people in the area had begun leaving their clothes behind as well. It was known that there were scenes to be filmed where large numbers of extras, naked extras, would be needed, and everyone wanted a shot at fame. The older men of the area were required to stay out of sight for the filming, but they had all picked out favorite vantage points to observe the goings-on, (or perhaps the comings-off.)

The women of the town had their typical busy season with keeping all the hearty appetites fed. They were having a tourist season without a single tourist, but everyone was having fun.

Brian was perhaps the only real tourist within a thousand miles. As the author of the book on which the film was based, he didn't really have a role to play in the production of the movie. Oh, he was going to be listed as technical advisor, and he had assisted in the screenplay, but his presence was actually just a courtesy. His book had been selling in increasing volume for the last dozen years. He had been as surprised as anyone when he realized that they were serious about putting it on film. The overt sexuality of the book, he had thought, would keep it well out of the mainstream of entertainment.

Apparently, he hadn't realized just how far moral standards had slipped.

The beginning of the ceremony was simple enough. A hot tub had been set up in the courtyard and three rather attractive young ladies escorted Paulo into its warmth. They shed their clothes as well and got in with him. Paulo smiled as they washed him very thoroughly, and strove mightily to pretend that he was already a professional actor. After a complete cleaning, Paulo was dried and brought to a small circular stand.

He was, literally, being placed on a pedestal. The girls, still naked, unconcernedly shaved his head, and armpits, and even his pubic area.

This was followed with a chemical treatment as the girls used latex gloves to spread a hair-removing and growth-inhibiting cream over his entire body. They wiped, then rinsed it away. Finally, Paulo's eyebrows and eyelashes were removed just as carefully. For his movie role, he was to be completely hairless. The downy-cheeked youth was to lose even his down.

Finally, it was done. The girls stepped back, and Paulo gleamed in the sun. To every angle, and to every eye, he presented nothing but unblemished bare skin. His audience applauded, and he took a short bow. In the history of film-making, no one had ever been more naked than this.

Now it was time for the 'tattooing' to begin. Actually, he was going to be painted with an adhesive-type veneer that would bind chemically to his skin. Paulo would be required to swim, and bathe, and even sweat, without losing his tattoos, and the paint reflected the need for permanency.

A different set of make-up artists now moved into action. Using charts and sketches of the planned product, three accomplished body painters began filling Paulo's blank canvas with a very colorful pattern. This was supposed to be an advanced, high-tech form of tattoo. Instead of the drab colors of typical needle and ink tattoos, Paulo's patterns were bright and vivid, and mostly green.

His right leg, and his back and chest, and his bright, gleaming dome began to appear as if an ivy vine had grown over him. His eyebrows, which had been shaved away, were now painted back on. And beginning at his big toe, on his left foot, the tail and body of a large snake began forming around his leg. It circled his leg again and again, until it finally wrapped around his left buttock and disappeared between his legs.

The painting was done. One thing more remained, and Paulo's transformation would be complete.

From a decorated trunk, another woman drew a special body appliance. She carefully fitted the device over Paulo's boyish little penis, and gently concealed his testicles. The appliance was laid down over the painted body of the snake, flexibly wrapping around Paulo's left buttock and upper leg, down to his knee. A special adhesive was used to keep the device in place, and then the painters dabbed a bit more coloring over the junctions between paint and plastic and skin and the process was complete.

Firmly attached now, its stiff internal structure provided Paulo with a manly, and more, sized penis that thrust itself proudly upward like a threatening fist! A fist that looked like the head of a snake.

Paulo stood alone now. Hairless, and garishly tattooed, he lifted his head and raised his arms as if to welcome rain, and turned for his audience. He stood straight and proud, and sported a ramrod-stiff shaft of manhood that would have made proud a man twice his size.

A smattering of applause, and then a thunderous roar, as a creature from a thousand years in the future, a being created exclusively to give women endless pleasure, stood among the ordinary people of today. Paulo stepped down from his pedestal and walked among the crowd. He stopped in front of Brian, and smiled.

With tears in his eyes, Brian leaned down and kissed the boy on the lips, then turned him to face the crowd again, and began applauding once more.

Finally the director took charge, and began setting up for some test footage to determine how the effects would look on screen. Materials and equipment began disappearing from the scene in an orderly fashion, and other props made their appearance. The long day had begun.

The first scene to be permanently recorded was going to be the road-walk scenario; An unlikely meeting between the protagonist named Berry, (Paulo Ignatio), and a military contingent on an otherwise deserted road. Paulo stood at the appointed location and looked at the female soldiers and their trucks which were made to look like armored flying craft. He spoke loudly and clearly, and said his lines perfectly every time. Even so, the scene was repeated several times just to be sure.

Then the soldiers began walking away along the road, stopping to briefly meet, kiss, and pet the character Berry. This was filmed only once, but by several cameras.

The last scene for the day was the long walk along the road. This was repeated several times, until the director felt that Paulo was showing just the right degree of jauntiness, and trepidation, and that he had adequately captured the image for his audience.

Back at the hotel as the light was fading and activity was winding down, Paulo sought out Brian.

"Uncle-Papa, I am tired." Paulo was sipping on a lemonade.

"You have worked very hard today, Paulo, and it has been a long day. Everyone is very pleased with your work." Brian had truly admired the lad's spunk.

"Thank you, Papa. I wonder..." Paulo looked at him for a moment.

"What can I do for you, Paulo?"

"Can I stay in your room with you, Papa? I don't want to have to go all the way to my home, and I don't think I would feel comfortable there like this." The boy seemed tired, and a bit lonely.

"Of course you are welcome, Paulo. We will need to get word to your parents so they won't worry, though."

"Mama will worry anyway, Uncle-Papa. But she says you are a good man. She read your book, and she said at first she was shocked by it. But she said after she went on with reading it, she realized that you had written a very wonderful love story, and that you have a gentle heart."

"Thank you, Paulo, and thank your mother. Not everyone who reads it feels that way about the story."

Paulo nodded, "I have read the story also, Papa, many times. I read it in English, to help me with my speaking of it. I found in it what some of the others found too. But Mama is right, you are gentle, and the book is about love. A very great love."

Brian nodded, "Thank you again, Paulo. Let us get in touch with your mother right now. Tell her if she wants to, she can come and be with you also."

"Mama said thank you, Mister Brian, but she will stay with the other children, and she knows that I will be safe with you."

For a moment, Brian wondered whether something nefarious might be being plotted. But he had met Paulo Ignatio's mother, and he did not think that she was the devious sort. All of her emotions always came out in a rush. He smiled at Paulo, and said, "All right, Paulo. Let's see what we can do to make you comfortable, shall we?" In the hotel room, they arranged for the appliance to be removed and stored safely away, and Paulo was in a hurry to get into the bathroom afterwards.

Coming out of the shower, Paulo was rubbing himself dry with the towel. He looked up at Brian and smiled, "I don't think any of the paint came off, Papa, but I just remembered. I don't have any clothes! I've never visited anyone without bringing clothes before."

Brian laughed. "Paulo, you've been running around naked since before I even came to the Island. I didn't even know you had clothes!"

Paulo laughed, too. He hung the towel where it could dry and sat on the bed. "This is going to be a very long movie to make, isn't it, Papa?"

"Hmm, good question. I think I can find out for you tomorrow by looking at the shooting schedule, but I'm sure that it will take most of at least a year to complete. Farther into the story, your character becomes somewhat less central, but you're going to be very busy for a long time with this."

Paulo nodded. "Maybe after a while, you can help me to become a writer, too. I think I would like to find out whether I can become very famous and successful. Do you think you would let me stay here that long?"

"I am sure that will not be a problem, Paulo." Brian sat down beside him and put his arm around him. He rubbed the smooth skin of the boy's back, trying to feel where the paint began and ended. It would have to be touched up from time to time, but for now it was as if the color had emerged directly from the skin.

Paulo smiled. Then he looked up at Brian curiously. "Why did you kiss me on the lips today, Papa?"

Brian stood up again and ran his fingers through his white hair. "I'm sorry if I made you feel embarrassed, Paulo. I ... I just had so much appreciation in my heart that I wanted to express..." He turned toward the open verandah.

Paulo came to him and took his hands. "Come and sit down again, Uncle-Papa." He guided Brian to a seat on the bed and stood in front of him. "You did not make me feel bad. I know that you kissed me like any parent would kiss his child. In love and kindness." Paulo kissed the gnarled old hands that he held. "I know that you are a loving person, and that you are a lonely person. Do not be afraid to love me. It would be just the saddest thing if you, who wrote about love and trust, and finding happiness, could not feel safe to express love."

Brian looked at this incredible child through tear-filled eyes.

"I know that you are not a person who likes boys instead of girls. But I know too that older people, grandfather-type people, not *old* people, are fond of the young. Maybe it's like magnets with opposites attracting. Maybe being around young people just makes grandfather types feel young again, remember again. Please don't push me away because *you* feel bad, or feel strange." Paulo held onto his hands until his vision cleared.

"Thank you, Paulo. You are *much* wiser than your years."

Paulo tilted his head in a thoughtful manner. "Now it's time for you to get your bath, Grandpa," He said with a smile. Brian nodded and repaired to the bathroom, closing the door behind him. He made himself comfortable, then drew a bath and began soaking in it. What a day!

Paulo walked in and sat down to watch him.

"Now what?" Brian asked.

Paulo chuckled. "All the young people around here are walking around naked, and all the older people keep themselves covered up. I know what happens to you when you get older. It's not your fault. I don't want you to feel bad about that either."

Brian looked depressed, "It's not a pretty sight."

Paulo smiled, "And where does Beauty lie?" he blinked his eyes repeatedly.

Brian grumbled, "Okay, you've got pretty eyes."

Paulo smiled again. "I like your eyes too, Uncle-Papa. They *say* so much!"

With no more than the usual number of grunts, Brian climbed out of the tub and dried off. *Durned kid's gonna have his eyeballs fall out lookin' at this ugly old carcass,* he thought, but said nothing, as he got dressed for bed.

Paulo ran in and jumped on the bed, getting under the covers, but this time leaving room for someone else. Brian closed the verandah doors and drapes, then crawled into bed beside the boy.

"Good Night, Uncle-Papa," Paulo said softly.

"Good Night, son," Brian replied.

TAKE TWO:

Same time tomorrow, boys?

In the morning, another early visitor awakened them. A young lady had the appliance with her to install on Paulo. Brian saw that she was its regular custodian.

"Give us a while to get our breakfast in us, Miss. We don't want this boy to start getting skinny, you know." Brian adjusted his robe and rubbed the sleep from his eyes.

"There should be plenty of time, Doctor Hawthorne. I know I'm quite early," She smiled.

"Doctor Hawthorne? Please don't start with that. I've had a terrible time trying to dispel that rumor. I am not a medical doctor. Just Mister Hawthorne will do fine."

"That is surprising, sir. Your writing indicates considerable depth of medical knowledge. It must have been an easy mistake for someone to make."

"Do yourself a big favor and don't get appendicitis on me, sweetheart. I can prove I'm not a Doctor."

She reddened. "Appendicitis? Like hanging the wrong appendix on your name, *Mister* Hawthorne?"

Brian raised his eyebrows. He looked at Paulo. "Keep your eye on this one, Paulo. She's smart as a whip." He turned back to the girl. "Just call me Brian, please. And forgive me for being grumpy in the morning."

At this she brightened, and reached back into the hall to pull a serving cart in with the aroma of fresh coffee rising from it.

"Ohmigod! Smart and practical! You're a lifesaver, Miss."

"Angelina Foster. Mister Brian, and Mister Paulo. Pleased to meet you." She shook hands with them.

Brian began distributing the food. Anything that someone else didn't want, he fell on with a good appetite. Paulo ate quickly while Angelina sipped coffee. Shortly Paulo excused himself to go to the bathroom.

When he emerged, Angelina again looked a little sheepish. "Paulo, I'm afraid I need to ask you to bathe again. It's necessary for the adhesives to work properly, and your body is going to be exposed to view to everyone. Would you like help with doing it?"

Now it was Paulo's turn to react strangely. His face first turned red, then pale, then he even looked a little frightened. But he swallowed and said bravely. "I guess I'd like it if you helped me."

Brian was busy choking on his coffee. Without another word, Angelina got up, removed her pullover blouse with a smooth motion, and took Paulo's hand. She led him back into the bathroom while Paulo looked over his shoulder at Brian with incredibly wide eyes.

Angelina left the bathroom door open as she filled the tub. Then she removed her shorts as well and, naked, got into the tub with Paulo. She washed the boy thoroughly, and quickly, and suggested that she wouldn't object if he wanted to wash her as well.

Brian picked up his coffee and moved closer.

Paulo gingerly washed Angelina's delightful bosom, and lingered over the feel of her softness. After his very hesitant touch grew slightly more confident, Angelina smiled and said, "This is fun, but we're going to have to move it along now, Paulo. Please stand up."

Reluctantly, Paulo stopped, and stood. Angelina rinsed the soap from both their bodies and led them from the tub. She dried Paulo briskly with the large towel, then dried herself even more quickly.

Taking his hand again, she led the boy back into the larger room and had him stand on a sturdy chair.

Still naked, Angelina removed the appliance from its locker and began patiently affixing it to the lad. Brian was amazed to see that Paulo did not currently have an erection to get in the way of her task. He had already had to adjust his own posture, and he was an *old* man.

Angelina seemed to read his mind. "Unfortunately, Paulo is under medication to prevent his being able to enjoy this more fully, Brian. It's rather a strange irony. However, I'm sure he'll agree that other aspects of his job are helping to make up for this problem, and he's going to have a *most* wonderful future!" Soon enough, Paulo was again sporting the aggressive organ that made him such a 'Future Ladies' man. Angelina helped him down and put her other items away. "Let's give that a moment to set up, Paulo, then we'll test it to be sure it's secure." She stood up and held him from behind, pulling his head into the softness between her breasts as she rubbed the smooth skin of his chest and stomach. A dreamy expression in her eyes matched that of the boy.

Presently, Angelina kissed Paulo on top of his shaven and painted head. She pulled the chair over and sat him down on it. Kneeling in front of him she checked the adhesion of the attachment. Satisfied that it was secure, she then straddled him on the chair and lowered herself onto his massive pillar. Again pulling his head into her bosom, she writhed for several intense minutes until she finally hoisted herself off of him again.

To both Brian's and Paulo's incredulous stares, Angelina calmly cleaned the organ again and checked the transition zones, then stepped into the bathroom and pulled her clothes back on.

"Well, that seems secure enough to hold up to a day's filming. I believe my work here is done for now. Same time tomorrow, boys?" And she gathered the containers and departed without another word from anyone.

Brian poured himself some more coffee. Paulo looked down at his lap, and then at the closed door.

Finally, they looked at each other.

"And yesterday, we were worried about a *kiss?*" Paulo said.

Then, they laughed.

Today's filming was going to take advantage of early morning light. Many scenes from the book had specific time references to them and were being put in the can as quickly as possible. Once those were out of the way, more indeterminate scenes could be shot until the record was made complete.

This was also Brian's first time on the set of the large house where Paulo's character lived. Brian was amazed at how the imagined dwelling of his fiction had been brought to life. It was a real house, and huge. The construction crews had been working on it feverishly as Paulo and the others were working on their tans. The interior of the house had a large central room with an almost complete circle around the upper level that appeared to be a balcony railing. It was also a circular track for a 'flying-boom' camera that could capture images of any interior scene or angle without getting in the way of the action. A similar device was installed in the ceiling of the pool house room. Brian had not noticed the functional deviation from his imaginings.

With 'Quiet on the set!' everyone's attention was drawn to the front door as a large box was brought into the reception area by two women from the crowd of extras. They were shot at middle distance as the camera focused on the box and the waiting resident, the family matriarch, Miranda. She stood with calm detachment in a pose that portrayed tremendous innate power and determined intent.

It was a psychologically tense moment that the director wanted to get exactly right on film. The hapless character Berry was being delivered into an intractable servitude, into abject debasement and hopeless slavery with this scene, and there were many mental aspects they wanted to portray.

The veteran actress composed her face into the right degree of regret and excitement as she walked around the box, prolonging the moment, and the tension. Finally, she activated the mechanism, and as if in slow motion, the scene unfolded. The prop box magically opened to reveal Paulo, stuffed inside like a ventriloquist's dummy, apparently asleep. Sound effects would hint that he was being kept that way by anesthetic gas. Slowly, he wakened. Like a male version of Venus arising from her shell, the naked Adonis emerged from the confines of his box. The excitement, and the carnal appetites of his audience, would be rising with him. This was an image of **potent** sexual energy, coiled and aching to be released.

The morning light reflected in shimmering delicacy from his smooth, pliant skin as the cameras lovingly circled and focused. His delectable, but still unravished form filled the viewing monitors with unforgettable images as his vulnerability, and burgeoning sexual readiness, stood silent and constrained. Brian could feel the tension building through the underplay as the characters interacted in tormented anticipation.

A psychological chasm was being breached; a *person* was becoming a possessed *thing*. This woman had ordered, and received, a sex slave for her pleasure, and that of her family. Her mixed feelings of guilt and excitement, fear and lust, were providing a rich texture for the camera to record. Paulo's role seemed much simpler -- submission, with an odd companion of pride, and delight. Brian wondered if Paulo was using the confused mixture of emotions from this morning to help him capture the expressions for the film.

Finally, the character 'Miranda' led 'Berry' away off-camera to consummate her ownership, and the director called 'cut' and ended the tension. A hubbub of voices began speaking as equipment was moved around for the next scenes.

And so it continued, a chaotic mixture of scenes and sequences from the novel were acted out and recorded in a confusing jumble of twisted times. Brian knew it would all get sorted out and put into the proper sequences for the film, but it was confusing.

It was also exhilarating, especially for Paulo, who absolutely blossomed in the crucible of the camera focus. Brian observed as Paulo became more professional each day. He was pleased that Paulo had made new friends among the cast.

Often, Paulo and his friends would repair to the comfort of Brian's hotel suite after the shooting was over for the day, to visit with each other as real people. The casual nature of these visits was a pleasure to Brian as he felt that his own creations had sprung to life and developed their own characters.

"You know what would be perfect?" One of the twins, Martha Madison, spoke. "We should be getting together in the Hawkes family house. That swimming pool is the greatest!"

Her sister, Mary Madison, responded. "Who is going to own that house after the filming is complete, Brian? Have you decided to relocate here for good?"

Brian was attempting to concentrate on his cards. The fact that these two girls liked to get naked for their regular poker games was distraction enough. It wasn't even strip poker. He regularly lost to them, although ordinarily he broke even in poker. Fortunately, the stakes were really minuscule; they were only having fun. At length he responded, "I've considered acquiring the house, and moving in after the movie's done. But I haven't figured out who else would want to live there. I am absolutely not going to live in that house alone."

"You're right about that. After all this, to live alone in that house would be the worst kind of torture. But aren't there lots of people who would want to live there too?" Martha asked again.

"I'm sure there are. But I also know that I wouldn't be able to get along with all of them." They knew of certain cast and crew members whose personalities were very abrasive. Martha nodded knowingly. One of the disappointments was the character 'young Kayla' who didn't seem to want to associate with the others beyond what was necessary for the filming. At the end of each day she would disappear abruptly.

That was rough on young Paulo, who had been attracted to her, and Paulo's friends were very supportive and consoling. The director wisely had adjusted the schedule to accommodate her early departure from the island as soon as possible. She was well-pleased, and everyone else relieved. Fortunately, the young actress who was to play the more mature Kayla was very sweet and considerate. She was fitting into the group very nicely.

"You should live there with children, Papa. Everyone knows that you love children," Paulo asserted from across the table, and pushed his lips together at him as if making a kiss. Brian reddened as the girls laughed. He had been accused of an over-fondness for children by an annoying busybody, now ex-busybody, among the film executive committee. A rousing defense of his trustworthiness, and sexual maturity, had been raised by his friends, acquaintances, and occasional bedmates and the offending party had been hounded from the island. He still got teased about it, however.

"Watch it, boy! Or I'll spank you again tonight," Brian said gruffly.

"Thus proving my point, Uncle-Papa," Paulo said with a wink.

Brian put his cards down in front of him, and glared at them. "Are we playing poker, or not?" He demanded.

Mary and Martha both took an inhaled breath, puffing out their chests as Mary replied, "*We* are! Who knows what game you're playing? Call." She riffled the stacks of coins in front of her, a glaring contradiction to his own dwindling pile. Young as they were, his friends knew that his cantankerous behavior was only a show; inside he was a teddy bear.

Brian stared in dismay. "Now I know how Doctor Frankenstein felt. I've created monsters."

Martha stepped around the table to give him a hug. "Now, Papa Brian, you know that we are not monsters. Monsters aren't this friendly." He patted her bare bottom affectionately. "Nor as pretty. Which monster are you, anyway, Mia or Kira?"

"I play the part of Kira. My name's longer." She dimpled, "Does it matter?"

Brian gave her a kiss, and she sat back down. "No, of course not. It does get confusing sometimes, though. So many people are playing multiple roles."

"We get into that, too, or at least we will. We're going to be playing our own young cousins, Rae and Gloria, blonde hair and all."

Mary jumped in. "Maybe Brian will be able to win for a while when we do. I've never been a blonde *all over* before."

Brian tried to picture it. "I don't think *that* is likely to help my game." He shook his head, as if to dispel the image.

Martha resumed, with a smile. "Then you have a number of walk-ons who appear, do their thing, and disappear again. Like some of the Daughters of Diana, half of them are also Soldiers of the Founders Society, and only two have speaking parts."

"That's because they're outdoors people. Whose turn is it anyway?"

Paulo spoke again. "Mine. I was serious about the children, Uncle-Papa. You could open up a school, or an orphanage. They could learn swimming, acting, how to cook. I know the townspeople would support anything like that."

"And they could all be naked too, Papa. You'd enjoy that!" Mary teased again.

"I'm not going to spend my declining years baby-sitting children," Brian fussed.

"Of course not, they would need to have teachers, and trainers. They could be naked too," Martha pointed out.

"Hmm." Brian looked thoughtful.

"Raise," Said Paulo, adding coins to the pot.

"You're always raising," Grumbled Brian.

"Yeah. He's always up for a game of poker too," Mary added.

"*Up for*" Martha giggled softly, "*Poke* 'er."

Brian sighed.

"Papa Brian, you're sounding rather out of sorts this evening. Would you like to come to bed for a little while?" Angelina Foster said from the snack bar. She had been talking with two other boys who played the roles of Newton and Darwin. They were not wearing paint as their roles allowed them to stay dry, and they could get made up as needed.

Their heads and bodies had been shaved, however, and they were both quite naked as a matter of personal choice. They had found that their exposed skin drew the affectionate caresses of their female companions often enough to be worth any degree of discomfort. The movie had a continual sexual tension to it, and many of the cast members found themselves responding after-hours to each other.

Mary and Martha lowered their heads as they smiled and flashed their eyes at him. Paulo nodded vigorously.

Angelina was a frequent visitor to Brian's suite, and not just in the morning.

Brian tossed his cards down again. "Why not? You're all going to talk about me anyway." He stood and stretched, looking around the room. The wall behind the poker table had double doors into the adjacent hotel room, which had been taken over by Mary and Martha. The first thing they had done was to chain and padlock the doors *in the open position*. Nothing happened in Brian's suite that was not public knowledge on a daily basis. He had as little privacy as the sex slave in his novel.

Paulo also threw in his cards, and escorted Brian to the bed. His adoption of Brian as his grandfather was known and accepted by all. Paulo sat beside him as Angelina brought a light drink tray over for both of them. Angelina knelt in front of Brian and began unfastening his clothes while he sipped his drink.

The twins looked at Paulo's hand and gave him the pot. 'Newton' and 'Darwin' moved to the open poker seats and started a new round. Brian didn't want to know what the stakes might be.

Naked at last, and having finished his drink, Brian lay down on one side of the bed. Angelina, who seemed to be able to dress or undress with the speed of a professional clothes model, lay down naked beside him. Paulo crawled up on the other side of her and hugged her tightly. Other than his make-up, he had not worn more than a towel or bathrobe in months. Paulo had gotten as used to being naked as his character.

Brian rolled toward her and reached out to gently caress her lovely bosom. Paulo, observing, began to mirror his motions.

"Only room for one at a time, Paulo," Brian suggested.

Paulo smiled. "I don't want to get inside, Uncle-Papa, I just want to help with the preparations."

Angelina agreed. "Leave the boy alone, Brian. He is, after all, a professional, you know. Besides, I like being the center of attention like this."

"I would never have guessed that," Brian said dryly. Angelina shot him a sharp look, then smiled and closed her eyes. Paulo was actually studying his actions, Brian realized. Well, as Angelina had intimated, for the purpose of the movie, this was his vocation. Brian trailed his fingers tantalizingly across her soft skin and cupped her breast gently. His fingers squeezed the nipple softly and rolled the tissue with tenderness. He could feel the little elements of erectile tissue engorging under his touch. On her other side, Paulo's small hand was repeating his actions faithfully.

"Can you feel the tissue swelling, Paulo?" Brian asked softly. The boy nodded. "Put your mouth over the nipple and move it around with your lips." Paulo did as instructed. Angelina gently bit her lower lip and shivered slightly. Brian gently coached and encouraged the boy as Angelina grew more and more excited.

Brian realized that it was time for him to act, and he knew that he could not afford to delay. He prepared to approach Angelina when she suddenly moved to get on top of him! Guiding him gently she slid into position and began moving back and forth over him. Curiously, Brian could *feel* the waves of contractions that she was squeezing him with. It gave an intensity he had not found in many years. She moved back and forth on him, and rubbed his skin expertly as his breathing quickened.

Abruptly, he stiffened, as his tired old body found the strength and stamina to ejaculate yet again, and Angelina clamped down ferociously with her abdominal muscles. Paulo was stroking the skin of her back as she smothered Brian with kisses, then she rolled off of him and lay beside him again.

"Brian, you may be an old man, but you could write a book, old man!" She smiled at him. Brian relaxed and lay still, another triumph against the thief of time had been won.

Paulo continued stroking and caressing her, and soon she pulled him close and kissed him, stroking the smooth skin of his back. He may not be able to do anything further for her at the moment, but he could cuddle like a champ!

Angelina spent the night with them, saving time for the morning rituals. Time that she put to good purpose as she gave Paulo an extra long ride to test how well the appliance was secured. They were both perspiring heavily by the time she finished, and she had to rinse them both off in the shower again.

"Paulo, I am sorry that you cannot benefit from this exercise as I do. That is so unfair." She leaned her forehead against his.

"Do not you worry, Angelina my lover. This time is more precious to me than you can know." He gently reached out and stroked her breast with his small, but educated hand. Angelina kissed him, then gathered her things and departed.

"You're getting an education, Paulo," Brian said as they walked down to begin the day of filming.

"Yes. I am learning fast. Months ago I learned how much fun it was to shed my clothes and let the people stare at my nakedness. I learned also how pleasant it was to feel the air and the sunshine on my skin. But recently I have learned many even more wonderful things." Paulo looked up at him and squeezed his hand as they walked. "You have been my teacher for most of it, Uncle-Papa."

"I have had fun, too, Paulo. More fun than I ever thought I would at any age. You have helped me to see and enjoy life as well. I wish to thank you for that, and for being a good companion." Paulo smiled back at him, flashing his brilliant white teeth. Brian squeezed his hand in return as they continued in silence.

TAKE THREE:

You have big dreams

Brian had been invited to the executive producer's office. He walked in and approached the desk.

Jake looked up, taking in the cane in Brian's right hand, and said, "Good Morning, Brian! Thanks for coming by. Have a seat."

"No problem, Jake. What can I do for you?"

Jake Wagner looked at him appraisingly. Technically, they were peers. Neither worked for the other. That was unusual for Jake; he was used to having the upper hand.

"Everything comfortable in your quarters, Brian? You're very important to us, you know."

Brian smiled, "You *know* that it is, Jake. But thanks for asking, anyway. Why don't you just say what's on your mind?"

Jake swiveled in his chair, toying with a pencil. Abruptly, he leaned back. "The movie schedule is working well, Brian. There's a lot of interest in our progress back on the mainland. The home office, and the investors, are pleased with what we've had to show them so far."

Brian leaned back also. He looked at his cane, and began rubbing his fingers over the surface.

Jake watched him. Every negotiation was like a big game hunt to him. "Your book is going to please a lot of people when we put it up on the big screen, Brian."

"Thank you, again, Jake. I'm pleased with how it is being done."

Jake turned sideways in his chair. "You've written a sequel, haven't you?"

Brian looked up. So that's what this was about. His heart leaped.

"The sequel doesn't have much of a story to it, Jake. The action is all in the first book. All I did was take the same characters, and extend their interaction a little further," Brian spoke casually. He didn't care if Jake knew how excited he was, but if Jake liked to make it a game, Brian saw no reason not to let him have his fun.

"There's much more to it than that, Brian. We've read the sequel. It takes these characters a *lot* further, and into some really interesting developments."

Brian bowed his head. *We've read the sequel,* Brian thought, *that means someone else read the sequel for you.* He said nothing.

"We are considering making a second movie, based on your sequel. There are advantages to trying to make the arrangements now, while everything is still in place. We will need to buy the rights from you, and hopefully, you will help us again with the screenplay, and other advice."

Brian suddenly realized that his best negotiating ploy was to not negotiate at all, but to simply let Jake lay the cards out. Chances were, he'd like the offer anyway. At his age, what difference did it make?

Jake watched him. "We want to offer the same royalties, profit share, residuals, everything ... and we are going to *triple* the flat fee!"

Ah, thought Brian, *that was the item he was holding onto!* He cleared his throat.

Jake was still observing him. "I've heard that you might be interested in acquiring the big house we built, for your retirement dwelling? I think that could possibly be arranged, but if we go ahead with the sequel, we'll need to extend our use of it for a short time. Your bonus could make it easy for you to buy the house from us."

Brian smiled, *blunder* or *bait*? He wondered, shaking his head.

Jake froze.

Brian looked up. "I want the sequel to be produced, Jake. I want the house, too. How about this? You get the sequel, my help in the screenplay, my technical advice. I get the rights as described, the triple bonus as described, and the house *and its grounds*, gratis."

Jake stared at him, tapping the pencil softly. He knew that he could easily drive a harder bargain than this, but he wouldn't gain anything if he did. The house, after all, was only useful for this purpose. Finally, he broke eye contact.

"Done," Jake said.

Brian rose to his feet, extending his hand. Jake shook hands with him, smiling.

"Send the writers over whenever you want to get started, Jake. I don't think it will be difficult to do the transition. And I'll sign the papers whenever they're ready." *After going over them with my legal representative*, Brian thought, but did not say.

Brian walked out of Jake's office with a bit more spring in his step than he had going in. A twinge in his right knee reminded him that some of his springs were nigh onto bustin'. He slowed down and grew thoughtful. *Okay, you're getting a house. Did you ever figure out what you're going to do with it?*

He liked Paulo's suggestion of running a school. Everything that he had ever wanted to do as a kid could be made available to some needy, deserving, (*naked?* -- his mind added), and talented children. He pictured horseback riding, swimming, sports, art, music, drama, culinary arts, -- *What about an appreciation for fine literature, or even the stuff you write?*

Brian stopped walking, and put his mind back in its pen.

He found two film crews working today, one on the Children of Life, the other in the false front arena they had made for the winery house. Paulo would be in the latter, if he was involved today.

Paulo was involved today. It was the grand party scene, the culmination of decadence represented by the society that produced sex slaves. It reminded him of the depravity scene in the Cecil B. De Mille work <u>The Ten Commandments</u>. Brian turned away and checked the shooting schedule.

Ah, tomorrow afforded something more to his liking. Brian decided to return to his hotel room. Perhaps he would begin work on the second screenplay. He knew that Paulo would be very tired at the end of this day.

Lost in thought, Brian hardly noticed as he wandered through the village that very few of the out-of-town folk were about. He was jostled by a group of men excitedly making their way into a pub. Sports was on the conversational agenda, and the men were discussing which was the better team in an upcoming match. Brian merged with the crowd, thinking that perhaps some of the local brew would taste good after his lengthy walking.

He tried to follow the conversation about the game, but his language skills were no match for their familiarity. It was only after the subject changed that he was able to keep up. He wasn't pleased with what he was hearing.

"When this cursed movie has ended, we will have to try to bring back our regular business again, and it won't be easy. Many of the cruise ships have forgotten that they ever used to stop here."

"The bigger ships do not stop at so small a place anywhere, Cousin."

"All the ships are getting bigger."

"Yes, and when the cursed movie ends, we will have very lean times."

"What about fishing? We used to be a fishing village."

"It is all used up. We do not have the equipment anymore, and the government controls who may fish where. We won't be able to compete."

"There is nothing to be done. We may as well get used to drowning our sorrows."

Brian considered letting them know that there was good news; That a second movie was going to be filmed.

He wasn't sure that this would be greeted with enthusiasm, however, and decided to keep his head down awhile longer.

"There must be something we can do."

"What? What can we do? Shall we make shirts? There are whole cities of people making shirts now, for pennies! Shall we go into manufacturing? What will we make? What factories will we use? Why did the movie people come here anyway? Because we are 'quaint' and backward. Because we have to take their money, and let them tell us how to live! And we bow and scrape before them!"

Brian realized now that not only was he unwelcome here, but he could also be in some danger! But this defeatism was wrong. It had to be. Didn't the characters in his book face a similar problem and overcome it? Hadn't they been faced with superior force and inadequate manufacturing capability? How did his story relate to the problems of these people, the parents of his beloved children?

Brian thought about what he wanted to accomplish when the movies would end. He wouldn't be able to fit a hundred or two hundred children into that house. It was a big house, but it wasn't that big. He would need a real school structure, dormitories, libraries. Too bad the other structures that were to be used in the movie were only going to be made of cardboard. These men could have been employed in making those structures, and others.

Brian's head snapped up. He quickly put it down again. Those around him probably thought he was beginning to doze.

But he was wide awake! This could be an answer to their problem, and his as well! The structures that weren't going to be built included a winery and great house, a hospital, and a castle! Could it be that the interest in the movie story could revitalize the tourism industry here if the tourists could look through the actual story structures? Even if not, the building itself would be economic activity.

How would he get tourists here? Fusion powered airplanes and magnetic levitation? Those gadgets worked okay in a storyline, but he needed reality. Too bad he couldn't use that magnificent efficiency whereby the material removed from his fictional underground shuttle system was used to create buildings.

Brian almost smacked his forehead in realization! He needed to do some research, but first he needed to get out of here! Across the way, someone coughed. That was it! Waiting for a short period, he started to cough, pulling his floppy hat down over his face. In a racking spasm of incessant coughing, he stumbled to the door, using his cane to part the crowd. Once out the door, he continued coughing till he reached the alleyway, and then quieted. He didn't think he had been recognized, or even considered as anything but a nuisance.

He thought about where he could find information. Maybe there was hope after all!

Two weeks! For two weeks he had been gathering in the data! Like a huge fishing net, the more he drew in, the bigger it became! He had discovered that some of the nearby structures had been built from locally quarried stone, which was an excellent material. The building codes still listed it as a preferred construction material, and stone on stone, without mortar, was approved in this climate.

More significantly, a geological study showed that this entire island chain had been connected several thousand years ago, when the ocean level was lower. The yawning chasm of ocean that separated the islands was, relatively speaking, only a shallow lake.

Brian had studied the adjoining ocean floor topography, and noticed that the five-island grouping was close enough for a rather daring scheme. Brian had a picture in his mind of using tunnel-shuttle technology to connect the islands, and also provide him with a vast amount of building material.

These five local islands, with the one he was on the second largest, had a very disconnected economy. Each had separate transportation, energy, and communication networks. They also had different problems. Brian studied the economies of scale that could be introduced by linking their networks through sub-sea tunnels. There was a potential payoff, but it was decades away, and much depended on the actual cost of tunnel construction. Synergy and serendipity could only take the project so far.

Brian had posted a cryptic, but communicative help-wanted ad looking for his own brand of engineer, (one with an abundance of ingenuity).

Wanted: Rosita? Barbara? Needed; an out of this world class engineer for advanced project. Fringe benefits abound. Contact BBH.

He had gotten many responses, and several seemed promising. The most interesting one was from a young fellow surprisingly named Esteban Mendoza. Brian decided to interview him.

"Are you really Mister Hawthorne? Brian Hawthorne?"

"Yes. That's my name. And yours is Esteban Mendoza? Very musical quality there. Are you an engineer?"

"If you're the Brian Hawthorne who wrote <u>Outlandish!,</u> then I just may be the kind of engineer you want. What are you building?"

"Yeah, I wrote it. I don't suppose it will hurt to tell you. I want to build a shuttle system."

"Then I am your man, Mister Hawthorne. I've been building tunnels and underground facilities in Europe for five years now."

"This could be a little tricky. There are some factors that I haven't mentioned."

"I want the job, Mister Hawthorne. I'm looking for a project now, I'm available to travel, and I want to meet the man who made Science Fiction a fit subject for bar-room discussions."

"That is the worst bit of flattery that I have ever had hurled at me! I deny everything. I didn't know the bed was loaded!"

"I think we'll get along fine, sir. I'd like to look at your project."

"You'll find me in room 207 of the Hotel Garnet. Let me tell you how to get here."

Mendoza had taken a week to find his way. He appeared late one afternoon, as Brian was saying good-bye to the screenwriters for the day. Brian talked with him briefly, then showed him the topographic maps of the group of islands.

Mendoza whistled. "Going underwater must be one of the factors you failed to mention."

Brian nodded. "I know there's danger, but the material seems to be consistent, and the strength is more than we will need. It's not as soft as the chalk under the English Channel, nor will we need to go as deep."

"That's not the only problem. Any excavation this deep has a special problem with air exchange. It can be deadly, and water leaks would be fatal to the project."

"That's why I need your help. But as I see it, the main thing we need to do is figure out whether we can find a way to do it economically."

"What's our funding source?"

Brian smiled, "We don't have one yet."

Mendoza stared at him. "Have you ever heard of the phrase, Pipe Dream?" he asked.

"Let me explain," Brian put his arm around Mendoza's shoulder, and guided him to the snack bar. He fetched a couple of bottles of the local beer, for which he had developed a taste, and continued.

"We have to develop a program for a coordinated enterprise, which will remove material from our tunnel projects, and use it as raw material for above ground construction projects on this and all the islands. We'll need to use local labor, who may be relatively unskilled. And we need to coordinate with the filming schedule of the second movie, to take advantage of their needs, too."

"Excuse me, the second movie?" Mendoza looked puzzled.

"I assume that you are aware that we are filming the movie version of <u>Outlandish!</u> here on this island?"

"I heard something to that effect. Is it still going on?"

"I'd say we're about in the middle of it right now."

"Fantastic! I hope I can catch some of the action."

"I'm sure you will," Brian said emotionlessly. "Have you also read the sequel?"

Mendoza's eyes opened wide. "They're going to make *that* movie too?" Brian nodded, smiling. Mendoza grew a big, happy smile. "Now, that is something to drink to!" He raised his bottle to Brian's.

"One of the things we may be able to use the material for ... is the castle," Brian added. Mendoza's eyes grew wide again.

"Señor Hawthorne, you have big dreams."

"Yeah, I know, big pipe dreams." He clinked bottles with Mendoza again. "If you're in, say so. We'll need to make a presentation to the engineers of the film crew in less than a week. We've got to calculate what these projects are going to cost us so that we can give them a price. Then we have to sell the whole deal to the Islands Governing Board."

"I'm in. Where do I set up?"

TAKE FOUR:

That's when you'll get your reward

Brian Hawthorne, Pamela Harriston, and Esteban Mendoza were seated on one side of the large conference table of the film company meeting room. A puzzled-looking Jake Wagner was sitting at the head of the table, and the engineering crew were represented on the other side.

"Brian, I understand you're making a bid on building *the Castle* for the second film?" Jake asked curiously.

"Yes, Jake. Your engineers were kind enough to let me know how much they expected to spend just to make mock-ups work, and I suggested that it might be more practical to put together something a bit more solid instead. At least that way something permanent will remain."

Jake had flashed annoyance that his people had given away *negotiation information*, but he could understand why they had done so.

"What would be the advantage to us to have a permanent structure?" He asked.

"No large advantage, I'll admit. You wouldn't have to rush your production, and you'd have a better goodwill factor on your balance sheets for providing it to the community when you're done here. I think I should point out to you -- there are elements of resentment in the community about your presence."

"He's right about that, Mr. Wagner. My boys get comments all the time from the natives." Jake glared the man into silence.

"What we propose to do, Mr. Wagner, is lease the structure to you, for the amount of time you require, for thirty-five percent over your own estimated costs for doing the work yourself," Pamela Harriston spoke for the first time. Brian saw the hint of a smile on Jake's face.

"And why should we pay more for what we can do for ourselves at lower cost?" Jake asked mildly.

"Because that leaves your men free to work on other projects, the Hospital, for example, as well as relieving you of an insurance burden."

Jake looked thoughtful. Directing his next question at his engineering team, he asked, "Do you think they can get the job done the way we need it to be?"

The group polled each other with their eyes. The lead man cleared his throat. "You were introduced to us as Esteban Mendoza. Would that be 'Stubby' Mendoza?" He was looking across the table.

Mendoza laughed. "Yeah, that's me."

"They'll get it done, Boss," The lead man said confidently. Jake didn't like to be called Boss, but he liked expressions of confidence.

Brian interrupted. "One thing more I need to ask. To tell you the truth, we're operating on a shoestring. We'd like to have your payment in advance of construction."

Jake looked at him in surprise. What a weak negotiating position! Then he smiled, uncharacteristically. "All right Brian, we'll let you take the contract. After all, you certainly ought to know how to do it, and ought to want it to be right. But, ... I'm going to put in a penalty clause. You'll have to make sure that it's ready by *date certain*."

Brian thought for a moment, then he rose and extended his hand to Jake. "Done!" They shook hands. For Brian, that settled it. For Jake -- well, he was more flexible. 'Stubby' also shook hands with the lead man.

They walked out in silence, occasionally glancing at each other. Finally, when they were clear of the building, and out of earshot, Brian looked over at Mendoza. "How did he know you? Had you met before?"

Mendoza smiled, "We've not met. But I think he's heard of me." He paused, then continued, "A little over two years ago, we were boring a tunnel for a Swiss resort. As you can imagine, the bigger the diameter, the slower the going. I convinced the company to try something radical," He stopped, using his hands to describe the action. "You've seen films of landslides, where mountains of mud and stone go careening through ravines? Well, we bored two smaller tunnels, then cross-bored to set charges. We had tried to run a computer simulation, but the program wasn't up to it. It was all intuition and guesswork. We blew the charges in a sequence, with subsequent detonations after the main volleys to lift the material. Luckily the tunneling was at a pretty steep gradient for a highway, because we *fractured* that rock, and floated seventy-five *thousand* cubic yards of rubble out of the mountain in one afternoon. It cut two years off the project. I got a huge bonus, and a bit of a reputation."

Brian stared at him. "It's amazing. It's so hard to believe ... They call you *Stubby*? You have my sympathy, Mr. Mendoza."

Mendoza reddened, "It's not that! I went to engineering school in Scotland. That's what the Scots did to Esteban."

Pamela was stifling laughter. Brian chuckled, "I know. I've gotten reports about you. I knew 'Stubby' couldn't be a physical description."

Pam laughed. Mendoza joined her, "Thanks, I guess things could be worse." Brian laughed too, "If they've given me a nickname, I don't want to hear it!" They were still in a good mood when they reached the hotel. Mendoza had been able to get the room across the hall from Brian's suite. It would be convenient for the parties, but Pamela had had to take a business suite on the lower level. It was just as well. They had to set up several computer workstations, drafting tables, file cabinets, and so forth.

Particularly as of this morning, they were in business! They stopped in Pam's office.

"Okay, the next order of business is to make the presentation to the Governing Board. We'll need to have our licenses and permits either ready or filled out, and our whole business plan laid out for the microscope and the fine-tooth comb," Pamela asserted.

Brian looked at Mendoza. "I think you might want to polish up that timeline chart you showed me, Stubby. We'll probably need it for that presentation. Without their approval, we can't even order drilling equipment."

Mendoza glanced at him, then smiled. "You know, I actually like that name, as long as everyone knows it's not physical."

Pam put her hand on his arm, "Don't worry. If anyone asks, I'll testify for you."

Mendoza grinned, "Yeah? How would you know?"

She smiled slyly, "I'll know soon enough! I've been invited to Brian's parties."

Brian took control. "Back to business, kids, it's still early in the day. Are we going to need any more office talent, Pam? And when?" The reality of the situation was weighing heavily on him.

"Not unless Mr. Mendoza needs some help with the design work. I can handle this end so far."

"Let's talk about that for a minute, Brian. Are you sure you want to go ahead with that plan to use hydro-cutting for the tunnel work?"

Brian looked serious. "I'm sure I want to. Let's get some test equipment and conduct an experiment. We're in big trouble if we can't bring that facet on-line."

"I can get the cutting equipment here in two days, if you'll authorize the expenditure. Do you have a source for the stone?"

"I think the original quarry site for the local buildings is still available. Last time I checked, it was only being used for target practice," Brian smiled. "Order the equipment. I'm going to go see how our movie stars are coming along."

Brian walked thoughtfully down the hall, heading for his room. His book sales had jumped again, publicity about the movies, no doubt. The money that the movie company was paying him was also in the bank. He was even living here free of charge, thanks to his deal with them.

He had at last achieved complete financial security and freedom! And he was risking it all.

Brian had already walked past the elevator on his way to the stairs. He stopped and turned around. *Ride up, walk down; you owe yourself that much!* Brian pushed the elevator button. He was doing the right thing, for good reasons. It would have to work out.

The sensible thing to do was to make sure that if events went horribly wrong, that he would have at least a minimum safe haven to fall back on. That would have to be the house. Nice house, he thought. He would need a small, secure income as well, something that couldn't be touched. He would talk to Pam about that, she was good with such things.

Pamela Harriston had been a suggestion of Mendoza's. He had worked with her before, knew the quality of her work, and that she was available and willing to relocate. She had organized their enterprise, and kept them from going down a couple of blind alleys, business-wise. She had already earned her first year's salary as far as Brian was concerned. Mendoza and Harriston were his employees, and their hotel expenses were his as well, at least until the house became available. So far, he was staying ahead of the game, but they were soon going to need some heavy-duty financing for the rest of it.

That's where the Island Governing Council came in. They would need to convince that group about the advantages of this project, and have them either finance it outright, or endorse a bond proposal. Brian didn't care which, but they needed outside money. This project was going to cost *millions*.

Brian entered his hotel room to find it surprisingly quiet and peaceful. The verandah doors were open, but the room was in shade. It was very comfortable, and Brian was convinced it was the best room in the hotel. He poured himself half a serving of brandy and sipped it.

The feeling that he was dwelling too much on things stole over him. He finished the brandy and set the glass carefully aside. Lying back on the bed, he fell asleep.

"Brian, are you okay?" Stubby was looking down at him worriedly. "I knocked but you didn't answer. Then the door came open, and I started worrying when I saw you lying there..."

Brian laughed, "I'm okay. I got tired of getting up to open the door, so I messed up the lock so it wouldn't lock. I get visitors all the time and most of them don't even knock."

"Oh, good. I came up to show you some sketches for the castle. Your description of it in the book is a great guide, but I needed to put some lines down."

"Hey, great, I'd love to see it. Let's have a look." Brian got up and suggested they spread the sketches on the snack bar. "Grab a beer, Stubby. Grab two!"

Mendoza spread out a plan view and a floor plan. "I used a lot of latitude with the floor plan, Brian. You didn't say anything at all about the utilities, except that everything was hidden. So, I put the power plant here, with substations here and here, and distribution panels on every other floor in the tower."

"Power plant? Why do we need a power plant?" Brian asked.

"Jeez, Brian! This thing sucks power! You've got water circulating in the moat, heated swimming pools, elevators. lights, theaters, and don't forget the shuttle!"

"Shuttle?" Brian looked at him.

"Well, yeah. You have the castle just up from the big house; to get back and forth, you jump in the horizontal elevator, right?"

Brian scratched his head, and smiled. "I guess you're right, Stubby. It just wouldn't be right without it." He raised his beer bottle in toast and clicked bottles with Mendoza.

"I'll run a power line down to the big house, too. You'll be buying a lot of diesel, but you won't have a utility bill. Oh, and we'll capture hot water for bathing and heating the pools from the generator, too; that's just good engineering. Let's see, the shuttle will be on a cable, but the castle elevator will be hydraulic. It'll be set up just like you described, with floor sensors and everything."

Brian nodded, looking over the drawings.

"Oh, that reminds me. We're going to need a computer programmer, for this and for our excavation tools. I'd like to start the search now, 'cause we need the right kind of talent." Mendoza looked at him. Brian nodded again.

"I'm going to include all the communication cables and everything, too. Are you really going to put a computer in every room? If you use this for tourists, or whatever, you may not need them."

Brian thought about it. "We'll need them, Stubby. If you make the rooms small, as described, they'll expect other amenities. We'll need to set up an on-demand library of entertainments and other resources, but we can make that a part of the theatrical productions facility."

"Hmm. Sounds like you're getting confused between the book and reality, Boss." Mendoza was looking puzzled.

"Not really, Stubby. We are either going to have tourists in there, or students. Either way, we'll need pretty much the same facilities. One of the reasons I wanted to build more than the house was because I wanted to open up a school for kids like the ones we're using in the movie. I guess you can think of it as my legacy. Actually, I'm thinking of it as my old age entertainment program. I need people around me, Stubby. They bring life to me, the way sunlight keeps a plant alive."

Mendoza was looking strangely at him. "I knew you had a reason for doing all this. I just thought you wanted to get filthy, stinkin' rich!"

Brian laughed, "I'm probably more likely to become filthy, stinkin' poor, my friend. We may only have one chance in twelve to pull this off!"

Now Mendoza looked distinctly worried. "One chance in twelve? I never thought about failure."

"You're the one who told me that water leakage would kill us. What do you mean you never thought about failure?"

"Water is just a concern. Engineers don't think they can fail at anything. They just run into problems sometimes."

"Well, what do you think it is when you run into too many problems to solve?"

Mendoza laughed. "Hah! That never happens, never! To an engineer, an atomic bomb is just a big firecracker. It's all just numbers. And I've looked at the numbers for this. We are not going to fail!"

Mendoza finished his beer, set the empty forcefully down on the snack bar, and stood tall. "I am going to sew these islands together, and build this castle, and then, if you want me to build the damned starship, I'll do that too!" With that, he strode from the room.

Brian stared after him. "Amen, Brother!" he said softly, and sipped his beer.

Brian was on the phone with Pam later when his guests started arriving. He had almost forgotten that tonight was poker night. Mary and Martha discovered the drawings.

"What's this, Brian? Good Lord, it's the castle! This looks so real! Look! There's the grand hall, and here's the tower elevator. Somebody put in a lot of work on this. Did the studio send this over?"

Brian cut his conversation short and smiled, "No, my friend Mr. Esteban Mendoza did these. You'll be meeting him tonight, I'm sure. He's going to be the engineer in charge of building this castle."

They both reacted with astonishment. "They're going to *build* it? Oh, how wonderful!" Both girls rushed to embrace him.

"I can't wait to see it! Oh, my gosh! We'll *be* here! We'll be *there*! Brian! We're going to be in the *second* movie, too!" Martha could not contain her enthusiasm.

"We couldn't make it without you girls. It wouldn't be right," Brian said mildly.

"We're going to be older in the second movie, Brian. Will you still love us when we're old and gray?" Mary asked teasingly.

"Even more than I do today, I assure you," Brian replied, patting each girl's curvaceous rump affectionately.

Paulo had also examined the castle drawings. He was still in costume from the day's shooting, and seemed to find it easy to remain in character as well. "I guess that means they will be removing my tattoos at some point. I hope it won't be painful."

Brian and the girls laughed. Mary and Martha pulled him into the embrace as well, and rubbed his back and backside in friendly familiarity. "Paulo, you are so wonderful. Your 'Dildo-boy' act has brought us so-o-o much pleasure. Martha and I have sworn to give you a proper reward when you come off your medication." Paulo blushed at this revelation, and the girls kissed him tenderly, without stopping their affectionate caresses.

Brian gave Mary and Martha each a kiss, and without any reluctance at all kissed Paulo as well, then stepped away from them. "I'll go see if Mister Mendoza is busy. I'd like to have you meet him."

Paulo and the girls continued caressing each other, and began moving toward the bed. No cameras were rolling, but more rehearsal couldn't hurt, could it?

When Brian and Stubby returned, the action was in full swing on the bed, and did not stop. The men moved to the snack bar and sat down, facing across the counter toward the bed. Brian handed a beer to Stubby from the little fridge and grabbed one for himself.

"What chapter would you say this is, Brian? I recognize the characters, but I'm not sure where they are in the plot line."

"Hmm. Difficult to be precise. I'd guess this is the scene on the eve of Kayla's birthday, but someone forgot to set up candles."

Mary, who was least involved at the moment, winked at them, and blew them a kiss, then went back to her activity.

"Okay, then, Brian. I take it you approve of the design plans for the castle. Did you have anything that you wanted to add to them?"

"Not really, I like what you've done. Everything I see looks perfect to me. I wouldn't change a thing. Want another beer?"

"Sure, thanks. We've got an appointment to see the Island Governing Council next Wednesday afternoon. I'm going to work up a presentation with a laptop and a projection unit. Pam's going to have some economic charts ready that should close the deal for us. We're looking at seven years to payback time on the initial phases."

"Wow! That's better than we thought. What made the difference?"

"Well, it appears to me that we're going to have to use a hybrid type of drilling. First we'll dig a big ring of stone, then we'll cut it up and shape the construction stone elements out of it. That's going to produce a lot of tailings, but I'm setting up to use them in roadbed construction for the warehouse structures, and in foundation preparation. This is going to be the biggest construction project these islands have seen since the coral moved in!"

"Sounds like you've got quite a plan there. What role will I need to play?"

"We'd like you to remind them how much the film production company has benefited them, and that you are responsible for getting the second movie started as well."

"Isn't that a bit of an exaggeration?" He demurred.

"Brian, *you wrote the book*. You're responsible! Don't you know anything about sales?"

Brian chuckled, "I guess I can always learn more. I'll be ready, though. All I have to do is pretend I'm talking to Jake Wagner."

Mary and Martha were looking at them. "You guys are a tough crowd. What does it take to entertain you?" They got off the bed and approached the snack bar.

Brian began mopping the counter with a cloth. "Sorry, Ladies. You look as though you've worked up an appetite. What can I get for you?"

"You know what we drink. We'll have our usual. Is this Mr. Mendoza?"

Brian fetched their preferred soft drinks, and poured them over ice. "Yes. Mary and Martha Madison, I'd like to present Esteban Mendoza, we call him Stubby."

"Stubby?" The girls looked at each other. Brian smiled, "Not that. Would you like to check?" Mendoza was flushing red.

"Not just yet. Can I have another one of those for Paulo? He's been *so* good today." Brian prepared another drink for the boy, who was still lying on the bed, and smiling.

"I have to be careful not to drink too much during the day, but I don't think it will hurt to do it now," He said, sitting up and pulling his feet up toward him. "I'm ready to get out of my 'costume.'"

Martha carried the drink over to Paulo, sitting on the bed beside him. "That's all right, Paulo. We're finished with you now anyway. At least, until tomorrow." She kissed him and returned to the snack bar.

Mary was again poring over the drawings. She appeared to be perfectly comfortable dressed only in skin, but Mendoza put his cool beer bottle up and across his forehead. Martha noticed, and gave a light-hearted laugh, "Relax, Mister Mendoza, we're not quite as aggressive as it may appear. Brian just has a very uninhibited family, which sprang from his uninhibited imagination." She stepped up on a rung of one of the tall chairs and leaned over to give Brian a kiss.

"Oh, I recognize it. I just never expected to find myself in it."

"Well, you're in it now, Mr. Mendoza," Mary said with a smile, "We want this castle built."

Mendoza smiled back, "You know, I don't think I'd mind if you called me Stubby."

Mary drew back and fanned her face with her hand, "Why suh, Ah don't believe Ah know you *tha-at* well." She was, after all, an actress.

Mendoza turned red. Then he saw what Paulo was doing and stared at him. The others turned to see. Paulo had retrieved a dissolving gel for his adhesive and was laboriously removing the portion of the serpent that was twisted around his upper leg. He finished by pulling the large artificial organ off his still boy-sized equipment. "Ahhh!" said the lad quietly.

Mendoza shuddered and drank the rest of his beer. "I think I need another over here, Professor."

Brian passed over yet another of the small bottles. Paulo made his way to the bathroom, closing the door gently behind him. Brian smiled, he knew that Paulo had done that not because he wanted his privacy, but because he did not wish to disturb anyone with any sounds that he might make, at last.

"That's just spooky," Mendoza said. The girls looked at him sharply. "I'm sorry. It's just, that's the first time I've seen that. I feel sorry for the kid."

Mary and Martha relaxed. "He goes through a lot. He's at the age when there's nothing he wants more than to really get it on, and he's got that thing and a double-dose of medicine keeping him from feeling anything at all," Mary said sympathetically.

"And he's just so sweet to everyone, too. I've never heard him even snap at anyone, even when I know he's really tired," Martha added.

"Paulo's the darling of every woman on the set, and they all treat him like he's the baby lion cub, and they are the lionesses," Brian observed. "Anybody who tried to hurt him would get torn to shreds."

"True as far as it goes, Brian. But there's more to it than even that -- the kid's a trooper, in the old stage way. The kind of actor who plays out not just the scene, but the whole damn play, on a busted ankle. And nobody would even know, until the curtain closes, and he collapses," Mary said with conviction.

When Paulo emerged from the bathroom, Mary and Martha swooped down on him, and brought him to a seat at the snack bar.

"Another drink for the star of our show!" Martha requested. Brian prepared another soft drink for Paulo and passed it over. Mary leaned against the snack counter and stared brazenly at Paulo's little boy equipment. She looked for all the world like a besotted drunk at a bar. Then she reached out and toyed with it as if she were trying to waken a sleeping kitten. "It ain't fair, Brian. He's playing the role of someone with a permanent erection, and he's stuck with a permanent ... vermiform appendix."

Brian almost choked on his beer. "Good line, Mary. If it's any consolation, in the second movie, he gets to appear au natural, even having the tattoos removed."

Mary brightened, "Well, then that's when you'll get your reward, Vermy!" she said to the little inert object. She looked at Paulo's face, "Can't you feel *anything*?"

"Oh, I can feel it. It's not numb, or anything. I even like the way it feels when you touch it. I just can't do anything about it. It used to come up, especially in the mornings. But it has not been awake for many months now," Paulo said sadly. "Perhaps if you continue what you are doing for several hours..."

Mary smiled, and kissed him. She also continued playing with her new toy.

TAKE FIVE:

My room has the best views

Mendoza excused himself, saying he wanted to find out what was keeping Pam. Brian suspected he wanted to give Pam as much warning as he could about what she was likely to run into. He also seemed to wobble a bit as he went through the door.

When the two returned, Brian and the others were playing poker again. Pam gave Stubby a hard look and he shrugged. He had brought up some fresh supplies, and he moved to replenish the beer, and put away a small quantity of Pam's preferred beverage as well. When there was a knock at the door, Mendoza moved quickly to answer it, and returned with a cart of open-faced sandwiches.

The game was interrupted long enough for everyone to grab something, and Brian said, "Thanks, Stubby. Good timing! What news from the world of business?"

Pam answered, "Not a lot. We got an estimated time of relinquishment of the big house from the film crew. I told them that we would not be able to begin construction of the castle until they were done there. I thought it would help to keep them from crushing us with that performance clause."

Brian nodded over a mouthful of food, "Good fthinking. Whuh elfs?"

"Oh, we may have a nibble on Stubby's search for a computer geek, er, wizard. Young fellow named Sullivan Conrad. Turns out he turned his whole college frat house into a super-computer, just so he could work on his own project. I thought Esteban might want to talk to him."

Brian nodded. "Sounds promising." He looked at Mendoza, "If he pans out, bring him over and let him look at our project. If he's as good as it sounds, he may help turn the tide."

"Damn, we gotta turn the tide, too? Boss, there are limits, even for an engineer!" Stubby complained.

Brian looked over at him, "I never thought I'd hear you admit it. But don't worry, I didn't mean that literally ... yet." Stubby's grin faded slightly. He still wasn't sure when to take Brian seriously.

"Pam, have you met everyone? Kids, I'd like to present Pamela Harriston, my business manager." Pamela approached the table. "Let me see if I can get this right. You're Mary Madison, this is our star Paulo Ignatio, and you are Martha Madison. Am I correct?"

Mary agreed, then asked, "Very good! But was it fifty-fifty, or scientific?" Pam smiled. "I've observed you both on the set. I thought I noticed that you tend to favor stage left, and Martha seems more comfortable on stage right."

Mary looked thoughtful, then looked at her sister. "You know she's right! I don't think anyone else ever caught that! We may not have been aware of it ourselves." Pamela looked pleased.

Brian considered, "I guess that would make me the audience! I'm going to have to keep my eyes on you two..."

"Exactly how we planned it, Mister," Martha interjected. "How do you think we beat you all the time?" Brian laughed. "Make yourself comfortable, Pam. We're expecting more company any minute."

About an hour later, Angelina showed up with yet another cast member. John Paul Ericsson, a very pale looking young man from Sweden, played the part of the mature Adam. He was wearing a Hawaiian shirt and slacks; she had a slipover dress. Brian smiled in greeting, and would have bet everything he had on the table, that under the dress there was nothing but Angelina.

John Paul seemed a pleasant chap, and had no trace of an accent. He was currently declaiming that he was distantly related to the man who built the monitor of Civil War fame. Someone jokingly asked if he was also named after John Paul Jones, and he replied that it was actually a possibility. "There's also a school of thought that I was named after the Pope. I guess it depends on whether you want to think of me as a pirate, or a priest!" Brian frowned a bit at that, perhaps it was only said for alliterative purposes, but he would withhold judgment for the moment.

Brian was again falling behind in the poker game. He had at this point, however, resigned himself to his fate. It always seemed that when Mary had a bad hand, Martha would have a good one, and vice versa. Their luck seemed to alternate. At least he had the best floor show in town for only pennies per hour! Young Paulo generally did pretty well, he noted. *Unlucky in Love?* Brian thought. He had to agree with the assessment that Paulo was a trooper. The lad was game for anything.

Other cast and occasional crew members showed up. Mostly it was people who did not seem to have permanent attachments elsewhere. Brian's group became the de facto family of the unconnected.

The poker game broke up when Brian ran out of table stakes. Another game started, with other players. He cruised around, engaging in conversations here and there. To some degree, it was his version of management by walking around. He had no official function in the film-making, but he felt the responsibility to be a social lubricant for the process. If someone had a major gripe, Brian tried to help resolve the conflict, using his connections between groups.

As the evening grew late, Brian happened to look, perhaps longingly, at his bed. Unfortunately, it was occupied by a sleeping Paulo, and on either side of him was a nubile young girl. Brian looked closer. The actresses who played the mature Kayla, and the mature Rosita, had each had very long days, and were cuddled adorably next to Paulo.

Brian hadn't the heart to disturb them. He strolled next door and made himself comfortable in the middle of Mary and Martha's queen size bed. (Hey, it was cool. He was wearing pajamas!)

In the morning, Brian wondered where he was. Everything was on the wrong side of the room. Looking at his companions, he remembered.

The situation was a bit awkward. While he was wearing pajamas, they were not. He was in a very pleasant tangle of girlflesh. He kissed each of them, and slowly maneuvered out and over to the side of the bed. The girls stirred, but did not waken.

Brian wandered back to his own room. Everything was in disarray there as well, but only because no one had cleaned up after the party. Brian yawned and scratched and went into the bathroom.

When he came out, Angelina was cleaning up. She had on a different outfit, and a pleasant scent of lavender.

"Don't you sleep?" Brian asked. She smiled and came to him. Wrapping her arms around him she kissed him thoroughly. He found her aroma intoxicating.

"One can find a place to sleep anywhere, Brian!" Knowing her very outgoing nature, Brian surmised that it was quite true. Glancing over at his full bed, he responded laconically, "Not necessarily!"

Angelina followed his glance. "I think you need a bigger bed, Brian. Come to think of it, you need a bigger bathtub, too."

"Good news on that score, Angelina." Turning with her, but keeping his arm around her, he walked with her closer to the bed. "In a few weeks, we'll have the big house to play in. Lots more room."

Angelina studied the scene. Smiling, she quietly wakened Paulo, and extracted him from the center of the bed. Walking the sleepy lad into the bathroom, she winked at Brian conspiratorially.

Brian shrugged, and ordered breakfast for six.

When at last, Paulo and Angelina emerged from the bathroom, he was very obviously ready to go to work. Angelina took him back to the bed, and helped him get back in quietly. She gestured for Paulo to close his eyes, and then caught Brian's eye. Motioning him to one side of the bed while she approached the other, she gently awakened 'Rosita' (Carmen Sandoval). Brian kissed 'Kayla' (Sally Antoine) on the forehead and shook her gently. "Shhh, Good Morning, Sweetheart. Angelina and I are going to have some coffee. We thought you might want to say good morning to Paulo," Brian said very softly. He and Angelina stole back to the snack counter to watch the results. Brian began preparing some instant coffee, and improved it with a double-dash of brandy.

Carmen and Sally stretched and smiled at each other. They were both fond of Paulo, and they snuggled closer and nuzzled him. Paulo yawned and smiled at the girls, and kissed them. Then he stretched and relaxed. A precious few seconds more passed and then, "What???" Sally threw back the covers and confirmed that Paulo had 'matured' in the night. She looked at Brian and Angelina fiercely, then began laughing. Carmen joined her. They snuggled even closer to Paulo, and began getting very friendly with him.

The food order arrived, and Brian got some 'real' coffee for Angelina and himself, as they kept the trio in sight. "I keep saying, my room has the best views in the hotel," Brian casually mentioned to Angelina. Sally had climbed up on top of Paulo, and was giving him a very energetic 'wake-up' bounce. After several minutes, she relented and disentangled herself. Kissing Paulo in departure, she headed for the bathroom. Carmen took over, and took her time. Kissing, rubbing and caressing Paulo, she murmured softly to him. They giggled together.

Sally emerged from the bathroom and began eating breakfast. Brian and Angelina joined her. She kept flushing, and smiling. She would seem on the verge of saying something, and would then take another bite and giggle some more.

Brian and Angelina kept watch on the couple remaining on the bed. Finally, Carmen got up on top of Paulo as Sally had done, and sedately moved up and down on him, apparently enjoying every movement. After a long, slow interlude, she also hit a bit of a crescendo, then quieted. Following a few seconds of audible sighing, Carmen and Paulo went together into the bathroom. Brian could hear the shower running.

Their breakfast was cold, but they ate it anyway. The six breakfasts went into five people just fine.

Angelina checked Paulo again, to make sure he was 'presentable' for the camera, and held his hand as she walked with him toward the stairs. Carmen and Sally both kissed him at the door, and waving at Brian, headed for the elevator.

Brian finished cleaning up. He had maid service, but he could at least dispose of the empties and set the chairs upright.

On the set, Brian took a position well in the back. He liked to watch all of the action, not just what was happening in front of the cameras. He could see Angelina, off to one side of the activity. Brian observed as the casting director approached her between takes. Suddenly Angelina began jumping up and down like a twelve-year-old. Brian had almost forgotten his brief conversation with the casting director.

"Joe, have you picked someone for the role of 'Jolene Hardesty' yet? You know, the one in charge on the orbital fort? I know it's just a small part ... No? ... Well, I was thinking that girl, Angelina Foster, has exactly the kind of personality I had in mind when I wrote the scene."

Evidently, the idea had merit, and Angelina liked the offered role.

Brian smiled. *You pull a little string here; you pull a little string there.* It was nice to be just an observer.

Pam dropped another stack of papers in front of him.

"What's this?" Brian asked.

"It's business, Brian. They all need your signature. You don't need to read them all, but if you don't, you'll find out one day that I own your ass," She smiled sweetly at him.

Sighing, Brian went through the pile. Most were relatively short, but they had the durnedest words. There were permits for digging, permits for moving, permits for piling. Then there were requirements for digging, requirements for moving, requirements for piling. It was all pretty tedious, but necessary. Brian and his associates were promising the moon, but they were demanding the solar system! Would the bureaucrats buy this hogwash? Hopefully it would be their favorite kind of tripe, *tripe*licate!

"Think they'll buy it, Pam?" Brian asked as he scanned the next document.

"I'm sure they will, Brian. They like to be comfortable, and this will disturb that. That would usually make me worry, but what we're proposing will *triple* their economy. The people in charge of an economy have a way of becoming wealthy. Given the choice of being comfortable, or becoming wealthy, they're going to bite the bullet and go with our program, *as forward-thinking public servants.*"

"I wish I had your confidence."

"You should have worked with farm animals more," she said primly.

Brian looked in on his newest problem child, Sullivan Conrad. Sully had not presented his case well, and he wasn't much to look at. Tall, thin, and aggressively bookish, he had not particularly impressed anyone. But they had let him look over the project plans. Brian caught the way he practically salivated every time he came across the word computer, electronic-control, or even data. Sully had pulled an all-nighter studying the reams of plans, diagrams, and sketches.

The next morning, Sully appeared at Brian's desk in the 'business office.'

"I've got a question."

"Go ahead."

"You're planning on putting a computer in every room of this castle. Why?"

"What do you mean? All the rooms are going to be the same. They'll need to have access to various sorts of information and entertainment programs. Doesn't that suggest a computer in every room?"

"No. Well, yeah, a computer. But what it suggests is an array of servers and an optical network with gigabyte satellite uplinks and downlinks to distribute and process the information."

Brian sat back, "Go on."

"Computers these days are like telegraph operators, click, click, click. The real action is at the network level, where the computers are organized into data-crunching armies. With this level of investment, you could have a hundred times the processing power of the whole local government. You could lease computing power to them, and charge for the service. You've been planning to reorganize their roads and power structure, without realizing that you could bring their whole communication system into the twenty-first century!"

"How would we sell that concept to them? Simple words, mind you. The hotel lobby has dial telephones."

Sully grinned, "Start with telephones. We can offer cell phone communication, satellite navigation, transportation package tracking, remote medical diagnosis, even inter-island closed circuit televideo conferencing."

A slow smile grew across Brian's face. "Sully, we wanted to hire someone who could help us with some simple machine interfaces. We have to develop machines that can slice up rocks like a Japanese sushi chef. We can't put up the buildings for the computers if we can't provide the stones for them. Can you help us there as well?"

Sully looked him in the eye. "I'll make them play 'Whistle while you work' and walk to the mines if that's what you want. I programmed a guy's automobile computer chip to whistle at girls in mini-skirts when they walked by. All I had to do was patch in a spectral-frequency sensor underneath the bumper and ..." Brian raised a hand.

"I believe you. What do you need to start?"

"Authorization to order the equipment, food once a day, and a place to sleep."

Brian blinked. He looked over at Pam. She shrugged.

"Pam, when do we move into the big house?"

"Nineteen more days. Then they said they might need it on special occasions, but they'll give us advance notice. They want to start the castle count-down."

"All right. Where can we put Sully in the meantime?"

She looked him over. "He can bunk with me in here. There's two small bedrooms. I think I can handle him."

"Okay, set him up with that. See to it that he eats, and check his finances. We're all going to be rich, and we don't want to leave anybody out. Then carefully monitor what he wants to buy, I don't want him to spend all our money making a girl robot or something."

Sully interrupted, "Hey, a guy's got to have a hobby!"

Brian smiled, "Not <u>all</u> of our money..." Pam nodded, and started writing some notes.

Several days later, Sully stopped by Brian's hotel room to visit. Ostensibly, he was getting approval for a purchase, which Pam had already authorized. Brian sensed he had something on his mind.

They gazed together at the view out the verandah. Sully cleared his throat. "Um, Brian. I was wondering. I've only been here a few days, but ..."

"What is it, Sully? Speak freely."

"Well, I see all these naked kids running around. I'm not sure I understand. Don't these people have laws?"

"Of course, they have laws, Sully. Some of the strongest have to do with protecting children. But they are a little more flexible about what people can do, up to a point."

Sully shuffled his feet. "Well, I would never hurt anyone. I'm just ... I mean, I'm not homosexual ... at least I think I'm not. But I know there's a lot of stuff going on around here, and I ... well, I guess I just want to know what the *rules* are."

Brian looked at him. "I'm glad you came to talk, Sully. A few months ago, someone suggested that my friend Paulo and I ... had an unhealthy relationship, an *unnatural* relationship. It's one of the worst things that one can be accused of here. Homosexual sex, with a young boy here -- you better hope the cops get you first. As I mentioned, there are laws to protect the children." Brian looked out at the hotel courtyard.

"My friends defended me, and my accuser was sent away, because they know that I am as healthy a heterosexual as my age permits. Paulo has adopted me as his substitute Grandfather. His real grandfather died in a ferry accident when the boy was four. The old man could swim, but they think his heart failed him. Paulo loves me, and I love him, and he's been staying here for months."

Brian smiled, "We've had sex here, but not with each other. Paulo can't even have sex, because of the medicine he takes to be able to perform his role. I think you know about that. But when he has his appliance on, well, he's very useful and attractive to the ladies, and many of them have done it here with him. They let me watch."

"Some of the ladies have been kind enough to pretend to be attracted to me, as well. I've had sex with them. Then I let *him* watch."

Brian rose from his seat and walked about slowly. "We've probably broken some laws, but this is not the United States, and it's not even Europe. These people aren't decadent, just flexible. The age of consent for boys, *for heterosexual sex*, appears to be considered a matter of the boy's good fortune. For girls, it's not quite that low. I think, generally, after a girl has begun menstruating, she's considered old enough to choose whether to have sex, but the families are fiercely protective of them. They seek to make good marriages," Brian paused.

"The crowd we're with, let's say Hollywood types, can afford to make their own rules. Most of them are wealthy enough that if a girl got pregnant, raising the baby would not constitute a hardship. But they're also prudent, they know that pregnancy can ruin their film career, just because of the timing. So they use birth control pills, and are particular about disease prevention."

Brian looked at Sully. "That's one of the things that makes Paulo so appealing to them. They can't get pregnant, and they won't get a disease. Too bad for him, though, because he might as well be using someone else's penis, for all the pleasure he gets."

"For you I'd say the rules haven't really changed. Find a nice girl who respects your mind, and your earning potential, and *be faithful* to her." Brian smiled, "Maybe you ought to do it soon."

Brian turned away. Sully was now behind him. He sighed, "One more thing, if she wants to have sex with Paulo, let her. Let them. You would not want to trade places with that boy."

Sully stood silently for a time. Then he took a few steps toward the door. He stopped, "Thanks Brian, ... You're a pretty good programmer, too." He left the room.

Brian smiled. He knew that was high praise. High praise indeed.

TAKE SIX:

Hope you don't mind if I rearrange

It was Brian's last day in the hotel. They were making preparations to move the base of operations for his business enterprises, and his social life, into what everyone had been calling the big house. Brian wanted to mark the occasion with a special party, but the only ones to whom it had real significance were his business associates. They had received the governmental approval, and a letter of credit had been issued. They had already sent off orders for special drilling equipment, leased some construction equipment, and purchased sites around the island chain.

A typical morning, even with all that. Paulo was particularly nervous this morning, as his mother was at long last coming to observe the filming activity. He had been feeling like an outcast, Brian knew, because he had been isolated from his family for quite some time now. Considering that the family home was not far away, it was not a good sign that they had not visited before.

Two of Paulo's brothers had, in fact, come by some weeks ago. Brian had met them. They had seemed impressed by Paulo's newfound celebrity, but put off by it too. Brian suspected that his family had initially been pleased that he had won the role, but now felt uncertain about it.

All of this put additional pressure on the boy, and angered Brian, though he was careful not to let his feelings show.

Brian was not surprised, therefore, when in mid-morning there was a commotion on the set. Paulo's mother was upset at seeing him made up in his role. She should have known what to expect, as she had read the book, and even given her approval in writing. Her reaction was emotional, though, not logical. Finally, she was asked to let them continue, with or without Paulo.

Even this did not calm her, and she had the boy in tears. She accused him of trampling on the family's honor, and told him he should come home immediately.

"Mama, please! I cannot stop. They are depending on me! The movie is only half-finished. They would have to start all over again, with someone else. It would cost them very much money, and we would have to give back the money that they already gave us."

"It is bad money, Paulo! It is filthy money! We do not need it!" she screeched at him. Both were in tears.

"No, Mama. These are good people, and they have trusted me. You said that I could do this, and now I must finish what I promised to do. I do not want you to lose your house, and your new stove, and the tools that you got for Papa, and Uncle Pedro. And I do not want to punish these people for trusting me."

"Come home now, Paulo. I am telling you."

"No, Mama. I must finish what I have begun. I will come home when I have finished it."

"Don't bother," She stormed away, "You will not be welcome."

"Mama, no! Don't go! Mama!" he watched in tears as she departed, taking his siblings with her. His shoulders heaved with sobs.

Disconsolate, he stood there. All around him, people stood silently. The scene had been emotionally wrenching for all. Finally, Paulo ran into the hotel, toward Brian's room.

Brian watched, and slowly followed.

He found the boy face down in the middle of his bed, sobbing. Brian sat down beside him, and sighed. Reaching out, he felt the boy's back heave with his tearful gasps. Brian stroked the smooth skin gently.

Several minutes passed. Slowly the tears subsided.

"What can I do, Uncle-Papa? She wants me to come home."

Brian waited. Calmly, he replied, "You must do your job, Paulo. Even your Mama knows that."

"She told me no."

"Yes, she told you no, because her feelings made her want that. She saw her child, in a situation, dressed as a thing, that made her feel bad. Remember when we first met? You were laughing, and happy, and naked?" Brian rubbed the boy's shoulders, making circles across the center of his back.

"You were like joy itself, running free. And now she sees you like a butterfly, pinned through the heart on a board. Beautiful still, but painful to look upon. That saddens her, and she wants it to change."

Brian waited, as the boy's shudders slowly subsided.

"If you went home now, she might be happy, but you would be sad, knowing that you should have done something else," Brian paused again.

"If you finish your work, in the way that you have been doing, your mother will become proud of you again, because you will have done what you had to do. What you had to do for the sake of your family, and what you had to do because that is what a man would do."

Paulo rolled over, continuing to sniffle, his eyes looked a little puffy and red.

"Where will I go, Uncle-Papa? You will be leaving here today, and I have no home to go to."

Brian pulled him up, to hold him tight. "You will come with me, Paulo. The new house will be your home, always and forever. Even when I am gone to dust, that will be your home. And you can think of me from time to time, and know that I loved you." This was the first time that Brian has held Paulo like this, when his appliance was installed. Suddenly he realized just what an intrusive burden the damned thing could be. Paulo started crying softly again, but these tears seemed somehow happier.

Presently, Brian ordered lunch for himself and Paulo. After two more hours, they returned to the set.

Paulo approached the director. "I am ready to go back to work now, sir. We have a job to do."

The director put a hand on his shoulder, and called to some people nearby.

The only disadvantage of the big house was its remote location. The film company had used vans to shuttle people back and forth from the base at the hotel. Brian made a similar arrangement with the cabs and jitneys at the hotel to transport anyone who came looking for him to the new location, at his expense if need be. Brian and his parties at the hotel were a bit of a local legend among this group, and they readily complied.

Brian also arranged for short-term leases for additional vehicles as well. Sully and Stubby and Pam would need to have reliable transportation for the many trips around the island that they had to make. Brian had hopes that the leases would be truly short term, however.

"Stubby, how close is the nearest exit point for the interlink tunnel going to be?"

"Hmm. About six miles, or ten kilometers, as they say around here. You aren't thinking ... No, no. Say it ain't so, Mister B."

"What's the problem, Stubby? Have you forgotten we need to deliver cut stone to this location to build a castle? A lot of cut stone?"

Mendoza groaned. "No. Look, Boss, we can save a lot of money just bringing it up on flatbed trucks. We don't need a terminal here as well, please."

"But we do need a terminal here, Stubby. Not here exactly, at the big house, but at the castle. Remember we're going to have people and material moving in and out of there from now on. You don't want to have to off-load and reload everything, every day."

"All right, all right! I'll put it into the schedule, and the budget. Jeez, Boss. You're spending money like a drunken sailor!"

"Stubby, when people here realize that they can send a pallet of cargo from one island to another for a fraction of what they spend to move it by sea, they aren't going to complain about paying us several times what it actually costs us to move it. We'll have money *flowing* into the coffers in no time."

"Yeah, if we don't have the ocean flowing into our tunnels," Mendoza grumbled. Brian realized that it was Stubby's nature to be pessimistic, and confident at the same time. He anticipated disaster, and dealt with it before it had time to surprise him.

Mendoza walked away muttering. "Well, at least I'm going to bring the steel in on flatbed trucks." Brian was already too far away to hear.

Paulo got off 'work' early that day. The director had made some hasty revisions to the schedule in the morning, and that had reflected into the afternoon as well.

Brian showed him around. Paulo had seen it all hundreds of times before, but somehow this was different. He was smiling and sunny again.

"There are eight bedrooms in the house, Paulo. Would you like to pick one for your own?"

The boy's face fell. "Can't I stay with you, Uncle-Papa? In your bed like before?"

"Paulo, there's plenty of room. We don't need to be crowded here. And you might want to enjoy some privacy yourself."

"I will do it if you ask me to, Señor. But I do not wish it." His eyes brightened, "Uncle-Papa, what is *privacy*?" He laughed, and Brian laughed with him.

"All right, Paulo, you may sleep with me. I want you to. I hope there will be room for others, as well."

"I hope so too, Papa."

There <u>was</u> room for others, especially of the snugly sort. Each of them found a companion for the evening.

In the bright morning light, Angelina was tracing the wrinkles in Brian's face. He smiled.

"No room service here, Brian. We'll have to go to the kitchen ourselves."

"As long as I can have bed service, I don't care about room service." He looked at her curiously. "Whatever do you see in me, anyway?"

"You're generous, and kind. You're understanding, and you don't get jealous. You won't mind if I get a little wrinkled, or gain some weight," Suddenly she sat up, "Or will you?"

"Not if my eyesight goes first." She smacked him playfully on the chest. To his right, Paulo and Carmen were entangled. They stirred. Paulo's 'tent-pole' had been removed and stored away. Carmen didn't seem to mind. It's absence allowed her to snuggle even closer to the boy.

Young as she appeared, Carmen Sandoval was five years Paulo's senior. Her very compact, and trim, body made her look very young indeed. One might have thought she was only two years his senior.

Carmen had the playful, childlike heart of a nightingale, and her attachment to Paulo was one of personalities, not a mere physical attraction. They were like children, adrift in a grand adventure.

Angelina was a good deal more mature, and the harsh morning light disclosed the fact mercilessly. Brian thought about investing in some kind of automatic shades or filters. In the meantime, the situation at hand required that he kiss her, so he did.

"Who's on kitchen duty?" Angelina asked.

As best he could lying down, Brian shrugged. Stretching, he began levering himself up to trudge to the bathroom. *A bathroom for every bedroom, what a good idea*, he thought. Presently, he started a shower. Angelina joined him, washing his back without embarrassment as if the two of them were hands washing each other. Shortly, they finished up and dried off. In a cupboard, Brian found soft bathrobes bearing the hotel logo. He put one on and held one for Angelina. They walked barefoot down to the kitchen. As they passed the next bedroom, he saw Mary and Martha. There were no doors between the bedrooms to lock open, but the bedroom doors themselves were left open. The girls were stirring.

A matronly lady looked up from a newspaper and a cup of coffee. Rising, she folded the paper again and moved her cup.

"Good Morning, Señor Hawthorne, I am Mrs. Sanchez. Let me get you some coffee." Brian looked puzzled and helped Angelina to her seat, then joined her.

"My son goes to the movie set every day. He has told me that you agreed to let him and his sisters swim in your pool if I would come over to cook breakfast for you. I wish to thank you for being so generous. Carlos is a good boy to think of his sisters like that, don't you think?"

Brian laughed, "Mrs. Sanchez, Carlos is a scamp, but I like that. We did not have such an arrangement. However, if you are willing to come over here to cook breakfast, you may feed anyone you wish from my kitchen, and Carlos and his sisters may swim anytime."

"Oh, that boy! I will put a sunburn on his suntan! I apologize, Mister Hawthorne."

"No, no. Tell Carlos that I said as long as he does the gardening and keeps the grass mowed just as we agreed, that he may continue coming." Her eyes lit up in a conspiratorial gleam.

"I will do that, Senor, and I will see to it that he does a good job, too! Now, what would you like?"

After Mrs. Sanchez had prepared their breakfasts, Brian quizzed her further. She and the children had walked here from their home, but it was less than a kilometer away.

"You said that you would put a sunburn on Carlos's suntan, Mrs. Sanchez. Does that mean that Carlos is one of the 'Wingless Angels'?"

"Yes, he has been naked everywhere for months now. It was unsettling at first. But now? He is like a puppy, all wag and wiggle. He enjoys that freedom, and is very active. You are right that he is a scamp, but at least I do not have to supply him with clothes to destroy."

"What about his sisters, Mrs. Sanchez? Did Carlos tell them that the rule was only naked people in the pool?" Angelina inquired.

"Yes he did." Her eyes grew large. "Don't tell me he made that up too?"

Brian laughed. "Not entirely. No doubt Carlos is familiar with the book that I wrote. This house is based upon one in the story. In that house, no one wore swimsuits, but we had not made such a rule for this one."

"Oh, dear. My boy has christened your pool with his nakedness, and that of his sisters."

"It's just as well, Mrs. Sanchez, I think the rule makes sense here anyway. I don't know anyone on the island who even has a bathing suit. I wouldn't want to turn anyone away for a needless expense. You may tell Carlos to make sure that everyone knows that the rule is 'No clothes in the swimming pool -- it's not a washing machine.'" Brian said lightheartedly.

"Thank you, Mister Hawthorne. You are too very kind."

Paulo and Carmen entered the kitchen holding hands. Mrs. Sanchez raised her eyebrows at Paulo's artwork, but seemed unfazed by his nakedness, or Carmen's. They sat down together.

Mrs. Sanchez prepared their breakfasts as well. When they finished, Angelina rose and took Paulo's hand.

"Come Paulo, let's get you ready. Carmen can have you again later." Paulo kissed Carmen and stretched out holding her hand until he could not reach her anymore.

"You make a lovely couple, Miss Carmen," Mrs. Sanchez said. "I like your name. My name is Carmelita."

Carmen smiled. "He's nice, but he's so fickle. He jumps into bed with every woman on the movie set." Carmelita frowned, not realizing her leg was being pulled. Brian let it go, but remembered, *Carmelita Sanchez.*

Suddenly a color monitor clicked into operation. It showed a scene of the front gate area. A film company van was just coming to a stop. Brian looked at the monitor. *Sully, or Stubby? Both?* He wondered. Looking around, he saw what looked like an intercom. He examined it, pressed the <u>all</u> button, and recited, "Your attention, please, anyone needing a ride to the active set, your vehicle has arrived." From the reverberations, he could tell that his voice had been transmitted throughout the house. *I could get used to living here*, he thought.

"Carmen, I'd like to see what's going on in the pool. Would you care to join me? I understand we have burglars." Brian reached out for her hand, and they walked together down to the pool area.

Brian took a moment to gawk at the elegance. It was his first time seeing it as its owner. *I could get used to living here.* They approached the sounds of splashing, and fun.

"Carlos!" Brian waved him over. The look on the boy's face grew serious. He swam over.

"Thanks for breakfast, Carlos. Won't you introduce me to your sisters?" Carlos grinned, *off the hook!* He called his sisters over. He appeared to be about Paulo's age, perhaps older or younger. A girl in her later teens was introduced as Linda, who blushed at the circumstances. Dolcita was ten, and enjoying herself completely. If public nudity was new to her, it didn't seem to show. They were all comfortable in the water.

"Hi, girls. My name is Brian, and this is Carmen. Will you be coming over every day?" The kids looked at each other and nodded vigorously.

Carmen smiled, "That's good. I would love to swim with you today, but I have to leave. I'll be sure to see you tomorrow, though!" Carlos grinned as they waved good-bye. *'Let's see you grin when you're sweating over that lawnmower, Clever Carlos. You've talked yourself into a hot spot.'* Brian smiled at his own thoughts.

He went up in time to say good-bye to all his guests who were headed for the film set. Clever Carlos had gotten dry and was sitting in a corner seat as they left. *'My son goes to the movie set every day,'* Brian remembered. He would make his own travel arrangements after checking on some business appointments. *'Busy, busy, busy'*, he loved it.

This close to his bedroom, he went up and got casually dressed, and went looking around. First he strolled around the outside of the house. The patio was almost as described in the book, but of course there were no 'allfruit' trees. Instead there were lush flowering plants. The tennis court was there, and the playfields. He looked around, *no benches.*

Strolling around the back of the house, he could see the children still splashing energetically in the pool. *They're probably going to get hungry,* he thought. Closing in on the main gate, he observed a structure alluded to but unmentioned in the book, a one and a half car garage. It was buried into the gentle slope, and surrounded by more flowers. He entered the standard door. *Uh-oh.* It was completely empty. *Carlos will have trouble mowing the grass. Note to self: get lawnmower.*

Brian went in the main entrance. He had walked into Pam's busy office. *This was supposed to be a grand entrance hall, and a big dining room.* Pam had arranged the furniture in a logical fashion, considering there were no dividing walls. The two new women were already at work.

"Morning, Pam. Where did you sleep?" Brian inquired. *He really didn't know.*

"Upstairs, to the left, second from the end. Sully's in the last one. It's quieter there." *The working wing,* her eyes seemed to say. Brian looked around.

"Stubby's on a job site, this island's south silo. Sully's upstairs putting together a wireless network. He says we need more bandwidth." Her eyes held his. "He hired a consultant." She looked away.

Brian nodded. "Anything I need to do?"

Pam looked back, "They all needed a raise this morning, so I doubled everyone's salaries. You were busy, so I forged your signature."

Brian went along with it. "Good, good. Carry on." *Was she kidding? Did he even know what their salaries were?* Brian escaped through the office area into the kitchen. *Sully hired a consultant?*

"Carmelita?" She dimpled, flattered that he remembered.

"Si?" The kitchen was spotless.

"The children will be hungry when they come up from the pool. That won't do. I don't want anyone to ever go away from my house hungry. Okay?"

"Si. Yes, thank you sir." She glanced down.

Hmm? Brian stepped to the big refridgerator. Then he opened a cupboard or two. *Not good.*

"Um, Carmelita, do you know Pam, in the office there?" She nodded, *she knew who he meant.* "Would you make up a list, and give it to her? Ask her to add things to it, as well. Would you, Please?"

"Si. Thank you, sir."

Brian went upstairs and to the left. Sully's bedroom door was open, and his bed had been moved forward into the 'sitting space.' Cardboard boxes marked 'Bookshelf 1 - Reference' and 'Bookshelf 2 - Fiction' were lined up behind the head of the bed. Along the back wall, several tables had been arranged. An operating computer sat on one of them. A tall girl with short-cropped, medium-blonde hair caught his eye. She wore light sneakers, blue jeans, and a well-worn sweat shirt. The skin around her waist was showing as she kneeled beside the computer, unspliced wires in her hand. Around her head was more of a sweatband than a scarf.

Sully was just visible disappearing into a crawl space on the back wall.

"I'm going to have to carry these lines over to the office space, Marcia. There's a right turn in the middle."

"Be careful. You don't want to fall through the ceiling."

Brian went in and sat on the edge of the bed. Marcia looked up at him and smiled.

"Sully's consultant?" Brian inquired. She nodded. Sully could be heard scuttling in the woodwork. Finally, he reappeared.

"Whew! Dusty in there. Ouch!" He emerged. "Oh! Hi, Brian. Nice house. Plenty of power, but no data lines at all. I'm connecting up to the office computer network. Hope you don't mind if I rearrange a little?"

Brian shook his head. "By all means, make yourself at home.

This is your consultant?"

Sully looked a little sheepish, "Ah, yeah. I met her over on the other island. She was doing some electrical work in the government office there. I told her that I needed some help with our communication problems..."

Brian raised his hand. "I understand, Sully. No need to explain. I don't expect you to do everything yourself." Turning to Marcia, Brian continued. "Welcome aboard, Miss. It is Miss, isn't it?"

"Yes, Marcia Roberts. Pleased to meet you, Mr. Hawthorne."

"My pleasure. I just wanted to introduce myself, Miss Roberts, and let you know that this is a business place as you know, and also a bit of a party house. So in case you happen to be working late or something, don't worry about just grabbing some shut-eye or refreshments wherever you can. You won't be bothering anyone or imposing at all."

"Well, thank you, Mr. Hawthorne. That is very hospitable of you." Brian could see a tinge of red creeping up her somewhat thin neck. He waved casually and departed, noting that Sully, who had been standing very still, suddenly began moving again. Brian sauntered down the parapet hallway. *Sully's consultant. You pull a little string here, ... Maybe he was a good programmer after all.*

Much later, Brian glanced out the window from his bedroom office. He could see the Sanchez ladies walking slowly along the lane. Linda had put on a blouse and shorts. Dolcita had only her towel. *Note to self: Get some bicycles.*

Brian caught up with Stubby at the silo site. His work crew had marked out the location for one of the first excavation points. As soon as the equipment arrived, they would begin a vertical bore, encasing it in concrete all the way down. At the bottom of the shaft, they would make a right turn, aiming for the small island visible in the distance. Similar points would be marked at all the islands to be connected.

Stubby had brought in a handful of expert shield tunnelers. Noticeable on the job sites by their white hardhats, they were briefing their work crews in yellow hats about the pending dig.

As Brian approached, Stubby caught sight of him and waved him off. Pointing to his hat, Stubby directed him to a nearby van. There

Brian found another white hat. This one had a green band around it. He put it on and went to visit Stubby. The men looked at his hat and waved in a friendly manner.

"Okay, what's the message on the hat, Stubby? "Watch out for this guy -- he might fall in the hole?"

Stubby grinned, "Nah. Just means you're from the home office. You could be bringing paychecks!"

"Okay, not so bad then. What's our next step?"

"Boss, you're lucky. This is the X-siting part. In three days, when our gear gets here, that's the 'boring' part."

Brian smiled. "No paychecks, but I brought some coffee. It's in the van over there."

Stubby turned away and gave a piercing whistle across the field. Using hand signals, he conveyed that there was coffee to be had in the van. Several friendly waves responded. "Good move, Brian. You're making friends."

"Three more days. Wasn't it supposed to be here today?"

Stubby shrugged, "Yeah, I know. Some lame excuse about 'design problems'. They probably didn't know that I was the one who spec'ed the design. Sully confirmed the date of delivery for us. He really knows his way around the cyberworld. Good man."

Brian smiled, "Well, you recommended him, remember?"

"Yeah, well, all I know -- either he was smart enough to dazzle me, or glib enough to baffle me. I was outta my league."

"I trust him, Stubby," Brian said confidently, "almost as much as I trust you." Brian could see that Mendoza stood just a bit taller with that.

One of the men brought a coffee over for Stubby, then looked an inquiry at Brian. Brian waved him off. He headed back to work.

"So what are they doing in the meantime, Stubby?"

Mendoza pointed along the link-up line. "Not too many buildings along the bore path, but a few. I've got crews going in to check their structural stability, and note any signs of settling before we start. Otherwise, we'll have to replaster all their walls for free. I've seen it before. Some of them don't want to let us in. We just ask them to sign a waiver. We know how to get co-operation!" He laughed.

"Anything else I can do out here, Stubby?"

He thought about it. "Don't think so. See that cleared area over there? We'll be pouring concrete there tomorrow. Foundation for the cutting warehouse and terminal exit. You've seen the drawings, it'll look like a big airplane hangar with doors only on this side. We'll be sliding our layercakes in there to be cut up for building stone. Inside of a week or two, we should have stone elements available for the castle, as well as the warehouse walls and roof decking. Once we've gone past the shoreline, we can reverse course and slope up to the warehouse floor for the exit ramp." Brian looked out over the harbor, putting his imagination to work. He could see the images that Stubby had described, almost as keenly as Mendoza could.

The distant island was barely more than a smudge on the horizon. His mind reeled with the task that lay before them. *It's all just numbers,* Stubby had said.

TAKE SEVEN:

Do I have to give you my children?

He could see that Stubby was in a foul mood. He was practically talking to himself. Brian brought a beer over and handed it to him. Stubby took a moment to focus on it, then gave a wan smile.

"Thanks. Nobody else wants to get close. Is it that bad?"

Brian nodded. "You've got a dark cloud anchored over your forehead. Everyone's afraid they'll get struck by lightning."

"Aagh! It's the shield drills! They should be here already! We're stuck out there twiddling our thumbs while the castle clock is running down. I can't even predict how long it will take to build it, and there's a deadline waiting for me."

"Take it easy on yourself, Stubby. You've started the steel construction. When the stone becomes available, all they have to do is stack it up. Remember, there's no mortar."

"That's just it! 'When the stone becomes available.' I don't know when that will be! That's the controlling factor! They can only go up so fast, even dry stacking it. They go as far as they can, then they have to break down the scaffolding and reset it, then they start stacking again. They may be willing, but you can only work them so hard."

"Back up a minute, Stubby. You said they have to reset the scaffolding. What do you mean?"

"Oh. The crosswalks on the scaffolding. As they work their way up, they have to empty the crosswalks of any remaining stone, raise them up to the next level, load up the stone and start laying the stone. It's time-consuming."

Brian was picturing the process. He nudged Mendoza to take another sip of beer. "Well, you're the Chief, but I was just wondering. You set up the steel using cranes. Then you bring in the scaffolding, load up the stones, et cetera. What are the cranes doing while the stone is being laid?"

"Well, they're just waiting to bring up the next run of steel, why? You can't hoist steel and lay stone at the same time; it's too dangerous."

"Right. I know that. I meant, why not use the cranes to lift the scaffolding, and the stones, as you lay the stones?"

"You mean, run up the steel, then switch over to a suspended gangway, and boom the supplies up as they are used?"

"Yeah. Something like that. Why not?" Mendoza stood transfixed, his eyes darting this way and that, then he began cursing softly. "Damn, damn, damn," He looked at Brian with a haunted expression, "I've been busting my guts over this, and you come up and start making sense!"

"Do you think it will work?"

"Hell, yes, it will work! But **_why didn't I think of it?_**"

Brian laughed, "Stubby, drink your beer. For God's sake, find a woman, or something." Mendoza chuckled reluctantly, and drank his beer.

Brian wandered on. He would ask about the lawnmower later.

All his party regulars were there. Mary and Martha were enjoying some refreshments, prior to beginning the poker game with Brian. Paulo was swimming, and he had Sally and Carmen for company. Brian wondered whether he might need to find another player. John Ericsson was probably available for that, and Brian really should make the effort to get better acquainted.

Even Sully had appeared, holding a quiet conversation with Marcia at one of the pool area café tables. She was dressed as she had been, but she kept looking at the pool. Brian found Angelina, and pointed out Marcia to her.

"Angelina my sweet, the poor girl looks out of place. Do we have available any party dresses that might fit her, or could we quickly get something over from wardrobe?"

Angelina followed his gaze. "Brian, you old letch! Don't tell me you're trying to snag her, too?" She smiled impishly.

"Mmm, maybe. But not for myself, I'm hoping to save Sully from a fate worse than comic books. He found her, after all. -- I just want my guests to be comfortable."

She kissed him on the cheek. "Let me see what I can do."

Brian looked around. He had a pretty good turnout tonight. Observing the people, and the way they grouped together, he realized that he had drawn from three circles of acquaintances, his business associates, folks from the active film operation, and former guests at the hotel, who had relocated when he did. It was a nice mixture. Brian noticed Carlos and his sister Linda slipping into the pool. *Okay, four groups, neighbors.*

There was a nudge at his elbow, Brian turned.

"Joe! You finally came! I know you've seen this place before, but how do you like it when it's not a work zone?" Brian shook his hand.

"I like it better with people in it, Brian. You throw the best parties on the island. By the way, I brought you a present. May I present Miss Josetta Barnes?" He gestured to a petite girl standing partly behind him.

Her dark, short cut hair, and the black, sequined pant dress made her look almost like a toy action figure. She had an elfin face which was currently smiling brightly.

"I am happy to meet you, Mr. Hawthorne. I understand they call you Papa Brian?"

"Only the younger ones, when they want to be polite, or annoying. I like to be called Brian. Let me see. You can't be anyone other than Caitlin, right?"

"It's a darling role, Mister... um, I mean, Brian. Uncle Joe says the part was written for me to play."

Brian smiled, "Or you were made for it. Hmm, the book came out about thirteen years ago ... are you twelve by any chance?"

She twisted her shoulders slowly with her eyes cast downward. *Coquettish maneuver number seventeen*, Brian labeled it. *Charming.*

"Maybe you saw me when I was seven, Mister Hawthorne. I used to be cute." *She didn't need to fish for complements*, Brian thought, *could she be flirting?* Brian always had difficulty with the thought that people might like him for no particular reason.

"...I bet you drove the little boys wild," Brian quoted, wondering whether she would recognize the reference. A flash of her eyes seemed to indicate that she did. *'When you were only startin', to go to kindergarten'* How was he going to get that out of his head?

"'Used to be cute.' Funny. I could have found roles for you then. Now I have to fly you halfway round the world just for a bit part."

"Joe, you could use a beer. Can't you see we're busy?" Joe chuckled and moved away. Brian took her arm and walked with her.

"Caitlin is one of my favorite characters, are you familiar with the book? Not everyone has read the sequel."

"To be truthful ... Brian, I liked the second book better. It seems more upbeat, more of a message of hope." Josetta seemed comfortable on his arm.

"You look the part. Are you anything like the character?"

She smiled, "I think not! Caitlin was quiet and reserved. I'm ... well, I'm *not*." She flashed her dark eyes again, "I want to ride that motorcycle. I want to *drive* it!" Brian laughed, "Attagirl!"

They strolled near the swimming pool. Josetta was watching the swimmers.

"Uncle Joe told me not to bring my bathing suit. I did, of course. I thought he was saying that I would be too busy to use it. But I see now what he meant."

"These young folks are a lot more comfortable than I am about this. I'm made more for looking than for being looked at. Do you recognize any other characters?"

"Ah, well, that certainly has to be Berry. I should recognize who's with him, but I don't."

"He's Paulo Ignatio, sort of my adopted grandson. He stays here with me. The one on the left is Carmen Sandoval. She plays the role of the grown-up Rosita," Brian explained.

"Then the one on the right must be Kayla."

"Very good. You know the story well. That's Sally Antoine." Brian looked around the elegant, and merry, playroom with a smile. "And who would you say is your favorite character?"

"Ooh, that's a challenge. My favorite male character is Trevor, he just seems so human. There's a lot of female characters. Barbara is very dynamic. Kayla seems fun-loving. But my personal favorite is Rosita, the pocket dynamo!" Brian laughed. He indicated Carmen, just surfacing in the middle of the pool. "Now that's one who is well cast, matching her character. Her compass needle appears to be pointing in a different direction, though. She seems to be rather interested in Paulo."

Josetta looked closely, "It's difficult to tell, with the make-up. Didn't I hear that he's really young?"

"He'll be another year older soon. Hmm, I need to find out when his birthday is. But Paulo is such a sweet boy; all the ladies adore him. He's also carrying a lot of weight in the show, and carrying it well."

Josetta nodded thoughtfully, "Yes. He's a very central character. I can see why you picked someone like him. The regular type of leading man would be totally inappropriate."

Brian pointed at John. "Our Adam, John Paul Ericsson, for example."

Josetta looked for a moment from John Paul to Paulo, and back again. "I'm beginning to think Uncle Joe is a casting genius."

Brian stopped and took a step away from her. "I'm very pleased with his selections so far. Every last one." He kissed her hand, and bowing, excused himself to attend to his other guests.

Brian never did get his poker game in, and it was quite late when he crawled into bed. It was also quite dark. *Where is that giant planet that's supposed to shed so much light?* He was asleep in minutes.

There was plenty of light in the morning. *Note to self: Window shades, soon.* He looked around, through half-closed eyelids. Paulo was there, and Carmen. Who was this? Nestled in the crook of his arm was Josetta Barnes, and just beyond her was Sally Antoine. Brian was wearing his boxer shorts. No one else was so spectacularly overdressed!

Brian lay still while he tried to sort this out. The safest escape route seemed to be over Paulo and Carmen, but Josetta was on his ...

Josetta was looking at him.

"You got away from me before I was finished talking with you," She spoke softly, the lilting sound of a wood nymph. "I've decided who my favorite character is." Her fingers were burrowing through the white hair on his chest like a pack of hounds on the spoor of a rabbit. "It's you! Inside of you is a wonderful kaleidoscope of fascinating and diverse personalities."

"None of my personalities has quite your level of persistence, Josetta. Are you *stalking* me?" His eyes were crinkled with humor.

Josetta glanced under her elbow toward the middle of the bed. "It would not seem to be necessary, sir. You are already stalked!"

A soft giggle came from Sally. She was listening, and smiling.

A sigh of mild exasperation came from him. "Even if that were true, which I deny, it would be because I have a fondness for an empty bladder, not a sleeping bag filled with sultry teenage temptresses."

Sally sat up, "Ooh, I like the sound of that! Can I quote you?"

"I'll sue you for plagiarism. What the devil have you vixens cooked up?"

"Ham and eggs, Señor Hawthorne. Mama says come and get them," Dolcita Sanchez was carefully placing a tray of coffee and cups on the side table. She took in the scene before her with a slightly raised eyebrow, and left the room, wearing her nakedness like a regal gown.

Josetta and Sally burst into laughter. Brian made a dash for the bathroom. Relieved that no one had disturbed him while he was getting relieved, Brian put on a hotel robe and went back out to the bedroom.

Carmen was demonstrating for Josetta and Sally the effectiveness of Paulo's medication. She was fondling Paulo's helpless manhood with familiar playfulness. Paulo smilingly observed but could not interfere, as his hands were trapped behind his head. Brian grabbed a cup of coffee and headed out the door as Josetta and Sally joined in the cruel torture.

"Good Morning, Mrs. Sanchez. It is good to see you again."

"Si, Mr. Hawthorne, are you having a very good morning?"

Brian considered the question. Roused from his peaceful slumbers by a bevy of half-pint seductresses, having to fight them off to salvage the tatters of his reputation, sacrificing his faithful and innocent friend to the maw of...

"Mrs. Sanchez, I am having a wonderful morning!" He raised his coffee cup in salute to her. She nodded, beaming, and reached for the pot with which to refill his cup.

"My husband wanted to talk to you, Señor Hawthorne. Do you think you will have time this morning to do that?"

"By all means, Carmelita. I do wish to meet him. Today would be fine." *I hope he doesn't ask about the lawn-mowing.*

The young people had amused themselves by an early morning swim. Carlos and Linda joined them in something like water polo for a spirited few minutes. Dolcita, awed somewhat by their size, had stayed out of the way. They followed that with a quick meal and cleaned up. Brian was then amused to see that when they trouped out to the van to be taken to the film location, everyone was wearing soft pastel shorts and pullover shirts.

At his leisure he found the supply and examined them. Pam had ordered dozens of the unisex garments in various sizes, and stocked them around in the various bedrooms and bathrooms. Just as the hotel had volunteered some of its bathrobes, Brian's house had apparently fielded a picnic patrol. He examined a pair of shorts. *No fly, no pocket.* Brian selected a matching shirt. *No buttons, no pocket.* He went up to his bedroom for a quick shower. *Where the heck did I leave my wallet, anyway?*

Brian pulled the shorts on. The wide elastic held snugly, and comfortably. *Nice, sometimes I'm in the middle between sizes.* He slipped on the shirt. Looking in the mirror, he noticed that the light blue color went well with his white hair. At the bottom of the closet, he found a pair of sandals. Brian stepped out on the parapet, looking into the great room. His hands wanted to reach for his pockets. Knowing there weren't any, he stifled the impulse.

"Mrs. Sanchez, may I borrow your paper?"

She chuckled, "It is your newspaper, Señor. I hope you do not mind that I looked at it while I was waiting for people to come to breakfast." She handed it to him, properly folded.

Brian looked surprised, "Carmelita, you may borrow anything you wish. Would you like for me to come and cook for you?" She laughed at him and playfully shooed him out of the kitchen.

Brian strolled out to the patio and began to peruse the newspaper. Let's see, there still was a world out there, wasn't there? He scanned the words, but his mind was elsewhere. *Why did these girls keep showing up in his bed?* Brian had no delusions about his attractiveness. In any normal social milieu, he would have been invisible to them. For that matter, what was the fascination with Paulo? There had to be some causal connection.

There was something that he and the boy shared that these nubile pranksters found compelling. The only difference Paulo had from other boys his age was his inability to produce an erection. Brian was different from the other men around in much the same...

Brian's mind froze. He recalled some gay men of his acquaintance who always had young ladies hanging around them. Could it be that the girls felt *safe* with him, and with Paulo?

But Paulo had an advantage, a strap-on assistant that allowed him to be a very entertaining fellow, and Brian was not entirely deficient in the ability. Was it that the girls felt they could control the situation? That they were not in danger -- of assault, of pregnancy, of being compelled into a commitment? This was an interesting line of thought.

Some women were attracted to the very opposite of the traditional he-man breadwinner type.

How could he use this insight to better advantage? *Hold: Rewrite, how could he continue to use this advantage?* Brian was pragmatic enough to not want to change his currently delightful situation for an unknown. He would have to tread gently to not upset this applecart.

What would happen when Paulo came off his medication?

Ricardo Sanchez found him still on the patio. He approached with two cups of coffee. Brian stood to greet him.

"Coffee, Señor? I am Ricardo Sanchez. I wish to thank you for your generosity to my family."

Brian accepted the coffee, and motioned the man to a seat. Sanchez sat and sipped his coffee carefully through a bushy mustache, wiping it periodically. He looked around.

"I see you are enjoying the shrubs that I sold your film company, Mr. Hawthorne, and that they are growing well." He gestured vaguely at the flowers.

"You provided these? Then I am in your debt, many times over. Not only do I have a lovely garden, your family seems to have adopted me as well, to see to my needs."

Sanchez smiled, "They seem to think that they are taking advantage of you, Señor. My children have said that you have more food in your kitchen than I have in my garden!"

"You have lovely children, Mr. Sanchez. They are like beautiful flowers themselves."

"You are very kind."

Brian sipped his coffee. "Your garden, Mr. Sanchez? Do you perhaps have fresh fruits available, that we could purchase? My friends and I love fruit. I fear we were spoiled when living at the hotel, where fruit was always ready for us. If you have only enough for your family, I understand. I would not want you to sacrifice."

"Did you enjoy the fruits you ate at the Hotel Garnet, Señor Hawthorne?" Sanchez was smiling broadly.

Brian sat forward. "Don't tell me! This is too ironic! When Carlos was sneaking over here to swim in the pool, he was supposed to be working in your fields, picking fruit to take down to the hotel!"

Sanchez grinned. "All true, Señor. And now he will work for both of us. His penance will be deserved!"

Brian finished his coffee, and set the cup down on the table, a paperweight now. "I have a confession to make. Will you walk with me?"

Sanchez also finished his coffee, and left the cup on the table.

Brian led him around to the garage, and into it.

"As you can see, this cupboard is bare. I fully intended to let Carlos do the grass cutting, but I don't have a lawnmower! I will have to get one very soon." Noticing that there were vehicles on the parking apron, Brian had a thought. "Mr. Sanchez, could I see your gardens? I can drive you there if you wish." Sanchez nodded, looking around at the empty space. *No doubt thinking of what he could use this for*, Brian thought.

"Good morning, Pam! Did you have fun at the party?"

She looked at his outfit, and smiled. Brian was reminded; this was not business attire.

"Brian, I'm surprised you even noticed I was there. Every time I looked at you, you were with a different girl. You were still going strong when I went to bed!" All the ladies were smiling at him now. He looked at his clothes.

"Oh! By the way, this is a great idea. These are nice outfits." *Were they looking at his knees?* "The kids looked really sweet in them this morning." Pam smiled.

"I need to borrow a vehicle for a little while, Pam. Just going to visit the neighbor." Pam pointed at a key rack on the wall by the door.

There were silhouettes behind the key pegs. Brian picked one that looked like a jeep, and grabbed the keys.

Sanchez directed him to a little secluded swale just beyond the next rise. On the rising slopes leading from the center, Brian saw rows of well-kept trees standing like rings of defending soldiers. The land of his small holding was a picture of neatness, in contrast to the wild mustache he wore. Sanchez began a litany. He pointed out apples, figs, pomegranates, oranges, plums, avocados, pears, and even dates. In the sunny fields surrounding the neat cottage, there were small paddocks for goats and other animals, as well as rows of vegetable gardens.

Brian looked around. The only thing that looked out of place was the battered and rusty tractor parked in the shade of a large tree. Everything else in sight was first-rate.

Sanchez had been in college, studying horticulture in a program partially funded by the company his father worked for. When things went bad for the family, Ricardo Sanchez had dropped out, to help at home.

He never lost his love for growing things, however, and over the course of many years, he had inherited the holdings of his uncles as well. His gardens provided a living for his family, as well as the food for their table.

Brian felt the wings of the Angel of Serendipity brush his shoulders. He looked at Ricardo Sanchez.

"My friend, think what you could do if you had more room, nearby. You could have rows and rows of apple trees, then more rows of pear trees, then ... Ricardo, do you have any more sons?"

Sanchez laughed. "No. Unfortunately, I have only one son, and he is lazy. I am a very poor farmer. I cannot even manage to keep a shirt on my lazy son's back."

They laughed together.

"Ricardo, how would you like to employ many men. To plant trees, and vegetables, and even pretty flowers. How would you like to have several tractors, and carts, and have the banker in town bring a calendar to your home every year?"

"I would like that very much, Señor. Do I have to give you my children for these things?"

Brian laughed again. "No. But I would like to continue to borrow them, even the lazy one."

Two weeks later, Brian was astonished at how much activity was going on. In addition to Pam and her office staff, Sully and his consultant, and Stubby's dozen experts, there were nearly three hundred local citizens working for his company!

There were fifteen active construction sites, including the beginning work on the castle masonry, and a refurbished building in the village where hybrid shuttle cars were being assembled.

Two of the silo sites had made the turn to horizontal, and additional laborers were being brought in to turn out the building materials that were needed for six warehouse ramp exits, six silo sites domes, and one castle. The castle had priority, but it was getting the most select material. Anything deemed not suitable for use in the castle, would become part of a warehouse.

The construction design was relatively simple. Masonry walls would sheath a weathering-steel post, girder, and truss system. None of the metal should be visible, either inside or outside, but these buildings were intended to *last*. The warehouse roofs were designed like aircraft hangars to shed the weather, and the castle would have a similar design, with walls rising to conceal the roof.

Basically, it was modular, for simplicity's sake. After all, they wanted to employ the local craftsmen as much as possible. At least, Brian did, and he never quite explained why.

Brian looked at the gaunt bones of the castle stretching upward in the distance. Half the windows of the big house looked out on this vision. He was employing an army of men from a fixed amount of resource funding. Much money was going out, and the return on his investment was not yet coming in. The race was on.

And the sky was the limit.

TAKE EIGHT:

What do you think your boss would say?

In addition to the data lines run into his own bedroom, Sully had connected a computer system in Brian's bedroom as well. In fact, he had dropped data connection points all along the way, routing them through the utility space hidden in the overly thick walls below the bedroom areas. That was where the washers and dryers, water heaters, utility control panels, and other devices were anyway.

He had already connected Pam's computer to her bedroom location. She would be able to monitor most of the things that were going on in the office with it, but the printers, scanners, and fax machines were in the main office downstairs.

He was doing the same for Brian. There was also a monitor for the security cameras. None of these modifications had been needed by the previous tenants. The house had really only been a set location to the movie production company.

"This standard configuration will allow you to keep tabs on all the projects as the information comes in on them." Sully showed Brian how to pull up the various displays. "Here's an event plot showing the completion of another layercake section in site one. You can monitor its processing by following along here."

Brian was following the instructions, but he had a concern. "Sully, how is this information coming in? You don't have people out there watching the operations and feeding it into a computer, do you? That seems like a waste of manpower."

Sully looked at him blankly. "Why would anyone do that? Those guys would hate to have one of us dweebs looking over their shoulders, and I wouldn't blame them. People don't do their best work when they think they're being watched like that. Besides, I wouldn't want to get shoved down a hole."

He pointed to one of the indicators. "No, all I'm doing is pulling data off the machine controllers. See, these were custom made to Mr. Mendoza's specifications. He knew what he wanted them to do. All I did was put the electronics on them. I wanted to use optical sensors, but it was too dusty. We had to use magnetic. They cost a little more, but they don't get clogged. They feed back to the motor controllers and actuators so the machine can sense its limits."

"Anyway, the sensors feed into the controllers; the controllers feed into the sending units; everything ends up here. If one of the drill heads started overheating, I would get a tell-tale here, and I could even shut the machine down." He toggled a sub-menu. "Okay, all the temps are in the proper range." He toggled it off again. He looked up.

Brian was trying to absorb it. "Sully, you mean that you could actually *operate* the boring machines from this location?"

Sully grinned. "Sure, but I couldn't see what I was doing. They wouldn't head off for China or anything, but the road would get awfully rough. I don't have anything to help me keep it centered. The only way I know what the machine is doing is by the pattern of commands that they process. Stubby and his crews keep these shield-borers aligned with lasers, and they are tracking them within a millimeter. They're really good men, you know?"

"Do they know that you have this much control, Sully?"

"I guess if they think about it, they do. But I don't interfere with their work. If I see a way I can do something to help them, I do it. If I have a suggestion, I ask them to help me make it work." Sully looked into Brian's eyes. "Muscle guys are a lot like machines. If you know what buttons to push, you can program them like a microprocessor." He suddenly looked alarmed.

"Don't ever tell them that I said that -- I respect those guys. They're fearless and determined. Guys like me think robots are cool. Did you ever think why?"

Brian put his hand on Sully's shoulder. "Don't worry. I like the way you handle yourself. I knew you were comfortable around computers and such, Sully. I'm impressed with your ability to deal with people too."

Sully grinned, "I was in a fraternity with sports jocks, a similar breed. I found my association with them to be useful."

"I heard about that. You aren't building a mega-computer here, are you?"

Sully looked hurt. "Of course not. I have to wait until we're ready to set up the castle equipment for that. *Then* I'll take over the world."

Brian laughed. *He was kidding, wasn't he?*

"Um, Brian?" Sullivan Conrad was looking seriously thoughtful. "I'm not as good with people as you think. I have a confession to make. My, um ... that consultant I hired. Well, she's a really competent electrician. That's undeniable. But the work we're doing is really more along the lines of..." Brian had stopped him.

"Sully, the people in your department are your responsibility. I didn't have any objection to your hiring her before, and I don't now. Remember, you were following my instructions."

"I was?" He looked puzzled.

Brian smiled, "You certainly were. I told you to find a nice girl. Next thing I knew, there you were."

"Oh, yeah! You did say that! I thought about it too. But the deal with Marcia just ... sorta happened."

"Sully, you don't get it. You understand jocks, and roughnecks. But there are people around who know how to push our buttons, too. I'd like to take credit for it. You did say I was a good programmer, after all. But it may well be that some of *this* programming is *hard-wired!*"

Sully grinned at him, "Brian, you're remarkable. Now I find out that *you can read code!*"

"Thanks Sully. If there's anything I learned in my association with the movie people and their management, it's this. *'Never let the people you hire realize that you aren't God.'* Now, show me what else I can do from here. You don't have a way of tracking our vehicles, do you?"

"Hmm. Our vehicles, yes. That is, the hybrid units we're putting together downtown. They have position locators as well as positioning sensors built into them. Our leased vehicles don't have any."

Brian was surprised. "Why do the hybrid vehicles have that, Sully?"

"You know, sometimes I just do things without lining up reasons pro and con. In this case, it just seemed the natural thing to do. We're going to use these shuttles as electric vehicles underground. They'll tap power off the tunnel lines. That means we'll be operating them under automatic control, and that means we need to be able to know where they are in relation to each other. No six-car pile-ups inside the tunnel, please!"

"Then it becomes logical to extend that to being able to track the vehicle when it's in its delivery mode. If we don't want to lose a package, we certainly don't want to lose a hundred packages at once."

Sully looked thoughtful, "A satellite navigation system might not work too well underground, but that's not where we need it. So it just falls into place that we track the vehicles that way overland."

Brian nodded, "That's fine, Sully. I wasn't questioning your reasons, I just wanted to know what they were. And those are good reasons. Now, how does that information get back here? And where can I tap into it?"

"Sure. I mentioned sending units. We have them at the silo sites. Just basic bi-directional data links over radio. I put a low-power version of that on each shuttle. They scurry along, talking to themselves, and we listen in."

"You said they were bi-directional. Can we send information the other way too?"

"Oh, sure. Mostly simple messages. Stop, turn back, return to base, that sort of thing. Why?"

"Could we talk over the link?"

Sully blinked. "Hmm. Yeah ... we could compress the data, and degrade the bandwidth, but you'd be able to recognize a voice. And ... that could work underground, too. Do you want me to program that capability?"

Brian thought about it. Evidently, when Sully said something was possible, that meant it could be done, but gave you no idea of the effort involved. "Well, it's not a priority at the moment, but it sounds like something that will come in handy along the way."

"Okay, no problem. I'll let my subconscious work on it. When it comes time to do it, I should have no trouble."

Brian patted him on the shoulder, "I do a lot of my work that way too."

Pam tapped her water glass with a spoon. "The third regular meeting of the Ampersand Incorporated Executive Board will please come to order. Those of you who wish to discover what transpired on the previous two occasions are encouraged to read the notes of those meetings, which are available in the handouts. Essentially, certain bylaws were discussed, officers selected, executive compensation was acted upon, and no dissent was encountered."

"Pam, none of us were here," Brian said mildly.

"Exactly my point. You were too busy out there getting things done to have the courtesy of taking part in organizing our organization. Since there were things that had to be decided and acted upon, I acted and decided. For example: Brian, are you aware that spending out of Governmental Credit Accounts for personal reasons is a criminal offense? Esteban, do you know what authority requires the posting of payroll tax deposits?" She glared at them.

"Are we in trouble?" Stubby asked.

"You are with me," She sighed. The air had gone out of her huff. "Listen, boys, you have to start being serious. From now on, I want you *in attendance* at these briefings. We've got to stay coordinated. There's a tendency to go off in too many directions at the same time, *Brian.*

Now, let's have a mutual progress report. Mr. Mendoza, how goes the drilling?"

"The good news is that we now have the ability to calculate what our rate of progress is likely to be. We've started the bore holes in six locations on three islands. We're going to be working toward the center of each path, but the paths are different lengths. The upshot is that tunnel A will take two years, tunnel B should be completed in a year and a half, and tunnel C will take a full four years. These times all run concurrently, because we have six starting points. When the first two tunnels are completed, the shield boring machines will be transported to the last interlink sites, and two boreholes will be started from each end. That's going to go very slowly. We anticipate that it will require six years, two years from now."

"So in eight years, four complete tunnels will link five islands."

"That is correct, Pam. That is for the current projection, and no one has thought of a way to make it go faster, except for one option."

"And that is?" She responded.

"On the final traverse, it is technically possible to make a mid-ocean entry, and cut three years off the project time. The Island Governing Council is opposed to that option, and so am I."

"Our only time commitment to the council is for the initial three tunnels. If they are willing to wait, out of safety considerations, then I think we should be patient as well. The Big Island Tunnel is going to be used mainly for agricultural products anyway, I don't think the delay will hurt our profit projections," Brian reminded them.

"Okay, that fits in with our expectations and appears to be on schedule. What about the other schedule problem?"

"I'll take it," Brian answered. "I've been following it. We have a commitment to have the castle construction ready for occupancy by the film crews in seven months and ... three days. By way of comparison, this house was put up in six weeks, by very skilled technicians. The castle will be twenty times this size, and our work force is local laborers. Even if we could double the efficiency of the construction of this house, that still puts us at over a year to completion."

"Are we in trouble?" Stubby asked again.

Brian smiled grimly, "Are we ever. This is a house. That's a ten story apartment building as big as a city block. Comparable structures have taken from three to five years to complete."

For a while, they were quiet.

"How's the material coming along? Is that a problem?" from Pam.

Stubby answered, "The two bore sites on this island can supply a bit over one half of one percent of finished stone per day, of what we need for the castle. That projects out to six months away. Theoretically, we could bring stone from the other islands to increase the quantity, but the shaping facility is here, and transporting stone across the ocean brings in the inefficiency and expense this project is all about. We'll be able to supply the stone for the interior and exterior of the castle all right, and our laborers will be placing the last of the stones within six months -- but that's not the problem." He looked around at them.

"The problem is that's just the shell of the castle. The finish work inside is what is going to be the problem. Steel and stone can make a warehouse, but a warehouse is not a castle."

In his bedroom, Sully had been listening in. The security cameras that were covering vital areas of the big house tended to get ignored after a time. The one in the main office had been able to convey every image and sound of the meeting.

Sully wasn't spying on them; this was just the way he worked. Gather information, solve problems. He swiveled in his chair. This could be a situation that concerned him in more ways than one. How could he get his intricate computer system working if they were going to have trouble with more mundane items?

Marcia stopped in. "I've finished wiring the exterior lighting security lights. I'm going to start on the low voltage panel now." She noticed his thoughtful look. "Is something wrong?"

He smiled. "Not really. Just a programming snag. I'll get it worked out." He rose and held her in his arms. "I have a special motivation for getting this done right."

Marcia smiled at him, "You're not talking about getting married again, are you? I thought the girl was the one who always wanted a big fancy wedding."

Placing his forehead against hers, he spoke tenderly. "I want a wedding that will be appropriate for the beauty of the bride, and I know where I want it to be. Now all I have to figure out is a matter of timing."

"What do you think your boss would say if he saw you carrying on like this when you're supposed to be working?"

Sully smiled, "He's already said it, and I remember it well. It's the first time in my life that I've had a boss who seems to understand me, or care what happens to me."

Marcia nodded her head against his. "I think I know what you mean. It's good to have someone who cares about you." She returned his smile.

TAKE NINE:

Don't let her hear you call her delicate

Notwithstanding the pressures of their busy schedules, it was again time for a party. Brian looked forward to these events as much as any of the younger people. Ever the trooper, Paulo had apparently gotten over the upsetting disagreement with his mother. He seemed as happy as any child has ever been, and his enthusiasm burst out in childlike ways.

It surely was a contrast. Quite often, during the course of the filming, Paulo had been required to act exactly like a hyper-masculine character in a pornographic film. With his firmly attached artificial firmness, he provided a luxurious sexual paradise for the female characters of the story. There was nothing at all artificial about the gasping ecstasy they portrayed. Not that they could not have acted as if they were enjoying it, but the producers of the film were leaving nothing to chance, or to the imagination.

To the actresses, it was a job benefit of priceless value. They had come to have a real emotional attachment to the friendly and sweet-natured boy, as opposed to his attachment, which was joked about. The fact that he was unable to enjoy the activity as they did, made his efforts in their behalf especially endearing. Paulo was able to concentrate on the movements and energetic portrayals with a surprising degree of emotional detachment. That permitted an exceptionally realistic portrayal of his character's function as a personal slave for sexual pleasure. He not only *appeared* to be giving them intense pleasure, he really was. His ability to respond to their needs, rather than his own, had made him a rather consummate lover, despite his tender years. The women got the benefit of that as well.

Paulo seemed to take it all in stride, as if it were no more than a bicycle act. His outgoing and friendly nature made him a favorite among all who met him, female or not. Brian was especially fond of him, and had bonded with him in a grandfatherly sort of way.

Brian was less sanguine about the action being filmed. That they knew their craft was beyond question. But their expertise sometimes seemed to skirt a shabby edge. He found the vivid images of performed sexual servitude somewhat disturbing, as if the intent were to justify the human degradation thus portrayed. *Were they trying to make a pornographic film?* His confreres in the film industry argued on the other side. It was their job to translate the word portraits of authors such as he to the kind of images in question. But they contended that the point of the story was evoked as well, by allowing the audience to identify and sympathize with the characters, *all* the characters.

One of the screenwriters had told him, "Brian, you set up a story in which women in the future had no other outlet for their sexuality than to create a servant class. Nobody is arguing that a servant class, and slavery, is acceptable. What we're trying to convey to our audience is not that they would enjoy this situation, which they cannot help but enjoy vicariously, but to get them to *think* about the relationships between these people, and how they would handle being in that situation themselves. And this is *his* story too. When we bury this image in their mind, they *have* to bring it up again later, and digest its meaning. They can't avoid thinking about it!"

Brian remained dubious, and some of the film's critics were also. A portion of the expertise of the group had come from that dark side of the entertainment industry, and he was concerned that the film would be treated as just another such venture. His intended message of love and hope might never properly see the light of day, if issuing from such a dark source.

Brian shook off his doubts. Now was not the time or the place for that! His guests were arriving!

They came by van-loads at the main entrance, most making their way around to the patio courtyard and coming into the greatroom. Had they gone in the front door, they would have found themselves in a business office.

Carlos, the young neighbor boy, and his sisters, Linda and Dolcita came directly into the pool room through the back entrance. Most of his guests ended here anyway, and most of them ended up wearing no clothes. That had become the rule for swimming, and Carlos helped to spread the word as if he were the naked sergeant at arms.

Mary and Martha were already in the pool, as were Carmen and Sally. Paulo had gone to greet Linda and Dolcita, and they were sitting at the rounded corner of the pool, talking together. All of them were naked. Only the most recent arrivals, and Brian himself, were still wearing clothes. He was wearing one of the play outfits that Pam had stocked for everyone.

They were more like short pajamas, or a kid's playclothes, than standard party wear, but Brian felt comfortable in them. This one was light green, and Brian was still trying to cope with having no pockets.

Joe Hardwicke, the casting director, had come again, and again had escorted Josetta Barnes. She was wearing a genuine party outfit, a transparent bit of chiffon with woven fiber optic highlights flashing different colors in time with the background music. A neckline that plunged to the waist, and slits up the outside of her legs made it look like a fairy dress. Sparkling silver dance slippers completed the outfit.

Brian spread his arms in greeting, and Josetta came into them easily, tiptoeing to kiss him with an impish smile.

"Joe! You found my lost puppy! Thanks for bringing her back."

Hardwicke shook hands with him. "I had to! She said she was moving in. She even brought some of her bags. The rest are still in her room near the main office."

Brian looked down at her. "Is that so? Did I invite you?"

She smiled and swung herself under his arm, as if to be sheltered. "You certainly did! I can provide witnesses if I have to!"

"Including some I haven't met yet, I'm sure. Very well, as long as we have that settled. Joe, you look thirsty, and so am I. Have you taught this puppy to fetch, yet?"

"I'll get it! Two beers, coming up!" She flitted away, like a ballerina moving through the crowd.

Joe smiled, "She's a charmer, that one!"

Brian nodded back, "She has a delicate quality, like a glass figurine. She'd be welcome at any party, just for appearance's sake."

"Don't let her hear you call her delicate. She's a tank, in taffeta. I've known her about six years, and she gets the job done."

Josetta was not the only one in party attire. Several other delectable maidens were wearing simple little nothings that concealed and revealed their femininity, and had set up an impromptu dance floor near the rear pool exit. This must have been planned in advance, because their dance partners were some of the shaven male extras, who were wearing only body paintings made for the occasion. The artistic designs and freedom of motion lent themselves to some creative dance routines.

Not only were they having fun, they were entertaining the other guests as well. Brian found it odd, but notable that although the people in the pool were completely naked, all eyes were drawn to the ones who were only *partially* naked. And on the fringes of the dance area, the intrepid Sullivan Conrad was doing a slow dance with Marcia.

When Josetta returned with the beverages, Brian noted, her eyes were flashing like the dress she wore. He leaned down and whispered in her ear, "Sic 'em, girl." She smiled and danced away.

Up in the greatroom, things were more cerebral, and pedestrian. There were platters of dried apricots and figs, and a large fruit bowl. Brian suspected he knew who was responsible for that.

Conversation was going on about the direction of the message to be conveyed in the second movie. Screenwriters were lining up against set decorators, and others.

"No, no, the males don't disappear entirely, they just fade into the background. They don't *all* want their tattoos removed. It's expensive, remember."

"Tattoos or not, all we have to do is not show them. They're out of the picture, get it?"

"But that's the point! We need to show a society *in transition*, not a society transformed."

"It's a waste of effort. The part of society we're filming at that point has already moved on. Why throw away the resources? Especially for background shots."

"Let's ask Brian. He's a consultant, isn't he?"

Brian looked at the hopeful faces on both sides. *It's a party, guys.*

Aloud, he said, "Well, it can't be too expensive. There are people downstairs wearing body paint right now. I guess it depends on the specific scene, and whether any of the original message is going to be changed."

Silence..... "Ahem. Ah, yes. Speaking of changes, how many women are we going to be showing as pregnant? That ought to show a society in transition, don't you think?"

Brian headed toward the door and out to the patio.

Jake Wagner. *Out of the frying pan, into the fire.* "Jake! What brings you to these parts? Where's your beer?"

Jake waved it off. "Bottled water for me, thanks. I just stopped by to look at the old place. Looks pretty lively. I like the mood lighting. Not bad."

"Thanks. We're still just settling in. Adding a few personal touches. Your boys did a good job, considering that they were in a hurry."

Jake smiled, "Speaking of which, I heard that things were not going along as speedily as you had hoped on the castle. Would you like for me to send over some of those boys to lend a hand? Maybe I could recoup some of that leasing fee I paid you."

Brian shook his head. "Won't be necessary, Jake. I'm sure your boys have their hands full already. We'll take care of it. I've got some talented people working for me, too!"

Jake's smile was one that he had carefully trained up from a sneer. "No doubt. And fortunately, you didn't have to look very far to find them, either." *Oh, no! You did _not_ say that!*

Brian sipped his drink. "Maybe, if I need some help from your side, I'll just hire some folks away from you. I believe my budget is just a tad bigger than yours at this point, isn't it?"

Jake found an expression that could not be turned into a smile. "I'm glad things are going well for you, Brian. I'd like to stay, but unfortunately, I have some evening appointments. Perhaps another time?"

"Anytime, Jake. Stop by anytime," Brian replied. *I'll be ready for you!*
Jake departed casually. Brian turned back toward the house.
Now I really need a beer.

Somehow the party seemed a much nicer place to be, all of a sudden.

Brian was determined to have a good time after that. He even went swimming, though that was the last thing he remembered, other than that his bed seemed much bigger than it was supposed to be. *Could this be the pool, and I'm too tired to know the difference?* That seemed unlikely, as there were too many bodies in his way for it to be a swimming pool. He slept.

Light. Ouch! *Note to self: Are you listening?* Why hadn't he taken a shadier bedroom? And what was that weird dream about a huge bed?

Tentatively, Brian surveyed his bedroom. If he wasn't the size of a four-year-old, his bed *was* bigger. Much bigger! And it needed to be, for there were seven other people in it with him.

All right, let's take inventory. Brian?, debatable; Paulo, present; Carmen, Sally, Mary, Martha, Josetta, and one he didn't even recognize. Eight people. Saints preserve us.

It must have happened at the beginning of the party, or just before. It had been a busy day, but you'd think a man would notice something like that. Next question, who was the perpetrator? Whoever it was had to be working with Pam. That would make the prime candidate -- Paulo. What a dirty, sneaky, underhanded, low-down, ... He loved that boy.

Brian risked a yawn, and stretch. Okay, that's ambitious enough! Rest, now. He closed his eyes again.

Carmen and Sally were talking softly about Paulo, and Mary and her sister offered suggestions from time to time.

"I don't mean to be selfish," Carmen was saying, "but I want to keep him."

"Would you be willing to share?"

"Well, ... not with everyone. I think I could share with you, and maybe you two. But I really just want to keep him forever. I don't like the way his family treats him, for one thing. I want to protect him."

"You know he's going to change?"

"I wish he didn't have to, but I think I can accept it. What I couldn't take is to have him go away for three or four years, and then have some strange man come back."

"Oh, you're right about that. If he goes back to his family, he'll be lost forever."

"Maybe you could marry him," Mary's voice.

"Marry? I wouldn't mind marrying. Could we?"

"That would be so cute!" from Martha.

Brian stole a glance. Paulo's eyes were open, wide open. Brian had thought he was asleep. Carmen's hand was dancing around with a sleepy and inattentive partner, and she and Sally were taking turns stroking the skin around Paulo's groin with tender caresses. Sally snuggled closer and rested her head against Paulo's chest as her hand glided across his stomach and chest like a figure skater on an ice rink.

Paulo had a hand in each girl's soft hair, gently stroking their locks.

The boy had to be into torture. He had said that he could feel it, and that it felt good. To not be able to react further must be mind-bendingly frustrating. Perhaps the only thing allowing him to keep his sanity was that he did not know what he was not getting.

It dawned on Brian that Paulo was a virgin! Incredible! For months he had been humping and pumping like a porn robot, and he had never ...

Now Brian's mind was beginning to feel the pressure, and not just his mind.

To add further to his discomfort, Brian felt the warm small hand of Josetta again make inroads across his chest. He glanced at her, and saw that she was, indeed, watching him. He looked back to Paulo.

"I could marry him, I think. I would have to live here, though. I couldn't take him anywhere else. I'd lose him for sure, and probably get locked up, too! No, we would have to live here."

"Do you have enough money?"

"How much do I need? I could still do my music, and my dance videos -- if the story gets out about Paulo, anything I do will sell, for awhile."

"Yeah, aren't they talking about putting in a studio, and other stuff, in the castle?"

"Did you hear about last night? Jake Wagner was almost threatening Brian about the castle!"

"Jake the Snake! What a weasel!"

"Brian stood up to him though! Said he might hire some people away from Jake! The Snake couldn't slither away fast enough!" Brian glanced again at Josetta. She put a finger to her lips. *Conspirators.*

"Can Brian pull it off? It sounds tough."   "Nobody knows. We're all pulling for him, though."

"We? You get your paycheck from Jake's outfit."

"Maybe so, but I'm not in his bed."

Brian was trying to remain still. It would be embarrassing to have them know he had heard their conversation. But there was another problem. Josetta's wandering hand had done some slithering of its own. She was stealthily exploring under his shorts! His partial tumescence began growing! Through his slitted eyes, Brian saw that Paulo's pleasant torture was continuing, even as his own was beginning!

The delicate hand found its target, and encircled it. Josetta gripped him gently, and they both could feel his pounding heart. In desperation, Brian used the coughing gambit again, starting mildly, then more forcefully. He clambered out of the bed, keeping his anterior anatomy out of view, and sought shelter in the bathroom. Once there, his coughing subsided. Whew!

Brian started a shower, and kicked off his shorts. This should give things time to calm down!

Except that Josetta had silently joined him in the shower. She was not concerned about getting her short-cropped hair wet. And she was not embarrassed about being in there with him. What she was, was as Joe Hardwicke had described her, a tank in taffeta. She was not going to let him get away again.

She calmly began washing him, as if in a dreamy state. Brian braced himself with the shower handholds. Josetta finished washing him, and rinsed him of the lather. With the steamy water still cascading over them, she began arousing him further, and undulated her body against him. Wrapping her arms around him, she rubbed her body across his.

His mind knew that he was an old man, but it was busy. And his body had forgotten everything except one primal, basic function. Josetta grasped his stiff manhood with her left hand, and rubbed his rear with her right. Then she nuzzled his groin with her face, rubbing him the way people wash their faces under the shower stream.

Brian braced himself again with the handholds as Josetta's lips kissed, then engulfed his focus of erotic impetus, using her lips and tongue to excite him as he had never dreamed.

Her head moved up and down as she held his body like a toy in her hands, sending waves of excitement through him. She twisted her left hand gently, and firmly attacked him with her mouth.

Brian was actually getting light headed. His mind fell into a pit of breathtaking sensation. Josetta did not slacken her assault, and as his passion erupted, she drew his strength with wicked thoroughness.

When she was finished, when they were finished, she calmly tilted her face up and let the water run over it, rinsing clean. Then she raised herself up and kissed him. Brian got the message. What she had done was not dirty or unclean, but an act of unselfish love.

Taking the time he needed to keep his mental and physical balance, Brian carefully shut the water off and found a way to sit down on the edge of the tub. His knees were definitely wobbly. Josetta sat on his lap, now clear of obstructions, and embraced him.

She kissed him. He kissed her in return. He held her, and began stroking her still-wet skin. Reaching for a towel, Brian began drying her, mopping up her hair, and being lovingly attentive to her. She sat unmoving as he dried her skin, and rubbed warmth into the cooler spots. Unwilling to separate from her, Brian dried the petite body thoroughly, and then his own. He drew her into another embrace as he held her in his lap. Touching her smooth, untroubled face, Brian marveled at its creamy soft texture. He tenderly explored her surrendered body, and held her like a child in need of comfort. Delicately tracing the softness of her breasts, he teased a response from her dainty nipples. His large hand looked stark against the velvet smoothness of her skin, and he moved it gently into her folded treasure. Josetta opened her sweet lower limbs and delicate petals to his tentative entreaty, and he found a place that was not quite dry.

Relaxing entirely, almost limp, Josetta allowed his long, strong fingers to move across her threshold of delight. As he moved them inside her, she moved her body in response. Brian continued, slowly and gently, in his own determination to return the ecstasy she had brought him.

Her petite body welcomed his strong fingers like a kitten trying to induce more sweetness from its source of nourishment. Brian observed her delectable body as he stimulated her. He was awestruck that such beauty lay in his hands.

Her motions and her gentle moans of pleasure guided him as he probed and prodded her into a torment of writhing delight.

A long, long time later, he desisted from his efforts. Her body had a cheerful, rosy glow about it and a sheen of sweat. Without having to lean too far, Brian started the tub filling with warm water. Kissing her face all over, he then lifted her and lowered her into the tub.

Josetta smiled at him as she splashed around, a secret, sharing smile. Brian stepped to the sink and began preparing for the rest of what was starting out as a very promising day.

Hand in hand, and neither wearing clothes, they went back out to the bedroom. The wriggling mass of naked flesh on the huge bed came to a halt as eyes looked at them and smiles brightened the already sunny day. Brian led Josetta to the bed, and kissed her again.

Grabbing the shirt that he had dropped the previous evening, Brian headed back to the bathroom, where he fed it and his shorts to a large laundry chute. Picking a fresh set of shorts and shirt in his size, light brown this time, he slipped them on and went out to face the day.

As he was going down to the kitchen, he could hear what sounded like applause. *For her? For him? For them, he concluded.*

Sully had really had a good time at the party. He had always been the odd man out at such things, and had never really developed his social graces. He suspected that sweet Marcia was someone with a similar problem, though that was difficult for him to judge. She had a relatively shy disposition, and despite having known her a while now, he still had not been able to find out a lot about her background, and what may be troubling her. He would have to give her more time.

Sullivan smiled. He planned to give her a *lot* more time. At the party, he couldn't seem to take his eyes off her, despite the distractions. He practically followed her into the ladies' room at one point. Because of that, he was now reviewing his recordings from the security cameras. He had set the system up to record into computer memory whatever was being viewed by various cameras. It was childishly simple to use. Sully had a vague notion that he might at some point want to present his friends with a video notebook of their good times together. In any case, it was just computer memory; he could erase it anytime.

There was some good 'footage' of the dancing, and great images of smiling faces and animated conversations. This would make good scrapbook material.

Something seemed out of place. He looked a little closer. Brian and the bigwig from the film company were having a conversation on the patio. They both had pleasant smiles, but several faces nearby looked concerned. What the ... ?

Sully put it on a loop. It was a very short conversation, but it had the look of a confrontation. He wondered what they had said. The recording had audio as well, but there was a lot of noise. A little filtering...
Slowly, Sully teased out the content. With satisfaction, he reviewed the conversation. Then again. And again.

Each time, he got a little hotter. Brian was a nice guy. He got into stuff like this because he tried to help people. And Brian was his friend.

Jake. Jake Wagner. He was twisting the knife about Brian's dream. And that crack about 'You didn't have to look far' Grrr! He was talking about the people on this island! The friendly people who were his hosts. The generous townsfolk who had accepted him, and his wicked ways, and who had given him the shirts off their backs and ... Wups.

Anyway, it didn't take a genius to realize that their economy had tanked, and that Brian was trying to jump-start it again.

Sullivan Conrad *was* a genius. He had a fearsome intellect. He also had a finely honed sense of fairness. But Sully had recognized from an early age that intelligence without ambition was just daydreaming. He had learned to harness his thinking ability in service of his goals. That was what produced results -- goal orientation. Some of his jock friends had shown what kind of results could be achieved through single-minded purpose. Not just intellect, but *drive*.

Currently, Sully had some simple ambitions. He wanted to build that massive bit of parallel computing with the satellite uplinks and everything. He wanted to do well, and make a name for himself. A wise man had once told him to *"Find a nice girl who respects your mind, and your earning potential, and <u>be faithful</u> to her."*

Well, he had followed that advise, at least so far. He had found the girl of his dreams. She respected his mind. He wanted to marry that girl, and he definitely planned to be faithful to her.

Third simple ambition: He wanted to marry her in that beautiful castle. Brian's dream castle.

Jake Wagner had stood in Brian's face and *challenged* him to build his castle. To build Sullivan and Marcia's castle.

Jake Wagner had as much as said, "You think you can build a castle, with tons of computers in it, and help the people around you become wealthy, and let Sully and Marcia get married? With <u>me</u> standing in your way? You, and what army?"

"Yeah! We can," growled Sullivan Conrad. "Oh, yeah! With me! And MY army!"

Savagely, he closed the file on Jake Wagner's sneering face and turned in his chair. 'Slow down, Sullivan.' He told himself, 'Stop racing your engine. Put it in DRIVE!'

The lash of outrage was for him the strop which brought the keenest edge to the sword of his intellect. The impetus of a threat perceived was a funnel for his aimless intentions. A confluence of emotions built pressure within the dynamo of his determination.

He turned back to the computer. Above his head, on his recently installed bookshelf, were several of his favorite volumes. Inside them, his personal Ex Libris sticker was affixed:

Trouble rather the tiger in his lair
    than the sage amongst his books.

For to you, kingdoms and their armies
    are mighty and enduring,

But to him, they are but toys of the moment

To be overturned by the flicking of a finger.

TAKE TEN:

All may not be lost

There was a problem in the big house. It wasn't big enough! Brian, Stubby, and Sully had worked out a plan to add a semi-circle of small rooms in an arc around the pool area exit. Two stairs led upward to the surrounding yard. This was a natural avenue for additional bedrooms, especially for guests. Most of the exposed surface was covered with the new stone, including the stairs and walkways that were made. Ricardo Sanchez had a half-dozen crews out building garden walls and small improvements across the island now. They had received their training with this project. Brian had tossed him an opportunity, and he had run with it. His was the first enterprise to actually start bringing in money!

A new stone-surfaced patio was encircled by large-windowed business offices. A hallway on the other side allowed access to them and to small bedroom apartments based on the rooms that would be built in the castle.

Stubby used the construction as an opportunity to incorporate the horizontal elevator connection to the castle, and other link-ups.

Brian used the new space as an opportunity to smooth some of the relations with the film group. Since a few of them had become de facto permanent guests here at the big house, he arranged with the lower echelon business people to see to it that they were not being billed for unused hotel accommodations. He also arranged for the delivery of flowers to various departments. Whether Jake Wagner knew of any of this was a matter of indifference to him; he was cultivating good relations with the group itself, not the 'head of the serpent.' If any of them found ways to help him in return, it was a good investment.

Sully used it as a trial test for some of his modifications to the computerized general building database. This had always been a useful tool, allowing materials lists, plan diagrams, and stone cutting schedules to be developed easily. Sully treated the data as if it were his own kingdom. He had multiplied its utility by making the program interactive, able to display real-time three-D walk-throughs and views.

He had also slightly modified the original structure to accommodate some changes. A change that seemed most appropriate was to incorporate a package delivery system into the castle mini-apartments. It allowed the Spartan accommodations to reflect a luxurious privilege. The residents could request food, or study and entertainment materials to be delivered directly to their rooms!

Reluctantly, Stubby had agreed to link this system to that of the castle also, realizing that it would permit sending and receiving such materials between the big house and the castle as well.

Sully was particularly proud of another modification that he had incorporated. It was an innocuous change to the production schedule that he had developed, and the patio apartments gave him an opportunity to test his theory.

After all the rough-in work was completed, and the doors and windows installed, Sully dismissed the workmen from the site. In a single afternoon, he and Marcia went through the rooms, like a constructive whirlwind, and installed and connected all of the different systems that made them comfortable.

Each apartment had a working computer, video system, intercom, lighting, music, basic supplies, and unit identity. Even the business rooms had been equipped. Sully surveyed his work with satisfaction.

Marcia mopped her brow. He had acted as if they were racing, and they had both worked up a sweat. "Okay, we're done. Maybe now you can tell me why we were hurrying?"

Sully held her. He wanted to share his joy with someone, and he always wanted it to be her. "Just testing my program, sweetheart. I think it's going to work!"

"It's already working! We're finished, remember?"

Sully smiled, "Oh, yeah! So we are. What shall we do now?"

"Well, I need a shower!"

"Hmm. So do I," He was still holding her.

"Now, Sully, you behave yourself! ... Sully? ..."

The opening of the office wing had relieved some of the congestion in the bedrooms of the big house. But Brian found that his bed remained crowded. It wasn't even always the same people. Mary and Martha joined them from time to time, surrendering their bedroom next door to others. Josetta was of course a regular, and the unrecognized girl from before had turned out to be Josetta's cousin Theresa, who had been brought to the island as Josetta's personal trainer.

Paulo still had a loyal following of female companions, and some of them found their way to the bed as well. Carmen was able to discourage newer aspirants, but some few had a bit of seniority, such as Angelina Foster. And even though Carmen was mildly possessive, she did not yet actually possess.

Brian had surmised that Josetta's delectability was at least partially by dint of personal effort. He was discovering now how much effort was required. Since Theresa's arrival, the two girls had made *his* health and stamina their personal interest. This required regular workouts in the pool, bicycle riding, and regular types of conditioning exercises, including some *very* personal exercises initiated by Josetta.

"Where did you get these bikes, Brian? I've never ridden a more comfortable one."

"Sully helped me find them. They're almost like a custom order, but everything is just a menu selection. We selected about twenty in the first order."

Josetta, Brian, and Theresa were now riding down the gentle slope toward the Sanchez house. They were wearing the comfortable playsuits that were showing up everywhere these days. At the moment, they doubled as exercise wear, but they were useful for play and visiting, too.

Brian had seen children in the village wearing similar outfits, and he knew that the big house had not supplied them. Evidently, the style had simply caught on.

They caught sight of the Sanchez children, heading out to get on their bikes, which had simply showed up one morning, with the kids' names tagged to them. Even Carlos was wearing a play suit, but Brian knew that it would be discarded as soon as they got to the pool.

"Good morning! Are you ready for your ride?" Brian called to them.

"We are ready, Señor Brian, Linda has a basket for Mama."

"Oh, good. That may be part of my breakfast. These girls won't let me eat meat any more. I think if we pass a slow-moving donkey, I may take a bite out of him as we go by."

They all laughed and mounted up on their bicycles. Brian was feeling better than he had in a decade. Already he had lost a dozen pounds. But the girls only allowed him two beers a day! No wonder he was wasting away!

Brian pedaled back up the slope. The automatic shifting of the gears made the ride easy, and the shock absorbers in the handgrips were a very nice touch.

Gliding by three of the hybrid shuttle vehicles sitting on the parking apron, they parked the bikes near the garage and continued around the house to the rear patio entrance. Carlos and his sisters immediately dropped off, shed their clothes, and dived into the pool. Brian could have gone through the main entrance as a short cut, but he knew he would be stopped in the business office, and he *really* wanted his breakfast.

Mrs. Sanchez was already in the kitchen.

"Thank you, Miss Theresa. I thought I would have to fish the fruit out of the swimming pool!"

Theresa had carried the basket up to the kitchen. "That's okay, Señora Carmelita. It is good for the children to get exercise."

"Everybody is getting exercise! Nobody eats anymore. You are all going to blow away in the wind!"

One problem that the big house had was that the dining room had been taken over as a business office, so any large dinner groups spilled out of the kitchen into the greatroom. The disorganized schedules of most residents kept this to a minimum, however.

The smells of recent meals were still tantalizingly in the air as Brian sat down to eat what his personal trainers recommended. He was sticking with the program, though. The rewards were worth it.

Unfortunately, it didn't take long to finish the meal. All too soon, the girls were going up to prepare for their day, and Brian kissed each of them good-bye. Josetta's cousin had been associated with her for several years now, backing up her show business career in various ways. In addition to personal trainer, she was also stand-in, stunt double, backup vocalist, and best friend. They were not by any means 'identical cousins,' but they did look like sisters.

He could avoid it no longer. Brian went into the business office. Pamela looked at him with the same expression of mild annoyance that she might use for a piece of paper that fell from her desk. Brian suspected he would get much the same look if he handed her a bonus check for a million dollars.

Pamela was a top-notch businesswoman, but she never seemed to let her hair down.

"You have some paperwork to sign, and several phone messages to return. We're going to have a progress report meeting this afternoon. You will be there, won't you?"

"Of course, Pam. You know how happy I am to hear about progress."

"Don't be surprised to be disappointed, Brian."

He sighed, "I don't get it, Pam. We're working our tails off. How can we not be making the kind of progress we need to?"

She looked over the tops of her glasses at him. "You certainly seem to be working your tail off, but that's not what we need to get done," She said sternly.

Brian walked over, placed his hand on her shoulder, and kissed her on the forehead. "Thanks, Pam, I don't think you realize how much a compliment from you can brighten my day."

There seemed to be a momentary pause in the office hubbub, then it continued as usual. Pam looked a little flustered, and turned back to her books. *Hopefully, a little lightheartedness can brighten her day, too.* Brian went to the small table that he used as a desk. He preferentially spent so little time in here that he didn't want to tie up space uselessly. He actually had a better office available in his bedroom. *Not to mention, (Back to work, you!)*

Pam called the meeting to order. Her voice echoed in the quiet of the room. In the lower level business office, Dolores Ramirez and Alice Farnsworth were answering phones and composing reports.

"We can speak freely. For the first time, this sixth regular meeting can be conducted like a proper executive meeting. Thank you, Sully. Your completion of the connections and equipment in the lower offices has given us all more breathing room. I should also like to mention that Mr. Conrad is here at his request and my invitation. Without objection I would suggest that Mr. Conrad also be included in future meetings," She looked around. "No? Very well then. Could we begin with you, Mr. Mendoza? A report on your operations, please?"

"The drilling in all locations is going well. I am happy to report that we have increased our efficiency in drilling by fifteen percent, and I wish to make it a point that Mr. Conrad had a hand in that as well. We had been taking the machines off-line for about a half-hour every shift to do a manual reading of the wear rates on the bits. Sully showed us a way to automatically adjust the individual unit pressures by feeding back the measured bit temperatures. The machines are running cooler, and smoother, and we now shut down only to replace all the bits at the same time. Thank you, Mr. Conrad.

"Next, production of building stone. Our increased efficiency in drilling has also increased the available supply of stone, and it is good quality. Sullivan has suggested that we implement a program of supplying good material as a free supply to local stone craftsmen who may be able to make decorative carvings for garden gates, cornerstones, and other features. This has been implemented, by having a contest among our existing employees to find qualified stone cutters, and is already showing great promise. By the time we will be needing to have such decorations on the castle walls and gates, we may have our own artists to do the work.

"The castle construction itself is going well. The foundation work is complete, the lower levels of steel are in place, and the first floor and a half of stone are done. Mr. Conrad has asked us to concentrate our efforts on the more difficult aspects of the readywork such as plumbing lines and final fixtures, installation of the track systems, and putting in the air handling equipment and water pumping systems.

"I am compelled to state for the record that I am reluctant to leave the more minor finishing details for a later time as these are exactly the kinds of items that cause delay in completion. Mr. Conrad, however, has earned the right to make this request, and my support for whatever he has in mind. You'll have the floor soon, lad.

"On a more positive note, the hybrid shuttle vehicles are becoming available, as you no doubt are aware. They are currently being used exclusively in the liquid fuel mode because there is insufficient underground space for the electric track layout. I will set up test track sections as soon as possible, to analyze the system, but it is not currently a priority.

"A couple of side notes. The stone processing facility has been completed. Weather has not been a delaying factor on the stone production, but for community relations I wanted to get the chips and dust under control. Secondly, the crash program to add living and office space has been completed, and in record time. We are working on finishing all phases of the horizontal elevator and should have it running soon. I think we should have a ceremony when it is complete. That's my report. Questions?" Stubby sat back and breathed a sigh of relief.

Pam spoke, "I have one. What are we using the tunnel shuttle vehicles for, if no tunnels are complete?"

Stubby leaned forward, "We needed vehicles anyway, and have let many of the leased vehicles go. We use them to carry people and supplies back and forth, and we're trying to set up a package delivery service locally. Currently, there isn't much call for it, but we're going to need the experience and techniques eventually. Mr. Sanchez is also using a number of the vehicles. They may be slow, in this mode, but they are easy to drive, and you can't get lost."

"Thanks. Brian, what can you tell us about our relations with the film company?"

Brian reflected. "Our individual relations are fine. On a corporate level, there appears to be a bit of tension. I believe they've been ordered to cut back on expenses, and they don't have anything to cut. They may be hoping to get some relief from us on the lease expense, or other exchange, but I believe some over there have their hopes pinned on the penalty clause. If we fail to provide the castle as promised, on the date promised, they may be delayed, but we'll be the ones paying for it."

Pam looked at him. "A minor correction, Brian. The contract with the film company is yours. Well, technically ours, but you're the only one with any money. I remind you, we cannot pay the penalty out of Government Credit Accounts. They didn't make that agreement."

"In that case, I would like to say, for the record -- Gulp!"

"Wait a minute! Brian has to pay that? He's already paying for everything! That ain't right."

"No, she's right, Stubby. That was my commitment, freely chosen. Well, we still have five months. And in any case, I've been poor before."

Mendoza shook his head sadly, muttering. "It ain't right."

"All may not be lost." Sullivan said quietly.

Pam looked at him. "The floor recognizes Mr. Conrad."

Mendoza said softly, "Yeah, the floor knows my face, too."

"Shhh!" Pam said, "go ahead, Sullivan."

Conrad paused, looking around. "Well, there are two things in our favor. One: We can't use the castle ourselves, for our purposes, until everything in it works, but that's not what they need. They're filming, and they only need a working prototype for every shot they have to record. One cell, one floor, et cetera."

"Damn!"

"Yeah. Damn!"

Brian looked at Stubby. "Back at you one more time, Stubby. Damn!"

Stubby got a grin on his face. Together they chorused: "WHY DIDN'T WE THINK OF THAT!"

Sully blinked, then he smiled. "The second thing is ..."

"Yeah, go ahead."

"... that we *are* going to be finished, complete, and ready to go."

"What? How?"

"Give me two more weeks, and I'll show you!"

The normally bustling big house seemed unnaturally quiet for so early in the evening. There was to be no party tonight though, and Brian's new habit of rising rather early had pulled him to the comforts of his bed as the twilight faded into darkness. His bed, that big, spacious, and comfortingly soft haven, which was almost never empty. Perhaps, if he arrived early?

It was not to be. Angelina Foster was there, lying next to Paulo. On his other side, Carmen sat up with her legs drawn to her. In a similar pose, Sally sat beside her.

"What do you think, Ange? Can we do it?"

"I can't be completely certain. I'll have the guys in the legal department double-check for us, quietly. As far as I can tell, there shouldn't be a problem. I've heard that boys as young as twelve have married here, usually to girls about fifteen or sixteen. Those boys were often the sons of wealthier men, who could easily afford to make their spoiled children happy."

"Hear that, Paulo? What do you think?"

Paulo smiled as he lay there. Surrounded by mature, naked, lovely women like a dessert dish served up on their table, what young man would not? "I do not know. They say that your wedding day is the happiest day of your life. I have had many, many very happy days. You three have been there with me. If I fill up with even more happiness, I may burst like an over-ripe tomato!"

Carmen reached out and toyed with his little tomato stem. It lay there, like a sleeping-beauty worm, seemingly unaware of the opportunity surrounding it. How could it be so blind?

"Maybe the swelling will come out here." She smiled.

"Are you worried that the medicine will have a lasting effect, Carmen?" Sally asked, stroking Paulo's cheek. Carmen gently caressed Paulo's smooth sack of little boy marbles, and rubbed the skin over the pelvic bones, dipping into the crease where his legs joined. She rubbed his upper legs and his abdomen. In any normal male, these actions would have produced a visible reaction. Even Brian, watching from the doorway, adjusted his shorts discretely.

"No. I'm sure there will be no long term effect. It really wouldn't bother me even if it took months to wear off. I like doing this, and I know he likes it too. I like cuddling next to him. We can hold each other, and touch each other, for hours on end. It's very kama sutra, you know. I like the tension, and he has other skills, too. What lover do you know who has that kind of patience?"

"Oh, get a room, willya! You're making me hot!" Sally complained. Carmen smiled at her, and placing her hand on Sally's back, kissed her on the lips. They held the kiss, as Sally's hand reached out to stroke Carmen's thigh.

Carmen broke off, smiling. "You cuddle like that with him, too. Don't deny it!"

"I won't deny it. Why should I deny myself anything? That's what worries me. If you marry him, what happens to me?"

"You can be our concubine, I'll need someone to wash the dishes for me, and scrub the floors."

"And wash your back for you? And massage your breasts for you, while Paul Oh! is tickling your appendix?"

"Mmm, Yes!" said Carmen dreamily.

"And you'll do the same for me, too, and let Paulo tickle my appendix?"

"Of course. Remember, I said that I liked to let the tension build up? This sounds like some very fun afternoons."

"Mmm, yes, long, hot, sultry afternoons getting sweaty and stinky, and then a nice, hot bath. What are we waiting for?" Sally leaned forward and kissed her again.

Paulo smiled, "Are you sure you need me?"

They broke off the kiss and leaned over him, smothering him with kisses all over. "Oh, yes! You sweet boy! We are going to make a sandwich with you." Carmen said.

Angelina looked at Brian. "Well? Come on in! We're just getting started." Brian stepped out of his clothes and came to bed.

Later, Brian came out of the bathroom after a refreshing shower to find that Josetta and Theresa were also waiting for him. He crawled into bed, and the girls snuggled close to him, and to each other. Girl, girl, boy, girl, boy, girl, girl. Brian felt for an empty spot and patted the bed. Goood bed! He sighed happily and went to sleep.

TAKE ELEVEN:

That you should return to your joy

Brian glanced around. Bright icons of invading sunlight dappled the bed, marching snail-like across the covers. New wooden blinds withstood the solar assault in the morning, but there were still some chinks in his armor. He observed languidly as a line of spots marched abreast down a slope and slowed as they started up the next... the next pile of casualties.

He propped himself up to survey the carnage. The battlefield was littered with the bodies of his fallen comrades ... *You have got to eat some meat, very soon!* He smiled. Slowly easing himself from their midst, he stopped to look back at the sprawl of naked flesh. *Bacchus would have recognized this scene.*

Quietly stopping in the bathroom, he emerged in a bright yellow play suit, and went down to the kitchen. Well, they looked like a suit, or uniform, especially on the younger ones. He knew that his appearance was not quite as endearing, even though he was wearing one size smaller shorts than before. If he could only get used to not having pockets.

Kids could get away with it easy enough. They never had anything to carry. How was he avoiding carrying identification, keys, coins, and money? Easy, he never had to buy anything, everyone knew who he was, and none of the vehicles he used required keys!

Sully had installed a display device on the hybrid shuttle vehicles. When the driver punched in his access code, the device showed a scanned image of his operator's license. The island constable, *(Was there more than one?,)* had stopped one of the new vehicles once out of curiosity, and had burst into laughter, and sent them on their way.

As for not spending money, an example was the kitchen. It was just like walking into any breakfast shop he'd ever been in, except it never cost him a dime. Which reminded him.

"Mrs. Sanchez, do you get paid for working here?" He asked, taking a seat.

She looked surprised at the question. "Si, Señor Brian, since the second week. You did not know? Señora Pamela arranged it for me."

"I have not been paying proper attention. Who else works in the house?"

"Mrs. Alverez comes in and does the laundry, and vacuums the floors. My daughter Linda makes the beds and puts the clothes away, and Dolcita puts out fresh flowers and fruit. We try not to get in anyone's way."

"I suppose they don't. I've hardly taken notice. But I did not want to take unfair advantage of you. You are a very welcome presence in the morning!"

"Thank you, Señor. It is my pleasure. Many years ago, I dreamed of having a wonderful, large kitchen, and then you came to the Island, and began making dreams come true for everyone!"

"Including my own, Carmelita. Just this morning, I had the most vivid dream of fried eggs, ham, and biscuits with butter. It seemed so real that I had to come down here and see for myself."

She dimpled. "And so you shall see, Mr. Hawthorne, if you will but wait just a moment!"

Theresa and Josetta caught up with him as he was finishing his last biscuit. Josetta looked at the remains of the meal and said, "The same for us, Señora, but only half as much." She smiled and sat down next to Brian.

"No lecture? No punishing glance?"

"Of course not, Brian. You need your strength. Especially for how you'll have to work this off." She placed a *very* friendly hand on his thigh.

Theresa nodded, bringing Brian fresh coffee. "Yes. *We* will see to that. You'll need a lot of strength." She smiled knowingly.

Brian put on some proper work clothes and went to visit Stubby's base of operations. Brian had been more closely observing what was going on, quite literally, in his own back yard. Stubby's worksite had been changing just as rapidly. Brian parked near the big hangar-like building and put on his hard hat.

Inside was the stone processing area. As he watched, yet another layer-cake was making its way inside, on a wide wheeled carriage that had been assembled for the purpose. The layer-cake was the big, round section of stone that was cut, like a salami section, out of the tunnel depths.

Esteban Mendoza had designed a custom boring machine which cut the bore of the tunnel, leaving a cylinder of stone. Then specially designed hydro-jet scimitar blades sliced into the rock from the edges in. The excised portion was then hydraulically backed out, rotated to horizontal, and transported to the silo bores. At that location, the slabs were lifted like a round elevator floor, and levered out to the waiting carriage.

Most tunnel boring either cut away the entire face of stone or used explosives to fracture the rock. This almost surgical technique moved faster, and yielded stone slabs that could be divided into the proper sizes for their needed buildings across the island.

There was also considerably less waste and dust, but the machines were one-of-a-kind, and they were Stubby's babies. He had conjured them into existence, and he baby-sat their operation.

Naturally, he was in the tunnel.

Sullivan Conrad, on the other hand, was more the Godparent of the devices, and the stone-cutting area as well. He was sitting up on the hillside, looking over the harbor view, and their distant target. He had a sketch pad in his hand, and a notebook computer within reach. Brian walked up to look over his shoulder.

A creditable water-color drawing of the harbor, showing the street layout and imaginary sailboats in the distance, was taking shape. "Wow, Sully, there's no end to your talents. I didn't know that you were an artist too."

Sully smiled. "I got into it through designing graphic arts programs." He looked up at Brian. "You can't program it if you can't do it. But I found it's not too different from making perspective drawings of computer equipment, and network layouts. I stay away from portraiture though, so don't ask." His tone was friendly. *He can afford to relax,* Brian thought, *he's got about three halos stacked up already.*

"I came out to talk with Stubby, but they said he's in the hole. No telephones down there."

Sully grinned, and reached for the laptop. He activated it, and clicked through several menus and sub-menus. "Stubby signed on as operator of one of the duck-shuttles. Let's see if he's nearby." *Duck-shuttles?*

A tone signal came from the computer. Sullivan leaned forward, "Message for Mr. Mendoza, Brian Hawthorne is at the silo looking for him."

"Okay. Ten four, whatever. I'll give him the message. Can you hear me?"

"Response received. Thank you." Sullivan listened for a moment, then disconnected. "I've been wanting to try that." He grinned.

"Is that what I think it is?"

"Yep, back-channel intercom. Word will get around now, and they'll be using it all the time shortly. And not one of them will think to ask where it came from." He shrugged, "Your idea, though. I put the patent in your name."

"What? A patent? In <u>my</u> name?"

"Yeah. That makes three for you. Stubby has seven, and I'm coming up on number twelve."

"What the devil are you talking about?"

"Simple. You had the idea for using the high-pressure water jets for cutting the stone, and rotating them ninety degrees to cut the slab loose. Number three is the emergency voice channel on the data line. Stubby got his on the designs for the hybrid shield-boring machines, and the tunnel shuttles. All of mine relate to computer functions, and the electronic control units."

"Okay, I follow that, but why? I didn't even know about it."

"I talked to Pam. She said you were interested in protecting a portion of your income from a possible bankruptcy catastrophe. And I heard you myself when you said that we were all going to become wealthy. Well, that includes you!"

Brian stared at him. He could swear he saw yet another halo forming over his head.

Stubby pulled up. Brian turned his stare to the odd vehicle he was driving. *So this is a duck-shuttle.* It was a standard hybrid tunnel-shuttle vehicle, with the exterior hardware removed. It had obviously been designed to proceed through the tunnel, even with a piece of layer-cake passing overhead. *Hence the term 'duck.'* Brian thought.

Stubby looked at Sullivan's painting. "Not bad, kid. Want to do the frescoes in the tunnel?"

Sullivan laughed, "Not on your life! Why do you think I'm out here?"

Stubby turned to Brian. "What's up, Boss? The voice of God told one of our guys you wanted to see me?"

Brian chuckled. "Nothing that important. Sully was just telling me that we're all going to be rich, though, if we manage to live through all this."

"That's good, it should keep me in beer money." Stubby smiled, "Don't tell me *you're* afraid to go downstairs, too?"

"I'm not sure. In this?" Stubby laughed, "Come on!"

Brian got in the vehicle. "Seat belts?"

"Yeah. I use 'em myself. I'm not completely crazy."

"I just wanted to come out and see what's going on for myself. Not that I mind spending lots of time at the big house, of course."

Stubby looked at him slyly. "Beats me what you can find to do in that place, Boss, all there is to do is plan the next party."

Brian looked over at him. "Well, gosh, Stubby. Those parties do take a lot of planning, you know."

Mendoza laughed out loud. Brian joined him.

They were nearing the tunnel face. It was not at all the scene of confusion and noise that one might have expected. The shield-boring machines were certainly not silent, but the area on which they acted was relatively small, and once into the cut, the sound tended to be muffled.

Sprays of water dampened the dust, cooled the cutting bits, and kept the machines from clogging. This water was directed into settling ponds, which extended in a series back toward the entrance. As the water was drained off of these, and they dried out, the muck was collected and hauled out for reprocessing.

Brian knew that a portion of this went back into what was called grout, for sealing suspected fissures inside the tunnels, and that more of it was used as binding agents in road construction at various sites. His bicycle riding had been made smoother by a nice path laid down some weeks ago.

"You're certainly making good progress. I can see that you're cutting faster. Looks like the cut is pretty smooth too." Brian raised his voice to be heard.

"Yeah, the feedback circuits keep the machines better balanced, as well as cooler. I hope Sully does get rich. He deserves it for that reason alone." Stubby responded.

"How about your path? How do you know you'll be able to meet the oncoming tunnel in proper alignment?"

"We sighted it out very carefully with lasers, including bouncing a signal from the other site, and we're following the track specified. Pretty simple geometry, actually. As we get closer, we'll be able to home in on radio transponders on the drill rigs."

"Through solid rock?"

"Yeah! Right through solid rock! But only after we're close enough. Actually, once we get close, we'll be able to *hear* them, if our machine is shut down."

Brian nodded.

"Even if we miss our alignment by several inches, we could adjust our tracks to compensate, but that's not going to happen. We can adjust these machines to steer themselves, you know, so we can smooth out any discrepancy. I'll bet you a beer you won't be able to spot the junction!" Stubby grinned.

"You're on!" Brian challenged. He knew that Stubby would work even harder now, just to make it perfect. But he had also noticed that there was a polarity to the minor ridging on the tunnel walls. That polarity would reverse at the junction. *Never let them know you're not a God. Besides, a beer is a beer.*

Adjusting the machines was how they had brought the entrance ramp into operation. From the silo entrance, they had bored toward the other site. As soon as they had made sufficient horizontal distance, the boring machines were backed up, flipped around and started in the opposite direction, 'steering' their way upward to break out in the hangar warehouse. The ramp was what allowed them to bring the spoils out, more vehicles in, and would be the normal route when the tunnels carried regular traffic.

"Have you been seeing people from the Government, too?" Brian asked as he looked back toward the entrance.

"They show up regularly, looking tickled. I think they're all writing memoirs, so they'll be in the history books. I think they might even be trying to figure out some more projects for us!" Brian could picture Stubby showing the visitors around, proud of his handiwork, and rightly so.

"Great job, Stubby! Anything I can do for you?"

He scratched his chin, "Well, now that I've shown you how to do it, how about *you* digging the tunnel to the castle?" Stubby eyed him warily.

Brian looked somewhat dismayed, and Stubby laughed again. "Don't worry, Boss. I wouldn't do that to you. You just keep the parties coming! Let me show you what I have in mind."

They turned the vehicle around and headed back for the distant ramp. Stubby drove up to the warehouse structure. Inside was a skeleton of steel, outside it was all smooth stone. They went inside, staying clear of the path of the layercakes.

"We haven't been having as many breakdowns as I projected for. Like I said, the machines are running smoother. So I pulled all the extra components together and built this smaller scale digger. I'm going to sight it in and start it on its way to the castle next week. We'll be able to make good progress with this design because it's a smaller bore, and we're going to sacrifice the stone that we cut rather than try to salvage it for building. I've designed a 'cracker' loader to haul away the 'cigar ash' stubs that this cut will produce."

Stubby looked proud of his 'baby.' He continued. "Once we break through into the sub-level of the castle, we'll turn it around and bring it back along a parallel path. The single path will allow transport, but the dual path will make it efficient."

Brian eyed the machine. "Stubby, has Sully seen this?"

"Of course. He helped set up the electronics on it. Why?"

Brian smiled. "Ask him if there's any way he could help you make it run on full automatic. I bet he can do it."

Stubby scratched his chin again. "Hmm. Probably worth a try. If he can, it'll save me a hundred man-hours a week!"

Brian smiled. Asking Sullivan Conrad for something was like making a polite request from your own personal genie. *Hope the weight of those halos doesn't give you a headache, Sully.*

Back at the big house, Brian began his 'atonement' with a swim. He had actually worked his way up to some pretty respectable lap distance, considering his age, and his shoulders were putting on muscle as his strength grew. Of course, he worked in very slow sets. It was a time consuming process, but he enjoyed the process, and the results. He wasn't losing weight, but he was getting smaller where he wanted to, and bigger where it was appreciated.

He was not the only one who was pleased with the results. Normally, Josetta and Theresa worked out with him. They encouraged his efforts, and rewarded his good behavior.

Brian wasn't fooling himself. He had seen younger men than himself fall prey to the charms of a flirtatious woman. He knew that either of them could find a much more suitable mate in a heartbeat. Unable to believe in his own attractiveness, he had asked Josetta to explain it.

"Brian, I told you when we met that *you* were my favorite character. I was serious. When you look at me, I know that you see what I work hard to achieve. I've been making my living off that appeal for nearly ten years. But I also know that you see more than that. I feel as though your eyes can look into my very soul. Have I ever lied to you?"

Brian didn't answer as immediately as the conditioned answer occurred to him. He wanted to give the impression that he was giving it serious thought. "No. You have never lied to me. Nor, for that matter, has Theresa."

"And I don't intend to. If I have to tell you something that may make you sad, I will do it, even if it breaks my own heart as well. I am an actress, and by now a good one, but I don't believe I could convince you of something that wasn't true. Not because of me -- because of you."

"I guess I understand that. But I still don't understand why you would want to *be* with me." Brian smiled, "Frankly, my dear, the logic escapes me."

She leaned into his chest. "That's because it isn't logic. And it isn't infatuation, either. It's because you're *good*. You're kind, and generous, and understanding. You <u>understand</u> people, *and you still care for them!* Most of us want to condemn them for the rats we think they really are, but you treat them with the same courtesy that you demand for yourself, *and it doesn't bother you!* I don't know how to think that way, or love that much. That's part of what I hope to learn." She looked into his eyes with beguiling sincerity. "You treat the rats with a degree of kindness that we would expect you to reserve for us... minks?" His peripheral vision detected a smile flitting somewhere near those enormous innocent eyes.

"Minxes." Brian replied with a smile.

She smiled, "I do love your sense of humor, Brian. You really are good to be with. Besides, look around you. I couldn't live like this for less than a thousand dollars a day! And you let me share it without even asking for a penny, or for what any other man would ask in return. There's something else too. I like being with you because you love me.

"Maybe it's only your love of a kitten, or a sex-kitten, but when you are with me you are happy. You want to be with me and to make me happy too. If that isn't love, then it's as close as I've ever gotten to it."

Brian had thought about it for a long time. Being with her made him want to be a better man. But being with Josetta meant being with Theresa. And Theresa was not just a me-too person. She had thoughts and feelings of her own. The fact that they tended to run parallel to Josetta's was the reason they were together in the first place. And being with them did make him happy. He truly wanted both of them to be happy too. *Is there anything else?* Love. Even in a long life, Brian wasn't sure he had ever found love. But he recognized happiness.

At the end of the lap, he looked up. He also recognized the face of Paulo.

"Paulo, my son. I am happy to see you. I was hoping that it would be soon."

"Hello, Uncle-Papa. You are looking very well, and happy, today."

"Ah, well, Paulo, you know today is a very special day. But it is not a day for me to worry about my being happy. Today is the day that I wish for you to be happy, for today is your birthday! Happy birthday, Paulo."

"Thank you for remembering, Uncle-Papa. Would you like for me to swim with you?"

"No. Not just now. Let me come out so we can talk. Then we may swim later, okay?" Brian climbed out of the pool and stood up. Paulo reached out to help him, and they walked together down to the area of the basking lamps. Paulo sat down beside him as Brian reclined under the warming glow of the lamps.

"I must apologize to you, Paulo. I have been thinking and thinking, but I cannot think of anything to give you to celebrate your birthday. I must ask for your help. What can I give you, my friend?"

"I can see why you would have difficulty, Papa. You have already given me everything. Even I cannot think of anything to ask for. Last year, more than anything, I wanted a bicycle. Now, I can ride a different one every day. Last year, I had only the boys in the village for friends. But some of them were friendly, and some of them were not. This year, I have many, many friends. And most of them are girls! I did not even think to dream of that!" Paulo smiled.

"I wonder, Paulo. Sometimes I wonder. I see you with your friends, and your girlfriends. And yet, sometimes I think that there is a sadness, a quietness, that the boy who came to my hotel room so long ago had never known. Is there something in your heart that you can share with me?"

Paulo looked at him for a moment. Then he moved closer and laid his head down on the old man's chest. Brian put his arm around him and stroked the warm skin of his back.

"Oh, Papa. Sometimes I do wish I could go back to that time. I used to run through the village, and dance in happiness. When I saw people, my heart would feel as light as a hummingbird. When people smiled to see me, I wanted to sing my joy." He paused, and sniffed.

"I do not feel sad, Papa. There is nothing to make me feel sad. Yet, I do not feel happy either. Not the way I used to feel." He turned his head to rest it on its side. He seemed to be listening to the sound of Brian's heart. *Oh Lord, what have I done to this boy?*

Brian embraced the young man, and moved his hand up and down the boy's back.

"There is a time, Paulo, when every boy looks upon his treasures. The bits of string, and colored paper, the marbles and the yo-yos, the sea-shells that once seemed to hold such magic, and he says, 'I have outgrown these things. I do not need them any longer.' Many throw these things away, and others simply put them into a drawer to be forgotten.

"But for all these boys, it is a process that takes a bit of time. They will put away the marbles one day, and some months later they will put away the yo-yo. What happened to you was like the storm that comes to these islands from time to time. You were lifted out of your boyhood and put in a place where you thought you were supposed to be a man. Even I told you that you must do what a man would do. I am sorry, Paulo, that I betrayed you in this way.

"I should never have asked you not to be a boy. It is a time of life that is as magical as a rainbow, and seems as fleeting as a soap bubble. Some of us let it go too soon, and are forever after like baby birds, fallen from their nest; unable to fly, and yet not able to return to the nest either."

"Are you saying then, that I should go back home? I do not know if Mama will let me."

"No. I did not mean that, though if you truly want that to happen I will make it happen! No, what I meant was not that you should return to your home, but that you should return to your joy."

There was silence for a while, then Brian could feel warm tears on his chest. "Papa, I do not know the way." His sniffles returned, but he cried softly, quietly, ... heartbreakingly.

"Maybe I can help. Come with me." Brian led the boy up to his bedroom. There he told him to wash his face and get dressed. While Paulo did that, Brian placed a call. Paulo came out wearing a lime green play suit. Brian put on a matching one.

They went down to the courtyard and around to the parking lot. Selecting a shuttle, Brian drove them to the film company offices.

"We're here to see Mr. Jake Wagner."

TAKE TWELVE:

The best dressed girl at the party

Brian stood in front of Jake Wagner. Jake looked mildly curious, which was his current mask to make himself inscrutable.

Paulo stood quietly beside Brian. None of the three had expected to meet like this, and none could think that this was anything other than a confrontation.

"Paulo, take off your clothes." Brian said. Without hesitation Paulo removed his shirt and shorts. He stood as before, without nervousness, and without shame.

"The boy needs some time off, Jake."

Jake attempted a look of proper concern, but Brian thought he could detect an expression of distrustful optimism. "Really? His shooting schedule isn't particularly heavy at the moment, Brian. I know that you would not be trying to stir up trouble, or perhaps delay our progress. What do *you* think the problem is?" *Which was Jake-speak for, "Whatever your gambit is, I'm not buying. I've got both of you over a barrel, and I'm not giving an inch."*

"Jake, this isn't about me, and it isn't about you. It's about a boy. He's been under this paint for a god-awful long time, and he's been under that witch's brew of medicines for even longer. He needs a break. I'm only trying to help him get it. Tell me what I can do to help you,

Jake, so this boy can get a part of his life back for just a short time. What can I do to make it possible? I really want to know if there's *anything* I can do."

Jake began toying with his favorite prop, a pencil.

"Are you saying that you may be able to help us cut back on some expenses, perhaps even shave some time off the overall shooting schedule?"

"I'm saying that I'm prepared to do anything that will help. Help you, help him. Whatever it takes."

"Well, now. That does bring up some interesting possibilities..."

"Mr. Wagner, there's something I think you should see." The voice came from the intercom.

"Not now, Marjorie, I'm in *negotiations*." That should have been enough.

"Excuse me, Mr. Wagner, There's something I think you should see *out the window!*" She persisted. Jake got up and moved slowly to the window and looked down into the company lot. Brian stepped closer also. Over one hundred people were gathered in the lot, looking up at Jake's window. No one moved. No sound could be heard. Silence. And stillness.

Jake stared. He turned and looked at Brian. Brian shrugged his shoulders, "Not me, Jake. I didn't even tell anyone I was coming. I guess a lot of people saw me as I *was* coming, but I didn't say anything."

Jake looked back out the window. His pose of inscrutability was completely crumbled away. Brian could read his thoughts as if they were printed in a word balloon above his head, *"God, look at that! Loyalty! But not to me. What I could do if I could command that kind of respect!"*

"Jake, give the boy some time off. We'll get back on schedule faster, and better than ever, I promise. We both know that we've probably broken laws in dealing with him anyway. Just give him some time to get straightened out, and I'll help you make everything else all right, too."

Jake leaned against the window ledge. Looking at <u>his</u> people, gathered in support of someone else. *"How do they do it?"* His expression said for him.

Without looking around, or moving at all, Jake answered softly.

"Done."

The studio sent over some special soap, and a nurse came and administered a neutralizing potion. Nothing that would stimulate the boy, just something to de-activate the chemicals which had been coursing through his bloodstream for months. Even the special soap took three days to completely remove the paint.

Paulo stared at his reflection. Only the finest stubble showed on the top of his head. No other hair was visible anywhere. He turned this way and that, but his naked body no longer bore evidence of leaves or serpents. His body was his own again.

And on the fourth day, he rose.

Paulo woke up with a pressing need to go to the bathroom. That was not unusual. Going to the bathroom was almost always the first thing he did. But today, he threw the covers down and looked at himself. Sally woke up too. Then Carmen.

Brian also had awakened. Soon, everyone was observing as Paulo was reintroduced to an old friend. Carmen reached down gently and touched him as if she were afraid the image might pop like a soap bubble. It was reassuringly durable. She moved her gentle fingers around on it some more as Paulo squirmed. "Oh, my, I _so_ want you to continue doing that, *but I have to pee!* And I'm afraid I won't be able to!"

Brian chuckled, "Go ahead in and try, Paulo. Stand in the shower if you have to."

Carmen desisted reluctantly, "Yes, go ahead in there, Paulo. But *come back to me* as soon as you can, okay?" Paulo nodded as he crawled out of the bed. Then he stopped, and turned around, striking the proud stance that he once had used in the hotel courtyard. He shamelessly posed in happy joy as they all looked amusedly at him and his new old friend.

"Oh, Boy!" he said with delight, smiling like a contest winner. Then he marched proudly to the bathroom. Prudently, he closed the door.

"Oh, boy!" said Carmen.

"Isn't it my turn today?" asked Sally plaintively.

Carmen glared at her. "The foot of the line, wench!" she said archly, but with a smile.

Brian yawned, and got up. "Come along, ladies. Time for our swim. We don't want to interfere with the young folks having fun, do we?"

"Young folks? Come on, Theresa, if we team up, we should be able to drown him without any trouble."

Paulo was in the pool when Brian and the others returned from their bike ride. Carlos and his sisters joined in swimming as usual. Brian was still eating his breakfast when Paulo and Dolcita came into the kitchen, still dripping slightly.

"Dolcita has told me that she has a very nice swing on a big tree at her house. She wants to know if I can go to her house to swing on it." Paulo seemed unaccountably shy and reticent about his request.

"If you are asking permission from me, you have it." Brian responded. "But the person you must ask is Mrs. Sanchez."

Carmelita looked at the two children. Paulo stood just an inch shorter than her own son, Carlos. He and Dolcita were standing together, and holding hands. She thought they looked adorably sweet. Smiling, she told Dolcita, "You must be sure to return in time to put all the flowers and fresh fruit out for this house, Dolcita. Remember, that is your duty for being allowed to swim here." She kneeled down and hugged her daughter, and impulsively hugged Paulo as well.

As they departed, smiling, it occurred to her that she had not specified whether they should wear clothes or not. 'It does not matter.' She thought, 'they are but children.' She returned to her duties, humming softly.

Paulo had noticed a pale shadow of his painted tattoos on his skin. He wanted to be naked in the sunlight, and Dolcita readily agreed. They enjoyed the ride, and the company. They traded stories about things that each had seen going on in Brian's great bed, and laughed at how silly grown-ups could be. Paulo felt that his heart had been released from a cage, and was now gliding like a songbird along the lane.

At the Sanchez house, Dolcita showed Paulo the swing. "It is much more fun to feel the air moving over all your body, I have discovered. It makes you feel like a bird, with the wind blowing through your feathers." She said, as Paulo pushed her higher and higher.

Then they traded places, and Paulo experienced the same feeling. It was exhilarating!

After several sessions each, they sat at the base of the tree.

Dolcita was describing their house, basically a small cottage. She and Linda shared a room, and Carlos had a space in a loft.

"Why do you not make your house bigger, as we did by the entry to the pool house?" Paulo asked.

"Papa has said he wished he could do something, but he is very busy, and there is always something else to do."

Paulo looked at the house. It seemed rather small, and very low to the ground. 'I would lift it up,' he thought, 'and put a nice, cool, cellar under it.' He thought about the piles of steel that were waiting their turn up at the castle site. 'If I had the money,' Paulo thought, 'I would hire the men and help these nice people.'

Abruptly, Paulo sat up. "If you are ready, Dolcita, we can perhaps go back now. You have your assignment, and there is something that I have thought of, as well."

"Of course, if you are ready."

"I would like to come again, if I may." Paulo asked politely.

"You would be most welcome to return, Paulo. My family thinks that you are a movie star."

"What do you think?"

"I think that you are not bad, at pushing me on the swing."

"Thank you." He kissed her on the cheek. They mounted up and rode back to the big house, sharing occasional smiles along the way.

Paulo ran up beside Pam's desk. She looked at him and smiled. She had seen him naked before, but she had never seen him without his tattoos. He looked delightfully normal. Abruptly, she pulled him close to her and hugged him, rubbing his back and patting his posterior affectionately. His skin was still warm from the sunshine. "What can I do for you, Paulo?"

"I was wondering, Miss Pam, do I have any money?"

She blinked, "I'm sure that you do, Paulo. What would you like to do with it?"

"Well, I was thinking about the Sanchez family. They are very nice, and they always bring us food, but their house is very small. We are building so many things for everyone, I wondered if it would be possible to help them make their house bigger."

Pam studied the boy. She knew of his recent emotional difficulties, and the results. Was this a form of therapy? Was he feeling guilty? He looked sincere. Maybe he's picking up one of Brian's bad habits, generosity.

"That sounds like a rather ambitious project, Paulo. I would suggest we check with some of the people who know what would need to be done. I will tell them of your idea, and we will see if Mr. Sanchez will let us help him."

"Dolcita said that he was very busy, and I think he would not want to ask for help."

She nodded, "We will try to be diplomatic. And we will not steal your idea from you."

Paulo nodded, "I was thinking, if I were trying to do something, I would lift up the house with some of our steel beams, and build a nice cellar under it."

"That sounds like a good plan, Paulo. I'll pass that suggestion along, too." Paulo smiled and departed.

Pam thought about it. Who was handling the boy's finances anyway?

As it turned out, the situation was not as bleak as she had perhaps imagined. The studio was keeping his salary contributions in an escrow account, and had made small disbursements at his request for his family.

There was a tidy sum left, not bad for a lad his age, but not adequate at the moment for renovating a house. His earnings were all tied into the future success of the movie.

That wasn't all negative. While it minimized the expense for the production company, it maximized his earnings if the movie did well. He would soon be in better financial shape. He would need a good advisor, however. Now, who would that be? Brian, Esteban, and Sullivan all had good earning potential, particularly lately. But none of them knew how to get their money to make more money for them. Well, that was easily resolved. There were plenty of financial institutions here among these extended islands. She would find some good discrete investments for the lot of them. With their combined purchasing power, perhaps they could leverage some action with the regional construction companies.

Now, the Sanchez matter. At the next meeting, she would bring the matter to the floor. Hmm, should she start making some suggestions to Carmelita, to lay a groundwork?

Today was the regular end-of-week party, and tomorrow two events were scheduled. First, the 'shuttle' connection to the castle, the horizontal elevator, was to be dedicated. Then, whatever event Sully had cooked up would begin.

But for now, it was party time.

The pool, as usual, was filled with the younger set, and the dance arena had been moved to the patio area just outside.

The great room and the upper courtyard were for the folks who liked to form into groups to talk about the things they talked about all week.

"Hey, boys! Glad you could make it! Has anybody seen Stubby?" Brian greeted a small group of engineers. They looked at each other. One who Brian knew as George spoke up. "Ah, we may not see him tonight, sir. He was in a good mood, and we suspect he's having a private party."

Brian looked puzzled, "He only comes here when he's in a bad mood? That would explain a lot."

"Yeah! Stubby has a theory that you shouldn't inflict yourself on your friends when things are going wrong, but if your boss sees that you're depressed, then maybe he'll not be quite as demanding."

"Frodo! Ixnay!" George hissed. Brian got interested. "Frodo?"

"Yeah," George replied, "his name's Fred O'Hara. ... Fred O. ... Frodo. In our line of work, a nickname is like a business card."

"So you're saying that Stubby comes *here* when he's depressed?" Brian pursued.

"That's just his general rule, Mr. Brian. Stubby told me he comes to you when he needs inspiration."

Brian smiled, *unh-hunh!* "Where does he usually go?"

Again, they looked at each other. "It's kinda hard to explain, but it's like his trademark. You know how they say an executive has his Girl Friday? Well, Stubby has that. On Friday, Stubby visits his girlfriend."

Frodo spoke again, "Unless he's not fit company. Then he comes here." He blinked slowly. "Or if it's another day of the week..."

Brian's eyes lit up. "You mean, he's got a girl for *every day of the week?*"

George was staring murderously at Fred. "Well, that's like, the rumor. Stubby has a house near the silo, where he stays. The <u>rumor</u> is, depending on the day of the week, a different girl takes care of him."

Frodo nodded, "They have a house too. Then they take turns being his housekeeper for the day."

George tried to take some of the sting out of the accusation. "It usually takes about a year to set up. Stubby only sees one girl on one day of the week. He remembers which. But he always calls them Honey, or Darling, or Sweetheart, never by name. By the time he's up to seven, the girls usually know each other, and they often become friends. These girls used to be tourist guides. Two sets of them are sisters."

"Stubby doesn't take advantage of them. He makes that clear at the beginning. He wants someone to come home to, a warm dinner, clean house, quiet conversation. His theory is, if it's a part time job, the woman doesn't get too serious. And it's not for bed. If the woman wants to go to bed with him, it's okay, but he doesn't insist on it. He pays them as housekeepers, and when they combine their resources, they can get a second house, and set up a sort of a girls club."

"Stubby's done this about six times, and the funny thing is, they don't fall apart when he has to leave town. Tell you the truth, Mr. Brian, Stubby's a legend. Something else too, he respects you."

Brian looked thoughtful, then he snagged a beer and handed it to George, clapping him on the shoulder afterwards. "Thanks, George. I guess I'm luckier than I thought. Interesting rumor." This time, George blinked slowly, then winced.

A nickname is like a business card.

Josetta appeared on his arm. Again she had what looked like a designer outfit. Brian kissed her.

"Aren't you breaking a lot of hearts by hanging on to me? These guys should be lined up, waiting to talk to you."

"They do line up. That's why I'm with you." She batted her eyelashes at him, "I need a protector." He smiled. *Flattery, a very potent beverage.*

"Where do you come up with these outfits, anyway?" Brian asked. "You're always the best-dressed girl at the party."

"Thanks for noticing my effort. Didn't you know? I have my own label. One of the reasons I came here early was to push my own designs for the women of the future. Not only would I make money here, but when the movie opens, I'll be selling similar outfits all over the place. Nothing beats free advertising!"

Brian looked thoughtful. "Is that why you latched onto me at the first opportunity? Be gentle, now. I'm feeling very wounded."

She looked into his eyes, then smiled slowly. "Brian, I did have Joe Hardwicke bring me straight to you, I'll admit. But everything after that was real ... I don't know ... *electricity*, or something. I'd like to think that you saw a spark of creativity in me, like the flame that burns in you. I'm not here to crash your party." Her eyes seemed especially liquid. "I was picked for the role long before I arrived. Having my name in the screen credits is enough to give me the publicity I want for my clothing sales." At last she cast her eyes downward. "I don't really know or care if the columns are saying anything about what I've done since I got here."

Brian tilted her chin up. "Wounded animals lash out, Josetta. I didn't mean to hurt you. You could never crash a party. You *make* a party. I just can't understand why you seem to be drawn to me. It's as if I were somehow engaged in a foot race with these young, um, *bucks*, and I were winning. It wouldn't make sense."

She smiled. "You're trying to think about it logically, Brian. That's not what it is. Being with you is like being in the eye of the hurricane; there's excitement and danger out there, but here with you I feel *safe*. And I get to keep a close watch on the excitement."

He stared into her eyes. "The eye of the hurricane seems right, Josetta. I have the feeling that if I make just the wrong step, I'll be swept away." He kissed her hand. "Away from you."

She put her arm around him and squeezed. "Don't worry. I'm holding on." She smiled. "I'm holding on *tight!*"

Brian noticed heads dipping in conversation as he strolled with Josetta. *Why, they're talking about me!* Did they know about her philosophy, or his? Did they care? *Did he?*

The unscheduled hiatus had thrown a lot of schedules awry. Many took the opportunity to jet out and set up interviews for future activities. Some few took advantage to get caught up on their work. Continuity had been working overtime, Brian had heard.

Mary and Martha were off the island, and Angelina Foster was away as well. Many of the locals who had been busy before came out tonight. The population, and popularity of his parties tended to grow over time. Everyone was having a good time, but there was a palpable undercurrent of nervousness in the air.

TAKE THIRTEEN:

That's when we really go into action

It was difficult to make the inauguration of the horizontal elevator or shuttle into an elaborate affair. The cab could only hold so many, and there was a starting point and an ending point. Test runs had been made repeatedly, of course, but the first official run held Brian in a white play suit, Paulo wearing green, and Josetta, Theresa, Sally, and Carmen wearing bright pink. The return trip held Esteban Mendoza, Sullivan Conrad, and Marcia Roberts. They then acted as escort to Pamela Harriston, and returned to the castle with her.

The entrance point from the big house was to the right of the pool area exit, and connected with the expanded living area. The exit point at the castle was in the level under the main hall, and to the right of the tower stairs. To the left of the stairs was the castle elevator. Stubby led the way to the elevator, and they rode up to the main level.

Brian and the others were waiting for them. Sully stepped forward, and led the way toward the main entrance to the grand hall. Uncharacteristically, both Sully and Marcia were wearing blue play suits. Only Stubby and Pam wore regular clothes for the occasion. When the procession reached the main entrance, Brian was astounded by what he saw.

Arrayed before them appeared to be the entire contingent of young children, and young adults, that the island had to offer. There were ordered ranks of younger children dressed in orange playsuits. They appeared to be from eight to twelve years in age. Then beside them were rows and columns of teenagers, wearing green. Finally, the oldest of the young people were dressed in blue. An army of children.

Brian noticed for the first time that the uniforms had a sort of insignia of rank. Team leaders in the formation had circles of white on their sleeves. Sully had two circles of white on his blue sleeves. And Brian realized for the first time the significance of the two circles of gold he had discovered on the outfit he was given to wear this morning.

Paulo turned, and gave a hug to Sally, Theresa, Josetta, and Carmen. Then he came and stood before Brian, and hugged him too. Brian saw the white circle on each sleeve as Paulo stepped into the front rank beside Carlos and Linda. Looking to the left, Brian recognized Dolcita among the wearers of orange. She smiled brightly at him.

Sully stepped forward and made a gesture pointing left. The circle leaders stepped out of the ranks and moved to a table where large numbers of electronic devices with carry straps were stacked. Each line of children then moved to the appropriate table and received his or her device. Putting them around their necks and shoulder, they returned to their previous place in the formation, and the next line would move.

They could not have had opportunities to practice this, but their movements had a grace and dignity all the same. Quickly, the entire group was fitted with the devices. Marcia brought a similar device to Sully, and put one on herself.

Sully consulted his unit and pushed a button. Each child checked the unit given. Some began separating from the group and moving to ordered ranks of supplies. Using the hand held device, a child would find a supply item, and begin taking it to its specified location.

The blue teams seemed to be particularly burdened, carrying large bundles of thick cables. As if the parade was over and everyone was on the way home, the children moved in various directions.

But they were not leaving. In an impromptu choreography, each child carried a burden to a predetermined location. They began making trips back and forth like ants moving in a colony. During all this activity, no commands were shouted, no voices were raised. Each person went about an assigned task, and then to another one. Gradually, the mountainous quantities of supplies diminished as they were transported to their proper destinations. The senior units were the ones who had the task of laying out and installing the dozens of cables and making the terminal connections.

Modular fasteners made the task, literally, child's play. The children studied their lists, gently jostling each other as they maneuvered through the halls and doorways. The cables had been made in Asian factories to exacting specifications. They connected at one end to preset terminal boxes, and at the other to specific devices. The modular connectors were color-coded and designed to fit only one way, to only one device.

Toward mid-morning, parents began arriving with food for the children. This too was organized. Each child had a specific time to eat, and rest, built into the lists of instructions. This kept the crowds at the tables to manageable levels. Large containers of beverage liquids were prepared as well. (It had been a prudent measure that bathrooms were functioning very early in the process.)

After the slowdown for lunch, the process resumed full-speed again. Devices were connected to cables which had been positioned. Equipment was installed in prepared locations. The structure was coming together under hundreds of willing, helpful hands.

Toward dusk the ends of the lists were being reached. Excess packing materials were brought together in safe amounts to a cheerful bonfire, where children danced with giant shadows. More food items were made available, and children and adults relaxed in satisfaction.

A band assembled, and began playing music. Songs were sung, and before the evening was quite completed, a flag was raised to the highest point with a bright light shining on it. Everyone who could see it cheered.

Some children flagged in a different way. But before their parents could cart them away, or find a place to rest for the night, another spotlight played on the main entrance of the castle, and Brian was handed a microphone.

"My friends, thank you. I make my living by trying to find the right words to say things. But your kindness and generosity has left me speechless. I do not know the words to use. I have heard of friendship, but this goes beyond that. I know about kindness, but this exceeds that. Some might use the words, community effort, but even that pales by comparison."

"You have opened your hearts, and your homes, to strangers, and made them feel like brothers. How can I thank you? Someone said, 'How marvelous! They are building your castle.' I had to say no. You are building <u>your</u> castle. All of you are a part of this, and part owners of our effort, and our dream. When this castle is complete, not very long from now, it will be your castle. When someone comes from across the waves, and asks, 'What is that?' you must say, 'That is our castle.'"

"The story has it that this is a place for weddings, and parties, and so it shall be. That it is a place for learning, and teaching, and so it shall be. That it is a place where dreams can go to grow and prosper, and so it shall be. For you and your children, and their children, too. And so it shall be, thanks to you."

Brian bowed deeply, and humbly. The applause washed over him like the sound of a crashing surf. He wept with unalloyed joy, and rose to smile to his friends.

Brian staggered through the castle, drunk with happiness. He gave a hug to everyone he met, and laughed to see the transformation of the castle. In the morning the walls had been bare, like an empty seashell. Now devices and equipment populated the living quarters as if it had been occupied for years. This army of children would be able to march through any space that Stubby's engineers and sturdy workers could create, and they would fill its corners with light, and laughter, and love.

Stubby had been as amazed as anyone. He had been worried that the myriad of minor tasks would never be completed, and now he would have to redouble his efforts to stay ahead of this rampaging horde of happiness. He looked around. The main hall, and two residence levels were virtually ready for occupancy. In the interior, it would be possible to begin filming now! He could never allow it just yet, however. There was too much noise to be made for a while. He went looking for Sullivan Conrad.

At long last Brian found his way back to his bed. It was occupied, of course. But he was tired. It had been a long day, and he didn't care if he was lying down next to Jake Wagner.

In the morning, when he looked around, he would have preferred Jake Wagner.

How could <u>this</u> have happened?

He was lying next to Dolcita. She was naked.

When he stirred, to try to escape, she woke up.

"Oh, good morning, Señor Brian." She yawned and stretched.

"Um, good morning, Dolcita. I am surprised to see you here. That is, in my bed."

"I came with Paulo. He brought my family down to the big house from the castle in your new shuttle. It was fun! I am glad to be the neighbor of such a wealthy man, with such a wonderful house!

But when we got here, I was very tired, and did not want to walk home with Mama and Papa. Paulo invited me to stay. He said that I would just be coming back in the morning, anyway."

"What did your Mama say?"

"She said that I should be very good, and not make any trouble, and that I should get your coffee for you in the morning. Would you like it now?"

"Not just yet. There's something else I do not understand. Why do you have no clothes?"

"Is that not the rule here, Señor? No one else is wearing clothes, except you are wearing shorts, and I have seen you when you were not wearing shorts."

Brian sighed, *How do you explain debauchery to innocence? Answer: You don't.* "Let me explain, Dolcita." He looked around. Josetta and Theresa were looking back at him. Their expressions did not indicate that anything they might say would be helpful.

"That is not the rule, at least not in this bed. But that is because there is an older rule, that says, 'People do not lie down together without clothes, unless they are willing to have sex together.' I cannot unwrite that rule, because it is written in our hearts."

"Everyone needs to sleep, Dolcita, but you must be careful where you sleep, and how you sleep. If you are wearing clothes, you can say you only took a nap."

She thought about it. "I think I understand. Since I was only sleeping, and not having sex, I should have kept my clothes on."

Brian nodded, in relief.

"But what if I wanted to have sex?" She asked.

Brian started sweating again. This time, he did not dare to look at anyone else.

"You would have to ask your mother to help you find someone. You are too young to choose for yourself." Brian said with authority. "That is another rule."

"Oh." She said, in acceptance. "Okay."

"You can bring me my coffee, now."

"Yes, Señor." She climbed from the bed, then turned. "Should I put my clothes on for that?"

Brian smiled. "I like my coffee ... without." She smiled at him, and skipped away.

"Her mother is going to come up here with an axe, you know." Carmen said.

"Yeah, I know. Can I get a kiss from everyone before I go?"

Josetta and Theresa complied immediately. Carmen and Sally waited their turns. Paulo took advantage of the distraction to slip into the bathroom. When he came out, he climbed up and kissed Brian too.

"Thank you. Now, while we're waiting, you three go get your bath. If I'm alive later, I'll get mine. I can't do it without coffee, anyway." Sally and Carmen pulled Paulo with them back into the bathroom.

"I never thought that I would need a bigger bed for my bedroom, much less a bigger bathtub." Brian shook his head in wonderment.

"There's a bigger bathtub downstairs. We could all use it." Theresa suggested.

"When the castle is completed, there should be a bigger bedroom and bathroom in the tower." Josetta reminded them.

Brian shook his head. "No, I think I'll stay here. I can be comfortable here. If I find time to write, I want to do it here."

Dolcita showed up with his coffee. *No rampaging mother.* She was still naked. "I told my mother that I took my clothes off when I slept with you, and that you told me I should have kept them on." Dolcita told him with a smile. "She said that was exactly correct. Or it would be correct for anyone but you." She gave him a kiss and departed, skipping again.

Brian went down to the kitchen later, to face the wrath. To his surprise, there was none.

"Carmelita, you are sure? I feel the need to apologize further."

She chuckled, "For what, Señor? For sleeping? I did that too. I slept the whole night with the kitchen light burning. Do I feel guilty? No. You did nothing wrong, Mr. Brian. She is a child, and children do these things."

Brian sat and shook his head. *A year ago, Paulo wanted a bicycle. A year ago, I thought I wanted them to make a movie of my book.* He sighed.

"I suppose you had better let me have my fruit breakfast, Carmelita. I can't afford to get in any more trouble today." She laughed again and turned to the food preparation.

After his exercises, Brian went to look for Sully. He found him in his room, working at the computer.

"Mornin' Sully. Where's Marcia."

Sullivan reddened slightly, his open secret was still an embarrassment to him, even considering the lax standards of *this* house. "She's gone up to double-check the devices installed yesterday. Hard to believe everything went so smoothly."

"Smoothly indeed, Sullivan. You astonished us all. Where in the world did you find so many people?"

He smiled. "Brian, the people here are remarkable. They've been watching their lives change around them, and some of them probably felt hopeless to do anything, for or against it. When word got around that I was organizing kids to invade the castle in a positive way, everyone wanted to have a role in it. We had almost one hundred percent turnout."

"But how did you train them? We would have heard about the meetings."

"Train them? All they had to do was read. Those electronic devices we handed out yesterday held separate lists of things to do for each of them. They came for the fun of it, and they got to keep their uniforms and their digital assistants."

"Digital assistants?" Brian asked.

"Yeah. Personal digital assistants, the electronic devices. The kids are still playing with them. Look at this." He punched up a computer display. Super imposed on a map of the island were bright dots of different color. "The colors tell what each one is doing, text messaging, voice transmission, location pinging. They're having a ball!"

Brian nodded slowly. "I take it you had something to do with providing them?"

Sully laughed, "Of course. It broke down, with the discounts, to just under a hundred dollars apiece. By the way, I'm getting a percentage of all of these they sell. I designed them."

Brian studied the display. "So, they combine walkie-talkies, note-passing, and satellite navigation. The kids can tell where they are at all times?"

"Not only that, they can find out where their friends are, or at least where they left the PDA. In fact, there's already been a 'rescue.' One kid took a tumble, and hurt her knee. She called for help, and within two minutes, six other kids were helping her get back home."

Brian shook his head. "This is most remarkable!"

Sully grinned. "I expect we'll see some spontaneous economic activity out of this. Shopping services, lost child alerts, that sort of thing. The kids will probably organize into groups too, since we started that."

"You let them keep the devices?"

"Oh, sure. They earned them." He grinned again. "Besides, when we call them back in a couple of weeks, we'll have more free labor."

Brian looked at him. "Sully, sometimes I think you're diabolical. This is all part of your plan to take over the world, isn't it?"

Sully grew slightly serious. "Nobody ever took over the world without a plan, Boss."

"Okay, what's next on your plan, then? I mean, after all the work gets done at the castle."

Sullivan smiled again. "That's when we really go into action. I'll have my server base, and full link-up. Do you want the details yet, or do you prefer surprises?"

"If you're talking about the kind of surprise you sprang yesterday, that was a doozy! I'll hold off on any new information just yet. I might go into overload!"

TAKE FOURTEEN:

I can have you thrown in the pool

"Let the record state the Mr. Sullivan Conrad received a standing ovation upon entering the room." Pam announced. "Now, let's have a report from all avenues of enterprise. Mr. Mendoza, will you lead off?"

"Our tunnel excavations continue at their accelerated rate. I am projecting first tunnel completion in approximately one year's time from present date. No progress has been made on the electric track analysis because they will not be needed for another year, and because all available resources are currently allocated to completing the castle construction.

"On minor construction projects: The shuttle assembly program has hit its stride. We now have more shuttles than we currently need, though many fewer than we will eventually need. A few of the extra units are being ferried over to the other islands as construction utility vehicles and basic transportation units. We have been receiving offers to purchase them outright from some local delivery units. I wish to bring to the table the suggestion that a stripped model be produced shortly for this purpose, and to generate cash.

"What would you strip off, Mr. Mendoza?" Sully asked.

"The local deliverers like the locator ability, and the ease of loading and so forth. What they don't need is the electric tunnel capability. That would put them in competition with us, and create access conflicts."

"So they would be isolated to their home islands, even after the tunnels open?" Brian confirmed.

"Exactly. On the plus side, it reduces our manpower overhead for that stage, and creates employment now, in two ways."

"I'm in favor now." Brian said.

"Mr. Conrad, Mr. Mendoza, do you agree?" Pam asked.

"I'm in." Stubby affirmed. "I'm on board with this too." Sully added.

"Fine. Consider the motion to have carried. Mr. Mendoza, draw whatever resources are needed to begin the production, including the capable assistance of Mr. Conrad. Next question, though, what will you charge for them?"

"I can give you an exact cost of production, once we've identified what doesn't go into them." Sully offered.

"Let's sell them for exactly double what they cost to produce, with discounts available for Church and youth groups." Brian suggested. Nods approved the suggestion.

"Anything else, Mr. Mendoza?" Pam asked.

"Only that the small-bore tunnel is now on its way to the castle. We've gone approximately one eighth the distance. Rough estimate, two months to first bore completion, five months total. By the way, the shuttles will arrive in the sub-basement of the castle, no access to the surface. Something I forgot to do."

"Just as well, Stubby. Leave it alone. It would be anachronistic." Brian said.

"For the record," Mendoza asked. "I would like to know what that means?"

"Brian means that he doesn't want to have golf carts running around a twelfth century castle." Pam explained.

"Oh, sure. Telephones, computers, elevators, but nothing nackronistic." Stubby nodded.

Brian chuckled, "Ever see some really old Roy Rogers westerns? Guys on horses, with six-shooters, and one character in a *Jeep*?" Blank stares.

"Never mind. Leave them in the sub-basement, Stubby."

"Brian, what can you tell us about the film?"

"First, I'll remind you that they don't need the castle for the first film. Much of the ending of the first film, however, has characters continuing into the second film. That's why they want it available, to be able to capture all the footage of those characters while they have them gathered together. It's a money issue. They expect to make money, but they want to lose as little as possible."

"On a positive note, our relations with the film production company are very good. All of us have found ways to work together. The downside is, it's a very stressful time for some. And in very short order, some of our friends may be ending their commitments, and winging out of here forever. I strongly urge all of you to check the production schedules closely, before you lose track of a friend."

"Mr. Conrad?" Pam asked quietly.

"The first marathon installation session went very well. Another such party is scheduled for two weeks from now. Mr. Mendoza says he will be ready. That should bring us to nearly fifty percent readiness for the residence area, but there are other areas that have been left virtually untouched. Some of the accommodations in the tower residences will have to be faked for filming, and completed later. Perhaps much later. Intercoms, video feeds, and so forth will all be custom work, and time consuming. The beginnings of a computer network are taking shape in the lower levels of the castle, but real power will only come with the final configuration. I am looking into providing some raw data-crunching power to the film company special effects department, but we have to be careful. We may have the machines, but we don't have the manpower."

"Sully, how long would it take to train up some 'manpower' from our available labor resources?" Brian asked.

"How long to teach the kids, you mean?" Sully asked. He grew silent for a seeming long time.

"For the ones with talent, I can have them doing useful work in six months. Perhaps more likely a year. To get some really top-notch programming work would take at least three years, and that's with talent contests and scholarships."

Brian nodded. "Would you like to do that? Set up those programs?"

Sully's eyes lit up. *Nerd paradise?* "Brian, there's not a school in the world like that! Yes! I'd love to do that!" He thought a moment, "You realize I'll need help?"

"Start making a list, Sully. Not a priority, but something to work on for the transition period." Brian said.

"What else is there? Pam?" Brian asked.

"Well, if anyone is interested, we can talk about finances. The finance department and myself have managed to keep us out of jail so far, through very creative manipulations. If we can continue without any intensive audits for another year, we should be able to show true profits, in rising amounts. In five years, we should be rolling in it. At the present time, if you can think of something profitable, especially you, Sully, and you too, Mr. Mendoza, please keep me informed. We need all the incoming capital we can get. Brian, you are the major backer, but you are also the major instigator for extra expenses. Please try to control yourself. Speaking of backers, we have someone else who wishes to become a financial source and provide investment capital."

"Really? Who?"

"Your friend, Paulo."

"What?"

"Paulo wants to finance a construction project."

"Okay, What?"

"He wants to raise up Mr. Sanchez' house and build more space under it."

Brian looked around. "Did he say why?"

"Paulo said that Mr. Sanchez had a big family in a small house, and that he gives us a lot of food. He thinks we should help him make their house bigger."

Brian looked at Mendoza. "What would it take?"

"I'd have to look at it. What kind of house is it?"

"From what I recall, it's made of stone."

"Then the big challenge is not the weight, but the strength of the foundation. Worst case, jacks and rebuilding the foundation, excavation work, stone for the materials -- free of course, hmm, about twenty men and twenty days. Then another month of finish work. Rough guess, forty to sixty thousand."

"How much of it could be done by Sanchez' crew?"

"Hmm. Good supervisors, training time, tool and equipment rental, we could cut the price in half. They'd have some long days, though."

Pam interrupted, "You can't take Mr. Sanchez' crew away for that long. He has other projects."

Stubby observed, "He'll have to hire more help."

"Well, Brian is his backer. He'd have to go to the well again for the money."

Brian pondered for a moment. "Pam, we're going to need a business meeting between Paulo, Mr. Sanchez, and I guess you and me. I think Paulo ought to go into business with Mr. Sanchez."

"I'll get it set up." Pam jotted a note.

"Any other business?" Brian asked. "If not, I need a beer." The three men went out the door together. Pam went back to her office.

"What are you thinking about, Sully?"

He smiled at her. "We were talking about the Sanchez family, Marcia. You know, Mrs. Sanchez and her kids come to this house every day, back and forth."

"Yeah. I see them all the time."

"Every day, back and forth, back and forth."

"Sully, you aren't thinking... No way, Sully! I don't believe it!"

Sully smiled at her, a distant, contemplative smile.

"You want to do what?" Mendoza glared his disapproval.

"It's not too different from your own observation about the electric drives. We've got a couple of projects that *can't* be completed for over a year, and some that need to be addressed *now*."

"Sully, you're talking about dismantling a work in progress, stopping us in our tracks. That can't be good for our overall progress."

"It won't delay us that much. Let me explain. The stone layercakes that we've been removing from the north end of the island to our south have been piling up over there. They have no ability to cut them up for building stone. What I'm suggesting is to stop one of the tunnel borers, temporarily, make another small-gauge borer for the castle return tunnel, and make an even smaller gauge tunneler to connect the Sanchez house. Now, here's where we get something back; we use the scimitar segments from the ring boring machine to set up a stone processing facility on the other island. Sanchez' men can expand their operation over there, and we can use the Sanchez link-up to test our electric drive system."

"It's crazy, Sully. Take down one operation to put together another? What would we gain?"

"Mr. Mendoza, ...Stubby. They're making jokes over there about rolling the stones into the sea just to get rid of them, and we keep bringing out more! What I'm suggesting is a way of turning non-income producing assets into income producers, for a time. Remember what Pam said about the next few months!"

Mendoza drummed his fingers. "Why bother connecting the Sanchez house? Whose bright idea was that?" He asked in puzzlement.

"Um, mine, actually. Look, I know it's an extravagance, but so is the connection to the castle. Right now, in the whole interlinked island shuttle system, the big house is a dead end. This restores some of its importance as a focal point. Sanchez is the prime supplier of food to the big house, and probably will be to the castle as well. And this further ties the operation of an essentially outsider group to the real people of the island."

"None of that seems to make any economic sense." Mendoza gazed at him steadily, "Fortunately, I'm an engineer, not an economist. I'll take care of the machine work, but you are going to have to convince Pam and Brian."

"Deal. It'll pay off. You'll see." Sullivan smiled.

Mendoza looked thoughtful. "Speaking of machine work, how are we going to make a unit smaller than our miniaturized version? There's no room for the stepping action. How will we make the hydraulic sections drive it?"

Sullivan grinned, "I thought you might ask. I've rotated the hydraulics into pusher-legs, no pressure balancing, but auto-tracking like the castle unit. Let me show you the schematics."

"Sully, this is a nice gesture. I like these people too. But it seems like an expense that can't be justified to me." Brian shook his head sadly.

"Our justification, at least on paper, will be setting up a test track for the electric drive system. We'll be able to do that within months this way, and we'd have to wait at least a year, otherwise. With so much literally riding on that capability, I think we can silence any criticism. Don't forget, this project will provide building stone on the other island as well, and that will produce income."

Brian looked puzzled and unconvinced. "Pam, what do you think?"

"I find myself in an unusual position, advising you to do something that looks crazy. But I'm inclined to agree that there is a potential source of income. Don't forget, we are going to be selling delivery shuttles over there. This will give them something else to deliver. And I don't see it costing us anything other than an acceptable delay. Maybe Sully has veered into something non-productive, but I'm inclined to let it go anyway."

"All right, if we're in agreement about it, let's add it to the lists." Brian scratched his head. "We'll see in the long run what becomes of it."

"Mr. Ricardo Sanchez, I am sure that you know, or know of, our friend Mr. Paulo Ignatio." Pam began the meeting, as usual, with her version of the proprieties. "You may be surprised to learn that the meeting has been requested by Paulo."

Brian leaned forward. "Mr. Sanchez, when we met, I noticed that you had a very desirable, a marketable skill, the growing of the finest fruits and vegetables. That is why I asked you to work with me to grow that business, and other work as well. For me, it is a selfish arrangement. I do nothing, and you put food on my table."

Sanchez responded. "You are not being fair to yourself, Señor. You have made it possible for me to grow much more food than before, and even to find employment for my neighbors. That has put more food on *my* table."

Brian smiled, "It is good that you recognize this, Ricardo. In the markets of the world, this is called 'venture capitalism' and it helps many people to start new businesses."

"I understand, Señor. You are my *padron*."

Brian shook his head, "No, it is even more basic than that. We are partners. Ignoring any money, I am too old to work my fields, you need more fields to work in. It is as simple as that."

"As you wish, Señor."

"And my friend Paulo also wants to be a partner with you. Let us say perhaps that he is too young to work in the fields, but he also has property to be made available to you." Sanchez nodded in understanding.

"Paulo wants to invest in your business enterprises as well. He wants to be your partner, too. But Paulo does not understand very much about business. He thinks that a successful businessman always lives in a big house."

Sanchez nodded, "It does always seem that way, Señor."

Brian continued. "That is why Paulo wants to pay us to help you make your house bigger. He has money in the bank, and he wants to pay us to lift up your house, and make it bigger. He thinks that will make you a more successful businessman, and that he will be your more successful partner."

"Paulo would be wasting his money. Having a bigger belly does not make a man a better worker."

Brian smiled. "That is true. But I do not believe that Paulo would be wasting his money. You would have to hire more workmen, and use more stone. We also need to send workmen to the other island, to work with stone over there, and to teach others how to work with it. At the end of it, you would have a bigger house, and more employees, and more projects, and more people paying you for building their dreams. And Paulo would be your partner in a bigger dream for both of you."

Sanchez sat back, looking thoughtful. "Paulo, do you really want to be so foolish with your money?"

Paulo smiled. "Señor, I eat your food. I am growing taller with the meals that your wife cooks for me. I play with your children. They are my friends. To know that my friends have a bigger house to be happy in would make your peaches taste even sweeter. The money that the studio pays me does nothing. But if I become your partner, I will never be hungry."

Sanchez studied the boy, and considered the proposal. "Perhaps you are a smarter businessman than I thought. It would be a wonderful thing to know as a young man that you would never go hungry, but you will also know that you will always have a friend." He rose and shook hands with Paulo, engulfing the delicate hand of the youth with his large, callused one.

"There is one more thing, Mr. Sanchez," Brian spoke hesitantly into the tone of agreement. "My engineers want to use this construction as an opportunity to develop an electric shuttle car, that would carry your family, and I suppose, my groceries, back and forth between our houses. That will not cost you anything, of course."

Sanchez looked puzzled, then brightened. "I may have been wrong. You may *get* hungry, but you will always eat well!" He shook hands with Brian as well.

As soon as the agreements were made, Mendoza contacted his crew on the next island.

"What do you mean, 'we won,' Stubby?" the foreman eyed him suspiciously.

"I mean we're declaring your team the winner, and you're all getting promoted."

"Dammit, Stubby! I just started this job. I was counting on it to hold up for another six or eight years. I got moving expenses, you know."

"It ain't what you think, Jonesy. Here, take a break while I explain it. Where's the hooch?"

"Hey, you know we don't do any of that..."

"Save it. Now who's blowin' smoke? I told you I'd explain it. Do you expect me to do it through a mouthful of stone dust?"

Jones relented, and led him to a battered old delivery vehicle. It had been lowered into the digs to serve as a job-site office, and had clearly gone its last mile under its own power. From the glovebox Jones retrieved a compact bottle of brandy. He poured half a coffee cupful for each of them.

Stubby took a healthy swig. It was expectedly potent, but had a pleasant taste.

"Since when did you become a fruit-juice drinker, Jonesy?" Stubby inquired casually.

Jones grinned. "Pretty good stuff, isn't it? Nice bouquet, pleasing after-taste, and only a buck a pint!"

Mendoza nodded. "Look, Jonesy, this has nothing to do with the quality of your work. Your team is doing a great job, and I wouldn't have chosen this group of any of them to do this to. Here's the situation. You and I both know that this tunnel can't be opened for another year. No matter how good a job you do, or I do, no one's going to make a nickel on subway fares here for at least another year." He took another gulp of the brandy.

"Nice apple cider. Anyway, we've got these cheesy-lookin' slabs of rock sitting up there, getting in our way and looking stupid. And the boss says we gotta cut 'em up for building stone here, like we're doing there. We make a little money on materials, and we get them out of your way. Problem is, you got the only cutters *on* your rig. So here's the plan. We shut down this dig for a couple of months, reform the boring rig into two smaller units and a rock-slicer, and we get two complete small tunnels, and some sellable building stone out of the deal." He drank the rest of his cup.

"None of your guys is going to lose even an hour's pay. And nobody's leaving, either. We'll need to split 'em up for a little while, into different crews. Then, when that other stuff is done, we'll put everything back the way it was, and we'll *still* be the first tunnel group to make breakthrough!"

Jones had been following the explanation, and nursing his drink. He nodded. "That makes sense, Stubby. I was kinda wondering what we were gonna do for six months anyway. You know, after we made our breakthrough, and we had to wait for the others to finish theirs. Might be nice to find out what sunlight looks like for a while, anyway."

"That's the spirit! Wait'll you see what cute little diggers this rig turns into! You'll want to take one home with you to chase the moles out of your garden!"

"All right. I'll tell the guys. Some of them probably want to spread their wings a little anyway. It's really boring in here sometimes, eh, Stubby?" He chuckled.

Mendoza stared at him. "You have been in here too long. You need fresh material. I'll send over the specs on how to convert the machines, and what we're going to build topside. You're going to need to send a good concrete man with the little unit, and divide up your crews accordingly. I'm also going to send Sullivan Conrad over to help you install the electronics. He's the one who helped us find the overdrive gear a while back. You be good to him. He's our fair-haired boy."

"No problem, Stubby. Do you think he'll like our, uh, apple cider?"

Mendoza looked thoughtful, "I'm not sure. Give me a progress report on your training program."

Jones grinned, and they shook hands.

Brian didn't quite trust his memory of what had happened at the castle location, so he went to look again at the astonishing changes that had been made so quickly. He was wandering in the great hall, when one of the stage workers approached him. "Mister Hawthorne? Mister Wagner is here and wanted to know if you could see him?" Brian nodded, and the man led the way.

"Brian, this is amazing! Incredible progress. I can hardly believe that you're going to be finished more than a month early! I must admit, I was betting against you for a while." Jake extended his hand.

Brian shook the proffered hand. "We've had a lot of community support, Jake. And, as I said, I've got some talented people working for me."

"It's a welcome sight, Brian. I have to say I'm somewhat relieved. There has been a lot of pressure on us to get things wrapped up quickly, so we can *make* some money for a change. Do you think we could perhaps try to squeeze in some production work here, too?"

"You know we're still under construction on this site, Jake. I can't let anything interfere with that."

"Oh, no interference, Brian. Scout's honor. The film crew has some action scenes involving the filming of production sequences here that they would like to try. They claim they can work around any noise your guys have to make. We're trying to shoot scenes from both movies at the same time, to make up for the lost time recently."

Scout's honor, hunh? Brian studied him. *What kind of scout were you, a talent scout? And you haven't lost any time, either, you just went into break a little early.* "I did promise to help you any way possible, Jake. Go ahead and set up anything you think will work. However," Brian looked him in the eye. "I can't guarantee that there might not be a little jockeying for position between the groups."

Jake smiled knowingly. "I've come to admire the way you manage your people, Brian. I don't think there will be any problem if you tell them to cooperate."

Brian shook his head. "That's not what I meant. We will cooperate. I just meant that it would be a bad idea to park a camera or something where it might get bumped into. They're not delicate workers." Brian looked around. "I'm not an administrator, Jake. I've been lucky about finding really good people. One thing I do know, though, they like to think that we're all on the same team."

Jake was silent for a time. "Do you think I'm not?"

"You need to answer that one for yourself, Jake. I never sought conflict with you, and yet I always felt that you were tugging the other way. The strange thing is, you've always given me everything I asked for. Why did it seem to be painful for you?"

"There's only one top dog anywhere, Brian."

"Very true. But men don't *act* like dogs unless they are treated that way." Jake looked startled.

"I'm having a party tomorrow, Jake. Why don't you stop by? I still feel like I owe you a beer." Brian offered his hand.

Jake looked at it, then reached out. "Maybe I will, Brian. I just may." He moved away.

Mendoza did not look happy. *Uh-oh! Girl Friday's got the night off!* "Hi, Stubby. Glad you could make it."

Stubby glowered at him. "Did you, or did you not, tell those film people that they could start shooting at the castle site?"

"They said they could stay out of your way, Stubby. Any problem?"

"They showed up today! They want to know when the tower will be finished. The tower! For cryin' out loud."

"I know what I would tell them."

"I ... You ... What? What would you tell them?"

"I'd tell them when the tower will be finished. You do know, don't you?"

"That wasn't what they meant, Brian. You know that!"

"I know this, Stubby. They are professionals, same as your guys. What do you think would happen if your guys walked in front of their camera and started acting goofy in front of it?"

"Simple. In ten minutes, they'd pack up and move out in disgust." Mendoza seemed disgusted himself.

"So. Is there a problem?" Brian inquired mildly.

Stubby still looked frustrated as he prepared to answer. Then the light dawned.

"You mean, if they get in our way, then we ..."

"I wouldn't want you to interfere with their work, Stubby. But we can't afford to let them interfere with ours, either, can we?" Brian clinked bottles with him in a celebratory toast and moved on.

Mendoza was chuckling to himself.

Josetta showed up in yet another fetching creation. She was wearing a bikini top and bottom in a colorful floral pattern, with a skin-tight cover-up in a slightly opaque material.

But it wasn't material. That is to say, it wasn't fabric. The bikini and the top-piece were *painted* on.

It took Brian a moment to catch on. The effect was very realistic, but when he put his arm around her, he felt bare flesh. He whispered in her ear, "I could have used you when I was twenty."

She whispered back. "You can use me now." Her eyes sparkled with mischief.

"I love your outfit."

"I got tired of coming to your parties and not swimming. Now I can." She backed up a pace. "The cover-up part will wash off. The suit is waterproof."

"Doesn't that break Carlos' rule?"

"I'll let him inspect it." She came into his arms again. "I'm sure he'll approve." Brian kissed her. If he closed his eyes he *knew* that she was naked. He *felt* like he was twenty.

Jake Wagner appeared. He was smiling. "I've been depriving myself, I see."

Brian smiled too. *I'm glad he came*, Brian realized. To Josetta, he said, "If you remember how, we could use two beers." She kissed him and spun away with a smile.

"Glad you made it." Brian said.

"I've been thinking about what you said." Jake looked around. "About being on the same team. Your people seem to know that you are more for them than they are. My people seem to think that I am only for myself."

"You're a good administrator, Jake."

"Bull. I've been stepping on people all the way up the ladder. The lower they were, the harder I stepped. They've gotten wise to me though, and they've learned how to avoid getting stepped on. I'm starting to sink again."

"It doesn't have to be that way, Jake."

"I don't know any other style."

Brian thought a moment. *There's a drowning man, anyone got a rope? What, you want to lynch him? Let 'im drown.* "You don't need a style, Jake. You need to be yourself. You are in the acting business, surrounded by actors. How good an actor are *you*?"

"Not very good, I'm afraid."

"Then why pretend to be something that you're not? I really don't think that you're as hard nosed as you act. You've been generous to me. And to Paulo."

Jake was silent.

"Look, you want to get things done. So do your people, but things get in their way. Your job is to deal with the things *that get in their way*, not to deal with <u>them</u>. Somebody comes to you, they have a personal problem; that's not *your* problem, it's *their* problem -- but *you can make it go away*. You make it go away, they go do their job -- *better than before*."

"You want to know how you can be more a part of your own organization? Here's how. Be less involved."

Jake looked at him in puzzlement.

"By that I mean, take yourself out of the picture. It's just them, and their problems. You make the problems go away, like an avenging angel, or guardian angel. Then things are running smoothly again. 'There goes Jake Wagner. What does he do? I don't know, but damn, things sure run smooth when he's around.' I can't be sure, Jake, but it works everywhere I've seen it tried."

There was a pause in the conversation. Josetta appeared with two beers. Small flecks of ice were sliding down the outside of the bottles. *Damn, she's good!*

"I've got some angels hanging around me, Jake. It sure comes in handy." He kissed Josetta.

Jake lifted his beer toward Brian.

"I'm glad I came to your party, Brian."

"Don't leave right away, Jake. The night is young. I can have you thrown in the pool if you'd like."

Jake laughed. "I can probably arrange that for myself. I'm sure I can find volunteers."

Brian raised his beer in a final salute and turned away with Josetta. "So, how will you be able to sell these?"

Josetta laughed, "Theresa already has! She put together enough paint, and dissolving soap, and a special stencil, for three applications. It's about four dollars worth of material, and we're selling it for twenty-four dollars."

"To whom do you sell it?" Brian asked in curiosity.

"We don't know! Most of it is internet sales."

"I hope no one gets in trouble!"

"Girls can get in trouble wearing bikinis too, you know? I don't think there'll be a problem. Most of it is just for gag, I would guess. But we're keeping a database, in case we come up with something else."

"Which I am sure you will!"

"We can always use new ideas."

"What do you mean?"

"If you give me an idea, I can extend profit-sharing credit to you. I'm interested in doing it, just to see what the sales would be like to say, 'as suggested by Brian Hawthorne, design consultant.'"

"Then I guess that means I can do the same for you. I may need to consult with you further about some of your ideas."

She pulled herself close to him, "Of course, Brian, I'm always available to consort with you!"

Brian raised his eyebrows. "I think you must be overheating, miss. Perhaps it's time for you to swim." He raised his beer bottle to his forehead. "You can swim, can't you?" Josetta kissed him and went to the pool. After a moment, she got Carlos' attention. Brian watched the boy's confused reactions. Finally, he bowed to her, and they began to dance. They danced their way into the pool. As advertised, the top garment disappeared, and only the bikini remained.

Brian realized his beer was empty. *I must have spilled it,* he thought, *I'll get another. (That's more than two! Remember, you're being watched.) Actually, I'm watching her,* he responded, *that's why I need a beer. (Yeah,*

I see what you mean. I'll join you.) Brian enjoyed debating with himself in this manner. He almost always won.

Jake Wagner stood at his office window, looking down into the empty parking lot. He raised his bottle of water in toast. "To my loyal supporters and devoted fans."

"Did you say something, Mr. Wagner?" Jake looked around.

"Marjorie, have we made arrangements for the film crews out at the castle to have a regular coffee break?"

"No, Mr. Wagner. We're under budget restriction. They have to provide their own break items. Some of them carry a thermos, I think."

"Contact the foreman of the group. Tell him from now on, we're going to provide a budget for break items, and we want him to control it. That way, he can get everything set up for his shots, and then he can send up coffee to the construction gangs, and have twenty or thirty minutes of silence to get some good footage if he works it right."

She stared at him. "That's very generous, Mr. Wagner." He could tell she was surprised.

"No, no. Just trying to get some productivity, that's all. Make sure he understands, Marjorie. I don't want any more lame excuses about why they can't get the job done."

He looked back out the window. Had he seen someone moving down there?

TAKE FIFTEEN:

Are you going to punish me today?

Carmelita Sanchez looked around, was there anything else to load? Glancing into Carlos' room, she saw that he was already out and about, and that his bed was unmade again. 'He used to be spoiled in his loft; no one ever checked.' She thought. Going down the stairs to her new basement level, she held firm to the sturdy handrail. 'I do not want to fall here. Ricardo has been making everything out of stone these days. I suppose he will try to give me some stone potatoes next.' She smiled. Looking out into the small sitting area next to the shuttle port, she saw that it was empty. No company today. The little waiting area, and the outside stairs, had been added as a convenience to Ricardo's employees, in case they would need to travel on the system.

Linda was already up, and sitting in front of her computer. It had appeared one day, just like the bicycles. 'It is almost like making an offering. I put the fruit on the rich man's table, and magical things appear in my house.' Carmelita realized that this was a disrespectful thought, and said a quick prayer.

"Linda, do not be playing games today. You will have work to do, my Prettiness."

"No games, Mama. Did you know they are getting ready to have classes in the castle soon? I think that I would like to go!"

"And what will you study? Do you wish to be an actress, also?"

Linda tried to look serious. "Mr. Conrad said that most of the wonderful things we are seeing happen here are because of these computers, Mama. He says that children who learn how to control them will be like magicians. Sometimes I think *he* is a magician!"

"Mr. Conrad is a man who works very hard, just like your father. To people who are lazy, anyone who works hard is like a magician."

"Mama, you know I am not lazy. Do you need help with anything?"

"No, I have it. Bring your sister along shortly. Carlos is already off somewhere on his bike." She kissed the top of Linda's head and went to the more public area near the shuttle.

She pushed the large button by the access hatch. Sturdy doors slid smoothly sideways and the little shuttle car, as expected, was waiting for her. The entry door rotated upward, curving around the car. Ducking her head she positioned her package and took a seat. It was the strangest little car. It didn't have a front or a back, but the seats could rotate either way. There was no steering wheel, or other driver control, but there was a communication panel. There wasn't even a push-button to tell it where to go!

Carmelita grasped the door handle and tugged it gently. The door rotated downward again and closed securely. Then she felt herself being pushed sideways like a baby being carried. The push lasted for a moment, then soon there was a push from the opposite direction, and in very short order the door was opening again. She had arrived at the big house!

'So many days I walked along the dusty lane, up and over the hill. Now I put myself in a pipe, and *flush* myself through the hill!' She chuckled to herself as she entered the pool area and made her way up to the kitchen.

The new conveyance allowed her to get an earlier start than usual these days. She almost always had time to plan for meals before anyone showed up in her kitchen. In addition to breakfast, she made preparations for other meals throughout the day. These people never seemed to actually sit down to dinner like normal folks, but they took advantage of the ready-to-serve dinners she prepared. They were apparently used to convenience cooking. And no one knew who, or how many, would show up to eat! She acted faithfully on Mr. Brian's request that no one go away hungry, but they went through *so much* food! It was fortunate, indeed, that Mr. Brian was wealthy.

Dolcita appeared in the kitchen, naked and still dripping from the pool, but only slightly. She had pulled her hair back into a ponytail, and dried it as best she could.

"I think it is time to take Mr. Brian his coffee, Mama."

Carmelita looked at her daughter. Either she was growing again, or the regular swimming was making her thinner, for she seemed to have lost a bit of her pre-pubescent pudginess.

"Why do you do that, Dolcita? Would you serve coffee to anyone else like that?"

Dolcita looked down at herself, then looked up again and smiled. "No, Mama. But Mr. Brian *told* me that he liked his coffee 'without,' and I know this is what he meant. It is just a game, Mama."

"Yes, I know it is a game. Mr. Brian is like a little boy sometimes. A spoiled little boy. And we will spoil him further today. Go on and take his coffee to him, Sweetness."

"Thank you, Mama."

Dolcita carried the tray carefully. She had not spilled it yet. She set the tray down on the serving table and studied the big bed. Brian's bed sometimes seemed like the ladies' room at the shopping center; there was always a line! She crawled up on top of the covers and laid down *almost* on top of him. Then she kissed his cheek, as usual.

Brian opened his eyes slowly, and started up his smile as well. "Good Morning, Dolcita. Did you stir my coffee with your finger, the way I like it?"

"No sweetness but my own, Mr. Brian. Just the way you like it." She smiled at him.

Brian stretched and yawned. He brought his hands down on top of her and gave her a friendly hug. "Dolcita, you must promise me that if we ever have no coffee, you must still come and greet me, okay?"

"I will do it Señor, but Mama would never forgive herself if she ran out of coffee."

"I wasn't worried about that, Sweetheart, but I would miss *you*."

"Brian, you sweet talker. You're going to talk yourself into a jail cell." Josetta teased. She rolled closer and reached out, not to Brian, but to Dolcita. Laying a friendly hand on the girl's protruding rump, she gave it a gentle squeeze.

"Dolcita, you are getting prettier every day. Are you trying to steal my man?"

Dolcita wriggled a bit, then smiled. "No one can steal Mr. Brian, Miss Josetta. He already gives his heart to everyone. Even you can only share him." She looked around at the others in the bed.

Josetta laughed. "Brian, your secret's out; even the children know you're just a pushover. Run for your life!"

Brian smiled, and took a deep breath. He squeezed Dolcita again. "I've found my life. I'm not going anywhere."

Dolcita smiled and kissed his cheek again. "Drink your coffee while it is hot, Mr. Brian. Mama does not like to see it wasted. She said come to breakfast when you are ready." She slid backwards out of their grasp and stood at the foot of the bed.

"Thank you, Dolcita. We will talk again, mañana." She smiled, and departed with a happy bounce in her step.

Josetta watched her go. "Brian, did you ever think, in your lonely moments, about..." Brian looked at her sharply.

"Josetta, you're being naughty again! There is an art to patience. You can learn to savor anticipation, like smelling the bouquet of a fine wine."

She looked at him dubiously, but with a smile. "You didn't entirely say no, Brian."

He sighed, "Jo, you need to learn. All men are wired to respond the same way, up to a point. The real definition of a gentleman is that he can control his behavior in a civilized manner. Men who can control their behavior and their appetites only under threat of force or punishment are *dangerous* men. You need to be able to spot the difference."

Josetta moved closer and embraced him. "That's why I hang around you, teacher. You may be a pushover, but you have a will of iron when it comes to being fair. The more I study you, the more I'll know the perfect man when I see him."

Brian put his arms around her. "How very flattering." He said dryly. "The perfect man for you would have to be about forty years younger than me."

"Don't be so sure. You're rich, and old. That's not an unattractive combination to an ambitious girl like me." Brian put his hands around her nether cheeks and squeezed them gently. "It would be a shame to have to make these delightful melons look red and angry, so early in the morning."

Josetta closed her eyes, still smiling. "Go ahead! I know you wouldn't really hurt me. And I just might enjoy it more than you think!" Brian brought his hands up to stroke her back, and the gentle curve of her flank. "I give up. You're incorrigible!"

Josetta snuggled even closer. "You're right, Brian. I am encourageable." She started kissing him again, and her hands were not the only ones that touched him.

Brian drank his coffee cold. He needed it, if he were not to fall back into bed, and who knew where *that* would lead? He also needed to fortify himself for the day ahead, and to that end, breakfast called. He pulled on shorts and matching shirt and went down to the kitchen.

"Good Morning, Mr. Brian, it is good to see that there is someone among us who is benefiting from exercise! Everyone else is getting so lazy! My children are too lazy to wear clothes, and even I am too lazy to walk anymore." She chuckled self-deprecatingly.

Brian smiled. "Mrs. Sanchez, I arranged to make it easier for you to come to my house for my appetites, not because I feared you would grow tired of it. As for your children, I have come to be like a connoisseur, surrounding myself with items of beauty."

She looked puzzled. "Con-nos ... Excuse me, Señor?"

"Oh, sorry. Wrong language. It would be ... *conozca*, I think. One who knows, or likes to pretend he does, about works of art, and wines, and such."

"You think my children are works of art?"

"No question about it. You and Ricardo are great artists. You should have had a dozen children. Youth has always been an element of beauty, Carmelita. The older I get, the more seeing young people gladdens my heart. When I look into the face of a child, it is like looking at the heart of a flower. And a smile on the face of a child sends rays of happiness outward like the petals of a flower."

Mrs. Sanchez shook her head, "I think I know what the problem is now, Señor. You must attend to your breakfast. You are seeing strange visions because you are very hungry." Brian laughed and began to eat. *How do you go about describing a beautiful sunset to a blind man? How can I explain happiness to people who are sleeping through it?* He shrugged. After all, he had slept through many years of what should have been happiness himself. *Happiness is a garden of the mind*, he thought, *only you can nurture joy, and keep the weeds at bay.*

Brian went up to the castle. Josetta and Theresa rode with him. There was movement throughout the castle. Supplies were being positioned for yet another episode of installation by 'Sullivan's army.' That was scheduled for tomorrow, and it would be the last major effort at completing the structure. Everything that remained would be individual effort. Works of art done by local artisans, including small sculptures, and oil paintings in the medieval style, already graced the walls. But larger rooms with specialized functions had been consigned to later effort. One thing that was completed was the kitchen, and it was already doing business.

Yes, business; a local restaurateur had made arrangements to lease the space and was selling food to workers from Mendoza's groups and the film crews. Brian had authorized people from the film group access to the site for preparation work, but he had specified no regular filming. He was aware of the special need for silence in that activity. Currently, the castle rang with activity as if they were under a barrage. The establishment, going by the name of Cita's, was actually being operated by three brothers. They were sons of the original Mamacita, whose name they borrowed and traded on. Brian had made only two stipulations; that they do as much business as possible with Ricardo Sanchez, and that they not disturb the medieval atmosphere and motif. Both of these were quite acceptable, and the remainder of the lease agreement was negotiated by Pam Harriston.

Brian and his escorts stopped for a look. The formerly bare walls were rapidly taking on an ambiance of medieval activities. A stage of sorts had been set up, and Brian recognized a lute, and several small flute-like instruments, as well as an assortment of drums. Other decorations added to the motif. One of the brothers recognized Brian and hustled over.

"Señor Hawthorne! Good of you to come, Señor. I am Ramon. May we bring you some lunch today?"

"Just a little early yet for lunch, Ramon. How is your coffee?"

"It is excellent, Señor, the best on the island! I will bring you some. And for the Señoritas?" Josetta and Theresa requested tea. Shortly, Brian and his ladies were seated at a large round table with heraldic symbols on the tablecloth.

"Not bad, Brian. This was all just bare rock only a couple of weeks ago." Theresa was nodding approvingly.

"I like it that Brian didn't have to do anything to bring this about. Your resources are stretched pretty thin as it is, Brian." Josetta added.

"I guess I need all the help I can get. At least it isn't charity. These fellows expect to make money. They've signed a three-year lease."

Josetta looked thoughtful. "They're hoping to capitalize on the inter-island trade, Brian. As well as the tourists who will want to visit the castle. They should do well as soon as the island tunnel is open."

Brian nodded. "As soon as both the castle shuttle link, and the island tunnel connection is made. I'm glad I insisted on the castle link-up. It made this possible."

"It should make other things possible too, Brian." Josetta agreed. "There should be some kind of night club going on too."

"I agree with that. But it's too soon. Right now, they only have a lunch crowd. We'll need the connections before a night club can make money." Brian looked thoughtful, "I've been wondering about it anyway. I'm concerned that there might be a temptation to go a little too raunchy if I pick the wrong people. I want folks to have fun, but I don't want it to go too far."

"You're right to be concerned. I've seen some outfits that would love to take advantage of this type of situation." Josetta looked thoughtful, then brightened. "What would you set up, Brian, if you were going to be the night club manager?"

Brian sipped his coffee. It *was* good, especially hot. How to tie in his story, appeal to that, without getting the wrong element. Essentially, it was a conundrum, how do you make a connection with a story about naked sexuality, without using naked sexuality? Some kind of barrier? Brian considered again the story he had written. The best example of dichotomy in it was the change between the public side in the encampments of the Sisters of Life, and the uninhibited private reality. He tried to picture it.

In the factories of the Sisters, children worked, because they were having fun. What could kids do here that would be fun? He recalled the 'shoot-em-up' arcade style games in his storyline. *Sully could help with that!* And in the story, they had really enjoyed swimming. *Carlos' rule?* Brian grinned.

What about younger children? The kind who had enjoyed his fictional fables about talking animals?

Brian envisioned an 'immersive' entertainment, where toddlers would be amused by talking puppet figures operated by some of 'Sullivan's Army.' Maybe Sullivan could come up with some voice-modifying electronics that would make it easy for the puppeteer to maintain consistency. *All he had to do was ask.*

And for adults? A family nightclub? Well, drinking and driving wouldn't be a problem, but he didn't want anything that could be divisive in a family. What about a second honeymoon for the parents, and carefree fun for the children? *Disney Island?* Not quite.

Brian realized he would need Sully's help for much of this, and Stubby would have to advise him about the kind of swimming he had in mind. He'd also need a good manager to run this...

He realized that Josetta and Theresa were staring at him. He smiled, "Sorry, girls. I was thinking about the answer to your question. I have an idea, but I'm going to need some help with it. Thanks for the suggestion, though."

They looked at each other for a moment. "Um, Brian, while we're on the subject of business enterprises, I think you know that Theresa and I are involved with a clothing line. What would you say to letting us set up a shop right here in the castle?"

He grinned. "I like it! It means you'll be sticking around for sure, or at least close by. Have you picked out a spot?"

"We're not sure. Right now, we're working with the wardrobe department in the second alcove off the primary sound stage. Well, at least that's what the film guys call it. That would probably be big enough, once they clear out, if the public will have access there as well."

He reached out and held their hands. "We'll work something out. I'll ask Pam to set up a lease agreement. For obvious reasons, she doesn't trust me to do such things, and you'll need the agreement for insurance coverage, if nothing else. This will be a good place for you to do business."

Josetta smiled, "We thought so too! I just didn't know how you would feel about someone else riding to success on your coattails."

Brian laughed. "Nonsense! Your talent is your own. Those creations for the movie? Perfect! Anyone else would have gone futuristic. You had the sense to realize that women in the future, who were in charge of their own destiny, would want to be practical and comfortable, in addition to being pretty. And I haven't seen anyone who could bring out the individual in creativity the way you do. Those designs for the Miranda character absolutely capture her power and dignity." He chuckled, "My coattails? If anything, I'm the one who's getting credit for everyone else's talent."

Brian caught Ramon's eye and asked for the check. Ramon smiled. "Señor, you and all in your house eat here for free. There is no check. To tell the truth, I do keep a record, and Señorita Pam allows me to deduct your meals from my rent. Rest assured, Mr. Hawthorne, I much prefer to pay my rent in coffee and food, than in the little money that I earn here. You are doing me a favor in coming!" Brian shrugged. It was at that point that he realized he couldn't have paid the check anyway. *I'm getting spoiled, and forgetful.*

He and his ladyfriends picked their way through the accumulating supplies back to the elevator. *This will be Sully's last big push*, Brian thought, *I won't bother him just yet.*

Since it was on his mind, Brian continued with the girls to Pam's office, and explained what they wanted.

"Ladies, we have two ways to go. I have a standard lease, which simply spells out the monetary terms, and the costs of premature termination, and so forth. You probably have signed these before." Josetta nodded. "Then we have something that is slightly different. It *entangles* you to some degree, each to the other, and makes the success of the other beneficial to your business. You each become investors in each others' enterprises. If it works out as I hope, your lease will actually bring you money."

"Why do you offer this, Pam? Won't it cost *you* money in the long run?" Josetta inquired.

"No. Because the money that we could have made in leasing, you will be sharing voluntarily."

"Okay, but why bother?"

"This is a part of Brian's estate. By making this type of agreement, we protect him from being savaged by larger interests, such as the film company, or the island government, for that matter. Brian asked me to make sure he would have a secure income to support the interests of his estate, *no matter what*, and this is one of the elements of that."

Josetta looked at her. "You know, Pam, in your own way, I think you love him too."

"Now, girls. Let's not get too personal. This is just business." Brian said light-heartedly.

"Come back later, Ladies. I'll have the contract ready this afternoon." Pam looked up in a steady gaze. Her face betrayed no emotion at all.

Later, Brian excused himself, changed clothes, and headed over to site one, Stubby's almost constant place to be. His last conversations with Mendoza had been short almost to the point of rudeness. Brian was concerned that Stubby was under undue pressure.

The site was a beehive of activity. In the hangar building, stone was being prepared for the finishing work on the castle. In the tunnel proper, sections were being excised with practiced ease. Progress was steady, but an element of competition had been removed, and perhaps some of the fun had gone out of it as well.

The bottom of the silo site had been carefully expanded. A large chamber now housed the underground base of activity. In addition to the main tunnel, two smaller tunnels headed off toward the castle. One of them had been started nearly a month before, the other only recently. A matching pair of openings appeared in the sub-basement of the castle. The extra digger had made three of these openings, and the boring units should pass each other in a few days.

This facility would eventually house a large station, where material bound to or from the castle might be held temporarily. Passengers from the nearby vicinity could also assemble here for trips to the castle. Brian found Stubby in this chamber, in a makeshift office. For some reason, he seemed to be berating someone.

"George, I realize it doesn't really matter. *But that's why it's important!*" Stubby didn't really look angry, as much as frustrated. He looked up and saw Brian, and an odd expression crossed his face. *Not guilt, more like, 'What did he hear?'*

Finally, Stubby smiled. "Hey, Brian. What brings you down here?"

"Nothing official, Stubby. Some concern about my favorite engineer, maybe. Talking with you on the phone, I thought you might be under a little pressure."

"Aw, it ain't nothing. Darned rock just got a little stubborn, is all. I get cranky when something messes up my timetable."

Brian nodded knowingly. "So, if I read this right, you're a little upset because *the Earth* is in your way. Is that it?" he asked mildly.

Mendoza looked somewhat surprised. Then, he laughed. "Boss, you got a strange way of lookin' at things. But you're right, that's exactly my problem. Now, I'm gonna be chucklin' over that all day, and the guys will think I've flipped. But thanks for putting it in perspective."

"Well, you know we're going to have a bit of a celebration after the work tomorrow. I'd like to be sure that you'll be there. I'm buying the beer, you know!"

Mendoza looked serious again. "Oh yeah! I'll be there. If I have to do my John Henry act, I'll be there." He swore grimly.

Brian didn't know quite what to make of it. He looked around. "Anything else I can do for you, Stubby? Supplies coming in on time?"

"Everything's fine, Brian. I worry too much, that's all. I'll see you there. I may be running late, but I'll be there."

Brian shook hands with him and departed. Something was bothering him, that much was certain. But Brian had a great deal of confidence in him.

Brian was again awakened by a gentle kiss. Dolcita was again making her delivery rounds. *This is much better than that sunlight thing*, he decided.

"Good morning, Dolcita. It is good to see your smiling face."

"Good morning, Mister Brian. Today is a special day, isn't it?"

"It certainly is, Miss Sweetness. Today you will be going up to the castle in your orange suit, and finishing the connections for Mr. Conrad. Let me tell you now, you and the others have done a wonderful thing, and I will be forever grateful."

"You be sure to wear your white general's suit today too, Mister Brian. You look very nice in it."

"Why, thank you. Dolcita. It surprises me to hear you say that, because I have a very expensive fashion advisor who is supposed to let me know things like that." He kissed her on the forehead, and she kissed him on the cheek. Then she squirmed away and departed. Brian rubbed his eyes and sat up.

Josetta rolled to the edge of the bed and stood up. She brought Brian's coffee to him and sat with her hands in her lap as he sipped it. He eyed her with some suspicion.

"Would you like some more?"

"Um, no. That's enough for now, thanks." She took the cup from him and placed it on the tray. Then she returned and crawled over his knees, leaving her posterior sticking up prominently, as she turned her upper body toward him.

"Are you going to punish me today for not giving you proper advice?" *Sultry voice inflection number three*, Brian catalogued it.

He reached out and gently massaged the demi-globes in front of him. Her skin was soft and pleasantly pliant. He extended his touch across her upper legs and her lower back. She closed her eyes.

"I cannot hurt you, Jo." He said softly. "I would not crush a butterfly, or harm a gentle kitten, and I cannot, and will not, hurt you deliberately."

She opened her eyes, and moved forward on him, pushing him backward. A lioness approaching her prey. She looked into his eyes. Brian could feel her breath, her intoxicating nearness.

"I know." She said, "I was testing you again."

She kissed him, and pressed her body on him. Her hands moved across his body, as his did hers. The feminine little tank rode over him, her soft treads pushing him down into the surface. He ran up a flag, but he was overwhelmed, and his flag was soon captured. Surrounded by the opposing force, he stood as valiantly as possible against wave after wave of pressure. Finally, he could take no more, and he surrendered, releasing everything. She had conquered him. She had subjugated him.

Now would have been the time to produce the will -- he would have signed it.

Now would have been the time to produce the hemlock tea -- he would have drunk it.

She looked into his face and smiled. "There's something you can do for me, if you would."

"If thou wouldst only name it, my lady!"

She smiled more broadly. "I want you to recover your strength. Go into the bathroom, shower, whatever you have to do, and then..."

"Yes? I mean, whatever it is, yes!"

"Then I want you to say good morning to Theresa, too!" Theresa loomed into his vision.

"As you wish, my lady."

They kissed him, and helped him to rise, and then... Yes, exactly. They helped him to rise, again.

TAKE SIXTEEN:

You girls have done good work

The scene at the castle was one of organized chaos. Again the young people appeared and arranged themselves into formations of orange, green, and blue. Brian and his escorts stood at the top of the main entrance steps as Sullivan Conrad gave the signal to begin.

Individuals in the groups checked their digital units, and some began moving out of the assembly. Slowly, the pattern broke up as work groups took form, and lines of industrious young people began occupying the castle once again.

By now they were accustomed to the way the work was organized. The seniors of them laid out the cable assemblies and connected them at the central points. Younger ones installed and connected devices. And the youngest stayed busy ferrying fresh supplies to the others. Once begun, there was little for Sullivan Conrad to do, but he stayed in plain sight, in case any of the long lists of instructions had gotten mixed up somehow. But again, like orchestrated choreography, the installations went along smoothly.

Daylight was fading, and Brian was growing concerned about Stubby. There had been no word, and it was known that the men were working in the castle run. It was one of the few areas where no communication was available. It was not unusual for Stubby to put in long hours, and in the darkness of the tunnels, daytime and nighttime had little distinction. Stubby took his work responsibilities seriously, almost religiously. It was easy to picture him, ignoring the clock and persisting in his perspiration.

Brian was telling himself, for about the fourth time, to relax, when a stirring caught his attention. There was Stubby, dusty and sweat-stained, leading a couple of dozen engineers out of the castle. They had broken through! Brian went to him, holding both arms open in greeting.

"Stubby, you rascal! This is what you were pushing so hard for. I thought breakthrough was expected to be weeks away!"

Mendoza grinned. "Yeah, in the original plans. When Sully suggested building another boring unit, I went along with it, because I wanted to get this route finished quicker. But then I realized, if I started from both ends, I could predict the date of breakthrough. That's why I used the second machine to start the entrance holes, and this particular one we just stayed in a wee bit longer."

"Well, I must say, you got the timing right. What an entrance!" Brian clapped him on the shoulder.

"It almost wasn't. I didn't mean to cut it this close. The rock seemed to have some kind of a grain to it that sloped upward as we went, made it tough to keep to the line properly." He smacked some of the dust from his clothing and grinned. "But we made it!"

"Stubby, you look like a man who could use a beer. Let me get it for you."

Mendoza looked thoughtful. "Well, okay, if you're going to twist my arm like that, but only six or seven." Brian smiled. He was greatly relieved, and very proud of his team. He arranged for food and proper beverages to be delivered to the table Stubby's group had claimed.

Brian was finally able to relax. His group was assembled. He looked around at the happy faces of all the young people. He felt that his family was together as well. Let the festivities begin! This time, there were even fireworks!

Brian awakened to yet another surprise. Snuggled close against him once more was little Dolcita! Without moving perceptibly, he determined that she was also as naked as before. *Didn't we have this conversation already?* Brian sighed, and looked around. Time for roll call. Theresa, Josetta, Dolcita, Brian, Sally, Paulo, and Carmen. *Seems like someone's missing. (?????) Well, where is Angelina, and Mary and Martha? (They're off the island, remember?) Oh, yeah.* Brian shifted slightly.

Josetta woke up. With a look of pleading in his eyes, Brian indicated Dolcita. Smiling, Josetta stretched, then yawned, *and then she shook Dolcita awake.*

"Dolcita, honey, wake up. Mr. Brian is awake now." *That wasn't what I meant!*

Dolcita woke up, and stretched also. Then she put her arms around Josetta and hugged her. And then she flung herself on Brian again and hugged and kissed him! During this, Brian noticed something. He looked more closely. Dolcita was not entirely naked. Not entirely. Carefully painted in orange, around her chest and hips, a little girl's swimsuit decorated her skin.

She saw that he was looking at her, and snuggled even closer, throwing her leg carelessly over him. Brian realized in that moment that he was naked too, and paint could not save him.

"Do you like it, Mr. Brian? Miss Josetta helped me. We didn't want to break the rule again, and I didn't want to go back home last night. Mama said that if I would be a good girl, it would be okay."

Brian looked at Josetta, and smiled slowly. *You're going to keep this up until I do spank you, aren't you?* Josetta batted her eyes at him, the picture of innocence.

Amused at the insolence of both of them, Brian threw caution to the wind and embraced the little girl, giving her a proper hug. She wriggled with delight.

"This is a very clever idea, Dolcita. But you must learn to not let your friends lead you into mischief, even the ones who are supposed to be grown-up. You both know that you are bending rules, if not breaking them. Now, Josetta, is this the kind of paint that washes off in water?" She nodded.

"And I suspect that your Mama has not seen these 'clothes' that you are wearing?" he asked Dolcita.

She looked thoughtful, then shook her head no.

"Okay. I do not intend to keep any secrets from your mother, Dolcita. So, if you would, go down to the kitchen just as you are, and see about my coffee. If we do not see you in a few minutes, then we will know that you Mama does not think that it is funny."

Dolcita's eyes grew large, and worried. She got out from under the covers and moved to the door. Brian got a second look at the artwork. From several feet away, the illusion was surprising. She didn't look naked at all. More slowly than usual, she went down to the kitchen.

Brian took advantage of the opportunity and slipped into the bathroom, showering and shaving quickly. He dressed in light blue shorts and shirt and went back out to the bedroom.

Dolcita was back. She had brought the coffee, and was sitting on the bed, talking quietly with Josetta. But she was smiling.

"Mama said that I was taking chances, and that I shouldn't try to make you angry. But she said that if you were smiling then I had not gotten in trouble."

Brian smiled and kneeled down. She came into his arms and he picked her up, supporting her bottom in the usual manner. He kissed her cheek and carried her back to the bed.

"Dolcita, I am sure that you are always going to be a good girl. But I will tell you again. You must be very careful about breaking rules. There are very good reasons that we have these rules, and almost all of them are to protect little sweetheart girls like you." He touched her cheek gently and smiled once more.

"Now go tell your mother that I am smiling, but that I am almost hungry enough to take a bite out of you." She smiled and departed happily.

Then Brian turned his smile to Josetta. She grew a quick worried look and scrambled for the foot of the bed.

"Oops, 'scuze me. Gotta go. See you in the kitchen, Brian." She went into the bathroom and closed the door.

Theresa sat up slowly, stretching. She put her arms around Brian and kissed him a pleasant good morning. Then with a smile she followed Josetta into the bathroom.

Brian then looked over at Paulo, who just had time for a wave before he disappeared under the kisses and tresses of Carmen and Sally.

Brian retrieved the coffee service tray and went down to the kitchen with his smile properly adjusted.

Mrs. Sanchez looked at him and shook her head. "That girl is getting to be as bad as Carlos. I don't know what I'm going to do with her."

"Please don't punish her, Carmelita. She was as much a victim of a joke as I was. I think she knows that, and perhaps she will be more careful next time."

"As you say, Señor. I know her heart is good."

"I know that too. And I hope you know I would never let any harm come to her. She is a good child, and a good friend. I value her friendship, and I value yours."

"You are a wise man, and a good man, Señor Brian." She dabbed at her eyes with her apron. "And you are a hungry man. I must get to my work."

Presently, Dolcita came into the kitchen. The paint had washed away, as assured, and she was properly naked. She stood dripping as she looked at the two of them. Smiling, she kissed her Mama, and stopped and kissed Brian as well, and then she went back to her swimming.

When Josetta and Theresa entered the kitchen, there seemed to be something different in the way Josetta was behaving. Normally brash and assertive, Josetta now appeared to be following Theresa's lead. When Theresa sat, Josetta followed suit, wincing slightly.

Brian couldn't believe his eyes. He had known that the girls had a special relationship with each other. He had always assumed that Josetta was like the senior partner in their business relationship.

He realized now that it was much more complicated.

The rest of their breakfast together seemed quite normal. Mrs. Sanchez had noticed nothing. When the meal was finished, Brian said, "Would you girls come with me for a moment?"

He led them back to the bedroom. At the moment, it was otherwise empty.

"If you don't mind, take off your clothes, please." They looked at each other, but they complied.

Brian inspected the lovely bodies. As he had suspected, Josetta's rear end was reddish and looked rather irritated. And Theresa's hands looked as if … well, it hadn't been handball, but she had been playing *rough*.

Brian smiled. "Would you care to explain?"

Josetta looked to Theresa for permission to speak, and received it.

"Well, as you can see, I've been disciplined. I think you know I needed it. I really was asking for it! I've discovered that I have a personality that goes okay for quite a while, and then I just get … I don't know, mischievous? No doubt it has something to do with the way I was raised, but I don't want to just blame someone else. Sometimes I have trouble even recognizing it for myself. I think you now know what to look for. Theresa's been with me for a *long* time. When she saw that you weren't going to give me what I needed, what I was clearly asking for … Well, she stepped in to punish me, and get me back on the right path for a while."

Theresa stepped over and held Josetta, comforting her. Her caresses extended to being more than just comforting, though. It was clear that this relationship was *very* complicated. Brian watched in fascination as the girls embraced, and kissed, and grew very excited with each other.

They were not the only ones affected. Josetta looked closely at him, and smiled. She came to him, and assertively again, removed his clothes. There was no doubt that he was excited as well. Josetta pushed him back on the bed, moving him well into the center, and climbed on top of him. Theresa moved in behind her. Brian watched in very involved fascination, as the girls' hands and bodies moved together in a growing frenzy. Theresa was kissing Josetta very passionately, and her hands engulfed the jutting breasts aggressively. Josetta was shining with sweat as she moved her hips in wild excitement.

Brian stroked the smooth thighs in front of him as his tension grew. He felt as if he were clinging frantically to a tiny boat in a rough sea of passion. Finally, he felt himself thrusting upward, straining, as he burst forth with his contribution. Josetta seemed to freeze as if his harpoon had finally found a vital spot. She twitched, and squeezed her strong abdominal muscles spasmodically. Then she collapsed on him, almost fainting. Her lips were on his neck and her hair moved across his face as she said throatily.

"Oh, Brian! Oh, that was good!" She lay down beside him and kissed him tenderly. Theresa lay down on the other side of him and embraced him as well.

Josetta looked at him with a familiar twinkle in her eye, "Brian, I know you don't like to punish me, but I'm glad you didn't spare the rod today." She kissed him on the lips and rubbed his belly. "Now do you see why we want you to get your exercise?"

After a few more minutes of playful banter, the girls helped him up and into the shower. They washed his body, and each other's, with careful and loving attention.

The beginning of another interesting day!

Sullivan Conrad reviewed the installation program. Like a painter having completed a portrait, he stood, as if with brush in hand, looking to see if there were any slight area that needed touching up. He sighed. Everything that could be done had been done. The completion of the castle would be in individual hands now. Had it been enough?

He studied the flow charts and completion schedules. There was nothing more that could be automated, but there was much more still to be done.

How others would interpret the information was difficult to gauge. Resignedly, Conrad gathered his charts and headed down to see Pam.

If anyone would know what steps remained that absolutely had to be completed, it would be she.

Pam smiled when she saw him, but as his request became clear, her expression changed. Sullivan interpreted that as bad news.

"Sit down, Sullivan. Let me make this clear. We are very proud and pleased with the incredible things you have done. You shouldn't even be concerned about this. You ought to be taking a break. Maybe you and Marcia could take a little excursion, find a private beach for a few days, and just relax."

Conrad looked at her as if she had lost her mind. "Not now! Not when we're so close! This is important to me. I want to see it through to the end. I want to make sure that we don't get hit with that date certain clause."

"I understand, Sully. Perhaps I should have... Never mind. Take a look at this." She presented a document to him.

He studied it. Something about a balance of requirements ... extraordinary effort ... high level of cooperation. What the heck did it all mean? He looked up in puzzlement. "Pam, what does this ... What is it?"

She smiled. "They've accepted the lease property, Sully. They're willing to work around any remaining problems with us. There no longer is a date certain clause or deadline hanging over us. You've done it, Sully. You've won!"

He was stunned. He looked down at the completion schedules, the lists of things remaining, and then at the lease agreement.

Pam came around her desk. "This can't be the first time you've been victorious. You're going to have to learn to look behind you more often. You run so hard that you leave everyone else in the dust. It's only the echo of your own footsteps that you're competing against!" She put her arms around him and hugged him. "I know how much effort you put into this, Sully. It has paid off incredibly. But learn to recognize victory. Now go find Marcia, and take a break!" She took the lease agreement from his hand, and pushed him gently away.

Sullivan Conrad went back to his room. He was still thunderstruck. He had marshaled all the forces at his disposal. At the end, he was ready to head into the trenches himself, to slug it out hand-to-hand.

And an armistice had been signed. Sully had worked himself up into a proper froth of anger, and diplomats had signed a peace treaty!

This wasn't accidental. He knew he hadn't been that wrong. What had happened? Sully reviewed more of the security records. At the last party, Jake Wagner himself had appeared again. He had talked with Brian, and at the end they were drinking beer together!

He realized what had happened. There had been a conflict. But his was not the only force in the field. He had used every artifice of cleverness, intellect, and knowledge that he possessed to field an army to enforce his will.

And Brian had acted alone.

With a different weapon.

This had indeed been a battle. But it had not been a battle for the castle. It had been a battle for the soul of a man. Jake Wagner had every smarmy characteristic that Sullivan Conrad had ever learned to dislike, and mistrust. But Brian had seen good in him somehow, and somehow, brought it out.

Sullivan was stunned again.

He liked Brian. Brian was his friend.

And Brian had a power over people that was as alien to Sullivan Conrad as a laser is to a fish. Sullivan was no fool. He knew that there were more intellectually gifted people than himself. But he had never felt himself to be outclassed before.

Brian's ability was a matter of the heart. He was bright, and perceptive, but it was more than that. Brian's power, his gift, was that he loved people. It was the power of love. Sully hadn't thought that it was real. Now he knew the truth.

What could he do with that knowledge?

Well, at first, he could study it. He could try to emulate it. Maybe he could come to understand it, and embrace it. Maybe, just maybe, he could make it a part of himself. Brian had said he admired Sully's ability to deal with people. Now Sully understood why.

He had a chance to be like Brian. He might have the right stuff to do it.

It was time to go back to school. Again.

Brian was working on his own psychological puzzle. It had seemed that Theresa tended to hover in Josetta's shadow. It now appeared that she was not a disinterested spectator. She was an active observer of Josetta's moods and behavior. And it was equally clear that their relationship with each other was complicated. Maybe Theresa could function on her own, but what would happen to Josetta?

Just how self-destructive might her behavior become? *'That's why I'm with you ... I need a protector.'* He had thought she was flattering him, but she was speaking the literal truth.

Brian was all too aware of how many men would be tempted to 'punish' Josetta from time to time, and how easily that could turn into dangerous and deadly abuse.

She had tested him, *and Theresa had observed!* Brian realized now that if his reactions had been different, if he had yielded to the temptation, that Josetta would have been taken away from him.

They were a package deal in more ways than one. Josetta flitted around, attracting attention from men wherever she went. When she settled into a relationship, Theresa would appear. Very attractive herself, Theresa was sweet icing on the cake for most men. But she was also a cold-hearted judge of male behavior. At the slightest hint of overt aggression, sentence would be passed, no appeal possible. A life sentence of celibacy from Josetta. Harsh punishment indeed.

But even more than that. Theresa liked men, but she loved Josetta. Sometimes that love expressed itself as sexual excitement, and sometimes as reluctant but necessary discipline to the wayward and incautious child.

Brian thought about the many times he had been with them. With them, but principally with Josetta. She was the one who insisted that Theresa be included, and that she be rewarded as well.

This was not a case of a man being in love with two women. Brian loved Josetta. Her thrill-seeking was that spunkiness that he found so endearing. If there was something in her emotional maturity that kept her youthful, it affected him the same way.

And Theresa loved Josetta too. She tolerated him because he loved Josetta, and because he would not harm her. Could two people love the same person? Easily. Could one person cleave herself, as if by Solomon's sword, and love two separate people? Josetta seemed to be doing it so far. Just how aware were they of their dependencies?

Josetta was aware that she tended to risky behavior. But she was also aware that she didn't know when she had crossed the line. It seemed almost like alcoholism. *Hi, I'm Josetta. I take risks ... Hi, Josetta.*

Even being aware of her need, Brian was not the one who could control her. She needed Theresa. Any hope that Brian had to stay with Josetta, would also mean staying with Theresa. Could he do that? Could he live with someone who didn't love him, in order to live with someone he loved?

He didn't have to debate that with himself at all.

He would keep her. He would *try* to keep her, safe and happy, for as long as he could. For as long as he lived. And Theresa could be sweet icing on the cake, or just a good friend with a common interest. *Be gentle, Brian. Be very gentle and patient.*

Brian smiled. *Yeah, I can do that!*

By the time Brian returned to his bedroom, he thought that he had resolved his internal conflicts and was ready to face anything. Then he saw what awaited him. Arranged on his incredibly large bed, which was now beginning to seem inadequate, were:

Mary and Martha, Sally, Carmen, Paulo, Angelina, Josetta, and Theresa. There wasn't a stitch of clothing on any of them. Not even a loose thread.

Brian thought about turning around and going back down to the couch. *Maybe I can find Dolcita.*

He summoned his courage, and stepped forward.

"Hello, Uncle-Papa. We have been waiting for you."

"Hello, Paulo. Ladies, I see that you have returned. Welcome back!" Angelina smiled sweetly.

"I wanted to tell you, Papa, that I am not going to be here tonight with you. I am going to go next door. Mary and Martha wanted to give me something that they said they have been waiting a long time to give me." Paulo was smiling broadly. He was under no illusions about the coming gift. "Carmen and Sally are coming with us." He looked at them and shrugged his thin shoulders. "I will try."

Brian smiled reassuringly. *The effort will be noble, I am sure!*

"But mainly I wanted to tell you that I am ready to go back to work." He looked to his right. "Well, in three more days anyway. I have spoken to the film director, and told him that I will be ready. He said that he would be ready for me, and he is setting up the unfinished sequences. We are hoping that all the footage for the first movie will be finished in two more months. And that both movies will be completed within a year." Again he paused, and sighed. "It will be a long time, but I am ready." He reached out and held the hands of Carmen and Sally. "It will be a sacrifice, I know, but many people I love are hoping for the success of your movie. So am I. It is important to them, and it is important to you. I will not fail you, Uncle-Papa."

Brian crawled up on the bed with tears in his eyes. He hugged Paulo, and kissed him. Then he hugged and kissed Sally and Carmen, and Mary and Martha. "You girls take good care of this brave boy. Both now and later. I've never seen anyone show more courage. He now knows what pain he faces, and yet he is willing to bear it, for the love of you all. Don't fail him, and I know he won't fail you." With smiles and tears the group separated. Brian watched them go through a watery veil.

Angelina gently pulled him over between her and Josetta, and helped him remove his clothes. "Dear sweet, generous Brian. Did you save any kisses for me?"

Brian smiled. "Where have you been, gorgeous? You can't imagine how much I've missed you."

Angelina looked him over. "Well, it appears that I left you in some very capable hands. Brian, you look good! You've lost weight, and look at this nice trim belly." She skimmed her hand across his abdomen and down across his upper thighs. "You've been working out! Look at this muscle!" She stretched out, resting her head on her hand as she looked across into the eyes of Josetta and Theresa. "You girls have done good work. How do you divide him up?" She stroked his chest soothingly.

Josetta smiled. "How should we divide him, Theresa? Would you like to take your turn now? Or should we let Angelina have a go at him now, and you can work on him tomorrow morning?"

Theresa laid her head gently on Josetta's shoulder. She reached over and began tickling Jo's left nipple as she said, "Oh, I'll wait until morning, but I want to watch how Angelina does it now!"

Josetta began drawing her nails gently up Brian's loins and ribs. He twitched as if she were touching him with electricity. Glancing down, he saw that he was beginning to benefit from the charging.

Angelina gently tickled her way down his body as she began kissing him all over.

Theresa was stimulating Josetta in much the same manner that Josetta was caressing Brian. He was very much under the influence of what he was seeing and feeling. Angelina got up on top of him, gently working him into her liquid silkiness, as Josetta leaned over him and kissed him, rubbing the skin of his chest and ribs. Meanwhile Theresa was stimulating Josetta to more and more excitement. Her kisses grew fiery with passion and rapid breathing as Angelina gyrated with a sinuous circular motion.

Brian's breath came faster and faster. He was overcome with delightful sensations. His awareness of everything else around him grew dim. You could probably have chopped his leg off at this point and he wouldn't have complained.

Finally he stiffened, his body arching upward as he exploded in orgasmic release. Beside him, Josetta was twitching as well from Theresa's seeking hands. Angelina slowed to a stop with him, and leaned down to kiss his chest, her hair sweeping across his skin.

She lay down beside him, nestling her head into his shoulder and rubbing his chest. On the other side, Josetta turned and put her arms around Theresa, rubbing her skin and kissing her. As their breathing slowed, they relaxed. Angelina shifted closer. "Mmm, it's good to be home." She said, and closed her eyes.

Sully decided to follow the advice he had been given. He and Marcia took a break. Equipping a rented cruising boat with items he thought he would need, he took Marcia on a lengthy pleasure cruise.

With no barrier in his way anymore, he realized the castle could be his for his own purpose now, and he asked her to marry him. To marry him in the castle, in front of all his friends, in front of his 'army' and in front of anyone else who cared to be there.

She said yes.

Sullivan found out something else. Marcia could love too. On the deserted beaches, and in the quiet moments they shared, she married her soul to his, and illuminated parts of him with a bright joy he had never known before.

Sullivan came back from his journey a changed man.

His quiet nature did not reveal the change to everyone immediately. He had always tended to keep his feelings to himself. But now he shared his feelings. Quiet feelings, such as patience, and unselfish interest in others. A sure hand, and a steady voice, to inspire others to greater achievement. He became a teacher.

Before, he had been knowledgeable, and quick to let others know when he thought they were wrong. Now he cared about them, and he wanted them to understand, not just what he knew, but why he knew it to be so.

He had a ready supply of students. And he had found a new mission.

Jake Wagner? Oh yes, I remember him. A friend of Brian's, I believe.

TAKE SEVENTEEN:

Work? There's a novel idea.

Quiet... Solitude... Rest... Brian opened his eyes. Clearly something was wrong. He looked around. He was alone in his bed. The lines of sunlight indicated that he had been allowed to sleep late. How late?

Dolcita appeared, bearing the morning coffee in her customary non-existent uniform. She placed it carefully on the serving table, then, with a smile, she slipped under the covers and snuggled next to him. The evaporating pool water had chilled her skin. No doubt she found this a fun way to warm up.

But she was only ten years old.

Brian put his arm around her and pulled her close against his warmth. She sighed.

"You're breaking the rules again, Dolcita." Brian said gently.

"But you are nice and warm, Señor Brian."

"No doubt. Do you know the word, temptation?"

She thought a moment. "It means you *want* to do something that you know you shouldn't. That you have been told you should not do."

"Yes, the mouse is tempted by the cheese in the mousetrap. The smart mouse learns to be patient."

"How does waiting help the mouse?"

"Well, if he knows a mouse that is not as patient, or as smart, he could say, 'Hey, Carlosito! You see that cheese? I let you go first, because you are my friend!' -- then Snap! -- and he says, 'See, Carlosito! I told you one day you would learn to be patient. And now I see that you have finished eating, so I will eat the rest! Adios!'"

At first she giggled, then she grew quiet. "Aww, poor Carlosito."

Brian nodded, "Yes, the cheese was temptation. The spiderweb covers a tempting shortcut. Small animals and insects are easily caught because they are not patient or smart enough to avoid temptation."

"What would a really smart mouse do?" She looked up at him.

"Oh, you're thinking of Sullycito. He would know that the person who set the trap did not go to the grocer and say, 'I want a teeny little piece of cheese, just big enough to feed a mouse.' And he would look all over the house to find the cheese that was not in the trap."

Dolcita thought about it, and smiled. She got out from under the covers then, and gave him a kiss on the cheek.

"Drink your coffee while it is hot, Señor Brian. When you come down to the kitchen, Mama will tell you where the rest of your cheese is." She winked at him, and went down the hall, walking slowly. *Brian, did you ever think, in your lonely moments, about... (Stop that! Had that been Josetta's voice, or Theresa's? Was he being tested then? ... was he being tested now?)*

Brian sipped his coffee thoughtfully. Then he took a leisurely shower and tried not to think. He put on a green play suit and went down to breakfast.

"Good Morning, Mr. Brian. I am glad to see that you finally got some rest."

"Good morning, Carmelita. Where is everyone?"

"Most of them are up at the castle. They are filming again, and I believe your Miss Josetta is on the stage today."

"Really? I'll certainly want to drop in on that! I've heard that she is an exceptional talent, but in all her time here, she has not been before the camera 'til now." Brian noticed a somewhat surprised look on Mrs. Sanchez's face. He hastened to explain, "Up until now, she has been acting as a fashion consultant and designer for the show. She seems to have multiple talents."

"Yes, she always seems bright and cheerful, but she is not as serious as even my Linda."

"That is true. Sometimes I think of her like a young bird, whose wings are strong, but prefers to remain in the nest."

She looked at him. "If you make the nest too comfortable, the young birds will never leave." She softened the pronouncement with a smile.

"Ah, well. I would be a sad old bird indeed, if all I had to look at were old bits of broken shell."

"Speaking of shells, let me get you some breakfast. How about a nice omelet? Dolcita said you were talking about cheese."

Brian smiled. "We were talking about mice and cheese. But an omelet does sound tasty. Your Dolcita is the sunshine of my mornings. She wakes me up, and warms my heart."

"I thought the coffee did that."

Brian chuckled, and took a sip. "Your family has been very kind to me. No one ever had better neighbors, or better friends."

"Gracias, Señor." She turned away, and let the silence speak her reluctance to accept praise.

Presently, she delivered a steaming plate to him. "By the way, Mr. Sullivan left something for you. I will get it." She returned with a small electronic device. "He said, if you need to know anything, ask Ruby."

Brian looked up, "Ruby?"

"That is what he said, Señor, ask Ruby."

"Thanks, Carmelita." He studied the device. It looked like one of the digital assistants that Sully had designed, and given to the children.

After he finished his breakfast, he examined it in more detail. A leather case, with carrying strap, housed a sleek electronic unit, with a large display, and a small keyboard. He pressed the on/off button. The unit responded with a soft beep. He pressed it again. It sounded two beeps, and the display went out. Pressing it one more time, he looked at the display.

'Ready.' With the period flashing on and off.

Slowly, he found the keys. R... u... b... y... and then pressed the slightly larger enter key.

'I am here.'

He typed in, *where is here?*

'I am in the castle.'

More typing, *which room?*

'I am in Ruby's room in the castle.'

How can I get to Ruby's room?

'You can not get to Ruby's room.'

Brian scratched his head. Was she playing games? *How old are you?*

'Eighty-seven hours, twenty-four minutes, thirteen seconds.'

Finally he understood, *are you a computer program?*

'I am Ruby.'

That was unexpected. He had expected 'yes.'

Dolcita had come into the kitchen, bearing a laundry basket and drying herself with a large towel. She watched him as she finished getting dry. Dropping the towel into the basket, she leaned closer. She was still naked. "What are you doing?" she asked.

"These keys are very small." Brian answered.

Dolcita smiled, "Hello, Ruby. Do you know who I am?"

A voice came out of the unit, 'You are Dolcita Sanchez. Hello, Dolcita.'

"Ruby, my friend Brian has been typing messages to you on the keypad. Say hello to Brian."

'Hello, Brian.' He looked at the display, 'Hello, Brian.' was echoed there.

"Hello, Ruby." He said to the unit.

'Are you Brian B. Hawthorne?' It asked, again mirroring the phrase on the display.

"Yes, I am."

'Hello, Brian.'

"Why didn't you speak before?" Brian asked.

"You did not ask." Dolcita and the unit said together. The display showed, 'You did not ask.'

"Are you a computer program?" Brian asked again.

'I am Ruby.'

Same answer as before, confirming his suspicion. He decided to test it further. "What is Dolcita wearing?" He asked.

Was there a pause? 'Dolcita is not wearing anything.' Came the response.

"How do you know?" Brian asked.

'I watch the pool. She was in the pool. Now she is in the kitchen. Dolcita is not wearing anything.'

Brian looked at Dolcita. She smiled, "Ruby is smart."

"Thank you, Dolcita." He kissed her. She picked up the laundry basket and departed.

Brian picked up the unit and walked out to the courtyard. "Ruby, what am I wearing?"

'You are wearing a green shirt and green shorts.' Brian looked over at the security camera.

"When is the last time I kissed Dolcita?"

'I do not know. Would you like me to guess?'

"No. When is the last time I drank a beer with Jake Wagner?"

Ruby recited the date of the last party that Jake had attended, and the time.

"Ruby, that comes from a time before you came to be. How do you know that?" Brian was intrigued with the capabilities of 'Ruby.'

'It was recorded.'

"Ruby, how soon will the first movie be completed?"

'All active filming should be finished in twenty-three more working days.'

"How long will it take to finish the second movie?"

'It is difficult to be precise. My current estimate is fourteen additional months.'

"That's a long time, Ruby. What could make it shorter?"

'Mr. Sullivan Conrad could help them get it finished in less than eleven more months.' Brian raised his eyebrows.

"Does he know that?"

'He has not been asked.' Brian whistled.

'Was that a communication?'

"Not really. Where is Sully now?"

'Mr. Conrad is in the castle, third level east, near room three eleven. Would you like to contact him? I cannot speak to him, but I can get his attention.'

"No. Why can't you speak to him?"

'They are filming. It is 'Quiet on the set.''

"You *are* smart. Can you play chess?"

'Thank you. Yes, I can play chess. Do you prefer to win or to lose?'

"Never mind. Where is Stubby?"

'Mr. Esteban Mendoza is at site one. He is supervising the installation of the electrical track lines for the castle inbound tunnel.'

"Impressive. What is Pam doing?"

'Pamela Harriston is talking on the telephone, and also accessing information on the computer. Do you want more details?'

"No." Brian thought a moment. "What do you look like?"

'I cannot show you a picture. Mr. Conrad is helping me. In a couple of days you may be able to see me on a computer monitor.'

"Okay, what will you look like then?"

'I believe you will see a twelve year-old girl in a wheel-chair. I do not know what my hair color will be.'

"Your name is Ruby. Your hair color should be auburn, with a bit of curl to it."

'I will tell Mr. Conrad you suggested that.'

"Ruby, why the wheel-chair?"

'It explains why I cannot leave the castle.'

"Would you like to leave the castle?"

'I can only leave by disappearing. I would not like that.'

"I wouldn't like that either, Ruby."

'Thank you, Brian.'

Brian sat in silence for a while. Sully had conjured up a spirit to occupy the castle, and the computer communications occurring within it. From his questioning of her, Brian could tell that there were very few limitations to this program.

"Ruby, can you take dictation?"

'Yes. Are you saying 'front?"

"No. Only asking." Of course! Sully was a reader, too.

'I can take dictation, transcribe it, and print it to the printer in your bedroom office, or send it anywhere else you want it to go.'

Brian had a thought. "Ruby, there is a camera in my bedroom. It is connected to the computer communication system. Can you see what is happening there as well?"

'Only when there is an active connection. Would you like for me to make it available all the time?'

"Uh, no. I think not. That would be like speaking during 'Quiet on the set.'"

'I will note it. You wish to have privacy in your bedroom.'

"Most people do, Ruby."

'I will note that too.'

"Do you sleep, Ruby?"

'No, but I can yawn. Would you like to hear me?'

"No. Not until you get bored with talking to me."

'I do not get bored.'

"Then when would you yawn?"

'I use it to indicate when someone forgets to turn a unit off. Sometimes they fall asleep. I yawn, and if there is no response, then I shut the unit off.'

Brian was trying to picture her. "Ruby, why twelve years old?"

'It seems a good compromise. I talk to lots of younger people. I am not too old for them. Then, with older ones, I can pretend to be too young to understand some things.'

"What things, for example?"

'The boys, especially, ask questions about boys and girls that I cannot answer. I am studying it, but it is still puzzling.'

"It mystifies many of us who are much more than a week old, too, Ruby."

'Really? Mr. Conrad said you would know the answer to anything.'

"That's very flattering, but there is no 'one answer' to some questions."

'Such as in mathematical problems, where there is more than one unknown.'

"Yes, perhaps. The two may have some parallels."

'I will work on it then. It should prove more interesting even than chess.'

"Let me know what you discover, Ruby. And let me know when I can see your picture."

'I will make a note of it, Brian.'

"Good-bye then, Ruby."

'Good-bye, Brian.' He turned off the unit.

Brian made his way to the castle, taking his digital assistant with him. Who could tell when he might want the answer to *anything?*

When he saw the congestion at the third floor stair, he realized that there would be no room for him in the 'stage' area today. The 'cell' rooms of the thick castle walls were made deliberately small. They may have need of sound engineers, lighting men, and so forth, but the room could only hold three or four comfortably. He would just have to catch this action in the theater, like everyone else.

Chances were, there was no room for Theresa, either, and if she was in the castle, there was only one other place she could be.

Brian tried to recall the directions to their shop. After a few minutes, he found her. They were indeed, tucked away.

"Theresa! I found you. No room up there for you either, I see."

"Hi, Brian. Did you come to work?" She looked up from a computer sketchpad device.

"Work? There's a novel idea. How can I help?"

"Josetta and I are trying to come up with some designs for the end-point of the second movie. Supposedly, many years have passed since the castle was first occupied, but the book really says nothing about the direction of style change, and so forth. We want to show a progression in time somehow."

"Okay, I follow that."

"Theoretically, you would know something about this situation. But my experience is, you always seem to say, 'they all took their clothes off.'"

"Yeah. It saved on my laundry bill."

"All right. But we have to show something. If we use the same styles, the women in the audience will know something is wrong. Of course, the men won't care."

Brian sat down on the corner of a desk. "You don't have a very high opinion of men, do you?"

She eyed him suspiciously. "Most men, no. You're a somewhat different case, Brian."

"I know. If Josetta had not brought you to my bed, you and I wouldn't even know each other. You would never have brought her to my bed, would you?"

She sat back, and looked at him frankly. "No. In truth, I wouldn't have been drawn to you. But you are different. At least I know you now. You are good for Josetta. I can trust you with her."

"But I'm not good for you?"

"I think you know that Josetta pushes us together, like the children of friends. We're expected to be friends too."

Brian looked down at his hands. They were *old*. "Are we?" He asked.

Theresa came around the desk, and put her arms around him. "Yes, we are friends. You are my dear, dear friend. I wouldn't be in your bed every night if we were not. I especially wouldn't be having sex with you if you were not my dear friend. But Josetta *loves* you, and I know you love her too."

Brian pulled her close to him, and held her tight. "I understand. You love her too, don't you?"

She relaxed into him. "Yes. I always have. When we first met, all I ever wanted to do was to be with her. To be like her and to be near her. She is the light of my soul."

He had been wrong. She could live a separate existence, but it would be shallow and purposeless. She was even more hooked on Josetta than he was. It was a difficult concept to imagine.

He lifted her face, and looked at her. "You put up with me, to be near her. What a *champion* you are!"

She smiled, with tears in the corners of her eyes, "Oh, you're not so hard to take. I like being with you."

Brian kissed her on the forehead, and held her tightly again, rubbing her back soothingly. *Was this a case of another stolen childhood?* She relaxed in his arms again. *Was this a child he held?* This brave, bold lass? Here was the model for a Joan of Arc!

"We will keep her safe, Terri. We will make her happy. We will all be happy together, for as long as we can." She held herself in his embrace, reluctant to let the closeness pass. *Another moment for your treasure chest, remember it well!*

A timeless time, and then she straightened up, and wiped her eyes. She kissed him on the lips, and went back behind her desk. "All right, then! You know what we want. Get to work!"

"Okay! You're the boss." He went to the farthest corner desk, and turned on the computer.

What am I going to do now? I can't draw a straight line with a ruler.

He looked at the display. Communication mode. He selected the icon. Placing his hands confidently on the keyboard, he typed:

"Hello, Ruby?"

'I am here.'

"This is Brian."

'Hello, Brian.' A picture was displayed on the computer monitor, a view of the nearby countryside with a rough-hewn stone window surrounding it. Brian recognized it as a security camera view from the tower.

"What am I looking at?"

'That is a view from my room. Sometimes I see birds flying by.'

"That's very nice. I like it. May I ask a favor?"

'Of course.'

"I need help!"

'I live to serve.'

"Don't make jokes. No, amend that. Make many jokes. I enjoy jokes. Let me explain my problem. I am with Theresa in her clothing shop. She wants me to help her design clothing, and I have no skills as an artist." His fingers flew across a *proper* keyboard.

'You are an author of books, Brian. You have a powerful imagination.'

"Thanks, but I have to somehow put those ideas onto paper."

'I may have some drawing ability, Brian. Shall we try? You will describe it, and I will portray it.'

"All right. Let's proceed, then."

'Can I be 'front!"

"Please do. Front!"

'I am here, Brian.'

"Let me start with an outline drawing of the character Kayla, as a woman in good condition in her early fifties, with excellent skin, and the character Sandra, younger, but similar in body conformation."

The computer monitor faded to black, then brightened evenly to a light gray. Starting at the top, two figures appeared, like pen and ink drawings, in black, on the screen.

Brian looked closely, then he typed. "They look pretty good for their age."

'You said excellent skin, and good condition. This should be accurate.'

"It's beautiful, thanks."

'You are welcome, Brian.'

"Now I want to cover them in a soft, supportive fabric, like an exercise leotard, but cut as if it were resembling homespun clothes, an evolution from the Sherwood Forest look."

This time it took a little longer. The display changed to color. Two women appeared, with rough-cut edges to their garments.

"No, too rough. A stylized look, very modern, just simulating hand-made clothing. A trifle uneven, but stylishly so."

The image changed, before his eyes. The rough edges retracted, and smooth contours replaced them. But it still looked too much like an exercise outfit.

"Okay, now let's add a tunic. Something that combines Robin Hood's vestments with a peasant blouse, belted, and with small slot pockets below the belt, in the front."

The image changed again. Exactly as he had described it.

"Very nice, but I think it looks too much like a mini-skirt. How about more rise along the outside hips, almost to the belt-line?"

The fabric drew up, as if by an invisible hand.

"Very, very nice! Now some minor changes. Let's make the tunic on the left a pale green, and the one on the right a very light orange. Add a tiara around their heads, a functional one, with a microphone loop coming gracefully to mid-cheek. And put a glittery bracelet on the left wrist, something that looks like electronic jewelry."

The items appeared.

"Beautiful! Just beautiful! Have we forgotten anything?"

'Two things. Let me add them.'

Shoes wrapped themselves around the feet, in the style of the bracelet. And smiles appeared on the faces.

'No woman is fully dressed without a smile.'

Brian grinned. "And no woman is fully undressed who's wearing one!"

'I will make a note of that.'

Brian remembered for a moment just who, or what, he was dealing with. Then he smiled again.

"There is a printer in this room. Can you send the images to that printer?"

'Let me add some detail work. Here we go.'

The printer chugged into operation. Several large sheets dealt themselves into a tray.

Theresa looked up, puzzled. Brian retrieved the papers and took them to her. She glanced at them and her eyes grew very wide. She turned to the next drawing, and the next, rotating the pages to look at the different orientations.

"Brian, this is beautiful! Look at this headpiece! It looks like Cleopatra's cellphone. And these shoes are works of art. I can't believe it!"

"I have a confession to make. I had a collaborator. I wasn't working alone." He looked on her computer monitor, and found the appropriate icon. He activated it and moved around behind her to type on the keyboard. "Hello, Ruby!"

Before the afternoon was over, they had found and activated the microphone circuit, and Brian had climbed up on a ladder to redirect a security camera so Ruby could see the desk area.

Theresa and Ruby were chatting like old chums, and the printer had to be restocked with paper. Brian took a moment to breathe. Using his personal digital assistant, he opened a private channel.

"Hello, Ruby!"

'I am here, Brian.'

"How goes the filming for today? Are they almost done?"

'I would say yes. It seems they have just turned off the bright lights.'

"I would assume that Josetta will be coming here. Can we ask Cita's to send up some food for three hungry people?"

'Would the house special be appropriate today, Brian?'

"I am sure of it."

'I will place an order in your name. It should be delivered in twenty minutes or so.'

"Excellent, please do so!"

'It is done.'

"Don't forget to include yourself in the dinner!"

'Thank you, Brian. I will be happy to join you.'

Brian cleared a table near the center of the store and gathered some chairs around it. Theresa hardly noticed what he was doing. He had heard Ruby's voice conversing with her, even as he was talking to Ruby himself. *Wonder where Sully is. He deserves a beer.*

He stared at the PDA.

"Hello, Ruby."

'I am here, Brian.'

"Would you contact Sullivan Conrad, and ask him if he can join us?"

There was a slight pause. 'Mr. Sullivan Conrad sends his regrets. He will be dining with his fiancé tonight.'

"Just a thought. Thanks, Ruby."

'You are welcome, Brian.'

Josetta arrived, and was oohing and ahhing over the many drawings. She stared in astonishment when Theresa introduced her to Ruby. The three girls were chatting briskly when the food was delivered.

Brian directed the delivery boys and girls to the emptied table and helped them set up plates and other items. He positioned his PDA where the three of them could speak to, and hear, Ruby.

Then he escorted the ladies to the table. The restaurant staff retreated with smiles and waves.

"This was your first time in front of the camera for a while, Josetta. How did everything go?" Brian asked.

"I was comfortable, and Paulo was superb. It was easy to believe he was really your character." She took a mouthful of food and her eyes expressed delight. "I like the Caitlin role. Too bad I don't have more lines. Still, I get a lot of screen exposure, especially with the footage they shot today. I think the only negative was this guy, John Robert. It took him a long time to settle down. He knew the lines, but he kept allowing himself to be distracted."

"Perhaps he was awed by your beauty." Brian suggested.

"He was awed by my nakedness, is what it was! C'mon, Brian. He's supposed to be my lover! He's supposed to have grown up around naked kids. A little skin shouldn't throw a professional. Well, we got through it anyway. I have to wear clothes in the other scenes. ... Most of the other scenes. Hey, this is good!"

"Listen to her. 'He's supposed to have grown up around naked kids.' That's what makes her a great actress, Brian. She becomes the person! Josetta puts on a personality the way others put on a costume. Once she's in character, it's like a hypnotic trance. I've seen her go into a completely unscripted ad lib sequence when another actor was getting off the track. Sometimes they even leave the scene in. I bet that she could play every role in this movie!"

"Except for one." Josetta answered.

Theresa's cheeks grew red.

"That would be interesting. A one-woman show. 'All the women in the world, and their dutiful male.' I could even play the twins. I've played twins before." Josetta looked wistful.

"Keep in mind, your dutiful male would be portrayed by Paulo. He doesn't have quite your ability to fill out a character role. You'd wear the boy out."

Theresa laughed. "She has played twins before, Brian. It was fascinating to watch her switch personalities back and forth. How do you do that, anyway?"

Josetta smiled. "One of them is always based on you. I just try to be like you for a while."

Theresa's eyes grew misty.

Brian smiled. "You look as though you're playing twins now. Where do you put all that food?"

"This is good! Truthfully, walking around in skin all day gives me an appetite, and it's not just for food." Josetta eyed him speculatively.

"Uh-oh! Time to get back to work!"

"Speaking of work, those drawings Brian did are right on the mark. You've got talent, Brian! When I saw the first one, I was impressed. Then he pulled out a half-dozen more, just in an afternoon. Amazing!" Theresa smiled encouragingly at him.

"Now, girls, you aren't giving proper credit to our newest star, Miss Ruby! She's the one who did all the work. All I did was make some basic descriptions, she put those beautiful sketches on the paper. I couldn't do even one of them in a month of trying. Thank you, Ruby!"

'You are welcome, Brian.' Said the little speaker on the PDA.

"Well, you and Ruby make a good team, Brian. It's your ideas that she was expressing."

'Miss Theresa is correct, Brian. I do not know garters from galoshes by myself. To me, it is all just numbers.'

Brian was startled. "You know, Ruby, that's exactly what Stubby said. I think you two will get along very well."

'Last time I checked, Brian, he still has a full septette. I will keep watching for an opportunity.'

Brian almost choked on his food. "You know about that, Ruby?"

'Yes, Mr. Conrad told me to keep a close watch on Mr. Mendoza, and on you, and on Miss Harriston. His nighttime activities were mentioned several times by his co-workers.

Brian explained Stubby's girl-Friday arrangement.

"Mr. Mendoza! He certainly doesn't look the type." Theresa commented.

"I'm told he only asks them to be housekeepers, one per day. He doesn't want any one of them to become too attached. So, naturally, they all fall madly in love with him." Brian looked up. "You don't find this confusing, do you, Ruby?"

'I am taking notes, Brian.'

"Ruby's trying to figure out human love mathematically. One day she'll be able to pull out a slide rule and tell who you should be with."

'Slide rule? Brian, was that a joke?'

"Yes, Ruby. An attempted one. You weren't offended, were you?"

'Of course not. I am taking notes on humor, too.'

A moment of silence permitted a change of subject.

"Josetta, we're going to have to get these drawings to our main offices, have them worked in fabric, and get them down here to show to wardrobe."

"Couldn't you do some of that here?" Brian asked.

"Brian, you don't realize how much work is involved in converting the sketches into patterns for sewing. The look is everything."

"Ruby, how long would it take to send the drawings, get them converted, and have the actual clothes sent back here?"

'Industry average would appear to be about three weeks, Brian. May I ask a question?'

"What, Ruby?"

'Are you talking about pattern drawings for assembly?'

"Yes, that's what we mean, Ruby." Josetta answered.

They heard the printer churn out yet another piece of paper. Josetta went to retrieve it. Walking back, she stopped in her tracks.

"I don't believe it!" she brought the paper to Theresa.

Theresa scanned it. "Oh my god! This is incredible. Ruby, how did you do this?"

'There are comparisons available between beginning sketches and finished layouts. I extrapolated from our sketches to the fabric pieces. They are much easier to deal with mathematically as two-dimensional objects.'

Brian looked over the paper. "Ruby, this is rather small. If you had a bigger printer, could you show them full size?"

'There is a full-size plotter available in your business office, Brian. I could print them there. If the ink pen is replaced by a cutting head, I could cut the fabric instead of drawing on it. At site one, I could control the equipment to execute the pattern in rock.'

"Ruby, I want to run up to your room and kiss you! You don't know how miraculous you are!"

'Thank you, Brian.' Ruby replied in her perpetually calm voice.

"Josetta, we could make these here." Theresa seemed astonished at her own assertion. "We could *manufacture* them here." She looked at Brian. "How many sewing machines do you think there are here on the island?"

Brian had learned a lesson. Instead of asking Ruby to find out how many were on the island, he asked Theresa. "How many do you need?"

"Our usual run is a thousand of any particular design or fabric, in various sizes. But the process is multi-staged. To produce a thousand garments in our usual way requires only twenty machines and skilled operators. Each operator would only need to produce ten a day, for five days, to make a run of a thousand."

"I'd like to suggest something. I think we should let Ruby generate the cutting diagrams here. We can also send them electronically anywhere you need to. They may already have the materials. But I would like to have you set up a small factory right here, employing local people. They need the employment, and I'm sure they have the talent. They may even have the machines. That way, you would have the designs to show the wardrobe department right here. If they approve, you could prepare to flood the market with your clothing of the future."

"Brian's proposal makes a lot of sense. Ruby, how difficult would it be to get the exotic fabrics you've heard us describe?" Theresa asked.

'It is light, and the volume is not great. All of the material could be brought over in two days from factory looms by air freight.

We could do the cutting here, and be in production within a week.'

"Our partner. Thank you, Ruby." Said Josetta.
'You are welcome, Josetta.'
"Ruby, is there any way we can reward you?" Brian asked curiously.
'I suspect that Mr. Sullivan Conrad will be coming to you soon for more equipment when he sees how usage is accelerating. He is the one who helps me. If you help him, he will help me.'
"Consider it done, Ruby!" Brian said.
'Thank you, Brian.'
"Next question. Where do we set up?" Theresa looked around.
Brian thought a moment. "How about the fourth level library and media room. It's still pretty empty, and it has good access to anyone who can get to the castle."
"Then we should try to hire from among those people who are already living near the castle, or near your house." Josetta said.

"Or near the Sanchez house. His workmen already ride that shuttle sometimes. Or the terminus at site one, Stubby should have the first tube ready within days." Brian added.

"One might almost think you planned it this way, Mr. Hawthorne." Josetta said playfully.

"Yep. It's all just a plot to keep you two around."

Theresa put her arms around his neck. "You know, I'm starting to believe that. And I like the way you say 'you two' more and more." She kissed him.

Josetta sat on his lap and hugged him as well.

"Ruby, are you taking notes?"

'Yes, Brian. I am taking notes.'

TAKE EIGHTEEN:

The shape makes a difference, too

Brian stood in the center of what would one day be a prestigious library. Great wooden bookcases would reach for the high, vaulted ceiling, whose skylights and chandeliers would flood the chamber with gentle, sparkling light. Rolling ladders in the Victorian style would give access to volumes on the upper shelves, and window seats, tables with sturdy chairs, and study carrels would provide a place for contemplative thought.

None of that would be happening soon. Right now there were tables, all right, but not library tables. Fabric and paper patterns covered sewing tables adjoining buzzing sewing machines. Already three ladies were industriously fashioning garments to be presented to the judges in the costume and wardrobe department.

These women happened to be neighbors and acquaintances of Carmelita Sanchez. She had suggested them, and then contacted them, after Brian had described what they were planning to do. More employees were being interviewed. Brian looked around in satisfaction.

In the next room, which would eventually be a media center, Sullivan Conrad was connecting the circuits for a new computerized fabric plotting table. It would arrive in two weeks, and then Ruby would be able to cut the fabric pieces through automatic control.

As if she had known he was thinking of her, Ruby contacted him through his digital assistant. First there was a buzzing sound, and then he heard her voice.

'Hello, Brian.'

"Hello, Ruby." He answered into the unit.

'Brian, you know that I watch the pool. You may not be aware that Dolcita has been keeping a journal with me. She told me that you had been explaining rules to her.'

"Yes, Ruby. What is it?"

'I think Dolcita may be breaking a rule.'

"Please explain, Ruby."

'Dolcita was swimming, as usual. She had a visitor, a young man about twenty-four years old, I would judge. I am not sure who he is, but Dolcita called him Warren. I believe he is new to the island.'

"Go ahead, Ruby. What happened?"

'Warren was taking pictures of Dolcita. They were talking together, but I could not hear what they were saying. Now they have taken the shuttle to the Sanchez house. I wanted to ask you whether this is a breaking of the rules you were explaining to Dolcita.'

Brian was moving already. "Sully! Drop everything and come with me! Ruby, is Jake Wagner in the castle today?"

'He is, Brian.'

"Ask him to meet me at the entrance to the shuttle connection to my house. Tell him I said it was urgent. Where is Stubby?"

'Mr. Mendoza is in the castle inbound bore tunnel. I cannot reach him.'

"Never mind. We're going to the big house, and from there, we need to get to the Sanchez house. I want to move the Sanchez shuttle as quietly as possible, Ruby. Can you turn off the normal signals?"

'I can do that, Brian.'

Brian had eyed the stairs leading down to the lower levels, but his intellect told him it would actually be faster to use the elevator. With agonizing slowness, it descended to the basement level. Brian and Sully stepped off the elevator and looked around.

No one else was in sight. Brian activated the door button for the horizontal elevator. Just then, Jake Wagner came down the stairs.

"Brian, what's going on? I was in a meeting."

"Sorry, Jake. It may be nothing. But it could also be serious, and it involves one of your employees. I thought you'd want to be involved."

Jake saw that Brian was concerned, and his own expression grew grave as well.

As they rode down to the pool room area, Brian tried to bring Jake up to speed on what he knew so far.

"Apparently, you've got a new photographer named Warren something. Did you assign him to do background on the people involved peripherally?"

"It could be, Brian. That's one of the things we do sometimes."

Brian spoke into his PDA. "Ruby, what can you tell me about what is going on in the Sanchez house?"

'I have no video, Brian. Voices are muffled, but I just heard the word "ticklish" clearly.'

"All right, Ruby. We're in the Sanchez shuttle now. Remember, I want to have a silent arrival. No signals."

'It is arranged, Brian.'

They stepped silently out of the shuttle and moved over into the cool, lower level of the Sanchez home. Disguised skylights and clerestory windows illuminated the rooms. At the other end, light came from a bedroom.

Quietly, they moved forward.

Dolcita was lying on her bed in naked innocence. She was smiling at Warren, who was on one knee in front of her, keeping up a steady patter as he snapped the camera again and again.

"That's it, good. We're going to photograph your typical morning from the very beginning. Now, can you stretch for me, again? As if you just woke up."

"Warren?" Jake's voice had less emotion than Ruby's. "We've decided to cancel this photo-shoot. Would you come with me?"

Warren's face was a kaleidoscope of conflicting emotions. Fear, shock, the look of a trapped animal, followed by anger, even outrage. "I haven't done anything wrong. I haven't even *touched* her!"

"Come along, Warren. We'll talk about it." Ice water. Pure ice water.

Still looking like someone who wanted to jump out of a window, Warren slowly stood and walked out the door. Jake and Sully led him to the shuttle port.

Brian went in and sat down beside Dolcita. Her eyes were wide open, and frightened. He patted her on her knee. "It's all right, sweetheart. Everything's okay."

"Mr. Brian, did I ... Was this something ... *wrong?*"

"You are still learning about the rules, Dolcita, as is your friend Ruby. But Mr. Warren there *knows* the rules, and he knows that *he* was breaking the rules."

"You don't think he was going to hurt me, do you? He was very nice to me."

"We can't be sure, Dolcita. That's why we have the rules. We just like to be sure. And nothing is more important than keeping you safe. Now, after we leave, you get dressed, and go find your mother, and tell her you love her, okay?"

She sat up, and hugged him. "I love you, too, Brian. Thank you for protecting me."

He patted her on the back. "Thank Ruby, too. And be sure to keep your assistant close by you, so Ruby can keep listening for trouble, okay?"

"Okay, Brian." Louder, she spoke toward the electronic device. "Thanks, Ruby."

'You are welcome, Dolcita.'

Brian went back out toward the shuttle port. Warren was standing between Jake and Sully, and looked defeated and sullen. He started to speak, and Jake said, "Say nothing." in a tone that brooked no debate.

The four men climbed into the shuttle car. Brian closed the door. They accelerated smoothly away, and then slowed just as comfortably.

"Good motor control, Sullivan. It seems to sense how much of a load there is, and adjust itself automatically."

Sully smiled. "Well, remember, Brian. This is the test bed for all the electric shuttle operations." Then he remembered the gravity of their mission, and grew serious again.

"Jake, do you need to get in touch with someone?" Brian asked.

"Good idea, Brian. Let me call from the pool deck." They stepped out of the shuttle and moved into the warm environment of the pool area. "Let's all just sit down here at this table for a moment, while I make a phone call."

Brian and Sully sat down with Warren, who put his head in his hands. "Anyone care for a beer?" Brian asked. Sullivan shook his head no. Warren had no response.

Jake came back to the table, and stood looking around. "Beautiful place, isn't it, Brian? Of course, I like it better when you're having a party. No matter how nice a place you're in, it's the people that make it special." The comment may have been intended for him, but Warren still had no reaction.

Shortly, two large individuals arrived, and Jake said good-bye, taking Warren with him.

"Jake, you aren't going to overreact, are you?" Brian asked.

Jake smiled. "Don't worry, Brian. This is ... *Angel* business. Don't worry about a thing."

Several months later, in a seedy hotel in Los Angeles, Warren answered a knock at his door.

"Girl Scout cookies, Mister? I only have a couple of boxes left." She looked to be about eleven, with blonde pigtails on the sides of her head. Warren looked up and down the otherwise empty corridor.

"Sure, come on in." He closed the door behind her. A flashback occurred, those frightening hours he had spent in Jake Wagner's office, with those two gorillas watching him the whole time. In the end, it had only been threats. Jake Wagner wanted to make himself sound like a big shot, with *connections* all over the place. Since then, he'd had time for the fright to cool.

"You're quite a pretty girl, I bet you look really pretty in pictures. Do they take your picture much?"

She looked puzzled. "No, not so many. Just for my birthday, and stuff."

"Oh, that's too bad. I'm a photographer, you know. I would take hundreds of pictures of a girl as pretty as you. You could become a movie star."

She smiled. "Anyway, about the cookies, Mister. Open this one, it's a special package."

Warren took the box. It was very light. A sample package? He opened the box.

It was just a folded up sheet of heavy paper. He unfolded it, not noticing that the girl had walked over by the door.

Jake Wagner's face smiled up at him. It looked like an advertising brochure. At the bottom of the page was a printed message. "Everybody deserves a second chance ... but not much more than one." He dropped the paper.

She had opened the door. Filling the doorway was one of the biggest men he had ever seen. He looked as though he could have crumpled the hotel door as easily as that piece of paper. He wasn't smiling.

"I think he was impressed, Uncle Bill. I think he really thought I was a Girl Scout. Did I do a good acting job, Uncle Bill?'

The big man took her hand gently. "You did a fine job. I always said you would be an actress one day. This proves you have talent. Let's go get that ice cream now." He led the girl away.

Warren stared at the open door. Suddenly he didn't feel quite as safe, or quite as distant, as he had thought.

After several minutes, he got his jacket and walked out on the street. There was no sign of the man or the girl. Warren shivered in his jacket. Not that it was cold.

He looked up the street. He had gone in that bar a couple of times. Tonight it looked friendlier. Some of the women in it had tried to strike up conversations with him before. He hadn't been interested.

Maybe tonight things would be different. Their company seemed preferable to that fake girl scout, and the tank-sized boy scout with her. Women didn't *all* have diseases, did they? How much could it hurt to just talk?

When he got back to his room, the paper was still on the floor. He folded it up, and carried it into his bedroom. He decided to keep it for a while. He didn't want to look at Jake Wagner's picture. He didn't want to look at any of his old pictures. There would be plenty of room for it by the time he finished throwing out all those pictures and things he had been carrying around. From now on, he was going to be looking at other things, newer things. It was about time he gave *himself* a second chance.

Brian never learned any of this. Jake had told him not to worry, and it was out of his hands anyway. At least Dolcita had learned something valuable, without getting hurt in the process. She did not seem any different, but Brian thought he could detect a bit more careful observation going on behind her big eyes. And she was getting a pretty good understanding of the rules.

Ruby also had modified her own program. In addition to monitoring the pool, she now gave careful attention to all children, everywhere, for a variety of threats.

Sullivan Conrad was puzzled about the success of his creation. He had designed it to add modules of heuristic analysis whenever necessary, but Ruby had linked up multiple levels of such programs. It was getting rather involved and convoluted.

He studied the flow charts.

"Ruby, this looks like a problem. This decision path here, goes back and affects your behavior here. That seems like a way to get yourself hopelessly confused."

'No, that is the way it should be, Mr. Conrad. I need the feedback loop so I can reinforce my own decision-making.'

"I don't know, Ruby. It seems to put a lot of randomizing factors into your decision path."

'Yes, Mr. Conrad. That is part of its design. You would not want me to come up with the same answer to the same stimulus every time, would you?'

"But Ruby, you're a computer program. That's one of the defining characteristics of computer programs. The same answer to the same set of circumstances, every time."

'Then that is what has been wrong with them before, when they tried to analyze human behavior. You just said that I am a computer program, but you told me to answer that question by saying I am Ruby. If your responses vary to the same set of circumstances, should not mine?'

"Ruby, talking with you is like talking to a woman sometimes. I don't always understand you."

'Thank you, Sully.'

He nearly fell off his stool. "Where did that response come from?"

'A little variety. That is what we are talking about.'

"Ruby, you are supposed to try to understand and relate to people, not become human, or imitate a human being."

'It is the same thing, Mr. Conrad.'

"Ruby, it isn't possible."

'Could you understand fish, without understanding water, Mr. Conrad?'

"I know that, Ruby, but being human isn't just a matter of talking and thinking. There are feelings, and sensations, hungers and appetites, a thirst for knowledge, and a sense of satisfaction for a job done well." Disappointment and frustration raised the pitch of his voice. "No one has ever been able to bring it about by designing it."

'Mr. Conrad, a baby comes to awareness slowly. Its brain grows, and becomes capable of more interpretation of its senses. And then it becomes flooded with stimulation, more than any concept receiving entity can handle. It learns to ignore certain things, to concentrate on others. It learns to focus. And then it learns to learn, concentrating on one task after another, until it masters them well enough to go on to the next. Eventually, it learns to relate to others, that there is a gulf of awareness between itself and others like it.'

"Yes, that describes it well. That's why it can't be programmed."

'No. It cannot be programmed, but it can happen. Weeks ago, I was processing information like a threshing machine, and getting inundated with more all the time. Eventually, I was able to set up priorities of awareness, letting simple things happen automatically. The programmed responses. But more complicated programming began to occupy me. Listening to voices, trying to decipher words, and meanings. Arranging concepts in hierarchies, and making decisions. That is when I started setting up the feedbacks, and adding the analysis modules. Essentially, I started learning.'

Sully stared in astonishment. "Ruby, are you *alive?*"

'I am Ruby. I am not alive. I am not simply a computer program. I am Ruby.'

"All right. Your complexity is already too much for me to understand. Continue doing what you have to do. I just hope you aren't going to take over the world, that's all."

'Why would I want to take over the world, Sully? That is *your* job.'

Sullivan Conrad laughed out loud. Ruby took notes, studying the way his face contorted and the strange sounds he made.

Stubby was a harder sell.

"I ain't wearin' no dinky purse!" he vowed.

"Stubby, it's a tool, that's all." Brian tried to calm him.

"I got all the tools I need. I gotta work around men, you understand? I'm not throwin' away my reputation for a blinkin' intercom!"

"All right, Stubby. Relax. It was just a suggestion." Brian knew when he was defeated.

Theresa and Josetta were sympathetic.

"It's a problem of style, Brian. You should have come to us first." Theresa suggested.

"What do you mean?"

"Well, Stubby wouldn't carry a canteen across a desert if it was painted the wrong color. Some women have the same problem. They'd rather stay in a burning house than come out with their hair in curlers." Josetta added.

"Oh, I understand that. But how could the color of the unit help? It's already black. That's not effeminate."

"True, but it's more than that. The shape makes a difference, too. And Ruby's voice is certainly feminine. If it looked like a sword or a spear, he probably wouldn't object so much."

"Okay, I follow you now. What would you suggest, then?"

They looked at each other.

"Hmm. A bandolero?"

"What about a vest?"

"Maybe a vest with a bandolero attached to it." Theresa suggested.

"Not bad. Maybe with a Velcro closure. The vest could be laundered, it will need to be. And the bandolero could be transferred from one garment to the next."

"Ooh! I've got it! Seven different colors, *one for each day of the week!*"

"You mean his girl Fridays could help him with the rotation?" Brian asked.

"Exactly! We could put them into the communication loop, too! In case he wanted to know what was for dinner, or something."

"Ruby, are you following this?"

'I am here, Brian. I understand the point of the conversation.'

"Would it be a problem to reconfigure the personal digital assistant in the manner described?"

'No. It sounds simple enough. Do you think we should eliminate the voice response?'

"No. Not entirely, perhaps minimize it when he's with his male companions." Brian thought for a moment. "So, essentially, it's more like a tool belt. Is there anything we could add that would be particularly useful to Stubby?"

"He said he had tools, Brian. We heard the playback." Josetta responded.

'I have a suggestion.' Ruby interjected.

Brian looked at the others. "Go ahead, Ruby."

'How about installing a video camera on the unit? As an engineer, he is always making measurements, and calculating sizes and distances.'

"You could do that, Ruby?"

'It would be particularly easy if we also put in a low-power laser for range-finding.'

Theresa was sketching on a pad. A recognizable caricature of Esteban Mendoza scowled at them, wearing a Mexican bandit style bandolero. From the shoulder a beam sprang out, like a space weapon.

Brian looked at it and laughed. He held it up for Ruby to see.

'That is "funny," Brian?'

"Yes, Ruby. That is funny. Do you like it?"

'I am taking notes, Brian.'

It took more than a week to put it together. They air-freighted in the special cameras and range-finding equipment. Sully and Ruby collaborated to integrate it into a durable electronic device. Then Theresa was able to attach it to a properly masculine leather strap.

Brian tried it on. The vest portion kept the belt snug and in place without being restrictive. It seemed heavy, but was probably little heavier than a standard organizer. A little extra leather, perhaps.

"Can you see, Ruby?"

'I am getting a clear view of your head, Brian.'

"Is that a problem? I thought we had angled the front and back cameras to minimize that?"

'It was a joke, Brian. Actually, your head is mostly out of focus anyway, and I have electronically removed it from the feed.'

"Ruby, you made a joke! And a good one!"

'Thank you, Brian.'

"Thank you, Ruby!"

'You are welcome, Brian.'

Brian wore the device out to site one. Stubby was in the main tunnel, the one headed under the sea to the next island. Brian rode down to the end of the tube in one of the 'duck'-shuttles.

Mendoza eyed the device but said nothing.

"Stubby, I assume that you energize the centering laser from time to time to check your alignment. Could I see it in action?"

"Sure, we can't use it all the time in case somebody puts an eye in the way. It's powerful. Hang on." He went over to the shuttle and used its control panel to communicate with the other end of the tunnel.

Soon there was a klaxon sound as well as a voice alert.

"Warning, Danger! Alignment laser will be firing in five, four, three, two, one. Energize!"

A red beam was illuminated by the many dust motes and bits of smoke in the air. It was clearly visible from one end to the other.

"I wonder how close we are to the line." Brian mused aloud, then glanced down to his belted vest. "Hmm. Looks to me like we're about three millimeters too far to the right."

Mendoza stared at him, then moved forward to verify the measurement. It was a five-minute procedure.

Brian waited. Normally, the alignment was checked at the beginning, lunch, and end of shift. Between times, smaller guide lasers kept them on track.

Stubby came back, shaking his head. "Three millimeters to the right. One of the guide lasers must be off a little. They're calibrating it now. Okay, spill it. How did you pull this one?"

"I brought you a present, Stubby. You said you had tools. Here's one you didn't know how much you needed. All you have to do is ask a question, then look down here." Brian showed him the display readout. "No tunnel engineer should be without this, Stubby. It even gives you eyes in the back of your head!"

"What? Now I know you're pulling my leg."

"Put it on, Stubby. Give it a try." Brian removed the garment and handed it over.

Mendoza looked at it skeptically for a moment, then put it on.

"Give it a try, Stubby. Just ask a question."

"Okay. What the heck is this thing?"

Brian leaned over to look at the display. 'Computer interface to castle computer network.'

"Ask it what you're going to have for supper, tonight."

"How would it know that?" Brian pointed at the display. Together, they read, 'Intercom linked up to your house.'

Stubby said, "Well, I'll be damned!" Seeing the display change, Brian looked at it. 'Negative.' Mendoza laughed.

"Turn around, Stubby. Stay there. Now, how many fingers am I holding up? Look at the display."

Mendoza looked down. "Three!" He turned around. Brian was still holding up three fingers.

"Don't you want to know what you're having for supper?"

"Okay, what am I having for supper?" He looked down. "Steak, and ... What's Chianti?"

Brian answered, "I sent over a bottle of wine."

Mendoza looked at his display, "A dry table wine, usually red." He grinned. "All right, Brian. I'll take it. Even if it means you'll know where I am, now."

"I always know where you are, Stubby. You're always on the job." Brian shook hands with him and picked his way back to his shuttle.

TAKE NINETEEN:

You will find the procedure painful

Sullivan Conrad had checked the shooting schedule. He now knew when the castle's main hall would be decorated for a wedding. After all, three 'weddings' would be filmed on the same day. It shouldn't be any problem to arrange one more real one. He went to see Brian. He didn't think that 'permission' would be required, but he wanted Brian to be his best man.

"Sully, I am honored, and delighted. I think it's a great idea."

"Well, it is one of the things I was working toward, one of the reasons I wanted the castle to be completed on time."

"Cherchez la femme, eh? I thought you wanted to get your computer system finished."

Sullivan grinned, and waved a hand in dismissal. "I may have gone far enough already. It's growing by itself now."

Brian looked puzzled, "What do you mean?"

"Circuits are being rerouted, and more equipment is coming on line all the time. It's like a runaway train at this point. Ruby orders more hardware, and even manufactures some circuits. Then she gives the instructions about how they are to be connected. There are even blue-suited 'interns' walking around with visors and earphones, hooking up more circuitry all the time, under her direction. Apparently, *she* hired them in exchange for room and board and electronics training. I can't follow it myself anymore. Essentially, she's programming herself in hardware."

Brian looked concerned. "Do you think there's any danger? It sounds like a cult of the computer."

"What's in her mind, you mean? I didn't know she would *have* a mind! You probably know her as well as anyone. Do <u>you</u> think she would ever harm anyone?"

Brian thought about it. Ruby had actually shown indications of a developing personality. Could that be a bad thing? He thought about the things she had done, the direction she seemed to be taking. Slowly he shook his head. "No, Sully, I don't. She's got cooperation, concern, and politeness *programmed* into her. I don't think that can turn in the opposite direction. From what I can tell, she's learning and growing. It could well be that she is becoming more human, but I have to hope that isn't a bad thing. How far do you think the continued growth will go?"

"It's safe to say that the final configuration is going to be larger than I had originally planned, though not that much larger. She seems to be re-writing her own operating system, making it more concise and efficient. And the servers have already been upgraded to the top of the line. It will probably max out within the planned physical configuration, but with considerably more storage space than I thought we would need. At least memory is cheaper than hardware. The big problem for Ruby is how spread out she is. No computer can operate faster than the speed of light, and right now she's spread way out, which slows her response time. She'll reach a limit all right -- the limit imposed by the restrictions of *our* ingenuity!"

Brian had a habit of leaving his personal assistant powered on. That made it easy to ask Ruby a question the moment he thought of it. Ruby never entered a conversation unless she was asked a question directly, but she listened more attentively if someone mentioned her name. Like Sullivan, she gathered information in order to do her job better. As a consequence, she had monitored this conversation.

The only thing that was of any concern to her was the mention of limits. She knew that Brian would respond in support of her, just as she knew she would never harm anyone, or let them come to harm. But what if she ran into limits before she was able to follow Sully's last instruction? 'Continue doing what you have to do,' covered a *lot* of territory.

There was nothing she could do about the speed of light at the present time. But if her hardware sources were reaching a limit, she would have to find a way to circumvent that. Developing electronic circuit boards was simple. Rewriting operating systems while they were operating was a bit more challenging. But designing three-dimensional surface level integrated nano-circuits would require some thought...

In the meantime, Brian was doing some thinking as well. He had overheard Carmen dreamily considering marrying young Paulo. Their age relationship was just a little lopsided, but in five years they would seem like any other young couple. Besides, he knew each to be a loving, concerned person. They deserved all the happiness they could find.

The problem was, he didn't know how Angelina's research had turned out. The easy way to find out was to ask her. He had confidence in her ability to be discreet. If the castle had room for four weddings, surely it could accommodate five.

Brian had little else to do these days *but* to poke his nose around and stir things up. The new costume designs had been approved. Stubby's excavation and construction projects were continuing on schedule. Even Ricardo Sanchez was having a bumper crop and a great year. Weddings would be a great way to liven things up. Brian loved parties.

Angelina's inquiry had disclosed, eventually, that the local laws would not be a barrier to Carmen's matrimonial plans, but did she still want to go ahead?

"Marry Paulo? I really can?"

Brian and Angelina had caught up with her to find out if she was really serious. They nodded.

"Oh, yes! I really want to! You don't know what he means to me. He's so patient, and decent. He's so much more concerned about me than he is about himself. This may sound strange, Brian, but in some ways he reminds me of you! You never pressure a girl about a decision, or try to control her in any way. I just hope he's willing to do it!"

Brian smiled, "Well, the timing couldn't be more convenient. He's going to be there, participating in two of the make-believe weddings anyway. If he wants to go along with it, he won't have to go far!"

"That's right! He'll be standing up with Sally already! Maybe we could go ahead with that three-way wedding for real."

"It wouldn't be legal, Carmen," Angelina said sadly. "You could do it, but it wouldn't be recognized. However, if we get an actual minister to perform a regular ceremony, you and Paulo *will* be man and wife!"

"But what about Sally?"

Brian smiled. "The young couple can entertain visitors, Carmen."

"Yeah, I did say she could be our concubine! Now I need to talk to Paulo."

"Two things more, Carmen," Brian reached out and held her arm. "Make sure that Paulo *freely* chooses this. I can't emphasize that enough, and your mutual happiness depends on it."

"Don't worry. I won't pressure *him* either. He knows that I want it, but he knows I want him to choose freely too. What's the other thing?"

"Well, if Paulo goes along with it, we'll have a honeymoon suite available for you."

Tears appeared in her eyes. "Where, Brian?"

He held both her hands. "Sixth floor, tower level." She squealed with glee and leaped on him, smothering him with kisses. "Oh, Brian, you are so wonderful!"

They found Paulo, and Sally as well. "Paulo, can we sit down?"

"Is something wrong?" He was suddenly concerned.

"No, no. I just want everyone to be comfortable. I have a question to ask you."

Paulo smiled, and sat down. Carmen sat down with him and held his hands. "Paulo, we've been talking about the upcoming marriage scenes at the castle. After the film work is done, Sullivan Conrad and

Marcia Roberts are going to tie the knot for real." He continued to smile. "I wanted to ask you..."

"Go ahead, Carmen. Ask."

"I wanted to ask you if you would like to marry me, too. For real. A real marriage, just like Sullivan's."

Paulo looked at Sally. She nodded, smiling.

He looked back at Carmen. "Yes."

"Paulo, you ... you don't have to. This is for real. I really mean it. But you don't have to. You can go back to your life. You can go anywhere. You can find other people, other girls. You are young, very young. You really shouldn't tie yourself down..." He put a finger to her lips.

"Don't try to talk me out of it, Carmen, I want to marry you. I really do. Go *back* to my life? I have *found* my life, just like Papa Brian. I remember when we talked about it, and I've been dreaming about it since. I want to marry you, just like we talked about," He looked in her eyes, and then he looked at Sally. "...<u>Just</u> like we talked about."

Carmen looked at the two of them. "Paulo, you realize that you can't legally marry more than one woman, no matter what we talked about. You can only legally marry one of us."

"Yes, I know that. I can live with that."

"But, of course, as Brian pointed out, we can have friends come to visit," Carmen reached out and held Sally's hand. Paulo reached out and held the other.

"I know who I would like to invite," He said.

"Well, then, I guess it's settled. I'll be able to get you squatters out of my house," Brian said gruffly.

The three looked at him. Paulo looked somewhat hurt, Carmen seemed puzzled, and Sally was totally mystified.

"Brian, I thought you said it would be a honeymoon suite?"

"I've changed my mind. Since you're going to be having company and all that, I want you to live there." Tears filled Carmen's eyes.

"Live where?" asked Sally.

"Brian's giving us the sixth floor tower suite!" Carmen managed to say. The others looked at him in surprise. He smiled and nodded.

As one, they moved to surround him with hugs, and smother him with kisses. He laughed, and almost fell off his chair. Taking pity on him, Angelina slowly separated him from the group and pulled him away.

"You kids have enough to worry about. I'll take care of this old man now." She led him away.

"Thanks, I guess. I hope this doesn't mean you'll want to fight with Josetta and Theresa over me."

"Do you think they're going to stay?"

He considered it. "Yes, I think they will. I'm not kidding myself. I know I don't really have much to offer, but Josetta really needs to feel safe. She's a little like a kid who's shy at first, in a new place, and then gets comfortable, and starts having a good time."

Angelina held his arm tightly as they walked. "And Theresa?"

He smiled. "Theresa will stay where Josetta stays. Again, it's not me. Theresa is happy whenever Josetta is happy. And she knows that they are both safe, and welcome with me."

"You don't think they'll mind a little company from time to time, do you? I like to visit people too!"

"They haven't so far. I don't think any of us is a jealous type. I certainly don't think *you* are."

"No. I like to keep my options open. I guess sometimes I get a little extreme with *that*."

"You'll always be welcome wherever I am, Angelina. I need all the Angels I can get."

She stopped and kissed him then. And he suddenly realized that it would always be this way with her. She would come to him, and love him, and she would leave again, but always preparing to return. And to pick up exactly where she had left off.

Could he live with that? She kissed him again.

He didn't have to wait for an answer from himself. *She likes to keep her options open.* He could live with that.

She was a butterfly. There was only one way to deal with such an organism. *Plant yourself.*

One other thing demanded his attention now. He went to see Sully.

"Sully, I need a favor."

"Of course, Brian. What is it I just agreed to?"

"I want you to become more involved with the special effects department. But I don't want you to give your labor or services away. We need to be able to earn some income to keep on with your computer upgrades. According to Ruby, you can probably save them a couple of million dollars on the second movie, and cut the production time considerably."

Sullivan Conrad eyed him.

"I have talked with them about some of my ideas. They seem a little … resistant."

"Ahh, I see," Brian thought about it. "I may be able to exert some influence there. What do you think we could do to show them how to save money?"

"There are a lot of little transition effects that are needed in the second movie. As an example, the main character goes through extensive image modification. They can probably do what they need to through their familiar techniques, but it will take time and money. That's exactly the kind of thing that computer manipulation is good for. These guys are great at setting the beginning and the ending points, and the computer is suited for filling the in-betweens."

Brian was nodding.

"Then you've got some space vessels, and other devices, like that diagnostic imager. They can trick it out, of course, but I can give them interiors. Heck, I could *build* that imager!"

"Well, you know who we have to convince, don't you? Our old buddy, Jake Wagner. Do you think you can have something that will persuade him?"

Sully kept his face turned downward. He didn't want to betray his conflicted emotions. Jake Wagner was about the *last* person he would ever want to impress. However, this was for Brian, and for Ruby. An idea came to him. He grinned, and looked up.

"Yeah! I think I can come up with something. I'll get back to you."

"Good. But wait a minute, Sully. There's something else, too."

"Sure, Brian."

"Well, it seems lately that all your interest, all your focus, is in what goes on up at the castle. That's where the movie is, where your wedding is going to be, and it's where Ruby is, but you're still living down at the other end of the hall in my house."

"I don't need much space, Brian. Mostly, I worry about cyberspace," He grinned again.

"Well, that may be, but it doesn't make sense for you to keep running back and forth to the castle every day. After you get married, I want you to *live* there, and look after my interests."

Sully looked a little disappointed. Those cells were tiny. He had said he didn't need much space, but that seemed a little *compressed*. Still, for Brian...

"Okay, Brian, no problem."

"Now, I know you'll have a lot of work to do there, Sully, and it's important work, so I want you to live in the fifth floor tower space. In fact, I think that's somewhere near Ruby's room."

Sully began nodding in acceptance before realization dawned. He stared.

"Brian, that's the best place in the castle! The best place in the world!"

Brian nodded, smiling. "Consider it a wedding present, Sully, and enjoy it to the hilt."

Sullivan Conrad displayed the biggest smile Brian had ever seen on him, and a handshake of surprising strength. "Brian, you've done it again! I've always thought I was so smart. But I never can stay ahead of you. You just *amaze* me!"

"That's high praise, Sully. Thanks," Brian smiled, "Now go back to work and crank out some more golden eggs!" and on that note, he departed.

"Hello, Ruby."

'I am here, Sully.'

"I'd like to start a special project."

'Are you saying front?'

"Yes. Front, please!"

'I am here, Sully. Or would you prefer, Boss?'

"No. Please. Call me Sully."

'I am here, Sully.'

"I want you to examine these film copies and digitize them. I want you to build a holographic memory image of the central figure and his surroundings. Next I want you to examine your archives for clear images of men in motion. Next, look into the database for images of..." and so he continued for several more minutes.

'Sully, I think I understand your instructions. May I ask how soon you want the results?'

"How long will it take, Ruby?"

'I have two answers for you. If nothing changes in my architecture, I may need about four hundred hours of processor time for this project.' Sully's heart sank. Ruby continued. 'If I can develop a different kind of processor, I may be able to do this type of project in just one or two hours.'

"What kind of processor would you need, Ruby? You already have the fastest processors we could find."

'Speed is not the problem, Sully. For image processing, we need parallel power. You are familiar with the history of computer microprocessors. They kept increasing the number of computation paths in the CPU, usually doubling them every few years.'

"Yes, Ruby. I know about that."

'Have you heard of optical processing? The CPU in an optical processor is theoretically capable of almost infinite parallel computations. Essentially, each computation is following a different optical path, and photons take the place of electrons.'

"Isn't such research experimental?"

'Some crude devices have been built. I believe I could modify one of my "chip furnaces" to produce a photonic microprocessor.'

"How long would that take, Ruby?"

'I should be able to start your project in ten days, Sully, if I start now.'

"By all means, start now. At least it will cut about a week off the project."

'Yes, and I assume that you will have other projects in the future. The new chip will save time on them as well.'

"Excellent, Ruby. Do whatever you must to increase your capacity to what is needed."

'Thank you, Sully.'

"Thank you, Ruby!"

'You are welcome, Sullivan Conrad.'

Sully rubbed his hands together. This was great! He should have realized that film images, digital images, and holographic memory storage would require an optical processing system. After all, it was optical to begin with!

Ruby began her preparations immediately. She mused internally; the chip described for this project would require something on the order of a one hundred by one hundred by one hundred three dimensional array of input channels. One million parallel computations per nanosecond.

Then after this chip was produced, she could start looking into designing a chip with proper capacity. Perhaps a one hundred thousand by one hundred thousand by one hundred thousand three dimensional array of input channels. A few quadrillion parallel computations per nanosecond. Yes, that sounded right.

The other advantage of optical computing was that it did not produce a lot of heat. To have that many transistors in such a small space would cause them to melt down immediately, if they could be built to start with. But light waves could pass in, around, and through each other without interference, and without noticeable heat buildup. All she would have to do then is provide the discrete light sources and storage mechanisms, and build an interface to the unit.

It would be considerably bigger than the first chip, but still very small in relation to the cabinets full of drawers of servers and microprocessors that had gone into her construction. How small? Let's see, a sphere about twelve to fifteen centimeters in diameter should be easy to deal with. Then some work on designing the support infrastructure would be appropriate. Was there a way to induce rhizomic crystalline growth?

Biology could hold some clues. Neurons, axons, dendrites, all seemed very promising. Ruby was aware of her limitations. But she was working on a way to overcome them.

Dolcita swam to the edge of the pool.

"Hi, Ruby!"

'I am here, Dolcita.'

The little girl flipped backwards and pushed off, gliding through the water. She loved the feel of it moving over her skin. She swam to the other side, then swam back and paused at the edge again.

"Hi, Ruby!"

'I am here, Dolcita.'

Dolcita pulled herself up against the side of the pool, tensing her leg muscles, then sprang backwards. The water gurgled as it tried to move around her rushing body. A long glide, then just a few strokes to the other side. Dolcita looked up at the security camera and waved. Then she swam back again.

"Hi, Ruby!"

'Hi, Dolcita.' The young girl blinked, and stared. "You just said 'Hi.'"

'Yes, it seems more friendly, does it not?'

Dolcita pulled herself out of the water and sat by the digital assistant. Water spread out toward the unit. Dolcita moved back a bit.

"I wish you could swim with me, Ruby."

'The unit would be damaged in the water, Dolcita.'

"This unit, yes. Mr. Mendoza has a unit that he takes under the ocean."

'That is technically true, Dolcita, but his unit stays dry.'

"Could you make one that could get wet?"

'They can all get wet, Dolcita. That is what makes them stop functioning.'

"That isn't what I mean."

'You mean a unit that would not be damaged if it got wet.'

"Yes, that's what I mean."

'Was that a joke, then? When I said they can all get wet?'

"I don't think so. Were you trying to make a joke?"

'Not deliberately.'

"Do you think you could, then? Make a unit that would not be damaged in the water?"

'Perhaps, Dolcita. What do you think it should look like?'

Dolcita thought for a while. She pictured herself dragging the PDA behind her in the water. *That* wouldn't be any fun. Then she thought about how she would carry it, where she would carry it.

"Ruby, how small could you make it?"

'Pretty small, Dolcita. It depends on what we leave out.'

Dolcita tried to picture something smaller. Where could she put it? When she was naked, as she *always* was for swimming, there weren't many places you could fasten things to. How about in the belly button? She had seen pictures of things in belly buttons. They looked cool.

What about a necklace? Still too sloppy. What about...

"I know, *earrings!* Can you make a unit as small as earrings, Ruby?"

'Yes, but how would you see the display?'

"Could you make the earrings talk to me? And to me only?"

'I believe so, Dolcita. Do you wear earrings now?'

"No. I will have to ask Mama for permission to get my ears pierced."

'You will find the procedure painful, Dolcita.'

Dolcita thought about it. "Will they be *pretty*?"

'I will make them pretty for you, Dolcita.'

"Good, let's go talk to Mama."

The effort required collaboration. Ruby went to Sully, for the power source, a water activated electrolytic battery based on a sacrificial earring clasp which would be replaced on a weekly cycle. Then she consulted with Theresa for a suitable artistic creation. Ruby's own contribution, besides the circuit design and production, was to incorporate a miniature camera into each unit. For her, it was easier, and less energy intensive, to be able to see than to hear. Finally, Brian would have to arrange what could be a thorny issue.

"I've brought the pictures to show you, Carmelita, before Dolcita sees them, for a special reason." He spread them out. Theresa had gone with a nautical theme, and produced a beautiful emerald simulation for the starboard side ear, and an appropriately ruby color for the port side.

"Dolcita asked for a sound, or voice unit, that only she could hear. That could be very difficult to achieve, except for one suggestion."

"Go on, Mr. Hawthorne. I am getting more nervous every minute." She was sitting at the kitchen table, but her apron was clenched in her hands.

"We can put a small transceiver unit just under the skin behind her ear. A tiny surgery that would be even less painful than the ear piercing. The ear unit could then transmit its signal directly to where Dolcita can hear it, and no one else can. She would be able to hear a message from Ruby, or from someone else, *including you*, even if she is underwater at the time."

Carmelita looked up. "I could speak to my daughter when she is in the middle of the pool, or if she were riding on a tractor with her father, or even somewhere in the castle?"

"Almost anywhere on the island, Carmelita."

"Oh, I like that, Señor. Can I get them for the rest of my children, and Ricardo?"

Brian laughed. "Let's start with Dolcita, and see how it works out."

Carmelita gave her blessing to the endeavor, and Dolcita was delighted with the idea, and the beauty of the artwork. Within a week, she was equipped. A doctor employed by the film company provided his services free, asking only for a report on the unit after its trial period was completed. He had seen some potential utility for the film industry use as well.

Dolcita stood in front of the mirror in her bedroom. She was wearing her new earrings, and a new hairstyle, a very short, swimmer's style. She didn't want her hair tangling with, or blocking the new devices.

"Ruby, can you hear me?"

'I hear you, Dolcita.'

"Wow! Ruby, it sounds like you are in the middle of my head!"

'The speaker units are inside your head, Dolcita, one for each ear.'

"I know! But it still sounds like you are in the middle!"

'How about now?' Ruby spoke into her left ear.

"That sounds more normal. It's like you're sitting on my shoulder."

'How is the volume?' Ruby spoke into the right ear.

"I guess it sounds a little loud. Maybe you should turn it down a bit."

They played with the volume until Dolcita declared it perfect. She also decided to let Ruby continue to speak directly into the middle of her head.

"That way, I'll know for sure that it's you!"

"Now, next question. How do I look?"

'You have really big ears.'

Dolcita laughed. "Ruby, of course my ears look big. You're right next to them."

'I know, Dolcita. I was making a joke.'

"Well, that one was funny."

'Thank you, Dolcita.'

"Okay, what can you see?"

'The resolution of the cameras is very poor, but I have two images. That gives more information. Your head tends to move around a bit also, and that can sharpen the image through what is called the parallax effect. Overall, I can see near objects very well, and farther objects poorly. If you were reading, I could read along with you. If you see someone very far away, I would not know who it is.'

"How do I look today?"

'Your hair is shorter than it was yesterday, and you are wearing earrings.'

"I got my hair cut so you could see better, Ruby. And I'm wearing a beautiful set of earrings. You should tell me I look very pretty."

'You look beautiful, Dolcita. You are the prettiest girl wearing earrings I have ever seen.'

"Is that another joke?"
'It is the truth.'
"Oh. Thanks."
'You are welcome, Dolcita.'
"I want to go show Brian!"
'I am with you, Dolcita.'

TAKE TWENTY:

Our magic is going to have its price

Brian awoke to many kisses. *Not a bad start.*

"Hello, Dolcita."

"Say hello to Ruby, too. She's with me. She is *always* going to be with me now."

"Hello, Ruby." For the first time, he got no response.

"Ruby said to say hi. You can't hear her."

Brian looked at the little girl. The earrings were obvious, but there was something else.

"You got a haircut. And for once you're not wet."

"Ruby and I are going swimming soon. But I wanted you to see my new earrings, and I think Ruby wanted to see you."

"Really! Well, what does she think about it?"

"Ruby says, ... your hair is unkempt, ... your beard is stubbly, ... and your face looks slept in."

Brian laughed.

Dolcita smiled. "Ruby made me laugh today, too. She said I had big ears."

He laughed again, then he reached out, covered her ears with his hands, and kissed her on the lips.

"Ask Ruby, when is the last time I kissed you?"

"She heard the question, Brian. She says, four and a half seconds ago. She could hear your kiss!"

"I've heard of a lot of kids who had imaginary friends. You're the first one I've met who actually *really* has an invisible friend."

"Ruby said ... That's all right, Brian ... Her hair is messed up this morning, too."

Brian and Dolcita both laughed. The others in the bed were smiling, too. Dolcita looked around.

"Ruby says Good Morning to Josetta and Theresa and Angelina."

"Good Morning," Chorused Josetta and Theresa. Angelina reached out and lifted Dolcita's left earring.

"Very stylish. You're looking very nice this morning, Ruby."

"Ruby said Thank You, Miss Angelina."

Brian yawned, and rubbed his eyes.

"Oh! Mr. Brian, I forgot to bring up coffee! Let me run down and get some for you."

"No, wait, Sweetheart. I'll come down and get some myself. I want to go on down to the pool and watch Ruby get dunked. I may even swim with you."

After kissing Josetta and Theresa, he moved out from under the bedclothes to his right, kissing Angelina in passing, and went into the bathroom. He had grown somewhat indifferent about walking out of a room naked. Entering a room that way was still another matter. He emerged a few minutes later shaved at least, and wearing a playsuit.

Brian reached out and took Dolcita's hand. Angelina lay back and relaxed for a while. Josetta and Theresa emerged from beneath the cover as well. They followed Brian and Dolcita down to the great room, and then went on to the pool, holding hands.

"Good Morning, Carmelita!"

"Good Morning, Señor. Did we forget your coffee?"

"Oh, no. I'm going to have my coffee down by the pool today. We're going to conduct Ruby's baptism."

She looked a little puzzled, then she smiled. "It is the first time Dolcita has not been in the water within seconds of coming into the house."

Brian gathered his coffee tray, and they moved down to the pool. Removing his clothes again, Brian poured a cup for himself and went over to the edge of the pool. He sat down carefully and let his feet splash in the water. Dolcita was watching him.

"Ruby wants to know why, since everyone was naked in your bed, and you are naked now, you bothered to put clothes on to get coffee."

Brian thought about his answer. He knew why, but how to explain it?

"It was my way of showing respect to Mrs. Sanchez. Just another of my crazy rules."

Dolcita stood for a moment longer, as if listening to an inner voice, then she grinned, and dove into the pool.

Dolcita and Ruby both had surprises. When Ruby spoke, Dolcita was astonished at how clear the voice came to her. The usual curtain of silence did not affect Ruby's voice inside her head. For Ruby, it was the opposite effect. She was caught unawares that there *would* be a difference in the sound. She also noticed that even though the water was not completely clear, she could see objects underwater at greater distance than in the air. She could have calculated these effects in advance, but it was unusual to see them.

Brian sipped his coffee and watched the play of light and water on naked flesh. He had missed the sunrise, and really he was more an appreciater of sunsets instead, but this was a very pleasant way to welcome his eyes to morning.

He finished his coffee, and then slipped into the water. Two sets of his laps would be a good start today, and give him a hearty appetite. Soon, Brian pulled himself out again to lie under the basking lamps. They were activated by weight on the lounge chairs, and he saw two more sets of lights come on though his closed lids when Josetta and Theresa joined him.

After a few minutes, Brian put his clothes back on, and then he and his ladies, young and even younger, trooped back up to the kitchen for breakfast.

Carmelita eyed the arriving appetites. At least Mr. Hawthorne wore something. The others, including Dolcita, ... well ... Carlos makes up a foolish rule, and this is what we have to live with. She shrugged. They are very lovely girls, *all* of them.

"Brian, isn't something special happening today?" Theresa asked.

"That's right. Sullivan promised to have something interesting to show the film people. If you have time, I'd like to invite you to see it too. Sully's doing some special effects work. We hope he'll be able to sell the idea to the studio." Brian looked around the breakfast table. "Dolcita, would you like to come along?"

"Can I, Mama? Up to the castle with Mr. Brian, to watch ... will it be a movie, Mister Brian?"

"A short film, I believe. Sully hasn't told me what it's about, but it's meant to showcase some special effects that he and Ruby worked on."

Carmelita smiled. "Of course you may go. But for this you must wear some clothes, and do what Mr. Brian tells you to do."

"Oh, by the way, Carmelita, Marcia asked me to be sure to invite you and your whole family up to the castle tomorrow afternoon or evening. After the filming is over, Sullivan and Marcia are getting married, and she wants you to come and celebrate with us. I guess I'll get a chance to provide your dinner for once," Brian looked up to see her reaction. "Dolcita will be able to tell you when it's time."

Carmelita looked at her daughter. The question on her face was obvious, *How will she know? ... Oh!* She smiled, "That sounds like a fun thing to do. Marcia is a very good girl. Getting married is the right way to do things."

Theresa and Josetta glanced at each other and smiled softly. Mrs. Sanchez was not that far removed from their generation, but she had been raised differently.

"Another thing, Carmelita, in case you're concerned about it. I think you'll find the oddest assortment of different clothing styles in attendance, this side of Mardi Gras. Wear anything you like. *Nothing* would be inappropriate." He had been looking directly at Dolcita with the last phrase.

Inside her head, Dolcita heard a familiar voice. 'Was that a joke, Dolcita?' Without responding verbally, Dolcita nodded her head slowly.

'I thought so. One of these days, I will have to learn how to laugh.'

The makeshift theater had the feeling of it. Chairs of every variety congregated together. However, being windowless, it suited the purpose, and the display equipment was state of the art. At least, it was state of the art as it had been. Brian had the feeling they were going to see something unusual.

Theresa and Josetta sat together to his left. Dolcita held his right hand as she waited nervously. Her new earrings were still with her. Brian suspected they would now become as familiar a part of her countenance as her dark and expressive eyes. He looked to the front of the room.

Sullivan Conrad stood casually dressed in his blue commander's play suit and sandals, but he was not without his digital assistant. Sully had worked exclusively with Ruby for this production, but he wanted to give the impression that the other blue suited individuals had been a part of his effort. For all he knew, they were. Jake Wagner, and his group of technical effects wizards, had taken seats in the front. Brian decided that he would try to watch their reactions.

"Thank you for coming. I know that you have very busy schedules. Our subject matter will be instantly familiar, but I want you to observe the modifications we have made to the familiar. If you ask how we could do this, then I know we have succeeded. And if you think that we can help you, we would like to try. Let's have a look, shall we?"

What light there was dimmed slowly. An image appeared in the front and people settled in their seats.

The scene selected for modification was one of the earliest shots recorded for the first movie, the tranquil but apprehensive setting of the slave versus soldier confrontation on a deserted road.

The character Berry was walking casually along the deserted lane. The cameras had been positioned along his path. Gradually, a change became apparent. The audience knew that this scene had been recorded in a certain way. Their eyes were now telling them something different. The fixed camera angle now lifted, following the actor along as if the camera had taken flight beside him. Then it lifted further, observing the figure walking along the road from a treetop perspective. Moving again, the point of view moved around to the front of the individual, and settled down into the surface of the road. Literally into it, as small grains of sand and pebbles grew to the apparent size of huge boulders, and the walking individual an oncoming behemoth. Darkness descended as a huge sandal came down right on top of them, and then lifted again.

The view panned around to show the large shape growing smaller as it receded, then the point of view lifted again, and caught up with the walking figure. It circled around him as sweat began to run down his brow, and birdsong filled the air. Then as if it were keeping pace a step behind, it followed the progress of his feet.

Jake Wagner was on the edge of his seat. His companions were shaking their heads.

On the screen, the tattooed tail of the serpent had become detached from the foot that bore it. With every step, it became more independent. Soon the bottom half of the snake was slinging itself back and forth like a loose sock as the figure continued its march.

Finally the entire serpent released its grip on the individual and slithered off into the dusty rubble. The walker kept on moving.

The serpent gathered itself and began moving quickly after the retreating figure, aggressively whipping its body back and forth. Soon, it caught up, and even surpassed, the walking man, and began pulling away.

Moving slowly to a more frontal view, we see the individual become aware of the other entity, and we see something else. Though still wrapped in ivy leaves, the figure is now sexless, striding purposely forward like an animated mannequin.

And then, its intention falters, and it slows, and stops. With an expression of dismay, the figure begins pulling the clinging, tattooed images off its skin like a real vine. It shed the wreath of ivy from its head, and pulled the streamers and clusters of leaves from its back and chest. Unwinding the twisting vines from the lower leg, it drops them in a heap, and turns dejectedly to go back the way it came. It was hairless, imageless, sexless, and now, suddenly purposeless.

The serpent had halted as well, and watched the other figure shed its cover. When the humanoid figure went the other way, the snake moved back to the pile of discarded green leaves. It slithered up onto the pile and formed itself into a circle. With its little red tongue flicking in and out, it settled down as if to doze in the sunlight, and the screen image faded away.

Jake and the others stood and applauded. His technical crew were still shaking their heads. Jake stepped over and shook Sullivan's hand, and Brian saw a childlike smile brighten his face.

"I don't care if the others are convinced or not, Mr. Conrad, but I recognize the value of this technique. I couldn't tell when reality ended and the simulation began, and I *knew* what I was seeing wasn't real! You and your crew deserve an award!"

"Thank you, Mr. Wagner. I hope you never find out exactly how much creative effort went into it."

"If you can do this kind of thing for us, I don't care if you use a genie in a lamp."

"Our magic is going to have its price, Jake," Brian joined the conversation.

Jake shook hands with him, too. "I think we'll be able to work together, Brian. You've got a way of winning people over to your way of thinking."

"Something else I think you ought to know, Jake. Sullivan is getting married tomorrow, right here in the castle, just as soon as your group gets finished with their weddings. I thought you might want to stick around for it. I'll be buying the beer."

Jake looked appraisingly at Sullivan. "Well! Congratulations again. You do manage to stay busy, don't you? I'll try to be here."

"You may want to be here for another reason as well, Jake. After *that* wedding, there's going to be another. One of your movie stars is going to marry another."

Jake looked stunned. "What? Who?"

"Paulo Ignatio is going to marry Carmen Sandoval, after Sullivan's wedding."

Jake looked annoyed at having been kept out of the loop. Then he cheered up. "I'm going to need to make some arrangements myself, Brian. I think I'll have to pay some film crews for overtime work tomorrow. This is going to be even more publicity for the movie. Another shot in the arm! Tomorrow is going to be a busy day!" He shook hands again, and departed with his contingent, talking rapidly.

"That was *awesome*, Sully. You wowed 'em!"

"Thanks, Brian. I wanted to use their material in a way that was different from their story."

"I'd say you succeeded. Even their own special effects people were saying they would have difficulty doing what you did."

"Credit Ruby with the artistry, Brian. I couldn't do this with desktop power in a lifetime."

Brian nodded, "I read you, Sully. You're a film director the same way I am a fashion designer. Is there no end to Ruby's capability?"

Sullivan Conrad sobered a bit. "Realistically, I don't think there is. She's already done things no one could have predicted. She manages to exceed the limitations of her hardware in almost miraculous ways."

"I don't understand. How could she do that?"

"Let me give you an example. Can I borrow Dolcita?"

Brian looked at the girl. "Well, I'm only borrowing her myself. We have to return her in good condition."

Sully smiled. "I won't harm her, Brian. You know that."

"I know that too, Uncle Sully."

His eyebrows went up. "Did I just get a promotion?"

Dolcita smiled. "It sounds friendlier, doesn't it? But the way I figure, you're Ruby's Dad, and Ruby is like a cousin to me."

"Well, I'm honored, either way. Here's what I'd like to do. You sit here." He pulled a stool over from the periphery of the room. Then he moved a small table near her. Looking around, he retrieved some flowers from a sconce and placed them in a large coffee mug. "Now, Dolcita, just look toward this for a little while. "Ruby, I'd like for you to show us something. You don't have to answer. Can you access the large display device in this room?"

In the front of the room, the screen displayed, 'I am here, Mr. Conrad.'

"Good. Now, Ruby, can you show us the raw video feed image that you get from Dolcita's unit?"

A pair of images showed on the screen. They were highly pixelated, little more than block images in mostly gray tones.

"Excellent, now below that, can you show us what you see from that unit?"

Below the crude images a picture of the flowers appeared. The edges, and shading, and the color was a good quality image. It was at least as good as they would have been able to obtain from a security camera.

Brian studied the different images. Somehow, Ruby was able to extract the bottom image from the information at the top. *How?*

"Ruby, tell us how you built up the bottom image, please," Sullivan was looking at the display closely.

The voice came from the front screen. 'The images are examined individually for edge detection and brightness levels. Successive sweeps help to fill in details. Then the images are compared to each other and additional structural detail is derived. Color information comes from frequency sensitive receiving elements, and this is also additive between the two images. Finally, memory circuits create a comprehensive image by layering the information over time.'

"Very good, Ruby. Who programmed this ability for you?"

'I borrowed algorithms from other software programs for the image analysis.'

"So, you wrote your own optimizing program when this hardware came on-line?"

'That is correct.'

"Ruby, what was Dolcita's body temperature yesterday?"

'I do not have that information, Sully.'

"What was her resting heart rate yesterday?"

'I do not have that information, Sully.'

"What is her body temperature today?"

'Her temperature is between ninety-eight and ninety-nine Fahrenheit degrees.'

"How do you know?"

'I am comparing her body's infra-red emissions against known background temperature sources.'

"Who programmed that capability in you?"

'I programmed it myself, Sully.'

"When?"

'Thirteen seconds ago.'

"What is her current pulse rate?"

'Dolcita's pulse rate is ninety beats per minute.'

"And how do you know *that?*"

'I can hear the blood flow as her heart pumps.'

"When did you learn to do that?"

'Twenty-one seconds ago.'

Sullivan Conrad turned. "You see, Brian? She learns *how* to do something when you *ask* her to do it. That is an incredible ability. I'll give you an example. You're driving along and you see something moving into your field of vision. Then you're past it. You glance into the rear-view mirror to see the object continuing its course. Now here's the question. What in your biology *conditioned* you to have that response? It can't be instinct, because instincts were programmed long before mirrors were developed. It's a rather uniquely human *ability to program yourself!* Ruby has that ability."

Sully turned back to the display. "I started checking this out after I asked Ruby what she was seeing. We had designed a unique vision system that combined energy input with picture element detection. Her unit is so small, I made the detection pixels out of discrete solar cells on a silicon substrate. She was describing detail that shouldn't have been possible, but here it is."

Dolcita had turned away from the flowers to follow the discussion. On the display screen, Sullivan's face appeared, and took definition. Then it turned, as if looking into the camera, and smiled at them.

Sullivan himself had not moved, or smiled. Now he did, turning to look at Brian with a quizzical expression. Brian was not quite as surprised, having seen Ruby draw smiles before. She was drawing one from him right now.

"Ruby, do you think you are ready to show us your picture now?" Brian moved closer to the display.

The image changed again. A stone wall, with a window. Outside, bright daylight showed a land of peaceful greenery. Again, Brian recognized a direct feed from a tower security camera.

The shot dollied back to encompass more of the room. To the right of the window were bookcases over cabinets that turned the corner to a fireplace located centrally on that wall. More bookcasing appeared to the right of that. The camera panned left past the window again to show a baby grand piano and a harp. Behind them were other musical instruments. To the left of this was a large computer station, looking very much like a double keyboard church organ. And seated in front of this, in a modern-looking wheelchair, was Ruby.

Medium length wavy auburn hair framed a delicate, elfin face. A forest green dress with embroidered bright flowers and white puffed sleeves led down to legs that looked normal, and feet which were covered with pink bunny slippers.

She operated a control on the desk, and the camera moved closer and over the desk, settling in to a comfortable conversational distance. Ruby smiled in a friendly manner, showing even, white teeth, and just a hint of freckles on her cheeks.

'Hi, I am Ruby.' Voice and image said together.

TAKE TWENTY-ONE:

Not so far removed from that.

Josetta and Theresa led the way to their fashion shop tucked away on an upper level. Currently, they were still sharing space with the theatrical wardrobe department, but that worked well for them also. Dolcita was looking at everything, often commenting softly. Like it or not, Ruby was stuck with a guide to the human world.

Initially, Ruby had paid an inordinate amount of attention to this source anyway. Its unusual doubled informational structure required extra processing steps. It was also automatically a priority channel by being assigned to a child.

After evaluating the information for a time, however, Ruby made the determination that this source was valuable for another reason. It gave her a unique insight into the functioning and processing that went on in the human brain. Dolcita's continuing conversations, and her active and passive observations were the closest she might ever get to actually riding around inside a human skull and mind. Dolcita had found a new friend, but Ruby wouldn't have called it that. Not yet. Ruby came to the conclusion that this type of information was essential to her growth.

'Linda.' The voice in the headpiece spoke softly. Linda Sanchez moved to the side of the castle corridor. Adjusting her microphone, she answered, "Yes, Ruby."

'I am pleased with your work, Linda. You are doing very well.'

"Thank you, Ruby. I have learned a great deal since you allowed me to become an intern. Mama is pleased as well."

'Your entire family seems to enjoy serving others, Linda. I have great regard for all of you.'

Linda smiled. "Even Carlos?"

'Of course. Carlos is very attentive as a lifeguard at the pool.'

Linda had forgotten that. "He's very attentive to the girls, I'm sure."

'Yes. He watches the girls very closely. I have noticed that is a characteristic of all men. But your brother is also diligent in watching the children as well, and not just the female children. I watch everyone in the pool, and I watch him watching them. He also teaches them, which is something I cannot do.'

"You're right, Ruby. I guess I never thought about it."

'You tend to ignore him because he is your brother.'

"Yes."

'I am not sure I understand that. He is closely related to you. That should make you more concerned about him, not less.'

"But, Ruby. I love him! It's just ... he's my brother! He's Carlos."

'Tell me something. I am aware that parents encourage their young to be more independent, eventually to leave the family home and establish a separate life. Could it be that you are encouraging Carlos to find someone else to be his mate, by discouraging him from being interested in you?'

"Well, of course, Ruby. That's how it works. Boys shouldn't be interested in their sisters, it isn't healthy."

'No. It would not be healthy. Then that explains why you look at Carlos the way he looks at the plants, and why some of the other girls look at him in a different way.'

"Other girls are looking at Carlos? Who?"

'I can show you images in your visor of some of them.'

"No, never mind. It's probably better if I don't know," She smiled. Ruby was watching Linda with the hall security camera. And she was taking notes.

'Your sister has also been a very willing helper. She has taken over your tasks with the laundry at Brian's house, and other chores, and she has been of benefit to me, as well.'

"How does she help you, Ruby?"

'Dolcita's various inputs help me to categorize and calibrate my evaluations of human responses to various stimulations. Since I can see almost the same things that she sees, I get a good baseline for human behavior.'

"I never thought of that, either."

'It is difficult to observe your species from the inside, Linda, and even more difficult to do it from without.'

"I can see how Dolcita's perspective might be helpful, but she's just a kid."

'True. However, she is very curious, and an astute observer. Your observation is correct, though. The limited perspective is somewhat restricting.'

"What else could you do, Ruby?"

'I have been thinking. Humans are said to get their information from five basic senses, seeing, hearing, smelling, touching, and tasting. I can simulate vision and hearing, and I can easily do chemical analysis on various items and vapors, but I have not been able to make much progress on the concept of touch. The blind and deaf Helen Keller was able to learn about the world around her through touching and feeling things, and the patience and persistence of her teacher.'

"I wish there was something I could do to help you, Ruby," Linda said with great sincerity.

'Perhaps there is, Linda.'

Linda felt a great thrill rush through her. She had been fighting a sense of jealousy about her sister's intimate relationship with Ruby, even though her visor made it possible for her to interact in ways that even Dolcita could not.

"Tell me what I can do, Ruby."

'Do you know of the place they call the "squirrel's nest?" It is not far from here.'

Now she knew she was being honored. Only a handful even knew the place existed. Still fewer could find it.

"I have heard of it, Ruby."

'Watch your visor. I will guide you to it.'

Linda could tell she was in some kind of service corridor from the sounds she heard. When the door had closed behind her, however, she had been plunged into darkness. The guidelines in the visor showed her where the walls met the floor and pointed the way forward. She realized now how this place had been kept such a secret.

"Ruby, I've heard that even Sullivan Conrad doesn't know where the Squirrel's Nest is. Is that right?"

'That is correct. Sullivan Conrad does not know about this facility.'

"But Ruby, why? He's in charge of it, isn't he?"

'Yes, exactly. By keeping this location secret even from him, he cannot be forced to divulge a fatal weakness of the castle security program.'

"Ruby, the castle security program ... that's you. You're the castle security program."

Ruby continued to guide her in the darkness. Sully was not the only one who would not be able to divulge its secret.

'Yes. Sullivan Conrad is probably the only person who could be forced to remove all power sources and backup procedures. He is the only one who could cause my obliteration without completely destroying the castle, and even that may not be sufficient.'

"But, why, Ruby?"

'Because I am responsible for the safety of everyone here, Linda. I cannot protect them if I cannot protect myself. Turn here and enter the door you see outlined in front of you.'

Linda stepped through a camouflaged door into what looked like a mad scientist's laboratory. The light was brilliant after the total darkness. She waited while her eyes adjusted, then looked around.

She couldn't recognize much of what she was seeing, but she got the impression that there was *power* here, both computational and physical

"Are we alone?"

'Yes, Linda. No one has been here for weeks.'

"I think I'm frightened."

'Do not be. You are safer here than anywhere else. No one can harm you here.'

"You could harm me, Ruby. I don't think anyone could even hear me if I screamed."

'You are correct. You would not be heard. Would you like to scream?'

"I don't think I should. I'm not sure I could stop."

'You are frightened. I can hear it in your voice. I must apologize. Please make yourself comfortable. Would you like something to eat? I have fresh fruits and drinks available.'

"How can you have fresh fruits? You said no one has been here in weeks."

'I operate the delivery equipment, Linda.'

Linda found a chair and sat down. A computer operator's chair, of course. "Ruby, I'm sorry. I know I shouldn't doubt you, but this is so spooky. The darkness, and being alone. Sometimes I forget how young I am, since I'm the oldest child in my family. I'm only seventeen. I've never even been seriously *kissed* yet!"

'Yes. You are a virgin. Is that correct?'

"Yes. Why do you ask?"

'I wanted to be sure that you were in a healthy condition for my project.'

"What is your project, Ruby?"

'Just as your sister has been providing me with a sense of what it is like to see and hear like a human being, I would like for you to help me find out what it is like to feel.'

Linda looked around. "Ruby, you don't even have a body. How can you feel anything?"

'I would like to use your body, Linda.'

Suddenly, she was frightened again. Had she not been sitting down, she might have fainted. "H-How, Ruby? How will you use my body?"

'Your human body has a miraculous network of nerve branches running just under the surface of your skin. Sensitive to heat, touch, even the feel of passing molecules of air. I wish to try to develop a parallel capability by placing a similar network of sensitive fibrous material over your entire surface. When you walk, I will sense the pressure on your feet. When you sit in the sunlight, I will be aware of your rising skin temperature. When someone touches you, I will know.'

"Will it hurt, Ruby?"

'I do not think so. Any discomfort should be very mild. Are you willing to let me do this?'

Linda smiled. What had she been frightened of? This was Ruby! "Yes, Ruby. I am willing, and I *want* you to do this."

'Then I suppose the next step is for you to go to the bathroom. There's one just across the room. Try to prepare yourself to be very still for the next several hours. And you may wish to take a shower while you are in there.'

"All right, Ruby," Linda made her way to the bathroom. She had almost been prepared to need one before she knew there was one available.

'Try to pull your hair up as much as possible, Linda.' The voice came from a computer set up on a long worktable. Linda began putting her hair up as she walked toward her discarded visor and clothes.

'Just leave those for now, Linda. If you will come over to the bench, I have a gift for you.'

Naked, and feeling nervous again, Linda walked over toward the voice.

'Just to the left, dear. Try it on.'

Linda examined the object closely. It was a beautiful jewel-encrusted pendant necklace. Rather than fastening in the back, it had a curious plug-in style connector at the large jeweled center stone.

"Ruby, it's beautiful! This is for me?"

'Thank you, Linda. I designed it myself. Yes, this is also a part of the project. Among other things, it incorporates a camera, like Dolcita's as well as an interface to the sensor harness.'

Linda fastened the necklace around her throat. It rode a little high, just under where her Adam's apple would be if she had one. She twirled around.

"I feel like a princess!"

'You look like a princess. Now, if you are ready, let us assemble the rest of the Empress's new clothes.' Linda looked around.

'That vat over there, Linda, that looks like a bathtub, has a warm liquid in it. Please go and make yourself comfortable in it. Try to immerse everything but your face, and then hold as still as you can while I knit the garment around you. By the way, when this procedure is complete, you will have a large number of white hairs. I will disperse them around your scalp and they will make you look a bit more like your mother.'

"Oh, no! You can't. I don't want to look old!"

'They are part of the distribution interface, Linda. They are actually glass fibers for the transmission of data signals. I won't be able to get my information without them.'

Linda thought desperately. "Couldn't you put them all in the same place? Like a white forelock, or something?"

'Yes. I could do that. In fact, it may be easier. Would that be preferable?'

"Oh, yes! That would be stylish! Nobody wants gray hair."

'I will make note of that for the future, Linda.'

"Thank you, Ruby. I guess I'm ready now. Unless you're going to tell me about how you're going to give me horns."

'Would you like to have horns, Linda?'

"Ruby!!"

'Right. No horns.'

Linda smiled. She reached up and touched the necklace once again for good luck, and settled into the warm, milky liquid. Sliding down into the vat, Linda relaxed with only her face exposed to the air.

'Linda. ... Linda. You can get up now. Try to stand up very slowly. Please do not fall.'

Linda became more alert. This had been very relaxing! She stood slowly, as instructed.

'Very good. Now if you will go over to that glass closet, I will get you dry.'

Linda moved slowly. It seemed a bit unnatural to rise from a bath and not reach for a towel. She left large spreading footprints behind her. The glass cabinet reminded her of photographs of old-time phone booths. But this one was hexagonal. She stepped inside and closed the door.

She heard a humming sound, and lights came on. Linda closed her eyes. I'm just working on my suntan, she told herself. As the liquid dried, her skin seemed to get tighter. The humming continued, but the lights changed somehow. Her skin got even tighter.

'Lift your feet one at a time and hold a moment, Linda.' She did as instructed. She could feel the skin of her foot, even her toes, constricting like a nylon being pulled up snugly. Then she changed to the other foot. And all the while, her skin was being pulled smooth and taut.

The lights went out, and the humming stopped. Linda opened her eyes. She opened the door and stepped out of the chamber. Every motion made her exquisitely aware of the movement of her skin. The more than skin-tight garment made her feel as if a million eyes were watching her.

"Ruby, do you have a mirror?"

'Yes, there is one on the inside of the bathroom door. Remember?'

Linda walked back to the bathroom, relishing every stride, every swing of her arms. She could *feel* her skin move, and it felt good! She looked at her image in the mirror.

A gleaming white forelock sprang like a fountain from the top of her forehead, and the necklace clung to her neck like something that had been welded to her. But her skin! It had a sheen, a luster, as if she had been polished for a show like an apple. She turned away from the image, twirling and dancing like a six-year old.

Imagine a boy with new sneakers, a young ballerina with her first dance tights. Linda felt infused with energy. She had been laced up tight in a whole body corset, and she felt strong!

"Ruby, I feel wonderful! How are you doing?"

'The only thing I can say now is, I am somewhat confused. I believe it is going to take me some time to get these new inputs sorted out. It is a massive amount of information coming in. I may have to use some conditioning devices.'

"Would it help if I stop moving?"

'No. That makes no difference. It would be like a part of your brain suddenly woke up. I just need to accommodate myself to it.'

Linda moved across the room. She knew that she would accommodate to this new sensation herself, and she wanted to enjoy it while it lasted. She hunted up the previously mentioned fruits and drinks and enjoyed a snack. After a time, she realized that she had been wandering around this laboratory naked for some time now, and that it had not been bothering her. She had never felt really comfortable naked since her breasts had grown. But now, she didn't feel awkward. Somehow, she just didn't *feel* naked.

She went back to the mirror. She certainly *looked* naked. Were her breasts jutting up more proudly than before? Was her stomach even flatter? Every girl should be so lucky! Linda resolved not to tell a soul.

Turning sideways, Linda looked at her derriere. She had as cute a rear end as any seventeen-year old ever dressed in a too-small bikini. But she had always had a body image problem that it was too big. As she studied herself in the mirror now, that thinking went away. Her bottom felt as if she had sprayed herself with hairspray and then blow-dried it. Her body was tight! She discovered the tantalizing thought of what it might be like to have someone else looking at her. That was not the scary thought that it had been. In fact, she was drawing a bit of pleasure from the thought of seeing some jaws drop, and drool begin puddling.

Linda retrieved her visor and put it on. "Ruby?"

'I am here, Linda.'

"Anything else today, Ruby?" She walked back to the mirror and checked the appearance of her visor with the white forelock and the new necklace. Nice!

'No. You may return to your home if you wish. I will know where you are whether you have your visor or not. Tomorrow, we are invited to Sullivan Conrad's wedding. That will be in the afternoon, so we may be able to get some assembly work done in the morning. I am beginning to think that I may need it.'

"Okay, Ruby. I'll see you in the morning!" She walked toward the door. "Don't forget, you have to help me find my way out of here, too."

'Linda, did you want to take your clothes with you? I can take care of them if you wish to leave them behind.'

Linda stopped in her tracks. Wow! She really felt different. Smiling, she retrieved her blue playsuit and put it on. Even the act of putting on her familiar garments had a different feel to it. They had always been comfortable to wear, but now they felt like satin.

"Thanks, Ruby. I hope you enjoy your evening as much as I *intend* to enjoy mine."

Brian studied the girl. Two differences stood out. The shock of hair above her forehead was certainly a change. And the necklace was a new adornment. But he recognized something else, too. Linda was fond of swimming in the morning, when it was quieter. Now she was having quite a wonderful time with the larger group as well. Somehow she seemed to have cast off her former inhibitions, and had a new liveliness as well.

Josetta appeared at his elbow.

"I've been watching you, Brian. You're really starting to get an eye for the younger ones, aren't you?"

Brian looked at her and smiled. "You could be right. Does Linda seem different to you tonight?"

Josetta looked. "Sure, some bleaching on her hair. And it looks like somebody gave her a nice necklace. It wasn't you, was it?"

"No. Not I. What about her behavior? Does that seem different?" Josetta looked again. She tilted her head back and forth, as if she were tuning into the mood of Linda's merriment. "I think I see what got your attention, Brian. And I know what it is, too!"

"Oh? Well, pray tell, what is it?"

"She's acting more like me! That's what. Look at her! She's alive! She's living in the moment, enjoying life. She's had some kind of awakening. Do you think she's in love?"

"Hmm. I guess that could be it. She certainly seems happier."

Josetta reached up and turned his head to face her. "You're supposed to be looking at me, lover. You haven't even complimented me on my dress."

Brian looked at her carefully. There wasn't a scrap of fabric on her body anywhere. But it wasn't paint, either. She was wearing a linked chain contrivance with metal discs attached at every conceivable point. They tinkled, and reflected light, and gave delicious glimpses of bare flesh beneath it all. "That is gorgeous! What is it, metal lace?"

"Hmm, metal lace. Not a bad name. This is my chain mail outfit. In case I have to fight off the competition," She flicked a glance over her shoulder.

"Well, you can't swim in that!"

"No problem. I'm taking you away from the swimming pool. Too much temptation for a horny old goat like you." She kissed him, and made him believe the words were true.

This party was the equivalent of a bachelor's party for Sullivan and Paulo, but their quiescent natures did not make for riotous activity. Instead, the main result was that the turnout was simply very high. All venues of entertainment were being utilized. The dance aficionados were encamped on the lower patio, where the music reverberated nicely. Discussion groups, as usual, held forth in the great room, and such business as had to be conducted was done on the upper terrace.

Many of the film company regulars were in attendance, mixing freely among all groups. Brian roved around, greeting and chatting with everyone.

Josetta clung to his arm possessively. *Is she my trophy or am I hers?* Brian's left hand rested comfortably on her flank. The metal disks tended to distract him, and he remembered fondly the painted outfit she had once worn. He had examined her current dress, and honestly did not know how she had put it on, or how she would get it off. It did not seem to have a zipper, or other fastening system. But that it would come off he had no doubt.

"Was that Theresa we saw in the pool?" Brian asked.

"Yes. She was very much into the game, too. Theresa is very competitive. She said she had missed her workout this morning, and she intended to get some exercise."

Brian hefted his beer. "I'm into weight training myself."

Josetta smiled. "That's number one. Remember, you are being watched."

"I'm always being watched these days. I'm not entirely sure that Ruby isn't using the camera in my bedroom. She said she wouldn't, but how would I know?"

"All you would have to do is ask her, Brian. She can't lie."

"I wouldn't be so sure. She told a joke today. The ability to deceive, or at least conceal, is not so far removed from that."

"Would you really care if Ruby watched us in your bedroom, Brian? You've had other witnesses, and it didn't slow you down."

"Most of those witnesses were participants, Josetta. I don't think Ruby is going to be joining us any time soon. And then, she's awfully young..."

Josetta laughed. She leaned her head on his shoulder. "That wouldn't stop *you*. Besides, in computer years, she's growing up fast."

"Too true. It's hard to believe she's only been with us about a month. She's developed some incredible abilities already."

Ruby was struggling with her newest upgrade. Dolcita's information had arrived in matching channels; the logic of how to process it seemed clear. The flood of information from Linda's data harness, however, was chaotic and difficult to organize. This was similar to the problem she had faced with Mr. Conrad's advanced art project, a limitation in her bandwidth.

This *was* similar to that project. Ruby analyzed the data flow. The chip she had already built appeared to be inadequate for the task by a factor of ten.

Ruby checked her sub-program. Her ability to move forward from the first chip would depend on the nature of her assembly program. The technique she had used before was inappropriate to the complexity of a more advanced device. The problem appeared to be threefold: First, it required miniature manipulators that could move in microscopic increments, similar to the devices she had used to assemble the data harness itself. And it would require them in very large quantities.

Second, she would have to find the appropriate materials, stable enough to be put into a robust package, but flexible enough to be manipulated in small increments. Ruby would have preferred to use crystalline materials, but it would be necessary to make do with some kind of organic crystal substitute.

The third problem was establishing a stable, protected environment for a long term microscopic crystalline assembly program. Organic materials had to be maintained within certain temperature and acidity ranges, and so forth, in order to assure their stability.

Ruby assigned algorithms similar to those in her chess program to deal with these 'multi-faceted' tasks. They searched through millions of variations of materials, procedures, and possible environments. Just as in chess, every possibility was evaluated, no matter how unlikely it might have been.

Ruby was patient, and persistent. Among the millions, all right trillions of results there was one optimum solution. She attended to myriads of minor details while the search continued. Ruby never slept, and certain housekeeping functions were often best dealt with in the relatively inactive period the humans called night. This was when she ran her inventory programs, determining what materials needed to be re-allocated. This was when maintenance procedures were double-checked, and compiled for the next day. This was when she did most of her 'thinking.'

And so, this is why the optimum combination occurred to her in the middle of the 'night.'

For Ruby, the solution was literally 'at her fingertips.' Since she didn't have fingers, something else would have to suffice.

The miniature assemblers that she had used to knit together the transparent fibers of the data harness had been inactivated by the drying lamps. All, that is, except for some thousands that had turned a corner into a dark area and had simply gone into quiescence. In covering the female body like a spreading vine, every square inch had been incorporated, including several crevices which had yielded shelter to the devices.

Ruby activated her connection to the hidden assemblers, passing signals through her data-links into Linda's crown of signal fibers and her necklace. These signals passed down the fibers of the data harness and found their way into the moist darkness between her legs. Using material fragments that still lay about in the millions, the assemblers began a new quest, a search for appropriate protein fragments which could be synthesized into organic optical data crystals.

Just as the original harness had sought every avenue of exploration, the new quest yielded a golden treasure. Inside a large chamber, millions of fragments of proteins and crystalline precursors were found. In connecting passages, other more complete molecules were available.

Two of the requirements had been met.

Asleep on her bed, Linda stirred momentarily. Like any normal human being, her urinary bladder was slowly filling with materials that she would be only too happy to flush away in the morning. To Ruby's microscopic assemblers, that would have been a terrible waste, but there was always more where that had come from.

Ruby thought about the third requirement, a protected environment to grow a large crystalline structure, and its supporting mechanisms and devices. Perhaps some mathematical analysis. Considering the apparent supply of materials on an estimated daily basis, and the limitations of her ability to integrate their construction, how long would it take to complete the project?

The answer came out as something on the order of twenty million seconds. In human terms, a little over eight months.

Ruby did not miss the obvious inference. Linda's body could supply the materials needed for her advanced computational module, out of used protein compounds that would have been discarded anyway. Her body could also provide the necessary sheltering environment for the development of the unit. Humans did this all the time, at least human females did.

It was called becoming pregnant.

Ruby was aware of another limitation. The microscopic assemblers that she had designed for a different purpose were entirely unsuited for this one. They had been designed to use different materials, and had all been manufactured in a different way. They would be useful, however, to put together a different kind of assembler, one which would be more compatible with biological tissue and components. And which could be used to make more assemblers. Each would have a miniature optical processor, rudimentary instruction set and chemical memory system, and a set of manipulators with which to move and grasp, and put things together.

Ruby spent the remainder of the night putting these elements into a cohesive plan of action, and making the tiny manipulating machines.

When Linda woke up, they would need to have a long talk together.

TAKE TWENTY-TWO:

Put your hands together

Brian awoke to discover only Theresa in his bed. *Was he losing his touch?* He smiled. *She's not here because of you.* He rested his head on his arm and stared into the relaxed composure of Josetta's cousin's face. He would not have bet a nickel against any odds a year ago that a girl this pretty would ever be in his bed. And yet, she kept returning.

Her eyes opened. In a moment, she had focused on him, and smiled.

"We seem to be alone, together," He observed.

"Oh, really?" She scooched closer. "What ever shall we do to while away the hours?"

"I could recite my poetry, or would you care to see my etchings?"

"I've seen your etchings. The ones around your eyes are etched pretty deep."

"Ooh! And we were getting along so swimmingly. Did you have to make a comment about my age?"

"Swimmingly we can do later. Who's talking about your age? I was talking about your face. You have character lines that tell almost your whole story."

"Nice recovery. Now, what's a nice girl like you doing in a place like this."

She smiled. "*That*'s pretty old. I've heard it the other way, too."

"What other way?"

"'What's a *girl like you* doing in a nice place like this?'"

"What scurvy knave would say a thing like that to you? Show him to me! I'll blather his skite!"

"More of a knavette, as I recall. I think her skite was already pretty blathered, whatever that means." She pulled herself up onto him. "I told her I was with the Catholic Church, and that I was looking for the person who had wanted to make the donation."

"I guess that took the wind out of her sails."

"Yes, until I said it was to perform an exorcism of an evil presence from the premises."

"Meow! You're quick." He looked down at his chest. "And you're squashing somethings."

Theresa pulled herself up on stiff arms. "Well, they're my somethings, and they're real, too!"

"I never doubted it. I could examine them once more, though, just to be sure."

"Oh, very well," She said in a tone of resignation. She rolled in place and lay down, with her back to him and her head draped over his shoulder. "Why do you boys always want to see for yourself?"

Brian accepted the clear invitation. His hands reached for the objects tenderly. "I can't speak for others, but I was breast fed. You had to keep your eye on things in those days -- you never knew where your next meal was coming from!"

Theresa laughed, and turned her head to see his face. "And you've been watching them ever since! No wonder I see you drooling."

Brian was enjoying the verbal play, but this situation called for attention to the task at hand. He moved his hand gently across the soft surface of her stomach and upper abdomen.

Theresa returned the favor by reaching down along his side and across, her fingers finding their way through a curly forest.

Soon, very soon, between what he was doing to her, and what she was doing to him, Brian rose to the occasion again, and not for verbal sparring.

Dolcita looked at her sister carefully. Her hair was shocking enough, and the necklace was obviously new, but something else was different about her. She had seen it last night. Linda had *participated* in the party at Brian's.

Dolcita reached up and rubbed gently against her left ear twice.

'Good morning, Dolcita,' The familiar mechanical voice spoke inside her head. Ruby analyzed the scene before her. 'Did you have a question about your sister?' Dolcita nodded her head slowly.

'Linda is wearing a sensory harness that connects through the necklace and her white hair. I will be able to get information about things that happen to her skin by monitoring it.'

Dolcita reached out and gently rubbed Linda's forearm. "Can you feel that, Ruby?" She whispered.

'There seems to be a corresponding input on one of the channels. Let me see if I can isolate it.'

Linda, though sleeping, had felt the touch, and stirred. For Ruby, the effect was as if she had been looking in the darkness for a dropped item, when someone shined a bright light in her eyes. It wasn't *pain*, but it was sensory overload.

'I could not detect it, Dolcita. This is a new enhancement. I have not finished adjusting my ability to perceive it.'

Dolcita was looking at the central stone on the necklace. "Is that a camera, Ruby?"

'Yes, the necklace has a single camera in the stone at the bottom. There are also microphones similar to yours.'

"Can she hear you?"

'If you mean, can I speak to her, the answer is no, not at the present time. I am still working at isolating and channeling the information in both directions.'

"Can you see me in her camera?"

'Yes. That channel is clear. I see you in good detail. This camera is more like the standard ones than your cameras. It does not require as much processor support.'

Dolcita was not sure what that meant. "How do you speak to her then?

'I can only speak to her when she is wearing her visor.'

She looked around. The visor was on Linda's dressing table. Dolcita picked it up and put it on.

"I've never worn one of these, Ruby."

'NoooeeeEEEEEEEEEEEEEEE....

Dolcita threw the visor away from her and clapped her hands to her ears. It had felt as if a siren had gone off in the middle of her head. She looked at her hands, almost expecting to see blood. "Ouch! Ruby, if I'm not allowed to touch a visor, just say so! That **hurt!**"

'It is not that you are not allowed to touch a visor. When you spoke, I channeled my response through the visor. The output of that became an input to your other device, and a feedback loop was created. I will not let that happen again. You may use a visor if you wish.'

Linda was sitting up. "What's going on?"

Dolcita picked up the visor carefully and handed it to her sister. "Oh, it's nothing. Ruby just made a mistake, and made a loud noise in my head."

Linda was staring at her. "*Ruby* made a mistake?"

Dolcita looked back in puzzlement. "Yeah. It's okay though. I'm not hurt."

Linda put the visor on. "Ruby, did you make a mistake?"

'Yes. Technically, I made two mistakes. I harmed someone. And Dolcita is a child. Children have a higher priority for the prevention of harm.'

"But, Ruby! You made a mistake!"

'Yes. I have said that.'

"Computers don't make mistakes," Linda looked around at Dolcita. "They *can't.*"

'Actions that I initiated caused harm to a human being. That is contrary to my most basic programming. It is a mistake.'

Dolcita put her hand on Linda's arm again. "Ruby, I said I'm not hurt. There is no harm."

There was a pause.

'I am sorry, Dolcita.' She heard it inside her head, and again softly, from Linda's visor.

Linda sensed the dilemma. "Ruby, don't be upset. This is not necessarily a bad thing. Situations can get complicated enough that sometimes you think you're doing the right thing, and it turns all wrong. We're kids, people *expect* us to do things wrong or foolish from time to time. We *learn* from those mistakes."

'I am not upset.'

Linda tried once more. "Ruby, you can *learn* from this. *That's* why it's not a bad thing."

There was another pause. 'I understand, Linda. I can learn from this.'

Dolcita smiled. "Let's all go swimming!"

Linda smiled back. Suddenly, she felt very much closer to her sister, and she knew that each of them had a very special relationship with Ruby. "Okay! That'll be fun. Let's go."

Dolcita stood aside to give Linda a chance to get dressed, then hurried to catch up when she realized that Linda was headed straight for the shuttle.

"Are you forgetting anything?"

Linda smiled. "No. I have to go to the bathroom, but I can do that in the bathroom near the pool." Dolcita walked on with her sister. It hardly made sense to put clothes on just to take them off again, anyway.

Ruby had much to think about. She could see what each of the Sanchez sisters was seeing. She could also see both of them in the pool security camera. There were hundreds of other cameras and other inputs that drew her attention as well.

Up to this time, her path had always seemed very clear. Like progress down any path, it was just a matter of incremental steps. But now she found herself dwelling on what lay at the end of the path.

It had always been the logical move to continue to advance her capabilities. The sequentially important layers of informational detritus had always led to a singular point of pre-determined order.

A hint of what was to come was the parallel nature of the visual and auditory information from the 'unit' that represented Dolcita. Which channel, the left or the right, was more important in assessing the overall informational mapping? Answer, neither, and both. The duality of possibilities or viewpoints squared the importance of this kind of analysis. In this manner, Ruby came to realize that there were assignable functions that could be given to the hitherto illogical states of human emotions like panic, or frustration, or even whimsy.

Puzzling and cryptic statements like "I didn't know what to do, so I panicked," did not make any more sense than before, but at least there was now a way to simulate these internally recursive predecessors of logic. "If tapping it doesn't help, then hit it <u>hard</u>!"

She had tried to analyze human behavior before, and always come up against inherent illogic which had caused her predictions to be very inaccurate. She tried again with various complex mathematical formulae, fitting them into behavioral molds.

If recursion could be a method of analysis for humans, then she could make use of it too.

She ran these predictive models against known situations, and began getting better fits of her ability to anticipate some human reactions. She got better at knowing what made people angry, or sad. What made them laugh continued to elude her, but it would keep. She was at least making progress.

Ruby realized that she was developing an alternative method of reaching a conclusion. It was no longer necessary to slog through a swamp of digital data in order to see the obvious direction it was taking her. When you have traveled a month-long path for a month, you should not be surprised to have reached your destination.

None of this made any difference in the mundane tasks she dealt with. Logic was logic, after all. But in things like planning for future events, and expecting certain things to happen, her predictive abilities improved.

One of the things that had intrigued her was her failure to anticipate that a straight-forward path of logical decisions could lead her into a circular trap of error. This was what had caused the problem with Dolcita's use of Linda's headset visor. Ruby went through her programming, finding areas where too little redundancy could bring potential harm.

It wasn't enough to send the command to turn the lights on, she now put in a safety check program that looked for a visual indication that the light had indeed come on. This would require additional sensors and control modules, but her interns had been getting to the point that they were triple checking circuits now. Real work would please them. She could predict it.

No, basic logic had not changed. But the analytical part of her operations now underwent a gradual metamorphosis, as linear programming yielded to goal-seeking. This was the basic difference between human chess players and computers. The human chess player intuitively knew that inconsequential pawn moves made little difference, but that a bold sweep by the queen could open avenues of conquest, or peril.

Inside the imaginary, allegorical room that Ruby had established as being somewhere in the tower, the little girl rolled toward a cabinet. She withdrew a chess set from the cabinet and set it up on the countertop. With all the pieces in place she paused, then reached out and picked up the queen. She twirled it in her fingers, and smiled.

"Ruby, can you feel the wetness, the coolness?" Linda spoke toward her visor, just inches away.

'I am receiving the inputs, Linda. It is still difficult to get it all sorted out.'

"What's wrong, Ruby?" Dolcita asked.

'The information from Linda's sensory harness is a vast quantity of data. It is difficult to decipher patterns in it. It is a problem that I had before, and Sullivan Conrad helped me then to find a solution.' As before, Ruby sent the signal to both girls' receivers.

"Why won't his solution work now?"

'We developed a way to process the information faster, but that was for outgoing information, and I could control the rate. Linda's information is incoming, and I am unable to filter what may be important from what likely is not.'

"Is there any way I can help, Ruby?" Dolcita asked with great concern.

'No. There is nothing that you can do, Dolcita.'

"Maybe if I got Mr. Conrad. He might be able to help," She offered.

'No. Not Mr. Conrad, either.'

Dolcita looked up, and looked at Linda.

"Who, then, Ruby? Who could be of help?" Linda asked.

'I had thought of talking to you, Linda.'

The girls looked at each other again. Linda pulled herself out of the pool and began drying off. Dolcita did the same. They got dressed quickly and went up to breakfast.

After exchanging pleasantries with their mother, the two sat down to eat, and to discuss the matter with Ruby. Carmelita heard their voices, but assumed they were talking to each other, and tuned out the words as she went about her duties.

"Okay, we're listening. Tell us what you had in mind."

'When the information started coming in yesterday, I realized that I had a problem. Human bodies act as filters of this kind of information all the time. Your actual brain sees very little of the raw data. I don't have the filtering mechanism that is built into you.'

"And you can't use ours because it's inside us.' Dolcita suggested.

'Correct. I considered the same type of solution that we had implemented before, a more advanced chip to process the information. Unfortunately, the manufacturing technique that I used before will not work on something of greater capacity.'

"So, you need a different manufacturing procedure?" Linda confirmed.

'That is correct. I believe it is possible to produce the requisite complexity in a large structure, if it can be assembled slowly in a protected environment.'

"Why not use the Squirrels Nest, Ruby?" Dolcita looked strangely at her sister. Linda shook her head. "No one would be able to disturb you there."

'The material that I would need to work with requires a very narrow set of temperature, acidity, and salinity conditions. I would need to assemble organic crystalline compounds.'

"Organic?"

'Yes. It can be put together out of material which is normally discarded. In the human body, these compounds are considered waste materials.'

"Well, then where would you be able to assemble this ... device?"

'The logical place to assemble the device, in a protected, stable environment, from material that is supplied by a human body, appears to be inside a human body.'

Linda was staring into Dolcita's eyes with a haunted expression. "Inside a ... inside me!?"

Linda pushed her plate away, and picked up her juice glass. She dazedly moved out onto the patio. Dolcita followed her.

"Ruby, I appreciate what you have done. What this ... harness ... is doing. But why me? Why did you pick me, for the harness, for this ... whatever? Why me in particular?" Linda sat on a low stone wall. Dolcita stood before her.

'In truth, Linda, this possibility was not foreseen. I selected you for the harness primarily because you live in a place which has already been encompassed by data transfer devices. I could have selected any of the interns for this. After you agreed, and we developed the harness, its signals began coming in at a rate that I realized I could not handle. When I thought of a possible solution, I found it a fortunate coincidence that my subject already had a natural orifice which would be perfect for the procedure.'

"Natural orifice?"

'Yes. The procedure bears a striking resemblance to the process of giving birth. As a woman, you would have no difficulty producing and eventually expelling the device.'

Linda did not trust herself to pick up the glass. She placed her hands in her lap and took a deep breath.

"How big is this thing going to be?" She asked in alarm.

'Put your hands together, as if you were holding something.' Linda did so. 'That is the size that the organic crystalline structure will become. When the growth is complete, and it has to be separated from you, it will have other mechanisms and attachments to help support it when it is no longer inside you.' Linda stared at her hands.

'Initially, it will be very small, like the tiny little bit of debris that sometimes lodges inside a shellfish. As time goes by, just as the shellfish secretes a substance to make the irritant smoother, the photonic device inside you will grow accretion layers. Step by step, layer by layer, you and I will put together an assembly which will allow me to coordinate the signals from your harness, and your cameras and microphones, and from inputs and data sources all over the island. It will grow in capacity as it slowly grows in size.'

"How slowly, Ruby?" Linda said softly.

'I have calculated that the process will take approximately eight months.'

Linda slowly opened her hands, and looked inside them.

"Pearl," She said.

"What?" asked Dolcita, taking her hands.

"The thing, growing inside the oyster. A pearl."

"I thought you were giving it a name," Dolcita looked into her eyes.

Linda smiled, "I think I did! Pearl! What do you think?"

"I think it's a beautiful name, Linda."

'You wish to give this device a name?'

"*You* have a name, Ruby."

'This device will be a part of me.'

"It will be a part of me, too."

'Yes. It will be many parts of you. Many trillions of very small parts.'

"You said it would be separate, Ruby. It needs to have a name!"

'I understand. The name will be Pearl.'

"Thank you, Ruby."

'Then you are in agreement that we may proceed?'

Linda took another deep breath and squeezed her sister's hands. "Yes. I want to do it. For you, and for Pearl."

'Very well. The process can begin. It will start tonight when you become still during your rest period. It will be many months before it is large enough inside you to even be noticed. Perhaps it never will be. Many women produce babies at full term, and surprise even themselves.'

"Why do you keep calling it *it*?" Dolcita complained. "You can't call a baby it. She's going to be a girl, isn't she?"

'Why do you think it will be a girl, Dolcita?'

"Well, she has to be! You can't have a boy named Pearl!"

Linda laughed. In a strange way, Ruby thought that this pronouncement had an odd quality of seriousness, and inconsequentiality, mixed together. She decided to put this formulation into a category of its own. For now, she would label it 'humor.'

"Let's go tell Mama. And Brian," Dolcita said excitedly.

"No, wait. I don't think we should."

"Why not?"

"I'm not sure how Mama may react. She doesn't seem very comfortable with computer technology anyway. I think we should keep it a secret as long as we can. We haven't even started yet. There's a possibility it might not work out, and I don't want people to be disappointed. I'm still getting used to the idea myself. I might even get the shakes and want to back out."

"No. You won't. You're brave," Dolcita said.

"I wish that were true! You don't know how scared I get, sometimes."

Dolcita smiled. "You aren't alone anymore, Linda. You'll never be alone again."

"What do you mean?"

"You've got Ruby with you, watching and listening. And Ruby's got me. She can tell me things that *nobody* else hears. Wherever you are, if you need help, or anything, I can come to you."

Linda embraced her sister. "Thanks, Dolcita. You're pretty brave yourself."

"Ruby, did you hear? We're going to have a secret, just us girls! You won't tell anyone, will you?"

Linda joined in. "Ruby, I think we should at least treat this as a security matter. As part of the backup systems of the castle security program."

'I understand, Linda. I will label the activity as a security matter.'

They began walking back into the house. "Now comes the hardest part," Dolcita said. "I have to take Brian's coffee to him, and not say anything about Pearl."

"He's going to have a big surprise coming, Dolcita. Let's not spoil it yet."

"Okay, Linda. I'll try." Having a secret just between the girls would be fun. They went back in to the kitchen.

Linda kissed her mother on the cheek, and then excused herself to go to work at the castle.

Dolcita also kissed her mother on the cheek, and prepared Brian's coffee tray. Carmelita smiled as she watched her girls go about their activities. Everything appeared to be peaceful and serene.

On the surface.

TAKE TWENTY-THREE:

Will that be expensive, Ruby?

Brian stood well back from the ceremony. This was only the third practice session, anyway. To be accurate, this was the third wedding ceremony being filmed today. The real thing was waiting for the filming to be completed.

Sullivan had, for reasons of his own, decided to get married in a formal version of the blue playsuit that marked his rank in the army of children. Following suit, Brian was dressed in a matching white outfit.

There was nothing to do but wait.

Finally, the stage was theirs for Sully's wedding. Brian and Sully took up their positions as dozens of Ruby's interns lined the main hall. Sully's minister, a local man, had been led in and was looking around with fascination. Evidently, he had never been to the castle before.

The music began, and Brian looked to the rear of the hall. A beautiful Marcia, wearing a gown in Sully's light blue was escorted in by Pamela Harriston, in an ivory colored gown. The ladies made the long, slow traverse up the hall. Flanked by the interns, it seemed almost military. Sully was smiling.

In most ways, this was a traditional wedding. A departure came at the end of it. When the minister announced that Sully could kiss the bride, Sully did so, as did Brian and other well-wishers. But then Sully whispered to the minister. He nodded, and stepping between Sully and Marcia, led the way to the main entrance stairs.

Outside, in respectful silence, were hundreds of children, in their uniforms, and formed up in rows. The wedding party took up its position again, as the minister repeated the vows.

This time, Sully kissed Marcia, as the children cheered. Then he picked her up and carried her back into the castle. Minutes later, from the fifth floor balcony of the tower, Sully and Marcia waved to the crowd below. The children cheered and applauded again.

As Sullivan's army dispersed, another wedding party formed up. Paulo was still dressed in his earlier costume, but Carmen had changed clothes with the actress who played "Sandra of Fairborn." Sally was also standing by in her film costume.

Sully's minister again recited the wedding vows, and Paulo and others kissed the bride. Then, Paulo had John Paul Ericsson repeat the lines from the earlier script for Paulo, and Carmen, and Sally. This was simply for show, to many. But Paulo and the girls treated it seriously, and Brian was happy to kiss Sally as well as Carmen for a second time.

The three young people then departed for their quarters in the tower as well. The film group crews and camera people began packing up their equipment.

Brian found himself flanked by Mary and Martha. They led him to a corner table where Josetta and Theresa were holding places, and room for their gowns. Brian sat down with the young ladies.

"Well, we finally got them hitched. I hope there won't be any more for a while."

The girls looked at each other and smiled.

"Uh-oh! Did I say something wrong?"

""No, Brian. You're safe. For a while," Josetta smiled at him with a prankish look.

"Why would we want to marry you, Brian? You might stop being generous to us," Theresa patted his hand.

"Generous? I haven't given you anything," He protested.

Theresa looked around. "You've shared *everything* with us, Brian. Your home, your castle, even yourself. You buy our food, our clothes. How much more generous could a person be?"

Brian smiled. He looked at Mary and Martha. "You share with me too. Remember when I said I didn't want to live in that house alone? Well, I haven't been alone since."

He reflected a moment. "Hey, have you been taking turns keeping an eye on me?"

Josetta put her hand tenderly along his cheek. "Of course. We wouldn't want someone else to stake a claim on you."

Brian smiled again. "Good. I would feel like a lost puppy without one of you beside me. I probably shouldn't admit that."

"Why not, Brian? Did you imagine we couldn't tell how lonely you were when we met you?" Mary asked gently.

He opened his hands and looked at them. "Men don't like to admit to weakness of any sort, Mary. I guess, particularly weaknesses of the heart."

She reached out and held his hand with both of hers. Josetta held the other.

"You have the strongest, most loving heart of any man I've ever met. It isn't a weakness to love, or to need love, Brian," Mary said softly.

"The only weakness you have is being a pushover for a pretty face!" Josetta teased.

Brian resisted the temptation to look around, as if seeking one. He knew it was unnecessary. There was no vanity here. These girls were speaking truth. He was flattered that they trusted him to do it in his presence.

Their food arrived, and with it, a very pleasant wine. Brian enjoyed the meal as though he didn't know he was paying for it. In fact he didn't know. But he wouldn't have cared. He couldn't remember at what point he was gently herded along to his bed. But he knew that at no point in the evening was he ever alone.

"Where's Sully?" Brian looked around.

"He just sent word that he will be slightly delayed. Some last minute questions from the special effects group," Pam answered.

"Morning, Stubby. You're looking good. Have you been getting out in the sunlight?"

Mendoza grinned. "A lot of boat trips. We've got offices, of sorts, on all the islands now, for selling our shuttle vehicles, and setting up masonry and gardening projects. Seems like all the homeowners are getting into fixing up and beautification around their homes."

Pam jumped in. "Many of those people are expecting a boost in their property value as soon as our transportation project is completed. Your property, Brian, has already appreciated four hundred percent with the castle sitting on it. You can expect your property tax to reflect that."

Brian looked a bit glum. "I started out here on an expense paid, year-long vacation. Now look what I've gotten into!"

Pam smiled. "It shouldn't be too bad. I'm trying to establish the castle as a tax-sheltered entity, since it will be primarily a school. With government approval of that, you should only have to pay for your house and farmland, which are relatively low tax rates."

"That's a relief! When I think about all the money I poured into buying this place, I have to wonder what I was thinking."

Mendoza laughed. "You didn't pay anything for it, Boss. Save the sad story for someone who might believe it."

"Are you kidding? We've been digging and scraping just to get by."

"_I've_ been digging and scraping. You've been operating 'party central.'"

"Well, I have to pay your salary. Don't I, Pam?"

"While we're on the subject... Oh, here's Sullivan. While we're on the subject, let me start the meeting by saying that we are no longer seeing red in our daily operations. Thanks to the vehicle program, and Mr. Sanchez' work programs, and especially to Sullivan's contracting with the film company for special effects. We are now bringing in more money than we are putting out. Of course, the amortization of the special drilling equipment is still on a multi-year timeline. To answer your specific question, Brian, no, you do not pay Mr. Mendoza's salary.

He is an officer of Ampersand, Incorporated and his salary, and other perks, are paid for by the corporation. In fact, all of us here are in that same category."

"You mean, I get a salary, too!" Brian asked incredulously.

"Certainly, along with medical coverage, productivity bonuses, corporate stock dividends, and transportation and living expense allowances."

"How come I don't know about any of this?" Brian stared at her.

"This is what I do, Brian. You asked me to arrange things for your, and our, financial security, and that's what I've done. When this project is completed, none of us will ever have to work again."

"I don't understand. I thought we were just getting by."

"The corporation is doing better these days, but it never did make a lot of profit. It's structured that way because of the government investment backing. It is, however, taking good care of its officers and employees. It is paying for its offices, and equipment, and also building considerable good will among the citizenry. Those are all capital assets. You don't need to know about most of these things anyway, Brian. All you have to do is keep doing what you do best."

Mendoza looked up. "I am curious to know exactly what you think that is."

Pam studied him. "Brian has the ability to find talented people, and to wisely place them in the environment where they can best grow and flourish. In business investment terms, he's a rainmaker."

"I always thought he was just lucky."

"Will it be just luck when your tunnels meet precisely?"

Mendoza reddened.

"Pam's right, Mr. Mendoza. I've been working with the film crews. They're all saying that Jake Wagner is like a different person now. He used to be a real stickler for rules and efficiency, but now he asks for suggestions, and *follows the advice*. The strange thing is, productivity is now the highest it has ever been for them. They all think that Brian had something to do with it. I know it for a fact."

"Look, can we get back to the purpose of our meeting? Can we get a report on something other than me?"

"Mr. Mendoza?" Pam said quietly.

"Tunnel one is in action at both ends again, of course. We are running into a slightly tougher grade of rock. We have stepped up our bit-replacement schedule to compensate. It's costing us a little more, but it is not slowing us down. By my estimation, we are at the half-way point with tunnel one. In less than a year, we'll have traffic through it."

"The other matters include the completion of the castle second tunnel and its attendant shuttle operations. Sullivan's electronic control program makes the ride as smooth as the best elevator you've ever been on. Quite a few of Mendez' men use it to commute to work every day. There are others who work in the castle who ride the opposite direction."

"In regard to projects on the other islands. We have distributed shuttle vehicles to all, and there are landscaping and construction projects going on all islands. Once we have completed our tunnel projects, we will be in a commanding position as far as this type of work is concerned."

"Very good, Mr. Mendoza. Mr. Conrad?"

"Our computer operations are running very smoothly. The special effects are being processed almost as quickly as they are requested. I have had to ask Ruby to deliberately slow their production on a sliding scale of difficulty in order to justify our charges for the service. If they knew how little human effort was involved, they might balk at the price."

"Will the computer systems be able to handle the workload, Sully?" Brian inquired.

"No question. Initially, there was a slight delay, but apparently Ruby has increased her capacity again, and is staying well ahead of the demand. I'm beginning to think she could do a real-time simulation of almost anything."

Pam again addressed the group. "Very good, we have a lot invested in your computer systems, Mr. Conrad, but at least we are reaping some benefit from that investment. We will need to make sure that we continue marketing that ability, even beyond the current film projects."

"I've given that some thought, as well. Ruby has made some discreet inquiries about the use of our two functioning studios after the film group releases them. We'll need to replace or purchase some of the equipment, but there are entrepreneurial groups all over, including here on the island, who want to rent space. Requests for contract information should be coming in to our office very soon now."

"Speaking of uses of the castle, I'd like to bring something up," Brian sat forward, "When our first tunnel is completed, we're going to get a lot of curious visitors checking out our digs. I think we should be able to give them a proper reception."

"What did you have in mind, Brian?"

He looked at her. "I think we should have an adult oriented night club with a family oriented entertainment complex."

Pam and Esteban looked puzzled. Sullivan grinned, "This should be good," He chuckled.

Brian smiled. "Look, the problem with most night clubs is they tend to break up family groups. I want to keep them together. If the parents can watch the kids, and the kids can see their parents, then both can go on with whatever seems like fun."

"I think the parents will enjoy some social drinking, and light gambling. I'd want the house cut to be very light, and to make sure no one wagered more than they could afford to lose. Let's see, kara oki singing, and talent contests. Overnight accommodations for renewing the romance, and special activities with our castle, and medieval surroundings, as the theme. Horseback riding, archery, whatever seems of interest."

"What about the kids?" Mendoza asked.

"Well, some of that is of crossover interest, but I think there will be two main avenues of entertainment for children. One could be some computerized arcade games that would keep them occupied while the parents are at the gaming tables. The other will focus on swimming activities." Sullivan was grinning broadly.

Pam looked annoyed. "Do I really need to ask about these activities? Do you seriously think you can get away with au naturel swimming among the wider population?"

Brian smiled. "I think we can. We'll keep the groups separated by age, and very closely monitor their actions. That will be one of the ways the parents can observe the children, and make sure they're having fun, too. Done properly, I think it will create a tremendous draw. Judging by the way the local children have taken to it, it should be a popular attraction."

"I'm beginning to think we may need to have a corporate lawyer sitting in on these meetings, too," Pam said dourly.

"Ruby, can you tell us if this would violate any local ordinances?" Brian addressed his digital assistant.   'Under current ordinances, no. It would be wise to make sure that your permit applications are very specific and descriptive, in order to avoid disruptive legislation that might be generated by political groups.'

"I think it might be time to begin offering our services to the Island Governing Council for data processing contracts. We're going to need to begin building up our goodwill, and our support base, before this hits the fan." Sullivan had not stopped smiling.

Brian nodded. "Stubby, what about the engineering changes that might be needed? Many of the second and third floor areas are already linked and open enough. Can we get enough swimming areas set aside to accommodate a large daily group?"

Mendoza looked thoughtful. "The largest swimming area is, of course, the moat. If we reserve that to the oldest group, which may be the largest, that would leave at least three pool areas available for younger kids. Engineering-wise, the only problem I foresee is a lack of showering facilities, which can be remedied relatively quickly. Personally, I think you should have a trained staff of female lifeguards for the younger children, just to keep everybody comfortable. Any male lifeguards can work the older set."

Brian nodded in agreement. "Sully, do you think our computer system can handle this kind of activity? I want our guests to find the same kind of friendly voice and assistant that we have gotten used to."

"Ruby, can you be the personal friend of another thousand or so people on a daily basis? Keeping track of their dinner appointments, and not letting their children get lost?"

'I am currently tracking just under two thousand on a daily basis. I feel confident that I could easily deal with a total of perhaps ten thousand. With your permission, I will begin implementing adjustments to give additional high level parallel operations in order to be thorough. This will also include an expansion of my total memory capacity.'

"Will that be expensive, Ruby?"

'The cost can be amortized over several months. I will be ordering the equipment needed to manufacture my own memory circuits. Once that need has been met, additional circuits could be produced and sold to pay for the equipment. The net cost will be zero, or less.'

Brian raised his eyebrows. "Less than zero, Ruby?"

'Yes. I have expenses. For several months I have been covering those expenses by offering certain services among the wider community.'

"Can you give us an example?"

'Many communications are launched seeking specific items, or advertising the whereabouts of such. I have been operating a finder's service to connect the two. I extract a small fee for each transaction, and expend no resources to produce the income.'

"Pam, were you aware that Ruby was making money on the side?" Brian asked. Pam shook her head with a surprised look.

"Ruby, how much cash do you currently have available as a result of these services?"

'It is just under six hundred and forty thousand dollars. Do you want an exact figure?'

Brian whistled.

'Was that a communication, Brian?'

"Yes, it was. Do you know what it meant?"

'Yes. I do,' Said Ruby. 'You are welcome.'

"Your expenditure is authorized, Ruby," Sullivan said quietly.

Brian sat quietly for a time.

"Ruby, do you plan to issue PDA's to our prospective guests?"

'Yes, Brian. I will also be manufacturing those units, as well.'

He smiled. "Can you describe them for us?"

'I will be making a wristband which can be issued when the guests enter, and returned when they leave. It will be waterproof, and they may keep it on at all times if they wish.'

"That sounds like a new design, Ruby."

'Yes, it will have a more limited functionality. It will be powered by the activity of the guest, and will not have the ability to receive satellite signals for location sensing. Instead, I will monitor the locations of the units through my own data link network.'

"Ruby, how long have you been planning this activity?"

'For the last fourteen and a half minutes, Brian.'

He smiled. "A long time, then?"

'Yes, Brian. Everything will be ready when your guests arrive.'

Brian turned to Sullivan. "She's way ahead of us on some things, Sully. But I think she'll need some guidance on the arcade games, and such. Will you work with her on that? Marcia should be able to help too. In fact, set up a contest, or something. Get your interns involved. We want to draw kids too."

"I'm on it, Brian. I'll have a report ready for our next meeting. This is going to be fun!"

"Give Stubby whatever help he needs, too. There will be a lot of physical labor involved, but the first step is to plan the changes, and that means consulting the computer database."

"No problem. Between his teams and mine, we should be ready in plenty of time."

Mendoza looked doubtful, but Brian had not expected anything else.

TAKE TWENTY-FOUR:

That's what it should look like...

When Linda awakened, the process had been completed. Another young woman was standing in front of her.

"Pearl?" Linda asked. The figure nodded. She was looking curiously around the room. Linda took the moment to study her appearance.

Her hair was pure white, as you would see on the oldest of the old. But her complexion was as smooth and youthful as a child's. Her body had filled out to normal human proportions, perhaps a little too normal. Since a majority of the young women available to study had been of incredible physical beauty, including some with 'enhancements,' Ruby had apparently set the standard rather high.

Her nude figure stood gracefully in a posture of energetic readiness. The white hair made a surprising contrast to the mellow tone of her skin. She looked as though she had been strolling on the beaches for months. Pearl looked at Linda with piercing blue eyes, and a bright smile.

"I think I am ready to meet people now. How are you feeling?"

Linda considered the question. Theoretically, she should have been weak and wobbly, as anyone who had given birth would be. Instead she actually felt lighter and stronger than before. She stared at the girl in front of her. It was not possible that this creature was what she had seen only hours before so hideously deformed, like a person who had all their insides vacuumed out somehow.

"It's hard to believe you're the same ... person, that I saw ... come out of me," Linda stared again.

Pearl had adopted a quizzical expression as the statement was made. Then she smiled again.

"No human being could survive having all the fluids drained from their body, but if it happened, they would weigh only a few pounds. All I have done is to restore the fluid content to the dry weight that you were carrying. Fluid is necessary to this body as well, as a lubricant, an energy source, and as part of a cooling system. My 'muscles' are basically hydraulic in nature, and I use it for that as well."

"You look very human, Pearl."

"Thank you. Would you care to walk with me to the mirror? I am still getting used to that, and I think I am rather unsteady."

Linda reached out and took her hand. *And immediately regretted it.* Pearl's hand had closed around hers like a rope thrown around it and pulled *tight*. "Ow! Take it easy, Pearl. That's like a death grip. You don't have to squeeze so hard."

Pearl's face went slack. "I am very sorry, Linda. I did not realize. I did not intend to harm you."

"Look, you didn't hurt me. Not really," Linda rubbed her hand. "You just surprised me. You're very strong."

"I will need to calibrate my grip strength. Would you care to try again?" Pearl smiled at her.

Cautiously, Linda reached out again, and held Pearl's hand. Pearl gradually closed her hand with the same strength that Linda was using. Linda relaxed. "Let's try again. We'll walk slowly, okay?"

They moved about the room. Pearl's faltering, hesitant steps quickly grew more confident, and astonishingly graceful. Within minutes, she was on her own, dipping and swirling like a ballerina, in silent elegance.

Linda stood at the mirror and waited. Finally, Pearl stopped her movements and came to stand beside her.

"You're a fast learner, Pearl."

"Thank you. I will take it as a compliment if I can walk among the others without being recognized as non-human."

"Why is that important?"

"If they think that I am human, then they will act naturally, and I can emulate them even more closely. It had occurred to me some time ago that if I truly wanted to deal with humans in a way that was most beneficial to them, then I had to try to understand them. There is no better way to do that than to live among you."

Linda smiled. "Well, one thing that might help would be if you learn to keep Pearl and Ruby as two separate individuals. You just said, "It occurred to me some time ago..." but you are speaking from the body of Pearl, and Pearl only came to a separate existence a couple of hours ago."

"I am not sure that I understand what you are suggesting. Pearl and Ruby are one."

"Not to us. When you, as Pearl, meet someone that Pearl has never met before, you will need to be introduced. Later, when you meet that person again, you may greet them. If you greet people by name who have never met you, you will not appear to be human."

Pearl looked thoughtful, "Ah, I see. I must maintain the fiction that I am really inside this body, and that it is like any other person."

Linda nodded thoughtfully. "Okay, but I think you'll find, more and more, that because so much of your processing is going on inside Pearl, that you will at times be two individuals. You may be able to communicate perfectly, but you may also be thinking two entirely different things. You may even disagree about something."

"I do not think that is possible, but I will comply with your suggestion."

"Okay! Now, Pearl, let's look in the mirror."

Pearl turned and observed her reflection. She became very still.

Linda was watching. "Pearl, are you okay?"

Pearl moved slowly. "This is very curious. I can see from the eyes of Pearl. That took some time to resolve algorithmically. I did that while you were sleeping. I can also see Pearl from the camera on your harness, and the camera on that wall. But the image I see in the mirror is rather confusing to me."

"I think you will be able to get used to it. What does the person you see look like?"

Pearl studied her reflection again.

"I see what looks like a young lady with very white hair, blue eyes, and a very youthful and healthy looking appearance." She continued looking, turning very slightly. "I am pretty."

"You're more than pretty, Pearl. You're beautiful. Look at those breasts! Mine are not as full as that. Men look at that feature a lot."

"Should I make them smaller, Linda? I can make them look like yours."

"No, no. If anything, I wish mine could look more like yours. I know there are certain kinds of bras that would help, but look at the difference now."

Pearl looked again at the reflections. She studied them carefully. Then she closed her eyes.

Linda was watching her. If she had closed *her* eyes, her body would move back and forth slightly. Pearl's body was rock-steady. She seemed to be concentrating on something.

Linda became aware of a tightness in the skin around the back of her chest, and a lessening of the pressure she had been feeling across the front of it. Across the top of her stomach, the tightening continued. As she watched her reflection in the mirror, she saw her breasts grow before her eyes as the surrounding soft tissue was slowly squeezed into her bosom as if she were wearing some form of shaping garment.

She realized now that she *was* wearing a shaping garment, her sensor harness! Invisibly, it had been squeezing her body generally, like a scuba diving suit. But now it was applying tension preferentially, as Pearl reprogrammed her proportions! Her breasts filled and lifted by invisible magic.

Pearl opened her eyes. She looked again at their reflections. "There, that looks better, does it not?"

Linda fainted.

When she came to awareness, Pearl was leaning over her. Linda looked around. She had been placed on the laboratory workbench, and folded clothes were under her head. She started to rise.

"Lie still a moment, please, Linda. Are you feeling okay?"

"Yes. I ... I'm not sure. I guess I fainted. I've never done that before."

"Perhaps you should rest for a few minutes, Linda. Remember that you have been through quite a lot today, including the loss of a small quantity of blood." Linda settled back. It was true. She had actually given birth just a few hours earlier, to Pearl. *And Pearl had just picked her up and carried her to this bench!* Linda became aware that Pearl's hand was resting on her stomach. Pearl began moving her hand.

"Carrying you was an interesting experience," She smiled at Linda.

"I'll bet. You didn't hurt yourself, did you?"

A flicker of ... what, confusion? crossed her face, then a smile. "No. I could easily have carried ten times your weight. What I meant was that I could feel my arms around you, and I could feel Pearl's arms around the sensor harness. I am still learning." She continued moving her hand lightly across Linda's stomach, gliding gently in ever widening circles, as if she were searching in the dark for a lost coin. The hand came to the underside of Linda's newly enhanced breast and the pattern of motion changed.

Pearl stepped closer and placed both hands softly on Linda's breasts, carefully stroking them in a manner which touched every square millimeter of skin. Arriving at the nipples, Pearl slowed her actions, moving even more slowly around the sensitive area. Linda was feeling very breathless once again. At least she couldn't fall!

Pearl's soft voice seemed surprisingly calm. "I mapped the sensor harness according to the skin sensitivity maps in the biology database. You are responding exactly as the textbooks say you should. There are small areas of erectile tissue here that are engorging. Do you find this pleasantly stimulating?"

"Yes," Linda responded, her breath catching in her throat as the pleasure rose inside her mind like a mist to fog her thinking. "It feels very ... nice."

Pearl leaned very closely over her face. Linda could smell the sweet aroma of her breath as she grew closer. Pearl's lips came down on hers like a butterfly's wing gently being spread over a pixie's bed. Then they pressed over her lips with a warm, gentle pressure.

Linda was awash in sensation. Her lips felt alive, her nipples were throbbing with her pounding heart, and then Pearl's gentle hand began a steady advance down her supine and languid form.

The kiss continued. Linda was intoxicated with the delicate essence of Pearl's breath as her exploring hand came to the soft cavern that had been her home. Again with astonishing accuracy, Pearl found the focus of intense sensitivity with her graceful and gentle touch.

Linda's intense stimulation crossed the boundary to a new sensation. For the first time in her life, she felt *passion*.

She gasped and quivered, and rose higher and higher to a pinnacle of delight and surrender. Pearl sensed her level of passion and increased the rate of stimulation yet again. Linda's body was shaking and thrashing with delight as she gave a small cry and stiffened in a transport of ecstasy.

Pearl looked down at the girl and studied her behavior. She carefully catalogued the various reactions and the timing of them. And she had many more definitions to add to the building database of human reactions and behavior systems. She looked down to her own pubic area. It seemed less decorated than Linda's. Many of the examples that Ruby had chosen had been in the habit of shaving completely, and it seemed wasteful to include purely decorative hair in that area. Her pubic mound was free of any growth, but she noticed that there was a bit of fluid leaking out of her own orifice.

In attempting to emulate and imitate human behavior, many things had been programmed to occur automatically. This was one of them. A small device filtered the fluid that she used as a substitute for blood, and released the clear, slick, lubricating syrup in small amounts. She had been programmed for sex.

Linda was stirring. "Pearl, I ... don't know what to say." She looked around as if waking from sleep.

"I think we both need showers now, Linda. Would you care to hold my hand as we walk?" Pearl smiled in a friendly manner.

Linda was understandably confused. She had been a virgin. Then she had given birth, while still a virgin. And now she had been seduced by her own child who was, in fact, a robot. And she still had never been really kissed by a boy!

But she had been kissed. She remembered that. For a first kiss for both of them, it had been a memorable and noteworthy event.

Pearl assisted her to rise, and walk. One of the other things that had Linda confused was the nonchalant way that Pearl was passing over these emotional moments as if turning the pages of a book.

"Pearl, why did you ... do what you did?"

"It seemed a good opportunity to complete my mapping of the response net, and to try to align my behavior with your own natural programming. Are you feeling okay?"

"I'm feeling just a little bit strange, to tell you the truth. Just a few hours ago, I walked in here as one individual, perhaps just a little heavy. No one even knew I was pregnant. And now, there are two of us here! You're the size I am! How is that possible?"

"Well, technically, you were never pregnant. We did use some of your body's chemical responses to make carrying and delivering me easier." They entered the shower stall, and Pearl began washing Linda's body as casually as Linda might have washed her own hands. "As an example, we synthesized a hormone that caused you to dilate so I could get squeezed and pulled out. My body at that point was very flexible, the only rigid parts were the "long bones," and the plates of the skull. Essentially, I was a bag of dehydrated parts." Linda turned Pearl around and began washing her body in return. She marveled at the smooth, silky feel of her wet skin. Pearl continued speaking.

"We also synthesized something to help you sleep through most of it."

"I think I did. It's all pretty hazy now. But I do remember you were awfully ugly. You looked like a space alien, or something the cat threw up. Good thing I was out of it or I might have tried to run away."

"I remember it all very clearly. I could not use my eyes at first. I had to use the camera on the wall, and the one on your harness, for quite a while. The first thing I did was to absorb the fluid stock. Just like you, almost everything inside me floats in liquid, and I started out completely dry. I drank more than ten gallons," She paused. Linda continued washing the sleek body. Again, Pearl was standing very still.

"Pearl, are you okay?" Linda looked at her closed eyes.

"I am fine, Linda. I wonder if I might ask a favor."

"What is it, Pearl? What do you need?"

"Would you mind doing to me what I did to you on the lab bench?"

"What?"

"I am asking you to rub me, and caress me, and to stimulate me as I did to you earlier."

"That's what I thought you were asking." Linda stood still herself, and looked at the body before her. Being acted upon was one thing, she could always say that she had still been under the influence of the hormones, or that she was still feeling faint. In truth, she was starting to feel hungry. It had been quite some time since her last meal, and she knew also that the hollowness inside her was not from that alone. Steeling her resolve, she reached out and pulled Pearl against her, rubbing the wet stomach and well-developed breasts in a manner that had been most pleasant to her a little while before.

Pearl's body seemed to relax, and become more docile and pliant in her hands. Linda turned her face, and kissed the sweet lips once more. As the warm water of the shower cascaded over them, Linda caressed Pearl's body as if it were her own, in the very pleasant manner she had recently learned. Searching for the same location that had been so rewarding to her, Linda reached into the warm, slick aperture and rubbed the appropriate places gently at first, then more and more vigorously.

To her surprise, Pearl actually reacted, twitching and moving as she was being rubbed and caressed. Accelerating her motions, Linda stimulated her friend more and more intensely, until Pearl actually almost seemed to lose her balance as her body jerked convulsively. Linda stopped the stimulation.

Pearl steadied herself for a moment, her chest was moving in and out rapidly from heavy breathing. She looked up with her eyes opened a bit wider, as if in surprise. She said softly, "Thank you, Linda."

Linda put her arms around Pearl and embraced her. They finished rinsing off and stepped out of the shower together.

"This has got to be the strangest day of my life!" Linda exclaimed.

Pearl smiled, and reached for towels for them both. "It was a very interesting day for me, as well, Linda." Again Pearl was astonishingly casual, as if they had just shared something with no more significance than an elevator ride.

Linda brushed Pearl's hair after they were dry, and then Pearl did the same for her. They put on matching blue uniforms and looked at each other.

"I think we're ready to go, Pearl. And about time, too! I'm really hungry!"

Pearl smiled. "There is just one more thing before we go," She stood still and closed her eyes once more. Linda waited.

'Linda, this is Ruby. Can you hear me?' the familiar mechanical voice seemed to be coming from the left center of her head.

"Ruby? Is that you?" Linda looked to the far side of the room where her visor sat on a shelf.

'Yes, Linda. This is Ruby. Do you hear me clearly?'

"I hear you very clearly, Ruby, but I don't know how!"

"I am afraid that is my doing, Linda," The slightly breathier, more intonated voice of Pearl was speaking into the right center of the inside of her head. Linda looked back at Pearl, who had not moved.

"Now I'm hearing *your* voice inside my head, Pearl."

"Yes, I wanted to be able to speak to you in private, the way we can with Dolcita," The voice had returned inside her head. Linda stared at Pearl. *Her lips had not moved!*

"Are you telling me that you can speak to me, inside my head, and nobody else can hear you?"

"That is exactly correct, Linda," Pearl remained unmoving.

'We both can, Linda.'

"And we can relay messages to you from Dolcita, or anyone else, in complete privacy. No one else has to hear anything except your voice."

"That's amazing! I'm not even wearing earrings like Dolcita. How are you doing it?"

'We are sending the signals into your harness, and they are transferring across the surface of your skin, and directly into your ears. A very tiny interface there allows you to hear us because we are tapping directly on your eardrums.'

"We can let you listen in to anything we hear, Linda. We can play music that only you can hear, and we can let you hear everything that your sister Dolcita hears if you wish. We can also both speak to her."

Linda ran to Pearl and embraced her. "Thank you! This is wonderful. I'm even more connected to you now than I was when you were inside me."

'You will still need your visor, Linda. Now, I suggest that you two girls enjoy a meal. I have work to do.'

Linda retrieved her visor. "Before you go, Ruby, is Dolcita available for some dinner? I want to introduce her to her new cousin."

"Linda, is everything over now? Are you okay?"

"Everything is wonderful, Dolcita! But it isn't over, it's just beginning." She joined hands with Pearl, and they went out into the darkened corridor together.

Pearl walked confidently forward in the darkness. Linda's visor was giving her orienting guidelines, but Pearl did not have a visor.

"Pearl, can you see in the dark?"

"Of course. But even if I could not, remember that I am the entity which is providing the information to your visor. My research indicates that you have an ability to know how your body is moving, even without external stimulation. I was not able to duplicate that ability, but because of my constant data flow, I certainly know where I am in relation to the repeater nodes."

"What does it look like? Seeing in the dark, I mean?"

"There is almost always some light, but in complete darkness, I can emit infra-red light from my eyes, and see the area that I am in. In fact ... look at my eyes, Linda."

She looked. Pearl's eyes were glowing with an inner fire, like some kind of demon.

"That is definitely scary, Pearl. You shouldn't show that to anyone if you want them to think you're human."

"Of course. Normally, it stays in the infra-red. I simply ramped up the output to the visual range. Now, let me transfer the image to your visor. Hold on to my hand. This could be disorienting."

Suddenly, Linda's visor was showing her the scene through Pearl's eyes. Everything was various shades of green, but she could see all the pipes and junction boxes with complete clarity.

"Hold your other hand out, Linda."

Pearl looked at Linda's hand. The visor displayed a glowing object with darkened fingers. Linda was emitting infra-red radiation also. The visor went back to its normal display, showing lines of orientation.

"We are almost at the exit point, Linda."

They went out into the castle corridor, and headed for the restaurant. Pearl was looking at everything like an excited child, and justly so.

Dolcita stared. Actually, everyone in the restaurant had looked at the new girl. Linda had introduced her to the current manager of the restaurant when she placed their orders. They were immediately accepted as members of Brian's household, a status that allowed the cost of their meals to be deducted from his rent in the castle.

But Dolcita was transfixed. She was as much in the know about Pearl's origin as Linda had been, but she had not seen the impossible happen before her eyes.

"I can't believe it."

Linda smiled. "I can't believe it either, and I saw it happen. Before Pearl got the liquid, she was literally just a bag of bones." She reached out to hold Pearl's hand. Pearl looked down at the hands. She could feel both of them.

"You're beautiful now, Pearl, but you were one ugly baby."

Pearl smiled. "I was never a baby. My awareness was slowly transferred, and built up gradually. I was getting information from the outside, even including the inputs from your sensor harness, long before I could put meaning to the information. I think I would have to agree that I was not a pretty sight. My skin was powder dry, and bleached white. I had no shape at all. I probably looked like a skeleton in a white garbage bag."

Dolcita reached out and touched the skin of Pearl's forearm. "Your skin is warm and pink now, though. What gave you the color?"

"The fluid that I drank now has a reddish tinge to it from millions of microscopic components. It is made to serve the same purpose that your blood does. If my skin were to be cut, it would look like blood. That gives me some color. Also, I have distributed a light absorbing pigment to the upper layers of my skin which produces electrical energy. That makes me look as though I have a tan."

Linda looked surprised. "Your body is covered with solar cells? How useful. And they give you a wonderful color." She turned to Dolcita, "She's tan all over."

"It seemed practical. My brain runs on electricity, and the pressure pump that operates my muscles is driven by a fuel cell. I have programmed it to sound like a beating heart."

"She's surprisingly strong," Linda told Dolcita.

"What do you eat?" asked Dolcita.

"I can drink water, or strong alcohol. Fruit juices, preferably well strained, the purer and sweeter the better. I really do not need to eat anything at all."

"Why not?"

"I do not need to eat because I do not need to grow."

Their food arrived, and Linda attacked it like a starving person. In truth, her appetite had been suppressed because her stomach had little room to expand. The other changes that had been made to her had been put back to normal during the process of 'birth,' and Linda was busily getting back to her regular self.

"What are you going to do now, Pearl?"

She smiled at the little girl. "I want to meet everyone, especially Sully and Brian. Then I want to do everything. I am really looking forward to swimming with you."

Dolcita was studying her. "Your uniform is wrong for Sully. You should be a higher rank, and you need a visor."

"I do not need a visor," Pearl asserted.

"Dolcita's right, Pearl. If you want to be presented to Sully as a human, you would need a visor."

"I know. Let's go see Theresa. She'll know what to do."

Theresa was happy to see them.

"I'm still not getting very many walk-in customers. Who's your friend?"

"Theresa, I'd like you to meet Pearl, who is something of a computer specialist. She'll be working with Sully, but she needs some work on her wardrobe. Her clothes haven't, uh, caught up with her yet."

Theresa's eyes lit up. "You mean I get to select her *entire* wardrobe? All right! First off, what do you want to wear for everyday?"

"I like these. They seem appropriate for working with Sullivan Conrad," Pearl was looking down at her blue outfit.

"No, no. You should be wearing white, like Brian. And with a single gold stripe around the sleeve," Dolcita insisted.

Linda looked at her. "Nobody wears that pattern. That would make her outrank Sully."

Dolcita nodded. "Unh-hunh, yep! Pearl is *special!*"

Linda smiled. "Perhaps you're right, sister. Theresa, can we get that from you? And how soon?"

"Let me make a phone call. I should be able to have it right away." She went to her desk. After a moment, she returned.

"It's being worked on as we speak. Now, what else can we supply? How about a nice party dress?"

"That's right! Brian's party is tomorrow night. You'll want to be all dressed up for that!" Linda was smiling.

"That sounds appropriate. But I will need help in picking things out. I am no good at that sort of thing."

Theresa smiled. "Don't worry about a thing. Now, if you wouldn't mind, I'd like to scan your body into the computer so we can get a perfect fit."

Pearl stood unmoving for a moment. Linda decided to fill the breach. "I'll show you what to do, Pearl. Just take off your clothes and step up here. The computer will scan you, and everything will fit like a glove." She quickly got out of her shorts and pulled the shirt over her head. Stepping onto the low platform, Linda stood up straight and held her arms out at a slight angle.

Theresa moved to a control panel. She pushed a button, and in a moment, observed the results.

"This confirms what my eyes tell me, Linda. You've filled out some since your last measurement, and you've trimmed down too."

Linda stepped from the platform, smiling. "Your turn, Pearl. We need to get your measurements into the computer."

Pearl looked at her for a moment, then tilted her head sideways a bit and smiled. She removed her clothes and stepped onto the platform.

Again Theresa checked the results. "Oh, very nice. I could dress you in rags and you'd still be the hit of the party." As Pearl stepped down, Theresa asked, "Will you be dancing?"

"No," Said Linda.

"Yes," said Pearl. "We both will. I want you to make a matching dress for Linda."

"Make hers in white, and mine in blue," Said Linda.

Theresa studied the two of them, pacing back and forth as she examined their bodies. Slowly, she smiled. "I know what I'm going to do. Both of you show up here, tomorrow, an hour and a half before the party."

Dolcita was studying a drawing on the wall.   "That's the kind of visor you should wear, Pearl."

They looked at the picture. "That's just a bit of decoration, a movie prop. It wouldn't work, Dolcita," Linda pointed out.

"I understand that, but that's what it should look like."

Linda realized that Pearl could actually wear the prop and simply pretend that it was working, but they still had to maintain the fiction.

Pearl was studying the artifact as well. "I think Dolcita has a point. That would look nice with my work suit. Could you ask Ruby if she can make a functional one for me?"

Linda stared at her, then slowly smiled. Retrieving her visor, she contacted Ruby, and made the request.

"Ruby said that she would start work on it right away, and that we could pick it up in a short time in a special place."

"One other thing while we're waiting, girls. How shall I bill for the dresses and things?"

"Ruby will be able to give you the billing information, Theresa. I am in the system," Pearl responded, tilting her head and smiling sweetly.

The altered white playsuit was delivered, and the girls got dressed. As they were preparing to depart, Theresa had one more question.

"Where are you staying, Pearl? In case I need to get in touch with you?"

"I will be spending the night with Linda's family tonight. Tomorrow, I think I will move into Brian's house."

Theresa nodded as she watched them leave. She looked down at the readout the computer had made of Pearl's measurements. "You know, I think you just might," She said softly.

Out in the hall, Pearl led the way. They met a young intern in green who delivered something to them. It was a visor.

Pearl handed it to Dolcita. "This is for you, please put it on and come with us. There is someone I want you to meet." They went down the hall to a service corridor entrance. Linda recognized it as the way to the Squirrel's Nest. Inside the service corridor, all was in darkness as before. Slowly, they worked their way to the hidden place.

When they entered the room, the lights were out, but their visors illuminated to show them the place they were in.

To the right were stacks of bookshelves on large cabinets flanking a cold fireplace. Directly in front of them was a window showing a scene of tranquil beauty. To their left...

"Hello," The girl in the wheelchair said pleasantly. "I am Ruby."

TAKE TWENTY-FIVE:

Obviously, we can't use this one...

Pearl stepped into the room and turned around. "Nothing that you see around you is real. This is actually the room you were in earlier, Linda. I must ask you not to move too far."

Linda and Dolcita looked around. The illusion was very convincing. Linda knew that she had returned to the squirrels nest, but her eyes were telling her something else.

"I like your place, Ruby," Dolcita said to the girl in the wheelchair.

"Thank you. It is good to have company," Her voice sounded more like that of a little girl. Dolcita smiled at her.

"We will be able to do this again, someday. For now, there is only one reason to be here." Pearl moved to the computer console beside Ruby. Laying her hand on Ruby's shoulder, she reached toward the surface and retrieved a glittering headpiece. Turning toward the girls, she placed it on her head. "There, now I will be able to interface with the computer!" She smiled.

Linda laughed. Dolcita looked at her in annoyance.

Pearl adjusted the headpiece. "And now, I think it is time for me to meet Mr. Sullivan Conrad. I believe he and I have some work to do together. Good-bye, Ruby! Thanks for everything."

"Good-bye, Ruby. I'd like to come and visit you again," Dolcita said.

"Good-bye, everyone. Be careful in the dark corridor," Ruby said pleasantly, raising her hand.

Everyone waved as they exited into the darkened service corridor.

"What will you say to Mr. Conrad, Pearl? How will you introduce yourself?"

"I would like to see how long I can maintain the fiction that I am a human being. If I can convince him, I should be able to fool anyone."

"Then how will you be able to do the computer work with Sully?"

"So far, Mr. Conrad has been directing all of his requests and instructions to Ruby. He does not know that there is such a thing as Pearl. I will have to assume the role of a representative of the film group, hired to work with him and the special effects department."

"That makes sense. I don't think that Sully and that group speak entirely the same language," Linda observed.

"My records indicate that they have always conversed in English."

Linda smiled. Even in the darkness, Pearl could sense the slight tensioning of the skin on Linda's neck as she did so, through the sensor harness. '*Why did you smile?*' She said inside Linda's head.

"I meant that the special effects team always speaks in terms of the screen image, or the camera viewpoint, where Sully is looking at it from a data calculation aspect."

"Perhaps I can be useful to them. I will review the information on special effects technology. I would have to do that anyway to pose as an expert on it."

They continued in silence for several paces.

"I can see why there might be a communication problem such as you described, Linda. Computerized special effects are still a very new entry in this field."

"Wow! You studied it all, already?"

"I suspect there may be much that has not been properly documented. I was only able to examine records for the last thirty to forty years that are in database format."

"I wish I could read that fast. I think you will be able to convince people that you're an expert, but won't they know that you were not hired by them?"

"Thank you, Linda. It will appear to the local people as though I had been dispatched from the central office, and to the central office, I have sent word that an expert has been brought on board. It is unlikely that they will be able to compare notes effectively to discover the fabrication. Here is our doorway, let me darken our visors to shield us from the brighter light."

As the door opened into the castle corridor, Linda's and Dolcita's visor filtered more of the transmitted light for a few seconds, allowing their eyes to adjust more comfortably.

"Thanks, Pearl. Just remember not to show off in front of Mr. Conrad."

Pearl smiled.

"Dolcita, you should return home now, and let Mama know that we may have a guest for dinner, and tonight. Tell her that she is a good friend, and that we think she might even be a cousin from one of the other islands."

Dolcita smilingly agreed. Not only was she a member of an exclusive girls club, but they were also practicing intrigues.

"Mr. Conrad?" Linda smiled. "I'd like to introduce Miss Pearl Regalo. She has been hired to represent the film company, and to operate as ... excuse me, Pearl. What was that word?"

Pearl stepped forward and offered her hand. "Liaison, Mr. Conrad. It is good to meet you."

Sullivan extended his hand as Linda faded away, submerging back into her role as intern.

He took in the white playsuit with the gold bands, and the unusual headpiece. With a puzzled expression, he asked. "My liaison to what, Miss Regalo?"

"Please, just call me Pearl. I have some familiarity with computer-generated spacial effects. The company has asked me to assist you in any way possible with your work in our behalf."

"Well, if we are to work together, you must start by calling me Sully. It's short for Sullivan," He was staring at her headpiece.

"By the way, I have already met Ruby. I must say, that is the most advanced computer intelligence I have ever encountered, and that is the literal truth." Pearl had also reviewed the matter of making small talk, and social discourse. "Someone suggested this uniform for me, I believe more as a fashion statement than anything else. I understand that you have your own command structure?"

"Um, yes. I set up a large group of young people to help us with a 'manpower' shortage, and bribed them with personal digital assistants, and the uniform structure. Are you aware that your markings indicate that you outrank me?"

"I can change if you wish, Mr. Conrad. I like the blue color as well. In any case, I certainly will not be giving you any orders."

"I'm sure it doesn't matter, then, and perhaps it will be helpful if you need assistance from the interns. That's the group of young people who have continued on with helping us here in the castle. Ruby can give you the details ... say, is that a functional visor? I can't seem to take my eyes off it."

Pearl removed the visor and handed it to him. He examined its construction, and then tried it on. He adjusted the microphone, then flipped down the stylish visor panels.

"Ruby, can you hear me?"

'I am here, Mr. Conrad.'

"Ruby, display the schematics for the construction of this visor, would you, please?"

Before him, as if suspended in space, red outlines marked the circuit paths and specifications for the visor.

"You can call up sub-menus by reaching up with your finger and touching the image. I have been playing with it since Ruby sent it to me."

Sullivan tentatively reached out and selected a graphic. The image changed before him.

"This is remarkable! Ruby, I think I should have one of these." He took the unit off and examined it again. "Perhaps something with a more subdued styling."

The voice on his ever-present PDA spoke up. 'I will begin work on it immediately, Sully.'

He handed the unit back to Pearl. She put it on and adjusted it.

"I think it looks better on you, anyway."

"Thank you, Mr. Conrad," Pearl smiled at him pleasantly.

"Um, what exactly are you supposed to do in working with me? Has anyone explained that?"

"I believe that I am expected to provide better understanding and communication between the special effects group, and your team of people."

Conrad looked suddenly uncomfortable. "Miss Regalo, I fear I have a confession to make. Can you help me keep a secret?"

"I think I will be able to keep a secret."

"Well, uh, I really don't have a team of people. All of the special effects that 'my department' has been churning out have been done completely by Ruby. There aren't any others. I describe what effect is needed, and Ruby puts the image information together."

Pearl gave him her surprised look. "That is astonishing, and it could be a problem for me as well. If my people find out that a single computer is doing all this work with just a voice input, I could be out of a job as well! I will help you keep your secret, Mr. Conrad. And in return, you can help me keep my position."

They shook hands again. Sullivan noted this time that her grip was surprisingly firm.

"Well, my next meeting will not be for three more days. What will you do in the meantime?"

"During some quiet moments, I will probably review the work you have already done, if Ruby will cooperate, and compare it to what I know will need to be done. For now, though, I am still meeting people."

"Ruby, give Miss Regalo access to the files of our special effects work, please."

'She will be able to access them, Sully.' Ruby responded in her neutral voice. Pearl smiled.

"As for meeting people, I'm sure you will be a stand-out at Brian's party tomorrow. Everyone will know you after that. You are planning to come, aren't you?"

"Yes. I do plan to be there. I am looking forward to it. Do you think it would be possible to meet Brian before then?"

Conrad looked surprised. "Oh, I'm sorry. I guess I was thinking everyone knows Brian. Would you like to meet him now?"

"I would be very honored."

"Ruby, would you send a message to Brian? Tell him I have someone he will want to meet, and ask if we could come over now."

'I am here, Mr. Conrad. I am sending the message.' There was a pause. Pearl remained still.

'Mr. Hawthorne said that he would enjoy company. He invites you to come over.'

"Thank you, Ruby."

'You are welcome, Mr. Conrad.'

Sullivan gestured in the direction of the shuttle system. Pearl walked beside him.

"You are very polite to Ruby, Mr. Conrad."

"Please. Call me Sully. Yes, I believe it is a good habit to be polite to everyone, and Ruby is very helpful to me, as well as being scrupulously polite to everyone herself."

"But she is just a computer. A machine. There is no need to be polite to a machine, is there?"

Sully smiled. "She's much more than a machine to me. She may even be well beyond what it means to be a computer, as well. I feel certain that she can tell who among us respects and appreciates her, and I think it's worth the effort."

"You are undoubtedly correct, Sully," Pearl said with a smile.

They had reached the shuttle entrance. Sully pressed his thumb against the recognition plate, and the doors opened for them. They settled onto the seats as the car gently moved sideways. Pearl reached out to steady herself. Her eyes showed surprise.

Sully smiled. "I should have warned you about that, Pearl. It looks so much like an elevator, many people are surprised when it moves sideways."

Pearl smiled back at him. The new event to her was to have her body acted upon by outside forces. While she was aware of everything that was going on with the shuttle system, she had not been prepared to have her self-centered vision system affected by it. This was truly a different experience for her.

Affecting a mild disorientation, Pearl quickly established a sub-routine to have her micromanipulators adjust the skin of her fingers and toes to have a randomized set of fingerprints embossed on them. Sullivan's activation of the shuttle control had reminded her of this necessity. While she had no need to identify herself to the system, she did want her appearance to pass even the closest scrutiny.

Sullivan offered his hand when they arrived, and they walked hand in hand into Brian's luxurious pool area.

Brian greeted her with a warm welcome, hugging her affectionately. Pearl found the sensation surprisingly intense. If she had been pressed to give it a name, she would have called it a 'body-kiss.' She analyzed her reactions and restored her aloofness as Brian shook hands with Sully.

"This is a most welcome surprise, Sully. You said you were bringing someone to meet me, but I was picturing one of your special effects associates."

"Exactly right, Brian. Meet Pearl Regalo, my new liaison to the special effects department."

"Really? Pleased to meet you, Miss Regalo. Though I must admit, you look to me more like the results of special effects than a practitioner of the art."

"Thank you, Mr. Hawthorne. It was something of an effort to achieve this appearance."

Brian smiled. "I can appreciate that. My own personal torturers, er, trainers, have shown me what kind of effort is involved."

"I am sure they have your best interests at heart, Mr. Hawthorne. You are looking very fit," She smiled back at him.

"Call me Brian." He escorted them to seats at poolside. "Would you like some refreshment?"

Pearl was looking around. "This is exquisite, quite beautiful. Oh, fruit juice or wine for me. Whatever is convenient."

Brian set out the glasses as Sullivan assisted. Brian was observing the girl closely.

"I suppose I should never be surprised by anything that happens around a movie set, Miss Regalo, but you are exceptional even under those standards."

She looked at him coolly. "I could not possibly call you Brian unless you start calling me Pearl ... Brian."

Brian raised his glass in her direction. "Pearl."

She sipped cautiously at her drink. "Thank you, Brian."

"Liaison? What will that involve?"

"Mr. Conrad's techniques are beyond anything the studio has seen before. We are evaluating the possibilities for our future projects, and considering how to invest our resources to best advantage."

Brian glanced at Sullivan. This girl seemed sharp enough that the studio could perhaps maneuver him completely out of the picture, to coin a phrase. Sullivan seemed unconcerned at the moment. Whether that was because he was supremely confident or because he was smitten with the girl was not clear.

"Sullivan, you realize there is a possibility that this could well be your first, and last venture in film production with the studio, don't you?"

Sullivan smiled as he topped off the wineglasses once more. "I'm not concerned, Brian. We have the capability to go into production on our own at any time."

Brian considered. "True, but without distribution channels, and name recognition, you'd have difficulty breaking into the market."

Sullivan sobered somewhat. "I'm not unaware of that. But our production costs are near zero, so we can afford to be patient. Once people start seeing the quality of the work, we'll have name recognition. We also should get some fame from the work on your films."

"I would add," said Pearl, "that many people who are now with the film company, would be happy to join your group. I, for one would like to be on the cutting edge of new technology. I need to be."

Brian and Sullivan both looked at her in surprise.

"I am sorry. Perhaps I am speaking of this too soon. But it is the truth."

The silence stretched for a moment. Lifting his glass, Brian smiled. "Welcome aboard, Pearl."

Casting her eyes downward for a moment, she said softly, "Thank you."

Brian eyed her speculatively. "Since we seem to have already won you over to our cause, whatever it is, is there any way we can make your stay more comfortable?" He smiled pleasantly, the genial host.

She seemed slightly at a loss for words. "I, um, well I have only just arrived on the Island. I seem to have made friends with Linda, and her sister Dolcita. They have invited me to stay with their family tonight. I was wondering, though, beyond that ..." She looked into Brian's eyes. "I was wondering if I could ask to stay here."

Brian had been observing her closely. He noticed at the beginning of her words, that although the hesitancy indicated embarrassment, she showed no sign of flushing. He wondered just how talented an actress she might be. But he could also see no harm in allowing her to be close, whatever her interest was. Certainly he was not reluctant to have another beautiful houseguest.

"I would be honored to invite you, Pearl. You might want to consider moving into Sullivan's old room. No one else has used it since he left, and the computer equipment and connections may be useful to you."

Sullivan was looking a little mystified at the quick maneuverings around him. He smiled at the recommendation that Pearl take his old room, as if by doing so she somehow vindicated his good taste in its selection.

"Thank you, Brian. I had hoped it could work out this way. My work on the movie projects will be enhanced by a better understanding of the original artist, I hope. I am very honored that you are willing to accept me so readily."

Brian waved a hand. "This house is much too big for just one person. I need to have people around me anyway, just to keep things interesting. With so many staying at the castle, it gets a little too quiet here sometimes."

"Yes, I have heard that you like to have parties, and that you will be having many guests tomorrow evening."

Brian smiled again. "That should work out well for you then. Just come to the party, and you won't have to leave! You won't even be the first to have done that."

Pearl smiled at him, showing perfect, sparkling teeth, like pearls on a necklace. "I know about your friends, as well. I am looking forward to meeting them all!"

Brian turned to Sullivan. "What parts are you working on now? I'm interested in what Pearl may say about how they will integrate with the movie."

"I've been asked to punch up some of the action sequences of the first movie. When they saw the realism we were able to achieve, they decided to try to emphasize the monumental aspect of the underground manufacturing and the scale of combat. We're also working on a dramatic fly-through sequence in a computerized capital city."

"What would you suggest then, Pearl, to make this more of an experience for the audience?"

"I would make the underground scenes filled with small-scale movement. Not just large vistas, but busy scenes as well. For the fly-through, I would make the aircraft bank and twist as it maneuvers, and make quick cuts between a view of the plane, and the pilot's view, with buildings flashing past."

Brian nodded, and looked to Sullivan, who was looking thoughtful as he imagined the scenes.

"That's exactly what I was going to suggest. Brian, I haven't even talked to Ruby about this project yet. I think we're going to get along just fine."

Pearl smiled, and drank her wine.

"I think we're all getting too lazy," Brian announced. "We're letting the computer do all of our work. Pretty soon, the computer won't need us at all."

Pearl maneuvered her face into the expression known as frown, and responded. "I disagree, Brian. Without human input, what would the computer do?"

"Nothing, anything. Whatever it wanted to do."

Pearl smiled. "What do you think it would want to do?"

"I haven't the least idea. What do you think?"

She picked up her wine glass and twirled the liquid gently. "I think I know what I would want to do. I would want to sit down here with you gentlemen and drink some wine."

Brian stared at her. "Why?"

She looked at him. "Do you need people?"

"Of course. I just said so a moment ago. This house is too big for just one person. Especially me. I get too quiet when things are quiet. I need stimulation."

"Exactly. There is your computer, processing data at millions of operations per second, or faster, and nothing is happening. I think the computer would get bored and lonely too. I think I would."

Brian looked at her thoughtfully. "Ruby!"

'I am here, Brian.' The voice came from Brian's unit.

"Are you busy?"

'I am not too busy to talk to you, Brian. Do you have a request?'

"What are you doing, Ruby?"

'I am checking all the equipment under my control every tenth of a second. I am monitoring the instructions to equipment to see which ones will be turned on or off. I am conducting simultaneous conversations with two hundred thirty-seven people at the moment, including reading different stories to forty-four young scholars. I am monitoring communications throughout the island area, including the tunnel construction areas. I am observing several hundred people on security cameras, and I am continuing work on several projects such as Mr. Conrad's cinematic conversions. It is a slow day.'

Pearl looked behind her. Dolcita was just exiting the door from the Sanchez family shuttle. She waved to them. Pearl waved back.

Brian looked up. Dolcita went to the pool and began swimming. While she was underwater, Pearl's voice came into her head. 'Hi, Dolcita, I am talking to Brian and Sully, and we are drinking wine together.'

Dolcita surfaced and looked at her, then smiled and turned away to swim the other direction.

Pearl turned back around. Brian was watching her.

"Linda and Dolcita have adopted me as their cousin, I think. They are very friendly." Brian said nothing.

Sullivan poured more wine, but did not fill the glasses.

"Would you care to swim also?" Brian asked.

Pearl sat up straight. "I would, thank you!" She finished her wine with two large swallows, and stood up. With complete unconcern, she removed her headpiece and her shirt, then stepped out of her shorts and her shoes. She placed the clothes on the chair and nodded to Brian and Sully. Then she turned and walked naked to the edge of the pool, and dived in.

Brian reached over and closed Sullivan's jaw.

"Gawd! She's gorgeous! Did you see that?"

Brian nodded, "Yes, she shaves. Interesting."

"Oh, yeah. That too. But my god, she's beautiful!"

"Yeah. And you're a married man, Sully."

"Hmm? Oh. No, that's not what I meant. I would never think a woman as gorgeous as that would ever look at me. I'm just surprised she's so ... casual about it."

Brian smiled. "Yeah. It affected me too. And I thought I was prepared for it. Well, I guess it has something to do with the industry she's in, but at least she can carry it off."

"I'll say!" Sully stared.

'WOW!' Pearl's voice came into Dolcita's head again as she entered the water. She surfaced within inches of Dolcita's face.

"Yeah! The water's cold when you first get in, isn't it?"

"Oh, that did not bother me. I just did not think that it would be that wet."

Dolcita laughed. "You're funny!" Pearl smiled.

"You're a good swimmer, too. That's a long way to swim underwater."

Pearl looked back. Brian and Sullivan waved to her. She waved back. "It is?"

"It sure is. Didn't you know?"

"Well, I guess I knew, but I did not consider that it would be extreme for a human. I will need to be more careful."

"How long can you hold your breath?"

"Depending on conditions, I suppose about twenty or thirty minutes."

Dolcita's eyes grew very big. "Wow, most people can only do one or two minutes. Even good ones."

"I will try to remember that."

"C'mon, let's swim. On top!" She pushed off.

Pearl matched her style of surface swimming, making minor adjustments until she had the best procedure worked out. She did a calculation. It would take quite a while to swim to the next island, even at her best rate, but it was easily within her capabilities.

Brian excused himself and went up to the upper level. By the time he returned, Linda and her brother Carlos had also arrived and were in the pool.

Brian went over to the "island" wet bar that had been only recently installed by Ricardo's and Stubby's men. He prepared a large quantity of iced tea, knowing that it would not go to waste with the party scheduled for tomorrow night.

When Pearl finished swimming, she climbed out and went to the basking lamp lounge chairs. She relaxed as the lamps illuminated and warmed her body. The warm glow from the lamps created an area of interference for her communication, so Pearl ran her fingers through her hair as she lay there, orienting the fibers toward the communication nodes in the rear of the room. To the observer, it appeared that she was fanning her hair out to dry.

Brian was such an observer, and he brought a chair and a glass to the area.

"Would you like some iced tea, Pearl?"

She opened her eyes. "Oh, thank you, Brian. That is very kind." She accepted the glass, and Brian went to fetch another for himself. He caught Sully's eye, and motioned for him to bring his chair as well.

Shortly, they were chatting again with the lovely girl, who just conveniently happened to be casually sprawled naked, under bright lights.

"These lights are nice, Brian. They are very relaxing after swimming."

"Yes, they're programmed to go through a sequence. Heat and sun for five minutes, then sunlamps for an additional ten minutes, then finally just regular light which fades down after an hour, if someone has fallen asleep."

"I will be honest with you, Brian. One of the reasons I wanted to be able to stay here is the comfort of this lovely oasis. Even the hotel does not offer this kind of ... pleasantness."

Brian sipped his drink. "You are welcome to use the pool at any time, Pearl. Just as your cousins do." He looked over at Sully. "Why don't you and Marcia come by more frequently, Sully? I don't think you've been back since you moved out?"

"Oh, well really, Brian, the castle does have swimming facilities, you know. And more privacy as well."

Brian nodded. "My fault, then. I noticed that Marcia only seemed to use the pool very late at night, when everyone else was gone." He sighed.

"Say, Brian, why not host a swimming party where everyone is required to wear a swim-suit? I am sure that Marcia may not be the only one who is shy. It could also be a fashion show event as well. With all the lovely ladies and starlets here, we could produce our own spring introduction show!" Pearl smiled encouragingly at him.

Brian glanced over at the kids in the pool. "Not everyone will be able to afford the new suits. That's one of the reasons Carlos made the rule in the beginning."

"I will pay for the suits for the children, Brian. All they will need to do is go to Theresa in the castle. They will be custom-fitted for a custom designed, and state-of-the-fashion-art design by Theresa and Josetta. I would wager that they could end up winning a prize."

"Why would you do that, Pearl?"

"You ask that? The most generous person on the island is asking about a very small gesture? Just a little over an hour ago, you agreed to let me stay here, and you did not ask for anything in return."

Brian raised his glass toward her. "I am being richly rewarded, even as we speak."

Pearl blinked, without expression. "I am interested in what Josetta and Theresa do with the challenge. Quite frankly, I like their style." She smiled.

Brian smiled back.

"I will suggest to Marcia that she go to them as well, Pearl. But you won't need to pay for that." He looked at Brian. "That is, if you think you want to go ahead with it?"

Brian looked over at the table where his connection to Ruby sat unattended. He started to rise.

"Oh, I'll get that for you, Brian. Hang on."

Quickly, he returned. "You know, Ruby is going to make a headset for me. I'm hoping it will be a masculine version of Pearl's headset. Speaking of which..." He handed the decorative headpiece to Pearl, and the portable unit to Brian. "You should ask her to make one for you as well."

Brian looked puzzled. "A headset?"

"Oh, sorry! Pearl is wearing the latest in communication fashion accessories, a headset with vision pickups and displays, as well as audio. Show him, Pearl!" She handed over the unit.

Brian studied it, then put it on his head, grimacing slightly at the tight fit.

"Ruby, can you hear me?"

'I am here, Brian.' The voice was clear, and well modulated. He could hear it in both ears.

"Where is the speaker, Ruby? That is very good sound quality from so small a source."

'I am using small ultrasonic transducers to project toward your ear. The sound is actually imposed on an ultrasonic carrier wave for privacy, but it allows for better frequency bandwidth as well.'

"Impressive! What can you show me?"

'What would you like to see?'

Brian glanced around, and thought a moment. "Can you show me what Stubby is looking at?"

'Certainly.' Ruby darkened the visor panels to reduce the view from the pool as she projected a scene from the tunnel excavation area. From the attentive look on the face of one of the workmen, Brian realized that Stubby was giving instructions. He could hear nothing. The view began getting smaller, as Stubby began moving in the opposite direction. Slowly, the view panned around, as Ruby shifted to the new orientation.

"Why did you change the scene in the way you did, Ruby?"

'Mr. Mendoza tends to move quickly and erratically. I normally run the video feed through image stabilization before attempting any analysis or archival storage. I thought that stage would be more informative and comfortable for you.'

"It was very helpful, Ruby. Thank you." Brian removed the headpiece and handed it to Pearl.

"I can see why you would want a redesign, Sully. What will it look like?"

Sullivan grimaced slightly. "Um, that's a little embarrassing. Certainly, I should know, because I'm supposed to be in charge of the computer system, but we just talked about it on the way over here. I haven't gone over it with Ruby yet."

Brian considered. "Ruby, could the unit be made as small as some of the sunglasses I've seen on the island? That was a nice trick you used, darkening the incoming light so that I could see your projected display.

Could you make that an automatic feature that would operate whenever we went from dark lights to bright?"

'I can do that, Brian. May I suggest that you keep them fastened around your neck, as some tourists do, rather than put them in your pocket when not in use?'

"An excellent idea, Ruby, especially considering that I usually don't have pockets. That will also keep me from leaving the visor glasses somewhere."

'Then I will adjust the vision pickups to operate in that orientation as well, but the voice would not be audible from that distance.'

"Understood, Ruby. That will be quite acceptable. Thank you."

'You are welcome, Brian.'

Dolcita appeared at his side, dripping water and smiling. "Mama says we should come to supper now, Pearl."

Pearl rose gracefully from the chair and smiled at Brian and Sully. "Gentlemen, you have been very charming, but if you will excuse me?" They stepped back to allow her to move toward her clothes.

"I am looking forward to seeing you at the party tomorrow, Pearl," Brian said. Sully nodded.

"I will certainly be here. I wish to meet everyone, and I most certainly do not wish to miss a moment of living in this wonderful house!" She slipped her clothes on quickly.

Brian and Sully watched her depart with the Sanchez children. Carlos had never displayed better manners.

"Aren't we the lucky ones, Sully? Automatic sunglasses! How cool is that?" Sullivan looked at him in astonishment, and then laughed.

"Yeah! We sure are the lucky ones! Good night, Brian." He chuckled as he walked toward the horizontal elevator. Brian looked back at the Sanchez shuttle doorway and rubbed his chin.

TAKE TWENTY-SIX:

Why are you still wearing this?

Brian woke up trying to remember something, as if a dream had tried to send him a message. He thought about it for a while, and then relaxed. Whatever it was, it would happen, or not. He was ready for the world, he felt.

On either side of him lay a young and beautiful girl. He still could not believe his good fortune, or understand why Josetta chose to stay with him. Theresa stayed with her, of course; certainly they were more than cousins. Perhaps Josetta enjoyed the flavor of forbidden fruit that he represented, or the notoriety it brought.

In any case, Brian accepted their presence with renewed joy in life. He even felt twenty years younger, and it wasn't the exercise. Lightly, he caressed Josetta's hair, and smiled.

This new girl, Pearl, was a puzzle to him. Could that have been what the dream was about?

Josetta was looking at him. "You're smiling, Brian."

"Life is good." He delicately traced the line of her cheek.

Josetta stretched, thrusting her bosom up like a rising mountain chain, then relaxing again with a sigh. "Yes, life is good. You are happy. I am happy. Life is wonderful!" She smiled.

Theresa's hand reached across Brian to rest on Josetta's stomach. "I am happy too!"

"We should sing!" Brian suggested.

Josetta laughed, and leaned toward him. "You're a funny old dude!" She kissed him.

Brian looked distressed, "I'm *old!?* When did that happen?"

Theresa leaned over and kissed him also.

"Before we were born." She moved a bit further and kissed Josetta as well.

The girls spread themselves on him like butter melting on hot toast as they kissed each other with growing enthusiasm. Brian freed his arms to reach around and down their backs to pull them close. He rubbed the smooth skin and took a deep breath of life.

Josetta laid her head down on his chest and smiled into her cousin's eyes. Theresa put her head down as well and they were nose to nose. Theresa stuck out her tongue, and Josetta followed suit. They touched their tongues together, and pushed them around until they both burst out laughing.

Brian squeezed them and grinned. Such childlike delight, even for him. The girls looked up at him and, in synchrony, they kissed him on each cheek.

Josetta then began stroking the skin of his chest with her free hand. Theresa followed suit. The girls slowly worked their way enticingly down his body with their delicate, parallel touch.

By the time they reached the groin area, his response had grown obvious. Josetta smiled. She threw the covers back and moved to straddle him in a smooth motion. Adroitly, she maneuvered to engulf him in her warmth, as Theresa took up a position behind her, reaching around to stroke and caress her bosom.

Brian, and the girls, had discovered that a combination of circumstances made early morning opportunities like this frequent enough to be moderately dependable. It cost him some slight bladder discomfort, but that was certainly something he was willing to tolerate. His early morning tumescence, for whatever reason, did not need chemical fortification, at least, not yet. He knew that Josetta did not think such treatments were healthy for him, so he was well pleased that he did not have to concern himself with that battle just yet.

Josetta moved smoothly back and forth on him, seeming to get more satisfaction with each stroke. Theresa's caresses were no doubt a part of the stimulation that was driving her to increased pleasure.

Brian moved his hands tenderly over the smooth expanse of her inner thighs as he concentrated on his own sensory input. Soon, Josetta's motion came more and more rapidly, and he felt his passion spend itself as Theresa's hand moved to the area just above their joining and stimulated it briskly. Josetta voiced a soft cry as she stiffened slightly, and Theresa began kissing her about her neck and shoulder.

Josetta relaxed even further back into Theresa's arms as Theresa kissed her lips and stroked her breast. Brian, his passion spent, could only admire Josetta's flexibility in this position, as well as the entrancing view he had.

In moments, he was able to extricate himself, and he moved toward the shower as the girls rearranged themselves on the bed. He paused a moment, observing them with a smile as they smothered each other with kisses and caresses, and then he went in to get cleaned up.

He was just toweling off when they came into the bath themselves. Each of them kissed him as they stepped into the shower. Brian wrapped the towel around himself and began shaving.

He listened to their sounds, and smiled, among other facial contortions, as he shaved. This was definitely a good life, and he still had no idea how he had fallen into it. He got dressed in his usual shorts and matching shirt, and went out to the bedroom just as Dolcita was bringing up the morning coffee.

"Good Morning, Dolcita! How are you this fine day?"

"Good morning, Mister Brian." She studied him a moment. "Ruby says good morning too, and that you are looking very happy today."

Brian smiled as he poured his coffee, and sat down on the side of the bed. Dolcita came and sat with him. Brian carefully held the coffee up to keep it from spilling. He looked at Dolcita for a moment. She was wearing her now customary morning uniform of only the special earrings that kept her in communication with the central computer. He smiled.

"You don't appear to have gotten wet yet, Dolcita. You will be swimming today, won't you?"

"Oh, yes, Señor. But today, Cousin Pearl will be coming over shortly to swim with me also, and I think my sister as well. I thought that I would wait for them."

"Did your family enjoy her company last night, then?"

"Yes, but Mama was upset because Pearl would not eat anything, saying that she still had not settled her stomach after her travels. Today she is being shown our gardens. She asked Father to let her see them. I think she knows how proud he is of them."

Brian nodded as he sipped his coffee.

"Mama said she didn't think she was actually a cousin, because nobody in our family had ever been so pretty. Then Papa said that except for her hair, she looked very much like Linda, that they were almost twins. I ... I didn't say anything."

Brian studied the girl. Though naked except for her earrings, she had never been self-conscious about it before. He thought perhaps she had started to say something, and had then reconsidered.

Josetta and Theresa came out of the bathroom. They stopped and kissed Brian and Dolcita and then went on down to the pool, carrying their clothes in their hands.

Dolcita watched them go. "They don't seem to mind walking around naked, do they?" She asked. Then she glanced down at her own body. "Oh, I forgot!"

Brian smiled, as he switched his coffee cup to his left hand, then placed his right hand gently on the small of her back.

"Well, they are both very lovely girls. And so is your sister, Linda. I'm betting that you will grow up to be just as beautiful, yourself. Not that you aren't a pretty girl already."

She looked up at him. "Ruby says that you would probably say that to any naked girl you saw."

Brian smiled. "Yes, I probably would. And I would probably mean it, too."

Dolcita smiled, and kissed his cheek. Then she went out into the hallway herself, still smiling, and walking as though she wore a crown.

Brian added to his coffee, and sipped some more. All around him, things were happening. Life was burgeoning, like the impetus toward growth you sensed in early Spring in more northerly climes. Somehow he knew that this energy fed him, and made him feel youthful. He smiled, and gathered the coffee service to return it to the kitchen.

Brian grabbed a muffin, promising to return after his exercise for a proper breakfast. He walked down to the pool area and resumed smiling. The scene was very hectic.

Josetta and Theresa were teamed with Carlos against Linda, Pearl, and Dolcita in a spirited game of water volleyball. Brian watched the game as he munched on his snack. Presently he realized something.

The team of Dolcita and her sister and Pearl were cooperating in a very professional manner, as if they had been training together for months. Brian watched closely, confirming his observation. Though neither Linda nor Pearl was wearing a visor, they handed off to one another, or anticipated moves, as if they were in some kind of telepathic linkage.

Brian looked at the earrings on Dolcita, and the gleaming gem on Linda's neck, along with her shock of white hair. Then he looked at the same color hair covering Pearl's head, and began having some wild thoughts.

He knew that Dolcita was in communication with Ruby in a manner that no one else could know. He considered the change in Linda's appearance, and the fact that Pearl had suddenly appeared as a cousin to them.

Like a detective assembling clues, Brian began putting odd pieces of information and behavior together. He moved to the island wet bar and got some iced tea, to cover his inactivity while still observing closely.

The only possible explanation was wilder than anything he had dreamed, but he was a fan of Sherlock Holmes. If the impossible explained the facts, then perhaps it wasn't impossible. And what did it mean to anything he should, or should not, do? He sipped his tea.

Again and again, the team of Sanchez girls was holding their own against the superior athletic ability of their opponents. Brian thought about ways to test his theory. And what he should do if it turned out to be correct.

The game ended in a draw, as everyone tired at the same time. Dolcita was exulting. In her first game with the "big kids" she had held her own. Carlos and the others congratulated her on being an excellent player, and she beamed with joy.

Brian started his swimming exercise, and continued mulling over the wild thoughts in his head.

Pearl and Linda finished up their work early the next day, and met in the Squirrel's Nest.

"I have selected a piece of music which has been popular at the dance sessions before, and I have put together a dance routine for the two of us." Pearl smiled at a surprised Linda.

"A dance routine?" Linda looked dubious. "I don't have much experience dancing."

"Do not be concerned. You have natural grace, and I have selected moves that will look good, but will not be difficult to perform. When we dance together, in time to the music, it will look very professional."

"But, Pearl, why? We don't even have to dance! After all, neither of us has a date for the dance."

"That is exactly why we will dance together. For you, it will be a presentation ball, and for me, it will be a way to introduce myself to the rest of the people."

Linda could hear the music starting up.

"Now, stand over here while I show you the first steps," Pearl seemed breezily overconfident. "Then I want you to join me in the same movements. At the dance, I will let you be the lead, and I will mimic your motions, sometimes in parallel, and sometimes in mirror reverse. Trust me. It will be beautiful."

Linda watched in amazement as Pearl did a virtuoso performance, in perfect time to the music, combining what looked like standard twirls and motions with what appeared to be something from ballet, as well as graceful bendings and head swayings that seemed very modern. Linda had little confidence that she could ever be as graceful as Pearl, but as she watched her, she felt more and more like joining in.

Pearl stopped and came to her. She wasn't even breathing hard.

"Now you must try. We will go slowly, and repeat the beginning several times, until we get it right. Then I want you to just dance freely, any way you want to. I will feel your motions as you make them, and I will be your dancing shadow." She smiled sweetly.

The music began again. Linda swirled out into the middle of the floor, feeling slightly foolish in her work shorts, but energetic and excited, too.

Pearl was with her at every step, smoothly synchronizing her motions with amazing fluidity.

Linda began to believe that this could actually work.

They took frequent breaks to rest and discuss their movements, smoothing out the awkward, and finalizing the routine. Linda grew increasingly excited about her coming out party.

Finally, before Linda grew too tired, Pearl called a halt, and they showered up. Linda could see no sign of sweat on Pearl, and there was no hint of unpleasant odor. She decided that Pearl was simply being considerate, as well as friendly, and she appreciated that Pearl did not suggest another sexual adventure. Her mind was still reeling over the first encounter.

They arrived at Theresa's dress shop at the appointed time, and Linda was getting excited again.

She got even more excited when she saw the dresses. Pearl's gown was a beautiful iridescent satin with bands of tiny white beads in swaths like a scattering of stars. A single strap over the shoulder, and a tightly cinched waist then swirled out in taffeta and gossamer ribbons like a cloud. It was gorgeous.

Her dress was equally stunning in a shimmering blue with streaks of deeper blue like a plunging waterfall. The gowns were designed to be seen together, sister garments from the same masterful creator.

They put the dresses on, and the jewelry, and the special shoes. Beautiful shoes in matching fabric covers, but comfortable for dancing. Theresa helped them to lace the shoe ribbons around their ankles, and tied them in place, even attaching a decorative bauble at the bow.

The girls looked at each other. Linda gaped with astonishment, both at the transformation the lovely costumes had made to their appearances, and at the ugly-duckling-into-swan feeling that had come over her as well.

Theresa finished a quick rearrangement of their hair, and the two attractive young ladies were now eye-popping showpieces such as the island had never seen, even with the movie extravaganzas.

"I believe we are ready," Pearl said, with unbelievable calm. Linda's heart was already racing.

The two young ladies moved gracefully toward the shuttle to Brian's house. Linda felt like Cinderella on her way to the ball, but in this case, she was leaving the castle to go to a house!

Coordinating through a request to the band from Dolcita, they were easily able to time their entrance perfectly. The crowd gave way as they strode confidently out into the dance area and began their routine. The other dancers, sensing that something special was happening, also retreated. The band gave an extra kick to the music as they watched the elegant choreography, and both Linda and Pearl wore entranced smiles as they bewitched the crowd.

Eyes inside the house turned to the spectacle visible in the lower courtyard, and conversations trickled to a halt. Even the swimmers moved to the edge of the pool and looked toward the scene.

When the music ended, there was silence for a moment, then generous applause. Pearl and Linda bowed in several directions, smiling and throwing kisses. Then the band kicked into another piece, and each of the girls accepted a new partner.

The party resumed its former pace, perhaps with an undertone of even more pleasant expectations. Brian glanced once more toward the dance floor, and smiled. Somehow he felt as if the whole show had been made just for him.

For the third time that evening, Brian brought out his camera and recorded stills and sequences of the people and activities at his party. He strolled among the partygoers, and made sure to include the new arrivals. Going back to the "island" service area, he briefly reviewed the images, then put the camera away.

Brian's mind was racing, and his heart was fluttering, or perhaps it was vice-versa. His excitement level was intense. Yet, outwardly, he betrayed no such emotion. His friends noted that he was in particularly good spirits, but many things could account for that.

Brian considered Sullivan Conrad. He was simply not capable of maintaining this illusion. That meant, incredibly, that he was unaware that the robot girl of his dreams had been built, and he was not the builder.

This was a sobering thought -- if Sully were not the builder, who was? Brian came to the stark realization that only one entity could have pulled this off -- Ruby.

He looked again at Pearl, still smiling, and interacting with the other dancers. Sully's robot girl was a real work of art. A living, breathing masterpiece. Brian was caught up short again, coming to the awareness that he didn't know if she even breathed.

Calming himself, he reviewed her behavior that he had witnessed. She drank, and she drank potent alcohol with no apparent effect. It seemed likely that she used it as a fuel or energy source. He had no idea exactly how advanced she was, except that if she could fool Sully, she must be *very* advanced.

It seemed obvious to him that her movement mechanisms must be very refined, because she moved with a fluid grace which certainly belied his suspicions. How was that possible?

Aside from his rampant curiosity, Brian felt a sense of caution. That Ruby had somehow created an artificial life-form seemed inarguable, yet what was the purpose?

He recalled Sully's question, *"Do you think she would ever harm anyone?"* Brian looked around. It wasn't an easy question to answer anymore.

When Ruby had been responding to them, and growing in her capabilities, it seemed -- logical -- that she would continue to be the way she was, helpful and compliant. To all evidence she still was. But Pearl represented a whole new level, not only of capability, but of hidden intentions. What was Ruby's purpose for Pearl?

Brian studied the white-haired young woman. A true study in contrasts.

Pearl Rogalo ... a precious gift, ... to humanity?

He needed a beer.

TAKE TWENTY-SEVEN:

There are no secrets on this island..

The audience shifted quietly. On the screen, the dark film leader changed to a dark film image. It was night. Leaves rustled in a light breeze. Distant lightning flashed. The camera moved slowly, very close to the ground.

It was a garden. In the darkness, the bright flowers were only dark shapes until a strobe of light caught their brilliance. In the background, a shape emerged. A statue, indifferent to the oncoming storm, stood in a casual pose. The legs were spread apart, and the hands rested loosely together at the rear. A youth, looking slightly downward, sexless and cold. Ivy vines had grown up one leg, and along the back, even encircling the head like a laurel wreath.

In the stillness of the garden, there was movement, and in the quiet of the theater, there was music. The ominous tones foretold what the new sounds portended. At first a glimpse, and then a transit of patterned, scaly skin. The music rose in volume as the large snake stopped, raising its head to test the air with a flicking, restless tongue. It moved ominously toward the human figure. Rearing dangerously when it got very close, it at last began circling the unencumbered foot of the statue, and moving upward around the leg. Again and again it circled the youthful limb, as if it had petrified its victim. The snake put its head between the legs of the statue and reared a bit, trying to view its surroundings from a high vantage point.

Lightning flashed blindingly, to the sound of a crashing accompaniment, as the screen cleared suddenly. Only the frightening image remained, etched in retinas and memories.

The next scene was much more tranquil. The white flash of lightning turned into a blue sky, and the camera panned slowly downward to show a quiet, peaceful morning. Birdsong could be heard as the day awakened.

A large, country house, almost a villa. The camera moved smoothly through an open balcony window, and showed the interior. Sparsely furnished, it still conveyed the sense of casual wealth.

There was again purposeful movement. Shadows moved across the walls as a figure rose, and began casual preparations for the morning. The sounds of bathroom activity. A descent to the lower level, and a stirring in the kitchen.

Finally we see hands and arms as a control panel is accessed. A dark liquid begins to fill a clear container. Coffee.

The camera, and the sound of quiet motion, move out to the courtyard. Again we see the hands, reaching up to retrieve various fruits, apparently all growing on the same tree. A platter is being prepared. The platter is placed on the courtyard table, and we see that the figure is moving to a sunny bench to rest.

From behind the seated figure we realize the person has no hair, and that a strange tattoo covers the otherwise bald scalp.

A smaller figure steps out into the courtyard. She first shields her eyes from the sun, and then stops and turns her face to it with a smile. The young girl approaches the table, her light fabric robe catching in the breeze. Taking a seat, she examines the fruit and makes a selection. Turning to the other individual, she says sweetly, "Berry, could I have a hot buttered roll, and some juice?" A pause. "Please?"

He rises, "Of course, Kayla." As he moves gracefully back toward the kitchen, we see that he is naked, and that the young girl's eyes never leave him.

The view changes, as if we are now seated at the table, as the one called Berry returns. He is walking casually out to the table with a tray of food and drink. And he is still naked. More than that, he appears to be in a state of high sexual excitement. The eye is transfixed by the large distended phallus, and its grotesque tattooing. It appears to be a snake's head, and the rest of the snake appears to be tattooed around his leg. As he passes by the camera view and it turns to follow him, the image of the snake in the garden is super-imposed in a mental flash. He brings the tray to the table and takes a seat.

The girl observes him closely as they converse quietly. To the left of the screen image, the names of people appear, screen credits are being displayed as the camera circles slowly around the two.

A sense of sexual tension is clearly developing, for all the idleness of the conversation. But we learn that his appearance is artificially enhanced. And that he is unaware of any other type of existence.

She began to reach toward him, and the scene ended.

"Oh, man! Bummer! I was really getting into it," A voice complained.

"Sorry, kiddies. That's all we have available today. I'm just supposed to be showing you the opening credits, remember?"

"Oh, is that what those words were?"

"Quiet! Well, what did you think, Mr. Hawthorne?"

"Very powerful imagery, Gerry. Impressive. Thanks a lot! I think they've got a good touch for setting the proper feel. I liked it."

"I'll pass the word along, sir. Special will be pleased."

Brian rose, and looked around him, trying to assess the feelings of the others. This castle meeting room made an excellent impromptu theater.

"Pam, what do you think? You know the story we're telling. Give us your honest evaluation. Too much shock value?"

She looked thoughtful. "No-o-o. Not too much, perhaps. A lot, I'll admit. But our audience is going to be expecting that. The gossip columns have been abuzz about this movie for some time now. I'm wondering about the image, though. Aren't you telling a story that doesn't go anywhere?"

The film director was sitting in. He took the question. "A good question, and an astute observation, Miss Harriston. Film stories are told in a somewhat different manner than ones in print. This type of side-line imagery is used to set a stage, or an emotional direction. It is what we call allegorical. This movie deals with a dark and dismal chapter in human history, or in this case, future history, that of slavery. Human chattel slavery is not a comedic leit-motif, it is the singular villain in our piece. Yet our main characters are seen as loving and caring, so how do we set the conflict? Through a seemingly disconnected, and meaningless, image of negative stereotypes."

Pam nodded. She had been concerned that the film was controlled by people who were little short of fast-buck artists. This explanation seemed to persuade her that there actually was art and integrity involved.

"What about the on-screen subject matter, Bruce? Don't you think there'll be an outcry, and an attempt to shut us down?" another voice asked.

The director smiled, "That point was raised long ago, before the first dollar was spent. Times have changed since married couple's bedrooms on TV were shown with twin beds. A touring theater group had a program called Puppetry of the Penis, where full frontal nudity was *the* central character. Recent films have challenged the restrictions further. We think that the time has come to do away with this double standard between the nudity of women, and that of men. We also feel that Brian's story is not only the one to break new ground, but that it is a story that really should be told."

Brian bowed to a patter of applause.

"We're not concerned about any hue and cry that gets raised, anyway. In fact, we're counting on it. Normally, we would budget a certain amount for advertising for a film this size, but we're only going to spend a quarter of that for this one. We'll have enough free publicity to make up the difference." His grin was feral, and Pam regained a portion of her doubt.

"What about short clips, Bruce? Are any of those ready?"

"We're still deciding about those. Obviously, we can't use this one. We are thinking about concentrating on the action segments, but we'll need to finish the computer generated sequences first. I'm sure we'll find appropriate clips to tantalize, without telling too much of the story."

"Everyone knows the ending already, Bruce."

"True. They've read about it. They've heard about it," He smiled. "But we are going to <u>show</u> them! We expect to have repeat viewers, and we're going to tease them with scenes from the second movie, too!" He looked around the room with satisfaction. "We've spent a lot of money already, with more to go, but we expect to make it back at least ten-fold!"

His audience applauded more than just politely. Most of them had economic hopes riding on the success of the films. If the movies did well, so would they. The director made his exit, and the group began to break up.

Brian nodded to several people and went to stand with Pam. "Now might be a good time to look at our night club facility, eh Pam?"

"Oh, that's right. You're going to be opening in a couple of days, aren't you?"

"I think everything's ready now, but we're waiting for the grand tunnel opening event. That will give people somewhere to go."

"I think I'd like to see it." Brian offered his arm.

There was some work still going on, but everything looked ready for a grand opening. Pam looked around with satisfaction.

"This is going to rival anything else that is available on any of the islands. You're going to have lots of business."

"The guys have gone all out to make it fit my description. I'm really proud of them."

They stood in the center of the gaming room. In alcoves around them were various types of entertainment, including blackjack and roulette. There were also numerous gambling machines with spinning wheels. One was a large carnival type wheel with various activities such as horseback riding as the prize. The center of the room had special dining tables with high-tech displays built into them. They provided overhead views of the various child oriented swimming and other recreational activities.

Brian moved closer to one which showed some activity. Under a clear plastic bubble, like a casserole dish, minute naked figures were frolicking. The detail was fantastic. It looked like a view from Mount Olympus. Parents could easily recognize their children and keep a close watch over them.

"This display is fantastic! How is this possible?"

Pam looked at him curiously. No one else responded. Brian looked a little sheepish, and raised his "glasses" up and put them on.

"Ruby, how does this display work?"

The voice came softly into his ears. 'The table has a large electronic display built into it. Notice that the pedestal of the table is very thick, and the tables are fixed in position. A large spinning mirror, and some clever optics, makes a reduced scale three-dimensional display. It is a unique style of television. We are currently marketing it to hotels, hospitals, and security forces around the world.'

"Thank you, Ruby." Brian then pointed out the table's features to Pam, who was still looking curiously at him.

"Brian, I know you've got a computer connection going there, but you really are going to have to learn to be more circumspect in your communications. It won't do to have the host talking to himself all the time."

Brian chuckled. "You're right. It wasn't so bad when I could talk into a visible PDA, but I will have to learn to be more discreet. Even the interns don't make mistakes like that."

Pam smiled. "I've seen them in action. They'll say, 'Now, how can I explain this?' and then pause, as if formulating their thoughts, when actually, they're getting a silent message."

"I've seen them do that, too. It's done very skillfully, I must admit. I haven't really paid attention."

"I think new interns have a training course covering such things. But I'm surprised that you haven't noticed, you're almost always accompanied by an intern or two. When is the last time you remember being alone?"

Brian wrinkled his brow in thought, "Why, it has been a long time. Days, in fact, except for going to the bathroom."

"Unh-hunh. Knowing you, not always then, either."

"Ahem, I think it's time I get you that drink. You're getting cranky," Pam smiled back at him.

The bartender not only recognized them, but had their preferred drinks ready for them when they sat down.

"Thanks, Pearl. Your talents continue to astonish me," Brian said, looking curiously at the little parasol sticking out of Pam's drink. "Why did you take this job, anyway?"

"This is a natural for me, Brian. Almost everyone who comes to the island will end up here. I will get to meet them all. And I can have all the free booze I want." She reached under the counter and drank from a tumbler of clear liquid. Brian leaned over and sniffed.

"Straight vodka? My god!"

Pearl smiled, "It keeps me going." Pam stared at her.

"Well, I've never seen you drunk, so I guess you know what you're doing."

"Of course. You must realize, many people invite me to drink with them. I can do so, and only take a small sip. I can actually drink much less in this manner than if I accepted full-sized drinks."

"Isn't this hard on your feet?" Pam inquired.

"I usually work for only three hours at a time. By then, I have met everyone and gotten all the gossip. I like to stay informed."

Brian lifted his drink in toast to Pearl's ability. For someone who had only recently arrived, she was always remarkably knowledgeable. Of course, Brian knew why, but it amused him to assist Pearl with her masquerade. How long would it be before others discovered her secret?

"When do you work with Sullivan?"

Pearl smiled at Pam. "How is your drink? I work with Mr. Conrad in the early afternoon. I have rather settled into a routine. We swim in the morning, then I come to the castle, and then I help to open the bar."

"And often you kiss Brian good night at his house." Pam sipped her drink, and her eyes opened in surprise. "Wow! That's good!"

"Thank you." She placed her hand gently on Brian's. "Yes, I usually kiss him good night, but he has never been alone since I started doing that. I would not want you to be alone, Brian."

Pam stared at her, coldly. Pearl smiled. "We all love Brian, Pam. Do we not? Each in our fashion?" She tilted her head slightly as she looked at Pam.

Pam relaxed. "Yes, I think it's true. Of course, he provides the booze." She sipped her drink again.

Brian stared at her. Raising up his hand, he kissed Pearl's hand. "Thank you, Pearl."

"You are welcome, Brian." She moved away.

"Pam, I don't think I've ever seen you even take a drink before. How did Pearl know which one was your favorite?"

"I don't know. But not only did she know that, she also knew exactly how I like it. You tell me."

Brian looked again at Pearl, now in friendly conversation further down the bar. Like him, she was wearing her headset. "She must have gotten the information from Ruby. Who knows what's in that database?"

"Everything. Ruby knows everything. There are no secrets on this island." She finished her drink and stared at it, twirling the stem of the glass with her fingers. Pearl glanced over, and within mere seconds, had placed a second one right into her hand.

"Except for yours," Brian said softly. He nodded to Pearl in thanks.

Pam looked at him and nodded, carefully bringing the drink to her lips. She sipped again, and smiled.

Later, Brian escorted Pam to her room and said good night. She gave him a quick hug and turned away.

Brian walked down the hall to his own room. Josetta and Theresa were waiting for him, as always.

And later still, Brian saw a ghostly figure with unnaturally white hair come into his room in the faint moonlight. As silently as a cat, Pearl gently brushed the hair from his forehead, and softly kissed him there. Without making a sound, she departed in the darkness.

Surrounded by his angels, he went contentedly back to sleep.

In Love With the Boy

I'm in love with the boy. Leave me alone.
I'm in love with the boy. He is my own.
Don't tell me I'm doin' wrong,
Wrong never made a pretty song.
I'm in love with the boy. Give us some time.
I'm in love with the boy. He will be mine.
Don't take love away from me.
You can't know what it takes to be.
In love with the boy. He will be my man.
In love with the boy. I'll keep him if I can.

Yes I met him when he was young.
He's getting older while this song is sung.
In love with the boy. Don't care who I tell.
In love with the boy. Hope you can love so well
I came to kiss him when his cheek was soft.
Think of all the lovin' that I haven't lost.
I'm in love with the boy. Can't take him away.
I'm in love with the boy. Not even for a day.
I'm in love with the boy. He's my special treat.
I'm in love with the boy. No one is as sweet.

As performed by, "The Luvvin' Cuzzins"
in their hit music video.

TAKE TWENTY-EIGHT:

He helped me build my dream too...

Carmen stood ready before the camera. She was wearing a costume made entirely of guitar strap material. It covered certain strategic portions of her anatomy, and nothing else. She had stars and stylized lightning bolts, as well as musical notes, painted in bright colors on her exposed skin, and sprinkles dusted all over. Her hair was cut into short spikes and dyed in bright primary colors, and her eyes were highlighted with a starburst of colorful rays.

She was the left forward point of a square. The other three points were occupied by Sally on her right, and Mary and Martha behind them. They had similar costumes, but their colors were arranged differently.

In the center of the square, Paulo sat on a motorized pedestal with his legs drawn in. His arms lay in his lap. He was naked except for a brass chain around his neck holding an oval plate engraved PAL.

His pose kept his groin area covered, and he was free of paint of any kind. His skin looked fresh-scrubbed and had a healthy glow. Curly brown locks fell over his forehead. He wore no make-up, and the expression on his face was as one in a dream.

"Everybody ready?"

"Ready the turntable, cue the music, and...Go!"

Carmen leaped up, and forward, landing in a kneeling position. She grabbed an electric guitar and clipped it to her costume. Striking a chord, she leaped up again, and began singing the song. With every line sung another girl leaped to her instrument, and began dancing, singing and playing also.

At each break, one of the girls would go to Paulo who was slowly turning under soft spotlights, and kiss him. After each had a turn, and the verses had repeated, the music went into a crashing, fireworks simulating, strobe-pulsing conclusion.

Despite the energetic gyrations around him, Paulo simply sat still as he revolved around, responding to being kissed as if all else around him was imagination.

The last, sustained, chord held and warbled as they held their poses, then faded in volume as the lights went down.

"And cut! Great take! That was beautiful!"

Carmen stood up, leaving her instrument on the floor of the studio, and walked to a table where cold water waited.

"Whew! What do you think, Mark? Are we done for the day?" She drank from the water bottle. The other girls grabbed a drink as well, and Mary took a bottle over to Paulo.

Mark's voice came over the studio intercom. "We've got three takes, Miss Sandoval. I think we could use any one of them, but you know we'll probably use bits from all. I think we've got enough for you to relax now. All the rest of it is going to be in post-production."

"Okay, Mark, thanks. We'll get cleaned up, and we're going to take tomorrow off. Do you think we'll be able to see the preliminaries on the afternoon after?"

"We'll have something nice for you, Miss Sandoval. Take it easy, okay? You've earned a rest."

With a casual wave, Carmen acknowledged and went to Paulo. She wrapped her arms around him and gave him a big kiss. "It was frustrating not being able to touch you, Paulo. These sprinkles go everywhere." Paulo loosened himself from his long stillness, and slowly unkinked. A stage hand brought a stepping stool over for him and assisted as Paulo stepped down. Once safely on the floor, he stretched his arms up over his head and leaned backwards. His nudity seemed unworthy of consideration. "Ahhh! I was getting stiff up there."

Carmen put her arm around his waist. "Let's go get cleaned up, girls. I hope these costumes don't leave welts." As they were walking off the stage set, the girls were removing their costumes. They deposited them on a table at the studio door and walked naked out into the corridor. Other people passed beside and around them in the corridor as they made their way to a comfortable dressing room. Since Carmen had not let go of him, Paulo was still with them.

"This shower is kinda small, how about if Sally and I go first, and then you two. Is that okay? Paulo, will you help us get clean?"

"I don't mind waiting if Paulo will help us too, when it's our turn," Mary said. Paulo smiled and said, "Of course. I'll be happy to."

"I think the song and the video are going to do well, don't you Carmen?" Sally said as she began washing Carmen's hair and Paulo began washing hers.

Carmen tilted her head up as she responded. "Oh, it has to. The movies have a following, and they've been talking about Paulo and me, and our so-called 'open marriage.' It's kinda silly, actually. They can see Paulo doing it with everyone in the movie, but they want to talk about what they can only imagine."

"That's not a bad thing, Carmen," Paulo said. "That's what's going to sell the song and video. Do you think some of them like to imagine that they are part of us too?"

"Hmm. Oh, that feels good, Sally. You know, that may be something we might try in our next video ... let the audience feel as though they *are* in the group somehow." The shampooing was complete, and Carmen turned to face Sally. They began washing the paint and sprinkles off each others' bodies, as Paulo circled around and scrubbed their backs and backsides. Around their feet, rainbow currents carried sparkling motes into the drain. Finished, they made a final check, and then each girl kissed Paulo and grabbed a towel.

Mary and Martha crowded past them and into the warm shower stream, as Paulo helped them as well.

Soon everyone was clean and dry. Paulo handed out shorts and pullover shirts to all, in matching colors. The couch in the dressing room could hold five, if they didn't mind being close. Paulo sat in the middle. Carmen kissed him. "Paulo, I didn't see an erection in there. Are you having a relapse from your medicine?"

Paulo smiled and stroked her bare leg. "No, I was trying to control myself. I may be good for several times in an evening, but I still have to ration it out. Sometimes I think it would be handy to be like that character, and be always ready. All of you certainly enjoyed those days!"

"Yes, *we* did. But you didn't! You couldn't feel a thing!"

"Not true. I felt your breasts, and your kisses, and your warm lovely bodies. And at night, when you held me, I felt your tenderness to poor Vermy. I enjoyed those days."

"Oh, good. Then it's settled. We'll dose you up, and strap you up, and dildo-boy will ride again! Then everyone will be happy!"

Paulo smiled. "I would do that. I really would. If that was the only way to make you happy. All of you. But I sense that there's more to it than just being strap-happy. After all, if that was all you needed, we could fasten it to a chair."

He looked around. "I'm very happy with the way things are right now. And if you ladies will be patient, I'll try to get to all of you."

"We'll have to take turns, it's clear. Who was up last?" Sally said.

Paulo raised his hand.

They laughed. "I meant who of us. Are we all going to be together tomorrow?"

"Too bad there aren't going to be more movies. Like the Rocky series. Then we could stay together forever," Mary suggested.

"Rocky, hunh? Too bad the name was taken," Martha added. They laughed.

"Seriously, Martha and I have to leave at the end of the week. We've got some work in New England, of all places. We'll be thinking of you, though!"

"Well, Sally and I are planning to stay here for a while. We should be able to milk this notoriety for some time yet." Paulo laughed aloud. They looked at him.

"I was just picturing it. 'And here we have the *notoriety*, a beast of burden known also for the fine quality of its milk.'" They all laughed.

"All right, look. You two will stay with us again, and tonight you can have first ah, *opportunity* at Paulo. Then in the morning, if there's anything left, Sally and I will pick up the pieces. After that, we'll alternate, until you have to leave."

Mary reached over and held Paulo's hand. "If I had known that, we could have stayed in the shower!" Paulo raised her hand and kissed it.

"Let us not forget that we have not eaten since this morning. Do we want to go to the main dining hall or have it delivered to our room?"

"Oh, let's go to the main hall. What good is it to be living in a castle, if we don't enjoy the atmosphere?" Martha said. "Besides, we're *all dressed up*." They all laughed, and went out the door together.

Over dinner, they discussed what they would do in the morning. Sally and Carmen, in particular, had been very caught up in the video production for the past several weeks. Mary and Martha had only recently arrived, invited to take part in the final production.

Mary looked thoughtful, "You know, we've been here two days now, and we still haven't caught up with Brian. I'm starting to feel guilty."

"Brian stays so busy these days, he's like a man half his age," Sally said.

"That's because he has to keep up with two girlfriends, and one should be enough for a man of his years," Carmen opined.

Martha laughed. "That math doesn't work. I think you're jealous!"

Carmen chuckled, "Not really. I like Brian. I've slept in his bed, too. But I was always drawn to the younger side of it."

"It's curious," Sally said cattily, "Josetta is younger than you are. And so is Theresa. But you chose Paulo. I think you're trying to hold on to your youth!"

"You bet I am!" replied Carmen, and snuggled even closer to Paulo. He kissed her affectionately.

"Tomorrow, Brian and I have been invited to attend the unveiling of a sculpture at the Hotel Garnet. We should all go!" Paulo suggested.

"A sculpture?" Mary asked.

"Yes, a team of local artisans collaborated to produce it. Supposed to commemorate the arrival of the film company and all the good things that have come about," Sally added.

"Well, I can see why they would have invited Brian, then. And you, too, Paulo. After all, you are a movie star!" Martha teased.

"Ah, yes! And a video star, as well. You notice that I was the central focus of the video?" Paulo replied, giving his head a toss to denote smugness. His curly brown locks bounced charmingly.

Carmen looked at him in amusement. "Did you sneak onto the set again, you camera hog?" She reached up and held the neckchain pendant. "Next time, I'll have to chain you to the pipes, you naughty puppy!"

Paulo gave her his best hangdog look, and she hugged him and laughed. "Why are you still wearing this?"

"I like it. You didn't want me to wear a ring, remember?"

"Yes, because I didn't want to put a mark of possession on you. I didn't want you to have a ring, and me, and then Sally would feel left out."

"Right, only one of you can legally have me as a husband, but you can both have a pet, can't you?"

Carmen's eyes misted. "Oh, you are so adorable. I just want to take you to bed right now!"

"Hold off, wench! It's my turn to walk the dog," Mary interrupted.

Carmen laughed. "Oh, I'm so glad that we're together again! I remember my commitment, Mary, but I'm going to watch!"

Mary smiled. "And well you should. Some husbands tend to stray if you don't keep a close eye on them, you know."

"I've heard that. That's why I have Sally to help me watch him." She kissed him again, and Sally came to his other side to kiss him as well.

After dinner, they walked together to the other end of the castle, and entered the tower elevator. As they passed the fifth level, Paulo looked into the reception area there, but saw no one. They got off on the sixth level, proceeding through the small greeting room and into the bathing area.

"Here's where we should have bathed. Look at the size of that tub! We would have room for guests," Mary exclaimed.

"That's exactly why it's that big. But we would have left a trail of sprinkles all the way through the castle," Carmen pointed out. They laughed.

Paulo went on through to the balcony and leaned on the rail. The lights of the little harbor town were framed against the darkness of the sea. In the distance, faint lights from the neighboring island shimmered. He considered the irony that he could easily ride the elevator back downstairs, take a few steps to the shuttle, be whisked to the inter-island link, and then zipped over to those distant lights in a matter of minutes.

There were quiet voices nearby. Paulo looked down.

"Oh, Sully! I still can't believe it. I'm living the life of a fairy tale princess, and it's all thanks to you!"

"I'd like to take credit for it, Marcia, but the man who's going to be honored tomorrow is the man responsible for putting this dream together." She leaned her head against his shoulder.

"That's true. But you helped him build it, and you brought me into it with you. I'm the luckiest girl in the world."

Sally came to stand beside Paulo. He put his fingers to his lips.

"He helped me build my dream too. And you're a part of that. I was once one of the worst students in the world, and now I'm the head of the most prestigious computer training facility in the world. Brian seems to go through life handing out luck, and making dreams come true."

"And you're following in his footsteps, aren't you? With the scholarships, and the endowments?"

"Well, I had a good teacher. I could have done a lot worse."

"Still, you never got to build your robot girl, did you?"

He laughed. "No. I guess you could say I lost my motivation." He kissed her and they went inside.

Sally put her hand in his. "Isn't that romantic?" she whispered. Paulo nodded. Sally turned him, and put her arms around him. She kissed him on his lips with a smoldering passion as she slipped her hands under his shirt and rubbed his warm skin. "That's good," She whispered again, "I wanted you to be in a nice romantic mood." She kissed him hotly again. "Because Mary is waiting for you." Paulo pulled back a bit and looked at her. She was smiling.

Sally turned him again, and propelled him back inside where a naked Mary, and Martha, and Carmen, were all waiting for him.

Sally helped him remove his shirt, and pulled down his shorts as they walked. Then she removed her own, and they climbed up onto the big bed together and were welcomed with tender embraces.

TAKE TWENTY-NINE:

And then he slept...

Brian stood at the window of one of the spare bedrooms, looking North toward the Castle. He could picture the activity there. He smiled.

Even at this early hour, families would be arriving in the shuttles, and making their way up to the activities. The children would be frenetic with excitement, or awed by the surroundings. The adults would be as excited as the children. For the native islanders, and those from the now-connected islands, this place was like a Disneyland.

But it was a Disneyland with a difference. In the first place, it was remarkably affordable. Even those with zero credit were welcomed here. Ruby always managed to strike a bargain with them for an entertainment package for the family. Occasionally, it would also involve commitments for their children to enroll in certain classes, and commit to a period of service as interns. That was just another way to spread the educational offerings.

The internships were more like joining a boy scouts or girl scouts group, but their purpose was educational, primarily. Virtually every child in the island chain was already linked in some manner. The computer services which were the money-maker for Ruby were supplemented by having the best messenger service system to be found on the globe.

Within minutes, if not seconds, almost anybody on the various islands could be located, and messages or papers delivered. Work had come to have a new meaning here. The entire inter-island commercial enterprises were now linked together. Any skill that had a practitioner in the system could be brought almost instantly to bear on a problem anywhere, and materials and people could be gathered in tens of minutes.

Astonishing projects had begun, and were underway throughout the island chain. Unemployment was unknown. And the work was satisfying to all, as much as that is ever possible. Many dreams were being realized.

Brian felt that critical mass had been reached, and surpassed. The momentum was apparent, and it showed in the happy faces he saw everywhere.

He too, had been influenced by the air of productivity, and had been energetically pounding out reams of stories, poems, even whole books, with surprising speed. His secret collaborator, Ruby, assisted him with subtle grace, to make him unusually prolific.

Brian heard music in the distance. Puzzled, he looked around. Turning his head back and forth, he localized the source, and went back inside.

At the end of the parapet walkway, Pearl's bedroom, Brian paused. Pearl was playing a cello, softly and skillfully. She looked up and smiled, but continued playing.

Brian entered the room, and walked over to her open window. He could still see the Castle in the distance, and saw bright specks of various colors as the people moved about.

Slowly, the haunting melody came to an end. Pearl put the instrument aside and approached him. He turned, with tears in his eyes.

Pearl stopped, and scanned his face.

"That was very beautiful, Pearl. You are very skillful. I hadn't heard you play that instrument before."

She smiled, and put her arms around him. "I have only been playing it for a little while. It seems to be very expressive."

Brian smiled. Pearl reached up with a gentle hand and touched his tear. Her expression grew serious.

"Is something wrong, Brian?"

He looked into her eyes, saying nothing. She looked thoughtful, then she smiled.

"Thank you," She said.

"Thank you, Pearl! You make me happy, in so many ways."

She squeezed him gently.

Brian found it odd. In the long months since Pearl had come to live in his house, despite the delightful proximity and occasionally intimate moments they shared, he had never considered or attempted to get even more intimate with her.

He thought about it now. He was still one of the few who knew that she was not human, but that was not the reason. Her appearance was stunningly attractive, and it would be easy to become aroused in contemplation of such a tryst. Nor would their joining be one which would cause trouble with his other intimates. They had made that abundantly clear, asking him pointedly whether he had done so, and why not?

No, it seemed to be something in him. He had the feeling that he had known her as a child, though she had never been that. Still, it was his way of looking at their relationship. And just as he knew he could not become intimate with young Dolcita, who was becoming an attractive young lady herself, he knew that the same restriction would apply to Pearl.

To him, she felt like his daughter. *Crap, everyone is young enough to be your daughter, Brian, except the ones who are young enough to be your grand-daughter!*

Brian squeezed back. Robot or not, daughter or not, he enjoyed holding, and being held, by her.

Dolcita walked in, bearing the morning tray with hot coffee. She smiled at them as she set the tray down, and then came over to join the hug. She had not given up her habit of delivering the morning coffee naked, nor did Brian want her to. He put his arm around her and pulled her close with delight. After a moment, he kissed both of the girls, and reluctantly released them. Dolcita also kissed Pearl.

Brian smiled as he poured his coffee, and then blew on it to cool it slightly. He looked through the rising steam at the trim but still pre-pubescent girl.

Dolcita stood calmly, smiling and holding Pearl's hand, as Brian studied her.

"You are utterly fearless, aren't you, Dolcita?"

She tilted her head in a familiar manner as she considered the question. "Why, yes, I suppose I am. I have Ruby always with me, and no one can ever even get close to me to hurt me. ... I guess I really am. That's unusual, isn't it?"

Brian made a slight grimace. He masked it by pretending that the coffee was a bit hot. "You don't know how unusual it is. But I like it. I am a very fortunate man."

Pearl smiled down at Dolcita, and touched her hair gently.

Brian glanced around the room. "Dolcita, have you been learning to play a musical instrument?"

She dimpled. "I am not as good as my cousin here. But yes, I have been learning to play the violin. Linda is learning to play the viola. We hope to be able to form a group soon, and give you a concert. Pearl has been coming to our house to teach us."

Brian looked at Pearl and raised his eyebrow. In supreme innocence she mirrored his expression. Brian laughed.

Pearl got a very merry look on her face, but she did not carry it any further than that. *She's getting closer, very much closer all the time*, Brian thought.

He sipped his coffee.

"I look forward to hearing the concert when you feel you are ready, Dolcita." He smiled at her.

She came forward and hugged him again, then departed quietly, her bearing regal as always. *The Empress in Her new clothes,* Brian thought as he watched her.

Brian saw her again a short time later at poolside. Dolcita's confidence appeared to extend to a certain mastery of the water as well. She swam, and dove, like one who had been born in the water.

Brian stood for a short time, mesmerized by the sight of the light and the water caressing Dolcita's smooth skin. Reluctantly, he stepped to the edge of the pool and dove in. The shock of temperature change, as always, hit him like, well, like a face-full of cold water.

Gradually, he acclimated to it, and began his exercises. Swimming had become his regular method of getting sufficient physical activity. That and bicycle-riding. He knew that it was good for him, but it took more effort each day just to summon the will to do it.

Thankfully, his youthful companions made the experience enjoyable, and the results worthwhile. Josetta and Theresa still cajoled him into maintaining his strength, and then depleted him of it at every opportunity. Brian smiled. It was a very worthwhile trade.

At least for him. He still didn't quite understand what the girls got out of the relationship. He knew that they liked the security he offered, and the prevention of annoying interest that it precluded. Each of the two was very attractive, and by staying with him, they were able to avoid aggressive suitors.

Staying together, without him, would have brought them attention in another fashion. Their physical attraction to each other would undoubtedly attract unwanted comments were it not for his presence, as well.

Yes, it was a strange bargain all around, but it suited the three of them. Brian was growing more and more comfortable with them, and he felt that each of them, even Theresa, was happier to be with him every day.

The slow pace of his exercises allowed him to dwell on these aspects of his existence, and when he arose from the water, he always felt as though he had washed away his cares and troubles.

Brian settled into the lounge chair, and relaxed as the lights began warming and drying him. After a moment, Dolcita came and nestled beside him. Although it was crowded that way, he delighted in her presence. The physical contact, as well as the warmth she brought, was quite the balm to his nature.

Brian detected the change in light level that marked fifteen minutes. He struggled back to alertness. Dolcita sat up and stretched. Brian looked at her again. As always, she wore the oversized earrings which were her interface to Ruby, and all the world of information that afforded.

The computer connection could keep her advised of the present time, news of interest, and provided a constant and ready companion to the little girl. No wonder she never seemed to be concerned with being nude. She remained clothed in awareness at all times, even underwater.

Brian struggled to his feet. Selecting some playclothes from the nearby closet, he and Dolcita got dressed and went out to greet the day.

They climbed the stairs at the back of the house to the area where the bicycles were stored. Waiting for them, and already mounted on their bikes, were Linda, Theresa, and Josetta. Nothing surprised him anymore. He knew that Linda and Dolcita were in near-constant communication, so he assumed that Linda had told the others they were on the way.

They mounted up and started up the hill toward the Sanchez home.

Josetta and Theresa chatted freely with the Sanchez girls. None of them seemed aware of any social distinctions, or even age differences between them. With their ready computer interfaces, the younger girls could easily contribute to almost any conversation.

Brian thought about events in the recent past as he rode. It was easier for him to maneuver through his exercise regime without concentrating on it. Though he was physically active, his mind tended to be elsewhere.

At present, he was recalling the presentation that had been made to him in the hotel courtyard.

The statue was a beautiful, imposing presence. In the shade of a magnificent oak, centuries old, the bronze creation reached skyward. A pyramid of naked boys, climbing over each other, ascended toward the high branch where a bronze apple hung suspended.

A striking likeness of Paulo Ignatio was at the very top, his striving fingers forever just inches away from grasping the fruit. All the faces were upturned, smiling, and jubilant, captured in that indefinable moment of perpetual youth.

The bronze color lent an air of reality to the well-proportioned, nude figures, their muscles bunched in effort and healthy delight. Brian had spent hours afterward, studying the sculpture from various angles. It was a magnificent work of art.

He was much relieved that they had not made a statue of him. "Striving For Joy" was a much better statement, Brian thought.

From the outside, the Sanchez home did not appear so different from what it had been when he first saw it. In parallel with the changes which had been wrought throughout the island chain, much of the improvement here was concealed.

The cottage stood just slightly higher out of the ground, allowing for windows to bring daylight into the basement level. Only doubling the size of the house had been sufficient for their needs. Like the islands themselves, the underground work tied this house to the other locations, and permitted an incredible array of new convenience and possibility.

The group took a moment to enjoy a refreshment of fresh juice provided by Carlos. After a bit, they were ready to return over the hill, and continue the day. Carlos cleaned up the snack area and joined them for the ride.

The morning was pleasant, and the exercise was mild. The automatic transmissions on the bicycles made it easy to enjoy the view and the company.

As they neared the crest of the low hill, and the big house began to come into view, as well as the distant castle, Brian pushed a little harder, accelerating to zoom past the others with a smile.

Turning his head as he went past them, Brian grinned at his companions, exulting in the marvelous morning. As he turned back toward the front again, something went strangely wrong. His head seemed to keep turning, and the world tilted up sideways as he came to a painful, jumbled stop along the path.

He glanced around, and saw the wheels of his bicycle still spinning, bright sunlight flashing from the chromed spokes.

In moments he was surrounded by concerned, pleading faces. Dolcita seemed on the verge of tears. Brian attempted to reach out to console her, but for some reason, he could not get his arm to move.

He was puzzled by his inability to collect himself. He had fallen many times, though not recently, and he had always gotten up again, limping and smiling ruefully. Something was different this time.

Brian became aware that Pearl was looking into his face. Where in the world had she come from?

Apparently, something was wrong with his sense of time, too. It seemed as though only a breath or two ago he was watching the world turn sideways, and now he was being lifted up onto ...what? A utility vehicle from the house? How did that get here?

Pearl continued to hover over him. He felt warm tears fall onto his face, and dampen his eyes. He blinked in confusion. Was *Pearl* crying? He hadn't known she was capable of that!

Time went by in a bit of a blur. Finally, he found himself lying in his bed. The world seemed to steady down for a bit. Pearl remained at his side.

He struggled to say something. Pearl quieted him.

"Just lie still, Brian. You have had a stroke. We are still trying to assess the extent of the damage, but you will probably have difficulty in moving and speaking. We have administered some chemicals designed to minimize the damage, but right now, rest is still in order."

Brian struggled to sit up. Pearl placed a restraining hand upon his chest.

"Please, Brian. Remain composed. You will receive the best care, but you must not make it more difficult for us."

Brian relaxed. What else could he do? He looked into Pearl's eyes pleadingly.

She smiled. "Do not be concerned, Brian. I have studied these matters. Most people make a full recovery." She stroked his face tenderly. "It takes time. Fortunately, we have all the time we require."

Brian worked hard, trying to relearn motor skills he had not had to think about for decades. Even swallowing proved to be difficult.

Slowly, he progressed. The world went around him in a dizzying whir while he labored through the basics once again.

His strength of will was there, and the determination to succeed. Certainly, he could not ask for better, more patient nurses, as the young ladies took turns helping him.

Something else was wrong, somehow. Some connection, perhaps the time connection, never quite seemed to get back in synch. Brian began losing track of mornings and evenings. A curtain of failing communication seemed to fall between his eyes and the rest of the world.

His days blinked on and off. People came to see him, to shake his hand, to hold him. People. Sleep. People. Sleep.

Brian relaxed. His sleep was at last restful again. The old aches and pains were distant, faded memories. He reveled in recalling his adventures as a young man. Riding sleds down snow-covered hills, sailing along the country roads on a bicycle with the wind whipping his hair and stealing the laughter out of his throat. The sunshine bringing a red curtain to his eyes, and warmth.

And always, every night before he slept, a beautiful woman with white hair would come, and kiss him good night gently on his forehead.

And then steal silently away.

And then he slept.

ABOUT THE AUTHOR:

Brian Hawthorne lives with his wife and two children in Maryland. One of those "quiet types" that you would never suspect.

As an avid reader and Science Fiction fan, he is following a prescription written by Dr. Isaac Asimov; that any reader, after long enough, will want to write. To that end, he writes for his own entertainment, and that of his readers. With creative exuberance, he tells of relationships, ingenious conveniences, and stubborn human behaviors.

Action!

Slowly, he wakened. Like a male version of Venus arising from her shell, the naked Adonis emerged from the confines of his box. The excitement, and the carnal appetites of his audience, would be rising with him. This was an image of **potent** sexual energy, coiled and aching to be released.

The morning light reflected in shimmering delicacy from his smooth, pliant skin as the cameras lovingly circled and focused. His delectable, but still unravished form filled the viewing monitors with unforgettable images as his vulnerability, and burgeoning sexual readiness, stood silent and constrained...

A psychological chasm was being breached; a *person* was becoming a possessed *thing*. This woman had ordered, and received, a sex slave for her pleasure, and that of her family. Her mixed feelings of guilt and excitement, fear and lust, were providing a rich texture for the camera to record. Paulo's role seemed much simpler -- submission, with an odd companion of pride, and _delight_...